Praise for Megan Hart and her novels

"Ms. Hart is a master . . . I am absolutely in love with [her] writing, and she remains on my auto-buy list. Take my advice and add her to yours!"
—Ecataromance

"Megan Hart is one of my favorite authors . . . The sex is hot and steamy, the emotions are real, and the characters easy to identify with. I highly recommend all of Megan Hart's books!"
—The Best Reviews

"Terrific erotic romance." <div align="right">—<i>Midwest Book Review</i></div>

"Unique . . . Fantastic." <div align="right">—<i>Sensual Romance</i></div>

"Megan Hart is easily one of the more mature, talented voices I've encountered in the recent erotica boom. Deep, thought provoking, and heart wrenching."
—The Romance Reader

"Probably the most realistic erotic romance I've ever read . . . I wasn't ready for the story to end."
—A Romance Review

"Sexy, romantic." <div align="right">—<i>Road to Romance</i></div>

"Megan Hart completely wowed me! I never read an erotic book that, aside from the explicit sex, is [also] an emotionally powerful story."
—Romance Reader at Heart

Pleasure

AND

Purpose

MEGAN HART

BERKLEY SENSATION, NEW YORK

THE BERKLEY PUBLISHING GROUP
Published by the Penguin Group
Penguin Group (USA) Inc.
375 Hudson Street, New York, New York 10014, USA
Penguin Group (Canada), 90 Eglinton Avenue East, Suite 700, Toronto, Ontario M4P 2Y3, Canada
(a division of Pearson Penguin Canada Inc.)
Penguin Books Ltd., 80 Strand, London WC2R 0RL, England
Penguin Group Ireland, 25 St. Stephen's Green, Dublin 2, Ireland (a division of Penguin Books Ltd.)
Penguin Group (Australia), 250 Camberwell Road, Camberwell, Victoria 3124, Australia
(a division of Pearson Australia Group Pty. Ltd.)
Penguin Books India Pvt. Ltd., 11 Community Centre, Panchsheel Park, New Delhi—110 017, India
Penguin Group (NZ), 67 Apollo Drive, Rosedale, North Shore 0632, New Zealand
(a division of Pearson New Zealand Ltd.)
Penguin Books (South Africa) (Pty.) Ltd., 24 Sturdee Avenue, Rosebank, Johannesburg 2196,
South Africa

Penguin Books Ltd., Registered Offices: 80 Strand, London WC2R 0RL, England

This book is an original publication of The Berkley Publishing Group.

This is a work of fiction. Names, characters, places, and incidents either are the product of the author's imagination or are used fictitiously, and any resemblance to actual persons, living or dead, business establishments, events, or locales is entirely coincidental. The publisher does not have any control over and does not assume any responsibility for author or third-party websites or their content.

PRINTING HISTORY
Berkley Sensation trade paperback edition / September 2009

Library of Congress Cataloging-in-Publication Data

Hart, Megan.
    Pleasure and purpose / Megan Hart.—Berkley Sensation trade paperback ed.
        p.   cm.—(Order of solace ; 1)
    ISBN 978–0–425–22969–9
    I. Title.
    PS3608.A7865P57   2009
    813'.6—dc22   2009022194

PRINTED IN THE UNITED STATES OF AMERICA

10   9   8   7   6   5   4   3   2   1

To CelticAngel—you know why!

To my super agent, Laura Bradford, and my super editor, Cindy Hwang, for helping this story find a home.

And of course, as ever and always, to Superman, since I wouldn't be doing any of this without you. Everyone needs an angel to tell them they're strong enough to do what they're meant to do and that they'll be able to fulfill their destiny. Dean got Zachariah, and I got you.

Acknowledgments

I could write without music, but I'm glad I don't have to.

"Angel" by Sarah McLachlan

"Blue Dress" by Depeche Mode

"Breathe Me" by Sia

"Dragonfly" by M. Craft

"Écrire L'amour" by Étienne Drapeau

"Gravity" by Sara Bareilles

"Hanky Panky" by Madonna

"Hide and Seek" by Imogen Heap

"I Will Be Here" by Steven Curtis Chapman

"Keep Breathing" by Ingrid Michaelson

"Little Fox" by Heidi Berry

"Never Alone" by Barlow Girl

"Parce Mihi Domine" by Jan Garbarek & The Hilliard Ensemble

"Piano Trio in E Flat" by Schubert

"Red Shoe Requiem" by George S. Clinton

"Set the Fire to the Third Bar" by Snow Patrol featuring Martha Wainwright

"Speeding Cars" by Imogen Heap

"Touch" by Sarah McLachlan

"The Way I Am" by Ingrid Michaelson

Five Principles of the Order of Solace

1. There is no greater pleasure than providing absolute solace.

2. True patience is its own reward.

3. A flower is made more beautiful by its thorns.

4. Selfish is the heart that thinks first of itself.

5. Women we begin and women we shall end.

Stillness

Chapter 1

Stillness Faine had never been assigned to a house so modest it didn't have a name. What sort of man was Edward Delaw, to hold such a high position within the Court of Firth and yet abide in a house as humble as this? She paused with her hand on the front gate to look it over before making her way down the crushed shell path to the front door.

"You be all right, mistress?"

She turned to look back at the driver of the carriage she'd hired to bring her from Pevensie station. "Yes, Thomas, thank you. Master Delaw is expecting me."

Thomas gave the house a dubious look. "You sure? He might've sent for you, if he was."

"I arrived early," she assured him. "The mountain pass thawed a bit sooner than anticipated. I was able to travel more swiftly than the Order predicted. I'll be fine."

He looked her over. She knew he saw a small woman with dark blonde hair pulled into a thick braid spilling down her back. She was clad in a dark plum traveling gown of modest cut and sturdy fabric. She carried a trundle-bag in one hand and her overcoat, too heavy for the early spring weather, in the other.

She wondered if her appearance disappointed him.

"Right." He nodded again and clucked to the horses. "Well, I'll be back this way tomorrow after, if you need a ride back."

She returned her attention to the house. Spring green ivy climbed redbrick walls, and the gabled roof spoke of cozy, tucked-away garret rooms. Smoke from the chimney wisped its gray tail against the background of blue sky.

Shells crunched beneath her soles, and ten strides took her to the front door. She smiled at the sight of the knocker, a pixie's face done in copper with the ring through its nose. Fine details showed the owner of this house had a sense of humor and style, too, no matter the lack of lavish wings and gardens.

She took a moment to center herself before she knocked. Each assignment was to be met face forward, but every time she faced a new patron her stomach churned. The trick was to keep her inner turmoil from showing. After all, a patron who sent to the Order of Solace for a Handmaiden had certain expectations.

She recited the five principles under her breath and calm overtook her. Before she could lift the knocker, the door opened so fast she stumbled. In the next moment she was pushed back by the man ejecting himself from the doorway.

"Later," he was saying over his shoulder. "Hello! What's this?"

In one swift motion he moved and spoke, reaching for her to keep her from falling. His fingers gripped her upper arm while the other hand came around to grab her wrist. He pulled. Nessa regained her feet.

"Who are you?" the man she thought must be Edward Delaw demanded.

He let her go, and Nessa shook the folds of her gown around

her ankles, straightening her appearance swiftly. "I'm your Handmaiden, my lord Delaw. You sent for me?"

"You weren't due for another fortnight."

"I was able to travel faster than anticipated. I trust it's not an inconvenient time for my arrival?"

"I'm just off to Pevensie to see Prince Cillian's latest toys. I'll be home later. See to it Margera gets you settled." He looked down at the worn trundle-bag at her feet. "Is that all you brought?"

"Aye, my lord, I—"

"Ah, yes." His lips tightened in what might have been meant as a smile. "Yes, the Order informed me I'd be responsible for providing for you. Very well. I shall make arrangements for that while I'm in town."

He started off down the path again, shouting out to the man who'd brought round a prancing black horse from the back of the house. "Oi, Peter! Hurry, lad, I must be off!"

Her new patron swung up on the back of the horse, slung the leather bag Peter handed him round his neck, and urged the horse into motion.

It wasn't the most illustrious greeting she'd ever had, to be sure. "Hello," she called as Delaw vanished down the lane.

Peter turned, eyebrows lifting. "Hello. Pleading your mercy, but— ah, yes. You must be the Handmaiden, and thank the Invisible Mother you've arrived."

"I am." Nessa paused as Peter strode toward her and bent to lift her bag. He opened the front door for her. "Though I fear I must ask . . . why so happy to see me?"

Peter chuckled and stepped aside to let her through. "Because he's a right bit of a cranky bastard, our lord Edward, and frankly, Mum and me is afeared if he don't get some solace, he'll rant himself into apoplexy."

"Ah." A simple enough answer, and not unexpected. "I'll do what I can."

"Mum! She's here!" Peter led the way down a short hall toward the back of the house.

The scent of baking bread and other good smells set her mouth watering. Her stomach made a loud, embarrassing noise. Peter laughed.

"Mum'll take good care of you. Get you fed. I'll take your bag up to your room."

"Thank you, Peter." Nessa smiled at him, and he gave an exaggerated bow and a wink.

"Mum!"

The plump woman bending over to pull something from the oven straightened, her cheeks flushed. "Sinder's Arrow, Peter, must you holler like you've been stabbed? Who's this, then?"

"It's—" Peter stopped. "Your mercy, mistress, I didn't catch your name."

"Stillness." She stepped forward to greet the other woman. "Stillness Faine."

Margera snorted. "Someone's parents on the worm, were they?"

Nessa took no offense to the suggestion her parents abused the hallucinogen-laced wine popular among the wealthy. "Stillness is the name I was given when I joined the Order of Solace. You may call me Nessa, if you'd prefer."

Margera gave Nessa an obvious looking over. "I'm Margera. The affrighted one in the corner's Abbie."

Abbie squeaked at being so singled out and backed farther into the corner.

"Hello, Abbie." The girl didn't return Nessa's smile, but Nessa took no offense at that, either.

"She's afeared you'll bite her." Margera jerked her chin at the girl. "Abbie takes care of the downstairs, here. I told her not to worry, that you were certain not to bite. At least, not her."

Abbie squeaked again and fled the kitchen. Margera looked after her with a shake of her gray curls. "She's tetched, I swear on the Holy Mother's Milk. Peter! You leave those sugar buns alone, else I swear by the Arrow I'll cut off your fingers!"

Peter muttered, grabbed up a handful of the buns, and fled after Abbie. Margera turned to Nessa. "He'll be the death of me. Do you have children?"

"No." The question never failed to sting, no matter how much time passed.

"I suppose you'll be wanting some food."

"I would be grateful, yes. I'm fair famished."

"You could use a hearty meal or two, by the Quiver." Margera's disapproval was clear in her tone. "A good wind could blow you away."

Nessa laughed. "Hardly. My last patron preferred me to be slender."

"The master don't like stick-figured women."

Nessa watched as Margera sliced a brown loaf and set the pieces on a platter along with a crock of butter and a flagon of milk. The cook added a meat pastry and gestured toward the rough-hewn table for Nessa.

"If it pleases my patron for me to be thicker, I'll do my best to be so." Nessa sat, mouth already watering.

"I expected a bit more paint and glitter." Margera bent again to the oven to pull out several pans of bread.

"I've been traveling a fair distance, and for a while. It would hardly have been convenient to gaud myself up for that, would it?"

Margera shook her head and handed Nessa a knife for the butter. "I suppose not. You'll leave off paint and primpery, but you'll starve or stuff yourself to change your body for a man?"

"I will do whatever I can to provide my patron with solace." Nessa thickly buttered her bread.

"Anything to provide him solace. Including servicing him in the bedchamber, aye?"

"If he requires it," Nessa replied calmly. The bread was delicious and settled her grumbling stomach straight away.

"So then," said Margera with a curl of her lip, "what makes you different than a whore?"

"Whores are paid for what they do," said Nessa without rancor. "I'm compensated for what I give."

"And what's that?"

"Solace, of course," said Nessa, and set her attention back to her food.

Night had fallen by the time Edward came home, exhausted, frustrated, irritated. Fury, at least, had passed several hours before, when he'd forced himself to realize it would do naught but give him a headache.

Cillian Derouth had to be the least fit young man ever to wear the crown of Prince of Firth. He was arrogant, vain, reckless, immoral, and, worst of all, intelligent. A stupid, reckless, and immoral lout could have been molded, convinced to reign in his debauchery, controlled. Cillian was smarter than nearly everyone around him, including his father, King Allwyn, all of his advisors, and his lordling companions. Smarter even than Edward himself, as much as it pained him to admit it. It had made Cillian dangerous.

But then, he'd always been so, even when they were lads in school, though then he'd been joyful, too. Time and circumstance had added madness to Cillian's list of other attributes, and Edward had no small part in the blame for that. No small part, but much guilt, and playing constant guard dog for his former school chum at the order of that man's father did naught to assuage it.

Leaving his horse in Peter's care, Edward went into the house, seeking a stiff drink and his bed. If he were lucky, he'd get the chance to sleep the night through without dreams. The line of light beneath his door stopped him with a startle, before he remembered.

She'd arrived today.

The Handmaiden. He'd forgotten. Edward sighed, aggrieved. Now he would have to speak to the woman, deal with her, when he wanted only the comfort of his bed. He pushed open the door, and stopped just inside.

She'd straightened his sitting room, which had not seen the attentions of a maid since he'd run the last one off for clumsiness almost two months before. She'd done more than tidy; his desk and the fireplace mantel, even the bookcases and his cabinet, gleamed, free of dust. She'd arranged his reading chair and the tapestry rug in front of the crackling fire, a small table set with a cup and teapot in front.

The woman herself knelt on the rug, one hand faceup in the palm of the other in her lap. Clad no longer in a dusty gown, she wore a deep blue dress with a high collar and buttons running from neck to hem. She looked up and smiled as he entered.

"My lord Delaw."

The kettle whistled. The Handmaiden got to her feet in a single effortless motion and took it from the fire. She poured steaming water into the pot and settled the cozy over top, then hung the kettle back in its place. Every movement smooth, precise, efficient. Still smiling, she came to stand in front of him. She had to tilt her head to look into his face, the tiny thing she was. Her eyes were the color of her gown.

"May I help you out of your coat?"

Edward knew a Handmaiden's function. He'd had to sign a slew of documents stating he understood his responsibilities to her and what she was to provide in return. He'd not hired himself some sort of glorified cleaning wench, nor a doxy, but something both and neither. He understood her function, but seeing it, her smile, the way she moved, knelt . . . the way she'd knelt . . . it was more than he'd expected.

He put up a hand as though to ward her off, though she'd not even done so much as reach to touch him. "I believe myself capable of removing my own coat, thank you."

She tilted her head, her expression curious. "If it pleases you. Though I'm here to serve you and would be well pleased to make you comfortable."

Edward stared a moment, noting the curve of pale brows and pink blush of her lips. "You're prettier than I expected."

Her smile widened a bit. "I'm happy my appearance pleases you."

She seemed to be waiting for something. "You made me tea?"

"Yes."

"Tea at this hour will keep me awake. I need sleep."

"It's of my own blend," she said gently. "Made of herbs that promote an easy rest."

Impressed but unwilling to admit it, Edward grunted. "Very well."

She was two steps behind him as he sat, but the wench managed to be in front of him before he'd had time to cross his legs. In silence, she knelt at his feet as she poured the tea and offered it up to him. When he took it, she sat back and placed her hands in that peculiar position in her lap once more.

He sipped the tea, which was indeed of pleasant aroma and sweet flavor. "It's good."

She smiled again. "I've run a hot bath for you. It will have cooled for your comfort when you've done with your tea."

Edward paused with the cup halfway to his mouth. "How have you managed this? The tea? The bath? You didn't know when I'd come home."

"True, but it's my pleasure and my purpose to know such things," she told him. "I wouldn't be a very good Handmaiden if I couldn't do something as simple as watch from the window for you to return."

He studied her. "What is your name?"

"Stillness, my lord."

He raised a brow at that. "An unusual moniker."

She smiled. "It's the name I was granted upon joining the Order."

"I see." He didn't, really. Edward knew the function of the Order of Solace, but little of its inner workings. "Do you like it?"

"My name?"

"Aye. Stillness. Do you like it?"

"I do," she said after a moment. "For stillness is a part of solace, is it not? Stillness is serenity, yet in stillness there can be action, as well, if it's the choice you've made."

She was correct, and none of the serving maids he'd ever had would have known to make such an observation. "Are all Handmaidens so named?"

"When we enter the Order, we're given names that reflect our Calling. You may call me Nessa, if you prefer."

"I don't. Stillness suits you." Her smile made him wonder how he could have thought her plain.

She tilted her head. "Thank you. And what shall I call you?"

This took Edward aback. "What do you usually call your patrons?"

Her blue eyes twinkled, reminding him of light on water. "Whatever they wish. My lord or lady, sir or madam, mistress or master."

"Not that," he said sharply, though the word sounded so pretty from her lips and brought to mind memories of pastimes best forgotten. "You can call me Edward. Or sir, should you prefer it."

Stillness ducked her head briefly. "It's your preference that matters, sir. Perhaps we shall discover together which you like best."

There was that twinkle again, something he hadn't expected. A sense of humor. Her ease with him was perhaps meant to relax him as well, but all at once the entire situation had made him anything but.

"Must you kneel?"

"It's called Waiting." Her answer came with the air of someone who's answered the same question many times. "I find this position comfortable and easy to maintain while I wait to serve you."

"Surely you don't do it when I'm not around."

Stillness gave him that tilt of her head, the twinkle. "I do sometimes, sir, when I'm not dusting or straightening or making tea."

Damn. The chit was clever as well. He looked around the room to hide the sudden gleam of interest he was certain flared in his gaze. "You've done that rather well, I see. The last girl rearranged everything. You've managed to rearrange nothing."

She laughed, tipping back her head but not otherwise moving from her position, and Edward watched fascinated at the play of firelight on her skin and golden sheen of her braid. "It was no easy task, sir. You left me quite a challenge, but I suspect there are few who can truly achieve solace in squalor."

The room did have a much nicer air about it. His gaze swept around it once more, then to the cabinet at the back corner. Made of heavy, carved wood, it blended neatly into the woodwork while also managing to remain a focal piece of the room. Perhaps only to him, as he knew the contents of it. She'd polished the handles so they shone.

"You may have free reign in these rooms," he told her. "But not in that cabinet. Understood?"

"Of course. The Order chose me for you based upon the documents you filled out. I hope I'll be a good match for you, but if there is anything you desire, or anything you do not, you must let me know." She didn't question, didn't even look at the cabinet itself, but merely accepted his command as though it was inconceivable to do anything else.

But then, was that not why he'd sent for her in the first place? He couldn't deny her appeal. Her serene voice and manner, the demure dress that nonetheless accentuated every supple curve, the shining braid of sunshine.

He put the cup on the tray. "I'd like that bath, now."

She nodded and got to her feet, again two steps behind him as he went through his bedchamber to the bath. He saw fresh linens on the bed, turned down invitingly, the pillows plumped and sprinkled with essence of gillyflower he could smell from the doorway. The tub of clear water steamed. She'd laid out towels and soap.

"You may—" *Leave me*, he meant to say, turning, but her fingers were already working the buttons at the front of his coat.

Stillness opened them as efficiently as she'd poured his tea, and something in her quick and easy movements allowed him to stand motionless while she worked.

"I haven't had anyone undress me since I was in short trousers," he murmured, looking upon her bent head as she tugged the coat from his arms and hung it neatly.

She looked up, working next upon his shirt buttons and the laces at his sleeves. "If ever I should do something you don't care for, all you need do is tell me and I'll stop at once. I shall endeavor to serve you so completely you need never want for anything so long as I'm with you."

She bared his chest, her small nimble hands cool on his warm skin. She eased his arms from the sleeves and hung his shirt next to the jacket. Next she went to the buttons at his waist, and Edward's pulse leaped. He hadn't had a woman's touch there in months.

"And you do this because you believe it will bring about the return of the Holy Family." He focused on words instead of how her hands felt against his belly and thighs when she knelt to pull down his trousers.

"Aye, I do so believe."

By the Arrow, at his feet, her face tilted upward to meet his gaze . . . his cock twitched in the confines of his underdrawers. He could imagine too well how hot and wet her mouth would be. Yet she was doing nothing to entice or arouse him.

She got to her feet. "You're not a believer?"

The chance to discuss philosophy with her and keep his mind from his burgeoning erection made him answer more fully than he'd have done, otherwise. "The story of Sinder and the Holy Family was made up by the priests to order compliance and regulate the behavior of men who need fear to keep them from running rampant."

She loosed the ties at his front and slid the final layer of linen down his legs as she touched the back of each calf, lightly, for him to step out. Then she stood again without so much as a curious glance at his nakedness and took his hand to lead him the two steps to the wooden grate over the floor drain.

"Only the men?" She waited for him to sit upon the bathing stool, then reached for the cloth and pail of soapy water.

"It's not often women who pillage and murder. A woman's crimes are theft or deceit."

She scrubbed and rinsed him quickly and waited for him to step into the tub of heated-to-perfection water. Her hand nudged him back against the curved porcelain, and he couldn't help the sigh that leaked from him as the hot water caressed him. Her fingers went to the buttons of her gown. She wore a thin shift beneath, and unlike the gown that covered her from throat to toes, the shift dipped low enough to reveal the enticing globes of her full breasts and the smooth flesh of her arms. A slit gaped to show smooth, pale thighs and a hint of curls slightly darker than the hair on her head.

She knelt by the side of the tub and lifted a cloth. "May I assist you?"

"Yes." Was this not why he'd sent for her? To assist him, in all ways?

Stillness smiled and added scented oil to the cloth. She moved it over his body. The steam from the bath curled the tendrils of hair that had escaped from her braid. Her cheeks flushed as she leaned over the water.

"Nobody has—" Edward stopped at the rough sound of his own voice.

She didn't pause in her ministrations. Her hand moved slowly over his body. She'd already cleansed him of grime. Now she soothed him. She nodded, her eyes fixed upon his.

"Nobody has touched you this way?" she murmured. "Taken care of you in such a way?"

He nodded, lost in the blue depths of her eyes. Her hand moved across his stomach and his cock thickened, though she'd not touched it. He let out a small groan. If she'd smirked, he'd have ordered her gone without a second thought, but she didn't. Her gaze stayed on his, solemn.

"My lord Edward, you are tense and fractious. Would you allow me to relieve you?"

He waited for her to touch him, but she didn't until he nodded and breathed a hoarse, "You may."

Then her hand closed around him and he closed his eyes to thrust upward into her hand. She stroked him gently from hood to base, dipping lower to caress his testicles with her palm. He'd wanted this from the moment he saw her waiting for him on her knees. Wanted her hand on him, that sweet pink mouth engulfing him, wanted to sink his aching cock deep inside her slick heat and fill her. He wanted to feel her writhe beneath him, feel her quim tighten around him, hear her cry out in ecstasy.

Edward opened his eyes, expecting to see the bored expression of a doxy but finding instead the face of a woman completely engrossed in her actions. Her breasts rose and fell with her rapid breaths. Water had turned the linen of her undershift transparent, her taut pink nipples clear beneath the fabric.

She smiled. "Does this please you?"

"Take . . . take off your gown." His voice had gone low and growling.

She did, and he sat up, reaching for her. She entered the water willingly, straddling him as he positioned her and sank inside her. She gave a small surprised yelp, perhaps at the suddenness of being so impaled, but made no protest.

"Did I hurt you?"

"No."

Her cunt was hot, as he'd imagined. Slick. Tight. Her body embraced him, and his cock throbbed. He thrust inside her once, twice, in reaction rather than conscious effort, and she murmured something wordless.

Edward stilled, finding his control. As much as his body craved the mindlessness of fucking, his mind didn't readily relinquish its focus. He moved again inside her, water slopping between them. Her breasts moved enticingly, and he closed his fingers on her nipple, tugging. She made that noise again.

He thrust inside her again, harder, seeking swift release. She let out a sigh as his fingers rolled her nipple, the noise so sweet and perfect his balls contracted.

He wanted to fuck, to grab, to press and pull . . . to bite . . . he gave himself up to the ecstasy and pulled her closer, his hand finding the base of her braid and pulling to expose the line of that beautiful throat.

His teeth found her skin. He had to taste her. Fill her. Fuck her. Own her. Her cries grew louder, and his senses sharpened. Heightened. Harder he thrust, hand fisted in her hair and his mouth sucking greedily on her skin. He grabbed her other breast, then found her nipple with his mouth and suckled that as well, moaning at her flavor, salt and sweetness mingled.

He was going to explode. He fucked harder. Limbs tangled. His knee banged the side of the tub. Water sloshed between them like the sea against rocks.

She cried louder and a thread of alarm brought him back to earth. He was being too rough. Too fierce. Yet he couldn't stop now.

Stillness let out a last, shuddering cry and hot liquid erupted from his prick. His mind wanted to go red with it, but he held back, knowing to give totally into such passion meant being lost.

He loosed his fingers from her hair and sat back, panting. Her throat bore the mark of his sucking, a small red-purple bruise. She would likely bear the signs of his attentions elsewhere as well, and he swallowed guilt.

He caught his breath and looked at her, expecting stunned grief or the glint of anger, both expressions he'd seen on the women he'd taken to his bed in the past. She was smiling.

"Handmaiden."

"My lord."

"Get off me."

Her smile faltered, but she did as he said. Edward, shamed of what he'd done, pushed her aside and got out of the now cool water. He dried himself. The looking glass showed his face, stern, flushed with self-reproach. He looked away. Behind him the water splashed onto the tile floor and he heard the slap of wet feet.

"Have I displeased you?"

He tensed, expecting a touch, but Stillness didn't touch him. That she was there to provide him with absolute solace didn't excuse what he'd done. He could have taken his pleasure without causing her pain. Without speaking, he left the bathroom, and her.

Chapter 2

His sudden change of behavior surprised her, but Nessa didn't hesitate to follow him. Her gown had remained dry and she pulled it on, doing up the buttons as she went after him on bare feet. She found him standing in front of the fire, no longer naked but clad in a loose spidersilk robe.

There were five positions of the Waiting, the folded position that was the staple of a Handmaid's existence. Nessa, uncertain what she had done to displease him, knelt with her heels beneath her buttocks and her body stretched out on the floor in front him, her hands placed flat on the ground next to her head in Waiting, Remorse.

"I plead your mercy. Tell me how I displeased you—"

"Don't. Don't do that."

Nessa looked up at him. "If I've failed—"

He stared at her, his expression unreadable. "What are you doing?"

"Waiting."

"That's not what you were doing earlier!"

"There are five positions in the Waiting," she explained, trained eyes taking in his tense shoulders and grimly curved mouth. "I was in Waiting, Remorse, for I've displeased—"

"You haven't! Get up!"

Her patron turned from her, breathing hard, his face still flushed despite the release he'd taken in the bath. After a moment, she moved forward quietly to put herself into the line of his vision. If he'd wanted her gone, he'd have ordered it.

A good Handmaiden did more than judge when to serve tea and how hot to run a bath, more than clean a messy room or help a patron dress and undress. The Handmaiden's purpose was to provide solace, for each soul that found it would send another Arrow to fill the lord Sinder's Quiver. Only when his Quiver was full would he and his wife and son, the Holy Family, return to bring peace.

There was more to solace than understanding how to create physical comfort. Handmaidens needed to create mental ease, as well. It took time, skill, instinct and intuition, and Nessa took no small measure of pride in her ability to guess the needs of her patrons, to offer them what they needed.

But what did her patron need? She'd thought her body, the release of tension. Yet his reaction, after, puzzled her. She'd failed. She needed to understand him more completely.

"It takes time," she said after a moment, voice quiet, "to understand what you need. I plead your mercy for having failed you."

"You didn't fail me." Edward's voice was cold. Distant. He kept his back turned to her.

"I'm here to serve you. But woman I begin and woman I shall end. I'm not a magicreator, nor a reader of minds."

He turned stiffly, giving her his profile. "I shouldn't have treated you as I did in the bath."

This gave her pause. "You didn't wish to make love?"

His short, sharp burst of laughter had little to do with amusement. "That was not making love. That was fucking."

Her mouth curved slightly. "Did you not wish to fuck me, then?"

"I did. I did wish it." He scowled.

"I don't understand."

He turned to face her, reaching out to flick open the hastily fastened buttons at her throat. He touched the base of her throat, where his teeth had left their mark.

She waited for him to speak, and when he didn't, Nessa wracked her brain to think of what he might wish to tell her. Her fingers touched the sore spot, which even now gave her a thrill at the memory of how he'd felt inside her.

"Are you worried about this?"

He nodded stiffly. "There was no need for it."

She spoke cautiously, treading with her words as carefully as she'd have stepped with her feet on uneven ground. "There was need, else you'd not have done it."

Her patron stared into the fireplace. "There is never need to cause another pain for one's own pleasure."

"It's a small wound, only," she hastened to assure him, but he wasn't willing to listen.

"No wound is small when done apurpose!"

Again, Nessa hid her smile. "I assure you, I wasn't harmed."

He looked at her. "The marks on your throat say otherwise."

She dared a step closer. "Sir . . . as your Handmaiden, I'm bound to serve you as best I can. To that end I will do what is needed, be it dusting your shelves or taking you inside my body. It is my purpose to do these things, but you must trust me when I say it is my pleasure, as well."

He didn't believe her, she could tell, and her sympathies roused for the man whose nature pulled him so fiercely in such opposing directions. She took one more step closer, taming him as one tames the fox in the field.

His face worked, fleeting emotion in his eyes she couldn't discern, before he stiffened and gave her his back again. "You are dismissed. I rise with the dawn. You may attend me then."

It wasn't her place to argue, and Nessa did as he'd told her without protest or a second look back.

A nd this one," said Cillian, "can be heated in the fire."

The Prince of Firth held up the long, thin metal rod, his green eyes alight with glee. He waved it, then hung it back upon the hook in the wall. He stepped back, admiring his collection, and turned to Edward.

"I do so love acquiring a new toy. Almost as much as I enjoy a new girl for my hareem."

"My lord Cillian," said Edward without pause, "one can only marvel at your . . . taste."

Cillian, unaffected by Edward's disapproval, laughed. "Ah, Edward, my dear one, don't tell me the sight of them doesn't get your cock fair to aching!"

"The girls or the toys?" Edward leaned against the heavy table and watched Cillian loosen the ties of his cravat.

"Both, of course." Cillian tossed the fabric to a naked woman who folded it neatly, waiting as the prince tossed off his jacket. She took that, too, and handed him a ribbon, which he used to tie back his fall of red-gold hair.

"You do have an exquisite hareem, my lord, but as for the other—"

"As for the other," snapped Cillian, "I know you better than you do, Edward. You long to have a woman on her knees before you. You yearn to watch the stripes appear on her skin when you flog her. You like to fuck her wet, hot snatch as she cries out your name and bleeds from your touch—"

"No," said Edward sharply. "You're wrong in that."

Cillian looked at him closely. "Perhaps not that."

When Edward said nothing, Cillian sniffed and took off his white shirt, tossing it without heed to the naked maid. "You can deny your nature to yourself, but you can't deny it to your cock. Tell me you don't get hard at the sight of that."

He jerked his chin toward the nude woman in the center of the room. Her wrists were bound to the cross of ironwood. Her unbound hair, the color of shadows, flowed over skin the color of milky tea. Her legs were secured at the ankle, parted just enough for Edward to glimpse the tangle of dusky curls.

"I'm not here to discuss my bedroom antics."

"No?" Cillian grinned and hefted the flogger in his left hand. He trailed the thin leather straps over the back of his right. "Why are you here, then?"

"Because your lord father wished me to discuss the plans for your upcoming appointment."

"As Minister of the Council of Fashion." Cillian swung the flogger. "Ah, the sound of it is as nearly wonderful in the air as against her skin. Don't you agree?"

"The Council of Fashion is no less important a post than any of the others."

Cillian stopped. "Spare me the merry ego stroke, Edward. I'm being granted the minister position to give me something to do besides fuck and drink and gamble. Isn't that right? And as my dear father doesn't trust me enough to give me a position which has real effect on the government of Firth, he's settled it that I'll get to oversee the length of trousers for the upcoming season."

"It's not my place to judge your father's decisions."

Cillian flung him a look so venomous it would have made a

man unused to such ire step back. As it was, Edward merely braced himself for the flood of cursing he expected to follow.

"My father," the prince said in a surprisingly even tone, "pays you to play nursemaid to me. Placate and soothe my . . . irrational urges. To keep me in line."

He smacked the flogger against his forearm, and though it left a red mark, he didn't even flinch. "Isn't that true, Edward?"

Edward had to admit it was. This agreement brought Cillian no joy, however, as evidenced by the cloud that crossed his fine features.

"My father pays you to keep me happy as well, does he not? Isn't that part of your duty, too?"

"No man can make another happy, my prince," said Edward with a hand over his heart and a half bow to soften the retort.

"Same as it ever was." Cillian snapped his fingers and a woman scurried forward with a jug of worm, of which Cillian quaffed a great mouthful. "And yet . . . not the same."

Edward had learned saying nothing was more often the better course when dealing with the prince. Cillian's answering smile was that of a man baring his teeth to barricade a scream. The prince wiped his lips and handed the jug back to the maid.

"When they deemed me fit to return to polite society," Cillian said, "it was with the understanding I'd never really regain the status I had before. No monarch wishes to wed his daughter to a madman, even one so dramatically recovered."

Cillian grimaced, looking around the room. He let the flogger's trailing tails caress his arm. When he looked at Edward again, his eyes glinted with anger but his voice stayed calm.

"He didn't want to have to do it, you know. Didn't trust you. Has never trusted you, Edward, not since we were lads in school. It's made your place difficult, has it not? Being out of the king's favor, settling for the shite assignments. You could've sought a different trade, perhaps, but your own father was desperate for you to hold a higher place than he had. Spice merchant, wasn't he? Got his place in court by sheer hard work. Is that right?"

"You know it is." Edward kept his back straight, face without expression.

"It's what fathers do, isn't it, Edward? Hope their sons are better than they? What do you suppose my father thinks of me?" Cillian's laugh sounded like breaking glass. "No, he didn't want you at all, Edward, my dear one, but I insisted. My old school chum would keep me under control. He didn't want it to be you, not after what happened . . . what we both know happened . . . but it had to be someone, didn't it? And so now you have a nice house out of the city, and your table is never empty, your wardrobe never out of fashion. It's been good for you, hasn't it, my dear one? Looking after me?"

Cillian's green eyes had gone dark with emotion.

"Yes, Cillian," replied Edward coldly. "It has."

They stared that way for a few moments, much being said without being spoken, and Edward remembered how he'd once called this man brother. Then, at Cillian's whim, the moment passed. He swung the flogger against the back of his hand. "Ah, such a sweet sting. Are you ready for it, my dear one?"

The woman tied to the ironwood cross murmured and shifted again, the pink slit of her sex glistening. Cillian looked back at Edward with a grin that belied the tension between them.

"I don't give a virgin's fart for the Council of Fashion, Edward. Not about the difference between peacock and sky blues, nor about the cost of wool and silk, nor about trade routes or any other of that rot. Someday I'll be King of Firth and until then, I'll play as I wish. You want to know my plans for the minister position? What if I decree that all women should wear nothing but collars and men attire themselves in cock rings and codpieces?"

"I think you'd have a difficult time garnering the support to pass such a decree."

Cillian sneered again. "Don't worry. You can assure my father I'll be certain to surround myself with assistants who do care. But my prick is straining the front of my breeches at the moment, so unless you'd like to bring me off with your mouth, I suggest you step back while I whip this lovely cunna in front of me."

Edward had no intentions of so servicing the prince and stepped back. Cillian laughed and strode forward. He paused behind the woman and with tender hands pushed her hair over her shoulder to expose her bare back.

"Just a little sting, my sweet," he murmured.

She cried out, body jerking at the first lash, and Edward couldn't help the surge of desire flooding him at the sound of leather on her flesh. The delicious aroma of sweet feminine arousal teased his nostrils. Cillian let the flogger fall again.

Edward would have avoided Cillian's playroom entirely, had King Allwyn not expressly bid him to attend the prince there, to make certain his activities never again went too far. It was, however, torture, made greater by Cillian's constant taunting. He wanted to leave, but the sight had riveted him in place. Cillian was a master at physical dominance. He marked the woman's back without hesitating, pausing just when her cries grew so loud Edward was certain she was unable to take another strike. The prince slipped a hand between her legs, working his fingers inside her, and she cried out, pushing back against him as much as her bonds would allow.

"Edward. Come here."

Edward obeyed, for though his mind might be reluctant, his body wasn't.

"She's so close to the edge. Her cunt's gripping my hand like a fist. She's going to go over."

The girl moaned, body trembling. The welts on her back stood out against the dun of her skin. Cillian pulled his hand out, slick with her juices, and licked his fingers.

"Her honey is sweet. I want you to taste her."

"My lord—"

"You're not married, my lord Delaw," interrupted the prince. "And I know for a fact you have no mistress. So give me no excuses about why you can't take your pleasure with this cunna, who'd be begging for it if I hadn't gagged her mouth."

"Cillian. I don't wish—"

"Do it," ordered Cillian, voice low and dangerous. "Do you forget, my dear one? What it's like to do this?"

"I don't forget."

How could he? No matter how long it had been since he'd taken his enjoyment that way, he could never forget how it felt. Nor the consequences.

"Come taste her." Cillian was teasing. Seducing. Certain Edward would give in.

Edward moved forward, his fury inflamed by the scent of the woman before him and his cock, straining despite himself in his trousers. "If it so pleases you, my lord."

"It does," hissed Cillian. "Put your hands on her."

Edward slipped a hand between the girl's legs and her thighs trembled. His fingers slid along her folds, eased by the honey trickling from her slit. He rubbed it with his fingertips, then found her clit. She was so wet, so swollen, so hot . . . though her back bore the marks of Cillian's flogger she didn't weep, didn't pull away from the pain but embraced it.

A despised and familiar heat swept his brain as he stroked her. The need to grip, to bind and bite and own . . . he let out a low groan as her cunt pulsed around his fingers. She wanted this, his hands on her.

"Fuck her with your hand," murmured Cillian, "while I kiss her with my lash. And together we'll make this cunna scream. Shall we?"

He didn't bother waiting for Edward's answer, but brought down the flogger again and again while the woman writhed as much as her restraints allowed. Edward gave himself up to the desire. He slid two fingers into her slick channel, his thumb rubbing her clit with every stroke. Breathing hard, his prick as hard as the ironwood bar to which she was bound, Edward stroked her to climax while Cillian brought the flogger down again and again on her skin. The woman sagged, muscles leaping and jerking as she came.

"The way we used to." Cillian's voice had gone hoarse with his exertions. "Do you remember?"

"I remember."

"You. Me." Cillian's lash came down again, and the woman cried out, hips leaping forward against Edward's hand. "We rutted our way through every whore who'd have us . . . and they all would have us, aye?"

Edward didn't look at Cillian. His gaze stayed fixed upon the woman. Cillian struck her again, and she writhed. Cillian let the tails of his flogger trail over her back, then leaned forward to blow a breath along the welts.

"Do you want to know what they tried to tell me when I was in the asylum?" Cillian moved closer to the woman, his voice soft as he caressed her hair. "A good man's cock didn't get stiff at the sight of dainty wrists bound with leather cord, or the sweetness of curving buttocks marked with the shape of his palm."

Edward's prick was still stiff, but now his throat went dry. Cillian moved his hand over the girl's skin, and before Edward could pull away, the prince had reached forward and grabbed his wrists, moving Edward's fingers over the pattern of welts while the girl moaned.

"You remember what it was like to do this." Cillian's whisper floated like spidersilk in the lust-scented air between them. His fingers guided Edward's over the girl's skin, so deliciously hot. Over her hip, the unmarked smoothness of her ass, lower to stroke her thighs. "Where is the Edward I knew? The one who made the cunnas beg him to tie them? Why have you abandoned me, my dear one?"

Cillian lifted Edward's hand from the girl's warm skin and pressed the sweat-slick handle of the flogger into it.

"This time," he said, "you flog her while I make her come."

Edward jerked his hand away so fast the flogger fell at his feet, and he stepped away like it was a snake poised to bite.

"You go too far, Cillian." The words hurt his throat and sounded strangled, not detached as he'd meant them to.

Cillian's eyes flashed as he bent to retrieve the flogger. "You of all people, my dear one, should understand how I would know when to stop. I know how far to go. It's you who—"

"Good day, my prince." Edward cut off Cillian with an exaggeratedly polite half bow.

Cillian turned back to his pet. "Do you believe what they told me? About what good men don't do?"

Edward paused at the door. "Yes."

Cillian's laugh was harsh. "And what of lying, Edward? Do good men do that?"

To that, Edward had no answer. As he left, he heard the smack of leather on flesh, and the girl cried out again. He didn't look back.

Nessa had spent the day making Edward's quarters as soothing as possible, an easy enough task as he'd furnished them already with taste and comfort. She'd added little, straightened and dusted much, then contented herself with reading one of his books while she awaited his arrival.

At the sight of him tearing up the lane, his horse galloping full-out, Nessa tucked away the book. The kettle was warm and would need no more than a few moments on the fire to boil, but judging from the way her patron strode out of the stable and toward the house, he'd need something stronger than tea.

She had the whiskey poured and waiting in the crystal glass when he slammed into the room. The door opened so hard it struck the wall before bouncing back, and a book fell from the over-crowded shelves. Edward strode into the room, his dark hair disheveled and clothes askew.

Nessa held out the glass to him without speaking, and whatever he'd been about to say cut off without more than the smallest noise. He took the glass and tossed back the contents, grimacing at the sting. His eyes gleamed. He threw the glass into the fire.

And then, he took her.

He backed her up against the wall and lifted her skirt to her thighs, one hand sliding between her legs while the other fumbled at his trouser buttons. His mouth found the soft skin of her neck and he laved it with his tongue before nipping.

The force of his embrace and the teeth were triggers for her, though he couldn't have known it. His kiss swallowed her cry. His hand parted her folds, and his cock nudged her entrance. She opened for him, hands going around his shoulders to lift her body and angle her hips to ease his entry, but though arousal bloomed inside her she wasn't yet wet. His questing hand probed her, a finger slipping inside, then out again to roll over her clitoris. She twitched with a small cry.

Edward took his hand from between her legs and moved it up between them. "Spit," he ordered, and she did at once.

In the next moment, his wet fingers caressed her, smoothed over her clit and inside, and he grasped his cock and thrust inside her. Edward moaned as he filled her, his forehead pressed to hers. His whiskey-scented breath brushed her mouth and she opened her lips to breathe him in.

His mouth found her neck again, sucking hungrily, and the feeling of it set her on fire. Nessa had long ago discovered the need inside her for just this sort of passion. Fast, hard, without mercy, every small sting one more thread in an entire tapestry of pain and pleasure.

She wrapped her legs around him, grateful for her previous patron's insistence upon a slender form, allowing Edward to lift her without strain. The bookcase against her back shuddered with his thrusts, the books digging into her back and making her squirm with ecstasy as much as his cock inside her.

As her first orgasm struck, she cried out and threw her head back. He bit down harder. His belly rubbed her flesh, teasing the postclimax sensitivity in a way that made her writhe, but in only a moment the pleasure built again and she hovered on the brink of another climax.

Edward rocked against her and shuddered, pumping inside her. His final thrust moved her so hard it cracked a shelf. His shout eased a final burst of bliss out of her body, and Nessa clutched him as their bodies twitched and tensed in mutual completion.

They stayed like that as their breathing slowed, until finally he put her down. Her skirt fell back around her ankles. A warm trickle of his seed and her juices ran down her thigh, tickling, and she smiled.

"Good evening, sir," she said at last, the first words they'd exchanged since he'd come home.

Edward had a hand on the bookcase, his head lowered as though standing took all his energy, and Nessa put a supportive hand on his arm. She pulled up his trousers to his waist and urged him with small touches to sit, then looked at him with concern.

"Are you well?"

"I plead your mercy." Edward accepted the second glass of liquor she handed him.

This response surprised her, and she folded herself into the Waiting at his feet. "Sir?"

Edward sipped the drink this time instead of tossing it back. "I shouldn't have used you so."

Nessa said nothing at first, calculating the best response. She'd never had a patron so reluctant to avail himself of all she had to offer. She'd had patrons who didn't desire her sexually, true, but never one who took his pleasure with her and apologized for it, after. "I don't understand."

Edward rubbed his forehead. "You're no doxy. The Order was very clear on this matter."

She was beginning to see his reason for distress. "I'm here to provide you with solace in accordance with the principles of my order. You required the service of my body, and I provided it. There's no need to plead my mercy."

He looked at her, reaching out again to touch the fresh marks upon her throat. "Stillness."

"Yes, sir?"

A faint smile quirked his full-lipped mouth. "Is it a Handmaiden's place to be treated so roughly?"

It was perhaps meant as a question without answer, but she thought carefully before providing him with one anyway. "If I felt you were being unduly harsh for no purpose but to cause me distress, I would have to judge if my distress brought you solace."

He met her eyes, expression curious. "And if it did?"

"For every patron to whom I provide absolute solace, one more Arrow fills Sinder's Quiver. So I believe and such is my goal. So if I believed allowing you to treat me harshly somehow brought you solace, I'd suffer the treatment with grace and the glory of knowing I was doing my part in bringing the return of the Holy Family.

However," she said, raising a finger, "if I believed your abuse was ill-guided and purely selfish, that causing me harm did nothing to ease you . . . then I would leave and return to the Order and you could be faced with fines for not obeying the confines of our contract. I'm not a whipping boy."

Edward reached for the hand that had pointed, and he took it between his two. "And what do you believe about how I have treated you thus far?"

Nessa reached to touch his cheek. "I believe you're a man uncomfortable with needing."

He put a hand over hers against his face, holding it there for a moment before taking it away and holding both hers between his. "I'm quite gratified to have you here to see to my needs."

"You needn't fret. I'm not made of glass. I don't break."

"How do you know?"

The challenge in his tone surprised her, but she met it. "Experience has taught me so."

"Experience with patrons?"

Her experience with the limits her body could handle had happened before she'd discovered her Calling. "Some."

"Is that something they train you for? The Order?" He seemed alarmed and disturbed, two states of emotion Nessa didn't wish to encourage.

"All Handmaidens are given the same basic training," she told him, hoping her calm would transfer to him. "But we all have our own specialized interests and abilities. Some are more patient. Some, better mannered. Though we're all trained to provide comfort, there are as many ways to do it as there are stars."

"Have you ever had a patron you didn't want to serve?"

She smiled. "It's not a question of want. If I'm assigned, I serve."

"But if you didn't like him?"

Nessa thought for a moment on how best to explain. "There are five principles of the Order of Solace. The last is women we begin and women we shall end. I'm a woman, but I am also a Handmaiden. I've learned how to be both at the same time."

"You put aside one part of yourself in order to become the other."

"When necessary."

With some alarm she watched his face tighten. Her words had upset him, somehow, and she didn't understand why. He let go of her hands, and she saw she'd lost him again.

"You might make me some tea, now" was all he said, and so that was what she did.

Chapter 3

inder's Arrow, man, you look fair busted." Alaric Dewan's blunt words made Edward look up from the mug of hot mulled cider he'd been studying and not drinking.

Alaric slid onto the couch across from Edward, his long legs stretching out comfortably as he reclined, hands linked behind his head of blond curls. "Frankly, Edward, you look like you've been rode hard and put away wet, as our dear Cillian likes to say."

"I haven't been sleeping." Edward sat back, forgetting the cider, which held no interest for him. The library at the palace was otherwise empty this time of day, and he'd sought a respite from the monotony of court to sit and think.

Alaric lifted one pale gold brow. "How so?"

Edward scrubbed at his face before answering. He hadn't bothered with a looking glass over the past few days, but if Alaric said he looked bad then he assuredly did, for Alaric was honest to a fault.

"I've had much upon my thoughts" was what he finally said, more to appease Alaric than to reveal anything.

"Oh?" Alaric leaned forward to snag a biscuit from the tray on the low table between them. He ate it as he did everything else—with unabashed pleasure and gusto. "How so? Allow me to venture a guess. Our dear Cillian?"

Edward shrugged, unwilling to discuss his relationship with the prince.

Alaric laughed. "He's been testing his dear papa again, aye? And therefore you. But there's something else, aye? Something at home?"

Edward scowled, annoyed but not surprised at his friend's insight. "Why would you say that?"

Alaric's shrug was too affected to be innocent. "Rumor has it you've secured a Handmaiden."

Edward made a low noise deep in his throat. "The members of this court are lacking in activity if they have the time to discuss my private affairs."

"So it's true?"

Alaric's frown left Edward unmoved. "I've no time to constantly train housemaids to properly clean and take care of me. I wanted someone who'd come already prepared."

Alaric snorted. "My good man, a Handmaiden is no housemaid."

"I know that." Edward frowned harder. Alaric *would* insist on being deliberately obtuse.

"But that's the only reason you sent for her? To clean your rooms and press your clothes?"

Edward said nothing, refusing to respond to such a slyly made comment.

Alaric reached over to flick the lace hanging in disarray from Edward's sleeve. "If so, she's been neglecting her duties."

Edward yanked his sleeve from Alaric's all too nimble fingers. "I haven't been home in two days. I've been sleeping in my court apartment."

"Why?" Alaric seemed genuinely puzzled.

Annoyed at having to explain himself but knowing his friend would pester him until he gave an answer, Edward said, "Because Cillian's had need of me, and I find it easier to concentrate on my duties when I'm here."

Because going home to Stillness meant giving in to temptation spurred by the time he spent watching Cillian live out his fantasies.

Alaric settled back on the sofa, this time propping his feet on the table, heedless of the way his boots knocked the cider jug. "When you have a warm and willing woman at home, waiting to grant your every need? I should think you'd be eager to get home to that. Not to mention how much it costs you. . . ."

"No more than any mistress would," Edward snapped. "And she expects nothing from me but what we've already contracted."

"You mean she expects no emotional ties," Alaric said, voice quiet.

Edward let out a curse and got up to pace in front of the fire. Having such a longtime friend had its disadvantages, particularly when that friend knew your past and how it affected your present.

"There's no harm in admitting it, old man. It's well-known that you avoid such entanglements."

"Unlike you," Edward said, turning, "who breaks hearts left and right?"

Alaric's shrug wasn't forced this time. "I do my share of wooing and bedding, but I leave my lovers grateful for our time together, not weeping. Besides, it's also well-known that Alaric Dewan is an exquisite lover but heartless as well, and anyone who accepts my wooing does so knowing a fuck is all they'll get from me."

"And you avoid liaisons with those who seek to change you?" Edward already knew the answer.

"It's always to our mutual benefit," Alaric answered without shame. "My lovers know what I am. But at least I'm honest with them, and they with me. And with ourselves, which is the most important part."

"You think me dishonest with myself?" Edward would have gone to blows with another man over such a statement, but Alaric . . . well, Alaric had been his boon companion for long enough to earn the right to speak his mind.

"I think you hide from yourself, Edward. Because of what happened back then."

Edward stiffened, though he'd known where this conversation was going the moment it began. "That was a long time ago."

"Aye, by the Void, eons ago, and yet you still haven't done more than take the occasional company of a doxy to ease your needs!" Alaric shook his head as though in wonder. "You're fair of face and form, with a well-filled purse and a good position in the court. Even if you seek not to ally yourself in marriage, surely you could set yourself up with a mistress?"

Edward looked into the fire. "Even a mistress who claims she holds no aspirations eventually wants to claim more than a monthly allowance."

"Unlike a Handmaiden, who is bound to provide service without reward."

Edward nodded. From behind him, he heard the sound of scuffling and in the next moment felt Alaric's hand upon his shoulder. He looked at his friend.

"It wasn't your fault," Alaric said gently. "You have to stop blaming yourself."

Mere words would do nothing to alleviate the years-long guilt. "I was there, too, when she died. I've as much fault as Cillian."

"You were a lad," said Alaric. "We all were. She was a whore—"

"She was a woman!" Edward's gut clenched at the memory of how she'd smiled when he'd asked her name, and how she'd not given it.

"She was rough trade and had been well used by many. Cillian has ever been one to push the limits." Alaric's fingers squeezed Edward's shoulder. "It was an accident."

"Does that release me from blame?" Again, Edward looked at his friend. "I don't think so."

Alaric hadn't been there that night. He didn't know what happened. Only Edward and Cillian knew, and one of them had gone mad from it and both became liars.

"You're the only one who doesn't." Alaric gave another squeeze and stepped away. "Go home to your Handmaiden, Edward. Allow her to service you as is her duty, if for no other reason than you've paid for the right to accept it. Get some rest."

"But Cillian—"

"I've had it from good authority that our dear Cilly has drunk himself into a stupor on worm and is passed out on the lap of Persis Denviel, that prat. Even his father doesn't expect you to be with him every moment."

Edward nodded, turning to face his friend and clasp his hand, having much to say but incapable of saying it. "You're right."

Alaric put his hand over Edward's briefly before releasing it. "Aye, and if not, you're no farther away than a swift ride. Go home."

Edward nodded. "I'll go."

Alaric grinned. "And mayhap I'll visit you tomorrow . . . see for myself this Handmaiden. I've never seen one. What's she like?"

"A woman," said Edward, thinking. "She's just like . . . a woman."

And though that answer didn't seem to satisfy Alaric, it was the only one he could give.

Two days had passed, and she'd waited patiently, for true patience was its own reward. Yet there could be no denying how much better it was when the door opened and Edward strode in. He didn't ignore her, but he didn't approach her, either.

"You've made a tangle of yourself," she reproached, watching him struggle with the laces at his cuffs. "Has no one attended you while you were gone?"

Edward stopped his struggle and allowed her to work the knots free. "No. I have no valet at the palace except for on formal occasions."

The lace came away in her hand and she folded it carefully and set it on the dresser, then moved to the other wrist. In moments she'd unfastened the rest of the laces on his shirt and moved to help him off with it.

"I'll run you a bath," she murmured, noting the dust on his skin.

"Very nice."

His praise warmed her, for she'd feared she'd been unable to satisfy him. She nodded and left him to start the water running. There had been patrons who'd never been satisfied with her efforts, no matter what she did. Something in their natures refused to allow them to find solace in anything. There was no shame in failing a patron like that, only in not trying her utmost.

Edward was different. He didn't seem unappeasable, and yet she wasn't certain what to do for him because he seemed so uncertain himself. She would have to try harder, that was the solution, and no other.

She looked up when he entered the bathing chamber, and the easy way he presented his nudity consoled her. He was relaxing in her presence. Becoming used to her.

She waited until he'd settled onto the bathing stool before kneeling next to him, gathering scented lather from the bucket and working it through the thick darkness of his hair, then rinsing it with clear warm water and combing it with her fingers to lay straight about his shoulders. She washed his body as well, as he relaxed with closed eyes.

"Sir, are you falling asleep?"

He cracked one eye open. "Aye, I fear I am."

"Then instead of the bath, you shall go to bed if that's where your body is telling you it desires to go."

His low chuckle warmed her as much as the praise. "Far be it from me to argue with my body or a woman, for I know I might be able to suppress my body but I can never win against a woman whose mind is settled."

The teasing tone made her smile and she held the fluffy towel for him as he stood. While he dried himself, she turned down the covers. Edward entered the room and looked toward the large bed with its four posts reaching to the ceiling.

"Would you join me? I'd like to have some warmth beside me."

She nodded and stripped quickly, as comfortable in her own skin as she was in any garment. She'd been scrutinized so often in her nakedness she'd have thought no gaze could move her, yet his did.

Edward's eyes trailed over her face and down the slope of her neck, her shoulder, down one arm to her fingertips, over her hip, her thigh, across her belly. It touched briefly at her sex, her knees, her toes, then back up to capture her gaze. He smiled.

"The first time I saw you, I thought you were nondescript," Edward said. "I unwisely thought you bland and symmetrical and dull. Neither hideous nor beautiful."

His words would likely have insulted another woman, but Nessa only nodded. "And how do you find me now?"

"You're not symmetrical. Your body curves and moves in a way that sets you apart from others." He touched the small crimson speck on her left hipbone, a spot the midwives called Kedalya's Kiss. "Your flaws make you unique."

"A flower is made more beautiful by its thorns." Nessa's voice dipped hoarse. "And to be fair, sir, you'd met me for but five moments before running off. Hardly enough time to discern anything about me."

He chuckled. "True. Let's get into bed, for I'm weary."

She nodded and dimmed the gaslights. He reached for her, spooning her against him. Nessa settled into Edward's arms, his breath warm on the back of her neck. He said nothing, so she remained silent. His breathing slowed. His hand rested on her belly. Her eyes drifted closed.

"I wasn't prepared for you, Stillness." She half turned but his hand pressed her still. "I studied the letters of information the Order of Solace sent, I reviewed the contract; to me all seemed in order. I knew what I was to provide and what I was to receive in return. And yet, I wasn't prepared."

She put her hand over his, her thumb stroking his skin. "Because I wasn't plain and nondescript?"

"Because I didn't truly believe you'd be able to help me."

Nessa timed her breath to the rise and fall of his chest against her back. "And now?"

He stayed silent for so long she thought perhaps he'd fallen asleep. When at last he spoke, his voice curled over her as deep and dark as the night itself. Like smoke. His words stroked her.

"Now I've become convinced I should at least allow you to try."

This made her smile and she nestled further against him. "I relish the challenge."

Edward chuckled again. "Say you that to please me or because it's true?"

"I think lying would displease you. So I don't lie."

"Have you had to make a habit of lying to your patrons in the past?"

"Lies, no matter how pretty the picture they paint, more often lead to grief than joy. So, no, I've not found it necessary to lie."

"But you have? If it pleases them?"

Nessa thought a moment, curling her fingers through his. "In the matter of whether or not a shade of rouge or cut of coat is flattering or not, I have perhaps been less than blunt in my answer. But if questioned as to whether a patron is right or wrong in some matter of manners or decision, though it might please them briefly to be told they are right if they're not, in the end it would only bring them grief to continue with poor choices."

"I didn't realize your duty was so tediously complicated." He moved their joined hands in slow, smooth circles on her belly. "How much effort you had to make to placate and anticipate."

"My entire purpose is to placate and anticipate. There is no greater pleasure than providing absolute solace. It's why I joined the Order of Solace."

He nuzzled her neck briefly. "How long have you been a Handmaiden?"

"Seven years."

He made a surprised noise. "You can be no older than—"

"I'm eight and twenty."

"I'd have thought you a good eight years younger than that."

Nessa stared into the darkness surrounding them and wrapped his arm a bit tighter around her. "The Order places no upper limit on the age of its initiates. There are those who come to their vocation years older than I."

Silence fell between them, brief and without awkwardness.

"Why did you choose it?"

"When I was ten and six, I wed the man my parents had chosen for me. After a year, we had a son, and I loved my husband for giving me such a precious gift, if for no other reason."

She did pause then, to gather the familiar threads of her story.

"When my son was two, he died of fever."

Edward's arm tightened around her. "My sympathy."

"My parents contracted the same fever and died. According to the laws of our township, all they owned passed to my husband, as I had no brothers to stand as heir. In a time when we should have clung to one another to palliate our mutual grief, he turned to worm and herb instead."

"And you?" Edward's tone was gentle.

"I . . . I was lost for a time, in my sorrow." Nessa closed her eyes, the darkness behind her lids blacker than the night-filled room. She thought of nights spent in stupor caused by worm and grief, of clutching the hands of strangers. She thought of places she'd gone and things she'd done to escape an inescapable agony. "And I found that being self-destructive, causing myself some small pain, I could distract myself from the greater."

He didn't pull away but she felt him withdraw, just the same. His fingers tightened in hers, almost painfully.

"And the Order? How did you find that?"

"My husband had squandered our inheritance and I'd taken a position as a kitchen drab. The mistress of the household had taken a Handmaiden. Her name was Tranquilla Caden, the first I'd ever met, and from her I learned about the Order and its purpose. I knew the story of the Holy Family, of course, how the lord Sinder walked in the Void and his footsteps made the mountains."

"And his breath the winds."

"Aye. And how he came upon Kedalya in the wood and fell in love with her, and how their love created a son."

"And there the stories differ."

She nodded. "Aye, they do. Some say she betrayed him. Others say it was our own strife that drove the Holy Family back to the Land Above to await the time when men and women no longer submit to hatred."

"But all agree that each soul on this plane that attains perfect solace sends another Arrow to fill the lord Sinder's Quiver, and when it's full, the Holy Family shall return."

She smiled into the darkness, her eyes still closed. "I do so believe. And I thought that providing others with comfort and solace would be the best way to find it for myself. So I sundered my marriage to my husband and joined the Order."

He turned her to face him, and she opened her eyes. Turned this way, the light from the window allowed her to glimpse his face. Edward pulled her snug against him, his expression somber.

"And now?" he asked. "How are you now?"

"I'm no longer self-destructive," she whispered. "And my sorrow has faded. But I will never stop grieving."

His hand passed over her hair, then cupped her cheek. "So what gives you relief, Stillness, from your grief? Is it still the smaller pain to distract you from the greater?"

"Yes."

He let out a low, shuddering sigh, and clasped her tightly to his chest. Nessa put her arm around him, the other tucked along her side. Her head fit just beneath his chin. His hands stroked her back, but the earlier calm his body had effused was gone. Now he jumped and hummed with tension, and she didn't know why.

"Why are you distressed?" She looked up at him and touched his face as he'd touched hers.

"Your story," he whispered.

"I plead your mercy," she said. "If I'd known it would distress you—"

"Shhh," he told her. "I'm glad I know."

And then as tenderly as any lover, Edward kissed her forehead. Her eyes. Each cheek, then her chin, before finally pressing his lips to hers. This gentleness undid her for a moment; her training failed her and she allowed herself the small, exquisite luxury of allowing him to comfort her.

His mouth touched her cheeks again, and when he kissed her once more the taste of her tears parted her lips in an apology he shushed before she had the chance to speak it. He kissed her slowly, urging her to open farther for him. At the taste of him, she moaned. His tongue dipped inside her mouth and she met it with hers. Edward grew hard against her, his cock hotter even than his caress. Murmuring his name, Nessa slid her hands into the silk of his hair at the base of his neck and shivered in delight as his teeth pressed her skin.

"And this," Edward murmured, nipping. "This small pain is the sort you seek?"

"Yes," she breathed, the word becoming a hiss of pleasure when his bite grew fiercer.

He rolled them, kicking down the covers to give her space to move on top of him. Edward pulled her astraddle his waist, and his prick rose hard between them. He rocked her forward so her clit pressed against him.

"What else have other patrons done for you? Have they bound your wrists?"

"Yes." She shivered with delight at the memories.

"Tell me of the time that gave you the most pleasure."

She moaned at the question and the sensation, words for the moment failing her, and his hand gripped her hip hard and denied her the pleasure of motion.

"I asked you a question, Handmaiden."

"I've had many patrons, sir, some more demanding than others—" Her hips rocked forward a bit and his grip tightened again, making her gasp at the sting.

"Answer my question."

"She bound my wrists to the post of her bed and tore my gown from neck to hem." Nessa's body responded to the memory; her nipples peaked and her cunt grew slick. "And then she used a riding crop to mark my back."

Edward's voice rasped and his thumb slid between them to

stroke her. "Your patron was a woman? A woman beat you?" His voice was now like shreds of silk, or the soft leather fringes of a flogger, trailing over her skin. "And she gave you the memory you most treasure?"

"Men are stronger," Nessa whispered, her body straining but staying still despite the nearly mindless urge to writhe. "But women, sir, can be crueler."

Edward groaned. "And this brought you peace, this woman's cruelty?"

"I found that beneath her touch I had the luxury of not thinking of anything else."

Edward thrust his hips beneath her. "Put your hand on my cock while you tell me this."

Eagerly, Nessa curled her fingers around the base of his prick, then slid upward to palm the perfect head. He let out a hiss as her fingertips caressed the small divot under his cock head, and the ridge around it. His thumb ceased circling her clit and instead pressed it in time to the beating of her heart.

"It gave her comfort to be cruel. In the privacy of her bedroom she could lay vent to the anger she wasn't allowed to display in public as a well-bred gentlewoman."

Edward's hand on her hip relaxed and he slid both hands to her buttocks, urging her with a touch to rock forward. She cried out again in relief at this permission and ground her clit against the base of his cock.

"You gave her solace by letting her hurt you instead of those she wished to." Edward grunted when her hand closed over his cock head and squeezed before moving back down the shaft.

"Yes."

"And you gained solace from your grief. What else did she do?"

"She beat me, one line below the next, so my entire back was aflame, but then she gave me a moment to rest. She pinched my nipples, one at a time, until I couldn't stay still, and she touched me—"

"Where?"

"Between my legs," Nessa cried as Edward's fingers closed around her nipple.

"With her hand?"

Another pinch, this time to the other nipple, and her clit spasmed. "Aye, and—"

"With her tongue?" His voice had grown rough as brambles. "By the Arrow, Stillness, she licked you? Tasted you?"

"Yes, yes, yes," she moaned, her head falling back as he twisted her nipples, and her clit danced against her knuckles while she stroked him.

Edward let out a strangled groan and rolled them both until he was atop her, pinning her hands above her head with one hand. "I want to taste you."

He was between her legs before she had a chance to do anything but breathe. His tongue flicked her taut flesh only thrice before his lips fastened on the sensitive bud and suckled gently. The direct sensation after so many minutes of indirect stimulation forced an ecstatic shout from her throat. Her hips thrust as her clit leaped beneath his mouth.

Edward slid first one finger, then another inside her, fucking her as he licked. Nessa moaned, spreading her legs wide and lifting upward to press herself to his kiss. Every muscle strained for release. His fingers twisted inside her, pushing just behind her pubic bone against a spot so sensitive her entire body jerked.

Heat flooded her. She braced herself for the waves of climax, but though her clit hummed beneath his still-working tongue, she didn't feel the familiar explosion of orgasm. This was something entirely new, slow waves of pleasure that built and built rather than diminished.

She'd been with patrons who lacked the skill to bring her to orgasm. Edward, however, was so skilled, so deftly talented with his lips, teeth, tongue, and fingers that he kept her on the edge without allowing her to spill over. All she could do was respond.

"I will be the one who keeps your mind from anything else," he said.

She was unable to do more than moan in answer.

Edward fucked her with his fingers slowly, twisting, then withdrew just as slowly and pushed apart her legs. In the next moment she felt his hot breath on her again, lower, against her sensitive perineum. His tongue traced the small area, sliding up to caress her labia and down again.

And then it happened. Always before, her body had reacted to sexual stimulation as it was now, by tensing and releasing in orgasm. Now, under Edward's attentions, she'd reached a point where she could no longer tense. No longer strain toward release. Instead, it was as though she had rocketed skyward and burst through the clouds to a clear night sky beyond. She floated, cradled. There was no more need to strain toward completion, no reason for her body to leap and jerk and vibrate. Everything had become . . .

"Stillness," Edward murmured, and kissed her sex as easily and with as much tenderness as he'd kissed her mouth.

The world disappeared for a moment, an hour, for eternity, she no longer could tell. She no longer cared. She was consumed.

Her body had responded faster and more delightfully than that of any other woman he'd ever had. She was perfection. This pleased him immensely, her ability to find that place. Most women could climax if given the time and the right caresses. Few could reach such a perfect climax of mind and body simultaneously.

After a moment he moved up her body to push his cock inside.

Earlier he'd wanted to fuck her hard, in a frenzy, but her orgasm had satisfied his need for swift release. His cock would better benefit from slow satiation this time. He thrust, moving easily in her slick channel. He licked the sweet softness of her neck and throat. Nipped. Her gasp sent delight from the base of his balls to the tip of his cock, lodged deep within her. He moved a little faster.

She raked his back with her nails, and he arched. His next thrust buried his prick into her all the way to the entrance of her womb, and she cried out. "You won't hurt me . . . take your pleasure harder, if it pleases you."

Edward was lost. So many times he had taken a woman to his bed, only to deny himself the release he sought in order to be certain he didn't harm them. He spent hours worshipping their bodies to climax after climax, only to stunt his own by holding back. He'd finally given up, taking no one to bed because nobody could give him what he wanted.

Until now. Stillness took what he gave and reacted to it. A woman could feign cries of pleasure and even train her body to replicate the internal spasms of orgasm, but no woman could fake the flush of real arousal that rose in her chest and throat. He didn't need light to see it, either. On Stillness he could feel it, the heat rising from her breasts and the throat he so loved to suckle. He fucked into her harder, reaching up a hand to grip the headboard, and she lifted her hips to match his motion.

An image of the girl Cillian had beaten rose in his mind; Edward twitched and groaned. The girl turned her face to look over one welted shoulder. It was Stillness, the flogger had become a riding crop, and the hand wielding it was his own. He cried out, hoarse, as his orgasm burst through him at the moment he envisioned bringing down the crop upon her back.

His body stiffened, his cock leaping and jerking. He felt each spurt of ejaculate as a separate, exquisite burst of ecstasy that made him shout out her name.

Her hands went around his back and held him close to her. He nestled his face against her for another moment before rolling off. The sweat cooled after a bit, leaving him chilled, but before he could reach for the blanket she had already done so. She pulled it up over both of them and curled her body to his, offering him her warmth.

And for the first time in many weeks, his mind gave in to his body's demands, and he slept without trouble until the morning light woke him.

Chapter 4

"Must you go to town today?" Nessa poured Edward a cup of tea and Waited at his feet for him to sip.

He shook his head. "The prince is spending the day with his father today."

"Is he very ill-behaved?" she asked, buttering a slice of simple-bread for him.

"Cillian? Aye, he is, indeed. But then he's ever been so, as long as I've known him."

She studied her patron as he drank the tea she'd prepared, learning as much as she could about him by the way he spoke and moved. Observation was a subtle art but necessary, and could only benefit from practice. This morning, she noticed, Edward was taking his time over tea. Not rushed. She wouldn't rush, either.

"Perhaps he'll grow out of it," she offered. "Even the rowdiest lads do smooth their manners with time."

Edward gave her an odd look. "He might, but I doubt it. He's been too long indulged to behave any differently, I fear."

She nodded a little. "Then his parents have done him no good service."

"No." Edward's mouth tightened for a moment. "No, I'd say they haven't. His mother died when he was a boy, and his father, I think, believed ponies and sweets would soothe tears better than a tender gesture or attention."

"When he was a boy? But I thought . . . I thought he was a boy."

At this, Edward let out a surprised chuckle. "Cillian is mine own age, Stillness, even if he occasionally throws a rather childish tantrum."

"Your pardon, sir; by the way you spoke of having to look after him, I thought—"

"No." A haunted look crossed his features. "He's not a lad. But apparently, he yet needs looking after."

This conversation was causing her patron distress, and so she moved to another topic with ease. "Have you finished your tea?"

"I have."

He watched her tidy up the tea and simplebread, and when she was finished, he gestured to her. "Come here."

She did, and Waited at his feet again, the back of one hand inside the palm of the other. She smiled as he looked at her, though he wasn't smiling at her. His hand reached out to touch the braid hanging over her shoulder.

"Fetch me the book on my desk."

She did without hesitating, without even thinking of why he'd asked her to do it. When she handed it to him, he didn't take it.

"Put it back."

Again, she did as he'd said, her obedience ingrained and the tasks he asked of her so simple as not to require thought. When she returned to him, she noted the gleam in his eyes. It flared brighter when she again Waited at his feet.

"Stillness," Edward said after a moment in which she sat silent at his feet. "Would you do anything I asked you? Without question?"

"Within reason. Though it's my goal that you need not ask, of course: that all you need be brought to you before you need it."

"How can you possibly expect to do that?" Her answer seemed to confound him, but she'd been asked it before and had a ready answer.

"Practice."

Edward shifted in his chair. Nessa tilted her head, watching him.

"I thought you understood this," she said when he didn't speak for some moments. "It was part of the contract."

"Aye, but seeing the evidence of it is vastly different than merely reading about it on a parchment."

Nessa smiled. "The Mothers-in-Service do their best to assign us to those we're best suited to help, you know. That I was assigned to you means they believed I was best suited for your needs. I'm your comfort, your grace. I'm what you need before you know you need it. I'm here for you."

His reaction wasn't unusual, but it moved her all the same when he let out a sigh and covered his eyes with his hand for a moment. Then he reached for her hand. His thumb traced an interlocking pattern of circles on her palm. "Have you ever been assigned a patron you despised?"

"Only one." She felt the shadows cross her expression at the answer, but could do no less than be truthful.

"But you served him, anyway?"

"Of course I did."

Her patron tugged her gently to sit next to him, though the chair was scarcely large enough for the two of them. "Did you succeed?"

"No. There was naught I could do to satisfy him, nor to bring him solace."

"Is that why you despised him?"

Shocked, she turned in the seat to look at him. "No! Of course not!"

"Is it because you despised him that you were unable to succeed, then?"

The answer to this question didn't rise so readily to her tongue. Nessa thought on it for a silent moment before answering. "No. Even if I had cared for him, I wouldn't have been able to change who he was. An embittered, violent man who thought the tragedy of his past entitled him the use of his fists."

His thumb paused in its circling. "He hit you?"

"Yes."

"His abuse was ill-guided and purely selfish," he said, echoing what she had earlier told him.

"It was." Even now, the memory made her cheeks flush. Vander Decamden had blacked her eye and bloodied her nose before she'd managed to fend him off with a kick to his groin. She'd left the day after, with the Order's blessing.

"A man who would use his hand upon a woman—"

"No, sir," she interrupted gently. "A man who would use his fists upon a woman in anger is not the same as one who brings her pleasure with his touch."

Edward looked at the hand he'd been stroking. His thumb pressed down, hard, leaving a red mark that quickly faded to white. "The difference is in the intent."

She said nothing, letting him be the one to lead. She could only offer him what he must be willing to take. She studied him, noting the rise and fall of his chest as he breathed, the way his tongue slid along his lips as he thought. The gleam of firelight on his skin.

"You like . . . you enjoy . . ." he said hoarsely, hesitating, "being bound."

"Sometimes." Nessa leaned closer to whisper her answer, her own breath coming a bit faster at the thought.

His thumb had begun its pattern on her skin again, and when he looked at her, Nessa's breath caught at the look in his eyes.

"Fetch me that length of ribbon from my desk. The one I took from 'round the package delivered yesterday."

She handed him the slippery length of ribbon within moments. Edward ran the material between his fingers as though testing it for strength or in admiration of its construction, she couldn't tell. When at last he held it up, the smooth coils fell from his fingertips to curl in his palm.

"Hold out your wrists."

She did. Edward took the ribbon and bound them, loosely, tucking the ribbon's edge but not tying it. He ran a finger along the ribbon, then the skin of her hand and wrist.

"You may go about your business."

"Sir?" Nessa hesitated, uncertain what he expected of her.

Edward smiled. "So long as that ribbon stays in its place, you shall be kept in my good graces. Should it fall, I will be displeased."

There were two reasons why this statement sent a thrill through her. The selfish one was that being so commanded called to that part inside her that craved the discipline of concentration. The unselfish one was because this meant he was, at last, allowing himself to take from her what she could give.

"If it pleases you."

"We'll see if it does or doesn't, won't we?"

Managing with bound wrists was no hardship, but keeping the ribbon round them was. He watched her carefully as she made and served tea and cleaned up after. As she mended a tear in his trouser hem and pressed a cravat. The ribbon grew looser and looser, allowing her greater range of motion, but never falling off.

"Stillness," Edward said at last. "Come fetch me this book."

He pointed to a volume high on the shelf, higher even than his head.

"The green book?"

"Aye."

This close, she could smell him, something spicy and masculine. A faint odor of herb clung to his clothes, and under it the scent of the soap he favored. The tea she'd made him added a hint of seductive warmth. She reached for the book, standing on her tiptoes to do so, knowing before she even tried there was no way she could reach. Her fingers brushed the edge of the shelf three lower than the one on which the volume he wanted sat.

And the ribbon, at last, fell away.

"I set you a near impossible task, or so I meant it to be," Edward murmured. "And yet, not until I forced your hand did you fail at it."

She didn't bend to pick up the ribbon at her feet. "Did you so wish me to fail?"

Edward reached to run a hand over her hair, catching the tie at the bottom of her braid and pulling it free. "Aye. I believe I did."

She stayed still as his fingers combed her hair free over her shoulders. "Why?"

He put a hand beneath her chin, tilting her face to look into his. "Because then I could have reason to be displeased, and yet I have found that even in failing me you have pleased me. I'm quite discomfited."

Nessa smiled. "So your purpose was served, after all? You're distressed?"

"Immensely." He moved closer, lowering his mouth to hers but not kissing her.

He took her hand and put it to his groin, against his heated hardness. His fingers made hers stroke up and down through his trousers. His lips brushed hers, and still, he didn't kiss her.

"Take off your gown," Edward said, voice rough. "I want to see you."

The way his breath gasped in when she obeyed was one of the

loveliest sounds she'd ever heard. He stroked himself while he watched her, and when she stood naked before him, he pushed his trousers down over his hips.

"Come here." He pulled her onto his lap, her knees pressing the back of the chair, his cock imprisoned between them. "Loosen my shirt."

She opened the buttons, exposing his bare skin. He pulled her closer to kiss her, and she sighed as her clit finally got the attention it had been craving. Edward gripped her hips, pulling her against him belly to belly. Her clitoris rubbed the base of his erection, and she shivered.

He helped her rock her hips more. Their kisses were slow, languorous, but not exactly gentle. His tongue slid inside her mouth, demanding she return the gesture, and his teeth grazed her jaw and throat every so often.

"Lift up."

He slid inside her. They both moaned. Nessa's head fell forward. Their mouths met, hungry for each other. His kisses inflamed her. The bites even more so. Edward's teeth found her throat again and he held the soft skin between them, torturing her with the anticipation of the sting.

He'd told her this wasn't making love, but it had become more than fucking. Their bodies moved in perfect tandem, her climax mounting.

"This feels good?" he asked.

"Aye, it does. . . ." Her words became a gasp when he circled more firmly on her clit.

Then, he asked no more questions, and they moved together, each seeking the ecstasy of release. Hers came first, a burst of sparkling bliss radiating through her entire body. Her cunt fluttered, and the next moment she felt the pulse of his cock and heard his cry of joy as he climaxed.

Her head found a place on his shoulder as his arms went around her, holding her close to him. She listened to the sound of his breathing. He softened inside her, but they didn't move apart.

"You shall have to try harder, sir," she whispered after a time.

"How so?"

She smiled, nestled in his arms. "If you truly wish me to fail."

Edward sighed and held her closer. "I know, Stillness. I know."

Then they said no more on the matter.

I s she a witch?"

Edward looked up from his book. "Who, Alaric? Your new conquest? She's a bit testy, or so I've heard, but a witch? I wouldn't go that far."

Alaric frowned and eased his long body into the empty spot on the sofa facing Edward. "No, not Larissa, though *testy* as a description of her is being kind. No. Your Handmaiden."

Edward, knowing it was useless to do otherwise, set aside the text he'd been reading. "Why do you ask?"

"Because I'd say she's woven a spell over you." Alaric grinned. "The change is remarkable. The ladies are all atwitter. Even our dear Cillian took me aside to mention it to me. He wanted to know whether you'd been overindulging in herb and worm, for your smile was so ready and bright."

Edward shook his head. "I'll tell him it's no indulgence but his own recent calm behavior that's allowed me this good nature."

"He won't believe you." Alaric reached to the table in front of him and snagged a slice of joba melon. "And if you tell him that, he's likely to head back to his usual ways sooner than later."

"Good point." Edward watched his friend devour the juicy melon. "Do you make love to Larissa the way you eat that fruit? No wonder she's testy."

Alaric rolled his eyes. "Nobody makes love to Lady Larissa, old man. If you count yourself lucky to be allowed to her bed, Lady Larissa quite clearly makes love to you, not the other way 'round."

"She sounds perfect for you, Alaric." Edward knew the lady in question, though not well. "She does all the work, you get all the benefit."

Alaric sucked his teeth free of the strands of melon before answering. "She rides me like a pony, crop and all."

Edward raised a brow. Further discussion on that matter became impossible as the library door banged open and Cillian burst through, followed closely by his latest lapdog, Persis Denviel. The two men carried jugs of worm and bowls of herb.

"Edward! Edward, my dear one!" Cillian had already been imbibing. His eyes were bright, the pupils dilated, and his pale cheeks flushed. He raised the jug. "And Alaric. Join us!"

"No, thank you." Edward shook his head. "I must ride home and I care not to need tying to my saddle to keep me aboard the horse."

Cillian made a face. "You needn't leave us, Edward. What have you at home that could replace the camaraderie and companionship of the palace?"

At that, Alaric let out a snort and sat up straight. Cillian's red-gold head swiveled toward the other man. Putting a hand on his hip, Cillian strode forward to peer more closely at Alaric.

"You know," he said, then glanced at Edward, "don't you? You know what's put such a smile on our dear Edward's handsome face. Don't you?"

Alaric smiled and bowed his head in deference to the man hovering over him. "It's not my place to say."

Cillian's mind was too sharp to be dulled by worm, and he cast a sharp-eyed gaze upon Edward. "A new lover?"

"Nothing like that."

Cillian moved forward, peering at him. His eyes traveled over Edward's body, his neatly tied cravat, the buttoned waistcoat and perfectly pressed trousers. The gleaming, polished boots. Edward shifted awkwardly under Cillian's bright, searching stare. Alaric had turned, as well. Persis had lit a bowl of herb and lost himself in the fragrant smoke.

"You're better put together. You've always been smartly turned out, Edward, but now"—Cillian leaned in to sniff him—"you smell taken care of. But not a lover? A wife? Have you gone and married some fortunate cunna, my dear Edward?"

"You know I wouldn't marry without informing you." Edward didn't like the bright madness in Cillian's eyes, the madness that said he wouldn't be satisfied until he had an answer.

Cillian reached out to stroke the ribbon clubbing back Edward's hair at the base of his neck. "You didn't do this yourself. You braid your hair haphazardly and tie it with frayed cord."

Alaric let out a chuckle. "He has you there, old man. You look positively tidy."

Edward scowled at Alaric. "My lord, I have—"

Cillian's fingers tightened on the bound hair. "Whist. Hush. This is a puzzle, and I dearly love puzzles. Let me figure it out myself."

He leaned closer, his hard grin showing all his teeth. His hand stayed in its place at Edward's neck. His eyes traveled over Edward's face, locking at last upon his eyes. He sniffed again, a deep, slow breath, and the grin turned beatific.

"You have a Handmaiden."

Edward kept his sigh in check by stint of long experience dealing with the irascible and irrational prince. "I do."

Cillian clapped his hands. "Oh, that's rich indeed, my good man! What is her name?"

"Stillness." Edward forced his voice to remain as neutral as his expression, though the prince's reaction made him want to cringe.

"Stillness." Cillian breathed it out, eyes looking upward as he seemed to ponder that. He looked back at Edward. "She is well trained, Stillness. You are clearly closer to solace already."

"Cilly," whined Persis from his sprawled position on the chair by the fireplace, "the bowl's gone out."

Cillian's shrewd gaze narrowed as he looked at Persis. Edward recognized that look, and if Persis knew what was wise, he'd not repeat the tone of voice he'd just used. Persis, however, didn't seem too wise.

Cillian looked back at Edward. "My boy seems to think I'm responsible for keeping his bowl lit."

"Cilly," Persis whined again, languid fingers lifting the bowl for all to see. "It's not smo-o-o-oking."

Edward reached a hand to grasp Cillian's sleeve. "My lord."

Cillian looked at the hand holding him, and for the briefest instant his lip curled. The green eyes blazed. Then, quickly as that, he smiled again and extricated his sleeve from Edward's grasp.

"Don't worry, my dear Edward," he murmured with a look across the room to where Persis was fighting to light the bowl again. "I won't hurt him. Badly."

Edward sat back with a sigh. "Cillian—"

Cillian turned, and in the split-second swiftness that was only one of the things that made him so unpredictable was in Edward's face. His lips brushed against Edward's cheek as he spoke, low, for only Edward to hear.

"Persis has come as willingly as all the others, my dear one. What he suffers is not unwelcomed. Do you understand?"

"I understand, my lord," Edward said, resigned.

Cillian stepped back, grinning. "Sure you won't join us? We have plenty."

Edward was no longer certain he'd be heading home, but Cillian's behavior made even more clear the necessity of Edward remaining clearheaded. "No. Thank you."

Cillian nodded and drew himself up, straightening his waistcoat. "I should be pleased to make the acquaintance of your Handmaiden, Edward. Perhaps I should think of securing one myself . . . though I must say I gain the same benefits from my current pets and for far less strain upon my pocket."

Edward smiled stiffly. "She's not bound to attend me in any place other than my house, as you well know."

Cillian cocked his head. "Then perhaps you must host a brannigan."

Without waiting for an answer, he went to Persis and yanked him up by the cravat, shaking him until the bowl fell from the other man's hands. Persis whined and struggled in Cillian's grip, but not too hard, and it was easy enough to see he enjoyed the attention. Still chastising him, Cillian dragged him out of the library and slammed the door behind them.

"Well," said Alaric when they'd gone. "It would seem you're going to have a party. Shall I be invited as well?"

Edward sighed and scrubbed his face with a hand. "Of course. You're my best friend."

"Am I?" Alaric sounded so oddly wistful it made Edward look up, but it had passed so swiftly he thought he'd imagined it. "Of course I am, you great prat. Who else would put up with your insufferable arrogance?"

Edward laughed. "I think of the two of us, it's you who are the master of that."

Alaric buffed his nails on his coat. "Ah, well. Maybe you're right. But about that brannigan: You don't want him meeting her." Alaric's gaze was shrewd. "You're afraid of what he'd do to her."

"Legally, he can do naught to her. She's bound to serve me only until our contract is sundered. If he violates that he'd have to face the Order of Solace, and their influence extends even here, to Firth."

"Wouldn't stop him from trying," Alaric put in. "He's crossed the Law of the Book before."

"This isn't the Law of the Book, this is greater than that. I don't think even Cillian is reckless enough to tempt it."

Alaric shrugged. "You know him better than I. But the fact remains, if he wants to meet her you'll have no easy time convincing him otherwise."

Edward nodded. "I know."

"But what of me?" Alaric's grin was infectious. "Do I get to meet her?"

Edward laughed. "If you like. You can come home with me today. Margera will make us a supper. We can play at quoites, the way we used to."

Again, a trace of wistfulness crept into Alaric's tone. "I've missed you, Edward. Missed those times. You've been gone for so long, I'm glad to see you're finally returning."

"Gone?" Edward's laugh was a little forced. "I've been here all along."

"No," Alaric countered. "You haven't. Not really."

They stared at each other. "I plead your mercy," Edward said at last.

Alaric reached forward to grasp the underside of Edward's elbow, forearm to forearm, as they'd so often done. "You have it. You were lost, that's all. I'm glad to see you've been found."

Edward gripped Alaric's elbow in return. "Aye. I've been found."

"Look," said Alaric, pulling away and giving the rakish grin that had tumbled so many willing partners to his bed, "Cillian's left the worm."

Chapter 5

H e was naughtier than ever you'd expect." Alaric waved a hand in Edward's direction.

"Hush." Edward took the glass Nessa had refilled and put his hand lightly on her hair when she Waited at his feet. "Don't listen to him, Stillness, he exaggerates."

Alaric scoffed. Nessa had decided she liked Edward's friend within a few moments of their introduction, and her good opinion of him had grown as the evening wore on.

The three of them had shared a delicious meal, prepared by Margera but served by Nessa in Edward's chambers. Now the men had opened the jug of worm, and the stories had begun in earnest.

"Don't listen to him," Alaric countered, holding out his glass to be filled. "He's gone half barmy."

"Only half?" Edward put a hand over his heart. "Alaric, your flattery makes my heart skip a beat."

Nessa watched their interplay curiously. Edward relaxed in Alaric's presence in a way she'd yet been unable to coax from him. She studied them both from beneath her lowered lashes, part of the conversation but not active in it unless asked a question. When Edward got up to stumble to the privy, leaving Nessa alone with Alaric for the first time, she helpfully poured him a fresh glass of worm before he could ask.

"You're not violating your contract by serving me?" His grin was meant to be teasing, but she sensed sincere curiosity in his question.

Nessa smiled and knelt. "I believe it pleases my patron to provide his friend with a full cup at all times, so no, I don't think so. Besides, it's done of my free will."

"Ah." Alaric settled back into his chair.

"How long?" She asked quietly.

"Since the first time I saw him," came the answer, and it pleased her Alaric made no pretense at pretending to misunderstand her question. "You?"

"Not quite so long as that," she replied with a small laugh.

He sipped. From the privy they heard the loud sound of singing and both turned their heads, then looked back at one another, laughing.

"But you do," Alaric said. "Love him, I mean. How could you not?"

Nessa shook her head slightly. "I'm his Handmaiden. Though it would appear I serve him out of love, I can assure you it's my duty alone."

Alaric leaned closer to her, one arm on his knee. "You never love your patrons? Or . . . I rather think you love them all."

"If it was only love they required, they wouldn't need the service of a Handmaiden. But yes, I have a necessary fondness for all those I have served. It would leave me quite coldhearted if I didn't."

"But it's not love."

They stared at each other in silence, companionable and non-confrontational, while she pondered on how to answer his question.

"There can be no place for love in a Handmaiden's life," she said finally. "To love someone only to be sent away, in the end . . . over and over again . . . what an unhappy life that would be."

"Why would you have to leave?" He sipped more worm, slowly, and Nessa had the sudden realization Alaric was far less intoxicated than he'd been acting. "If you were in love with your patron, and he with you? Couldn't you stay? Does it not ever happen?"

Nessa frowned. "It happens."

"You disapprove?"

"The relationship between a Handmaiden and her patron is very special. It can lead to strong emotions, sometimes on both sides. Yet one must never forget the relationship is a contract. It has a purpose. If I provide one day, one hour, one moment of absolute and ultimate solace for my patron, I've done my part. My responsibility returns to the Order to continue in the task I have set myself to assist in bringing the Holy Family back to this plane."

"You haven't answered my question, Nessa. What if you fall in love with your patron, and he with you? What then? Your love gives him absolute solace and then . . . you leave? Doesn't that make waste of your intent? What happens then?"

"My purpose is to provide solace. Not even the Order believes it's possible to maintain such a state infinitely. Solace can be a fleeting thing or something rather more permanent, but no man or woman can be in a state of solace at all times, forever."

Alaric reached for the small bowl of herb on the table, and Nessa took up a flame stick from the fire and lit it for him. He watched her put the burning twig to the full-packed bowl, and he waved the fragrant smoke toward his face, inhaling deeply before sitting back with the bowl still in his hand.

"I think you've again sidestepped me, though I'm too full of worm to figure out how," he admitted. "But it seems like a very lonely life."

She answered quietly. "I know the purpose of my life, and that makes it bearable."

Alaric leaned forward to run a hand over her hair, his fingers stroking the long braid hanging over her shoulder. "Would that I had such a purpose," he murmured. "It would surely aid my own yearning for what I'll never have."

Before she could answer, a crash from the bedroom set her on her feet. With Alaric so close behind he nearly tread upon her hem, Nessa went to the source of the noise and found Edward staring in befuddlement at the chair he'd apparently kicked over on his way out of the bath chamber.

"Bother," he said, looking up as they came in. "This piece of furniture seems to have attacked me."

Nessa went to him and took his arm. "Sir, you are a bit unsteady on your feet. Maybe I should help you to bed."

Laughing, Edward pulled her into his arms and bent to nuzzle her neck. "Oh and aye, that would please me very much indeed."

This made her laugh, too, at his out-of-character giddiness. Nessa put her arm around his waist. "Lean on me."

Edward stayed still, refusing to move though she tugged him. He laughed. She laughed. Alaric, leaning in the doorway with his arms crossed, laughed.

"Allow the girl to put you to bed, you daft bastard," said Alaric. "Before you make more of an arse of yourself."

"Stillness would never think me an arse," said Edward staunchly. "She is my Handmaiden and thus bound to see all I do as a delight."

Nessa shook her head with a teasing sigh. "Oh, my lord, you have read the contract incorrectly. I'm bound to do no such thing."

Edward gave her such an affronted look it sent Alaric into another burst of laughter. "No? Do you not think my every action charming? My every word witty? My every . . . everything . . . ahh . . . shite. Put me to bed, before I make an arse of myself."

Nessa knew her laughter was undignified, but she couldn't seem to stop. Perhaps the smoke from the herb had affected her a bit, though she'd done no deliberate inhaling. Or maybe it was the sheer delight she felt in the room, pouring off these two men, such good friends.

"Come on, then, you ruddy prat, you're breaking the poor lass's back. Get on with you." Alaric crossed to Edward's other side and slung an arm over his shoulder, easing a bit of Nessa's burden. "To bed with you before you fall over."

Indeed, the two steps the three of them took did result in a fall when Edward tugged his companions with him onto the mattress. They ended asprawl in a tangle of limbs and bedclothes, and the room rang with merriment once more.

Nessa disentangled herself from a loop of sheet and Edward's arm to prop herself on an elbow and look down upon him. Alaric had rolled onto his back upon Edward's other side, arms and legs flung wide.

"Edward," Nessa said. "You are utterly destroyed."

Edward's hand snaked up to cup the back of her neck, his fingers sliding into her hair. "I am, indeed."

"Your head will ache upon the morrow," she murmured as he tugged her closer.

"The one above my shoulders may, but I don't intend for the one below my belt to face the same fate." Edward pulled her down to brush her mouth with his. He took her hand from his chest and settled it on the bulge in his pants.

She glanced at Alaric, who hadn't moved, his eyes closed and his chest rising and falling slowly. "Sir, we are not alone."

"Huh?" Edward got up on one elbow to look to his other side. "By the Void, Alaric, you're asleep? What manner of fool have you become?"

Alaric cracked open an eye and turned his head to look at his friend. "If only I were not walking on the clouds right now, I would give you a smack for that accusation."

"Handmaiden," said Edward. "It would greatly please me if you would help me off with my clothes."

Nessa smiled. "Indeed? You care not to sleep in your clothes?"

Edward smiled, too. "I do believe I have already indicated I don't intend to sleep."

"Ah." She looked over at Alaric, who had rolled onto his side, facing them. "And what of your friend, my lord?"

Edward looked at Alaric, then back at her. "It wouldn't please me for my friend to be lonely, Handmaiden. I should find myself very far from absolute solace should I know my dear friend Alaric was left distressed."

She couldn't hold back another giggle. She looked at Alaric, who'd now propped himself on one elbow to avidly watch the conversation. She didn't balk at being asked to allow someone else to touch her, but there was something else of import, here, and that was the emotional tie between Alaric and Edward. She sat up to look at them both, one to the other. Alaric was in love with Edward, but her loyalty wasn't to Alaric. It would not please Edward to leave his friend distressed, but worm and herb could prompt the tongue to spew what would normally have been kept hidden by the heart. Would it please Edward if this night convinced his friend to reveal the depth of his emotion?

"Handmaiden?" Edward slid a hand up to cup her breast. "Have I asked you for something you are unable to provide?"

Alaric looked at Edward, who was still staring up at her.

"Edward and I have been boon companions for a long time. Naught could change that."

The answer to her unasked question was enough, and she nodded slightly when Alaric met her gaze again. "Then it would please me greatly, Edward, to help you both out of your clothes."

"Ah, Stillness," said Edward, "you do make me happy. Every day I thank the Prince of the Land Above I sent for you."

Her fingers worked the buttons of his waistcoat and then his shirt. Parting the fabric, she ran her hands across his bare skin. "Sit, and let me take this off."

He did, obediently. Alaric didn't wait for her to assist him but was already shrugging out of his shirt and tossing it to the floor. He took the ribbon from his hair and let it fall like a shower of gold across his shoulders. The next moment she'd done the same to Edward's and the river of ebony, like raven's wings, made a dark contrast to Alaric's blond ripples.

Nessa pulled off Edward's shirt as he kissed her. The kiss deepened as she tugged the fabric off his wrists, and when they were freed he put his arms around her. Both men had disrobed to skins while she remained fully clothed, and Edward pulled away from another searing kiss to shake his head.

"This will not do. Alaric, you're swift with the ladies. Help my Stillness off with her gown."

"My pleasure." Alaric grinned. "Come here, Nessa."

Cool air caressed her as the front of her gown parted. Alaric put a hand to her face and tilted her head to kiss her fully while he used his other to pull the dress off her arms and push it down. His tongue slid inside and teased hers to explore the hot cavern of his mouth.

The bed shifted beneath her knees. Edward knelt behind her, his mouth suckling the back of her neck. Hands covered her breasts, fingers pinching her nipples to stiffness through the fabric of her shift. At last she knelt, naked, with one man in front of her and the other behind.

"Touch her," Edward ordered. "Feel how hot and wet she is, Alaric."

Alaric's hand slipped through her curls and stroked her, then moved to dip inside. "She's so tight—by the Arrow, Edward, how do you last more than one good poke with her?"

Edward kissed her shoulder blade. "I'm a better man than you? See how beautifully she responds?" he murmured, lips moving on her skin with every word. "Put another finger inside her."

Alaric did. Now she knew something else about Alaric. Not only did he love Edward, but he also gained his pleasure from submission. Edward's hand pushed her thighs wider again, then came round the front, too. With Alaric's fingers inside her and Edward's on her clit, Nessa couldn't suppress her low cry. It became louder when Edward's soft kiss on her shoulder became a bite.

"She likes that," Alaric said.

"She loves it." Edward licked the small wound. "Kiss her, Alaric. I want her whimpering."

Alaric bent to capture her mouth again, and Nessa had no need to fake a reaction to please her patron; two mouths, four hands, two erect cocks brushing against her, all were enough to make her body respond without effort.

Alaric swallowed her cry with his kiss. Edward locked his fingers in the hair at the base of her neck, holding her still while he rubbed her.

"Put your cock inside her, Alaric."

With two men to lift her, two to turn her, Nessa needed to do nothing but allow them their freedom. Moving together as if they were of one mind, Edward and Alaric shifted closer to the edge of the bed until Edward supported her from behind and Alaric's feet hit the floor, his prick still inside her.

"Smooth piece of dancing," Alaric commented, twisting his hips to adjust himself.

Edward laughed, his breath hot on her back as he pushed his body against her, a leg on either side of her hips. His cock rubbed the line of her spine as his hands crept round to cup her breasts.

"With such skilled partners," Edward said, "How could this be anything but?"

Alaric chuckled and thrust inside her again, making her moan. She let her head fall back again onto Edward's shoulder. His mouth latched on to her skin, teeth nipping hard enough to send pain-pleasure shudders through every limb.

"Does this please you?" Edward whispered into her ear after a moment.

"Yes," she replied immediately.

"And this?" His hand returned to her clit and pinched it lightly with his finger and thumb.

She could only utter a wordless reply, but he chuckled and continued. Her cunt clasped Alaric's prick in a way that made Alaric grunt and grip her hips harder.

"Shall we let her come, Alaric?" Edward's voice had gone deep, shadowed, like a thick forest. "Or shall we make her wait for it?"

"Sometimes the longer you wait for something, the more you love it once you have it."

Alaric was looking at Edward. Reflected in the mirror on the dresser across from her, Edward was looking at Alaric. She saw her own face, eyes glazed with desire, saw her body held between two others. She saw Edward turn his gaze to her, felt him turn her head to kiss the corner of her mouth, and the moment, whatever it had been, passed.

"I think," murmured Edward into her ear, "we should let her have her joy, Alaric. She can always have more, later. Come for us both, Stillness."

There was no difficulty in obeying him; in fact, she had no choice. She was already tipping over the edge into ecstasy. She cried out, body arching and taking Alaric in as deep as he'd go. Bright flashes danced in her vision as every muscle leaped and quivered.

Alaric groaned, his thrusts becoming ragged. "By the Arrow!"

"You can feel every ripple, can you not?"

Alaric made no answer as he pumped. Nessa floated down from her place in the clouds, smiling when Edward kissed her again. She was happy to lie back in his arms and accept the joy her body had granted.

"You have well pleased me," Edward told her, with another kiss. He looked upward toward his friend. "And so have you. Handmaiden, I fancy feeling your mouth on me. Alaric, take the chance to taste her now. Unless you'd rather finish inside her?"

The question sent a thrill down her spine, and she looked toward the blond man. He shook his head and withdrew, slowly, and gripped his erection in a fist.

"No, old man, I think I'd very much like to taste her." Alaric grinned smugly. "I told you I could last more than a moment inside her."

"Oh, a competition is it?" Edward laughed. "We'll see."

Again, Edward orchestrated the position, his commands slurred but firm and made in such a manner both Nessa and Alaric hastened to comply. Now, with Alaric on his back beneath her and Nessa on her hands and knees, Edward leaned against the headboard and offered his prick for her to taste, and she took it eagerly.

"Very good." Edward's voice went rough. His fingers wove into her hair and he held it away from her face as she suckled him. "You are such a very, very good girl, my Stillness. My Handmaiden."

She might have forgotten his intoxication if not for these murmurings, this litany of praise. In his drunken state, Edward had become someone different than the man with whom she'd been acquainting herself for the past fortnight. This Edward was free and easy with his commands, with his teeth, with his demands of her. He wasn't shamed by them.

Edward's hand tightened in her hair, the small pain making her climax even fiercer, and she shuddered so hard the headboard rattled behind him. Breathless, blinking in shock, she lifted her head as Alaric moved from beneath her to kneel behind her.

Alaric slid into her with a load groan, echoed by Nessa's and a low one from Edward as she bent her head to take him in her mouth again. She was out of control with arousal, her body so much at the mercy of another. She craved oblivion such as this, but had more often found it beneath the kiss of a crop. In pain. She'd never been able to lose herself so totally in pure ecstasy before.

The men filled her completely and left her no room for thought of anything but this, them, of their taste and smell and the touch of their hands on her body. Of fingers twisting in her hair, pulling it as tears of delighted discomfort leaked down her cheeks and the taste of them mingled. Of hands gripping her hips. Fingers pinching her nipples, twisting, making her cry out again and again.

Nessa opened for them both as Alaric moaned his release and Edward climaxed without a cry, a moan, or a shout, merely a whispered, sibilant murmur . . . her name. Stillness. The sound of it made one last tremor pass through her. Then, cradled between two very smug and smiling men, she laughed.

"We amuse her," mumbled Edward. "Alaric, she must not have had enough from us."

"Give me time to breathe and I'll be ready to go again," Alaric assured her, still grinning. "Just 'ware the Order doesn't come after me."

"I think you're safe," Edward said, winding lazy fingers in Nessa's hair. "For I did request it of her, after all."

That comment Alaric answered with a snore, which made Nessa and Edward laugh again, so fiercely the bed shook, and sometime after that, Edward eased inside her and made her cry out his name in hushed tones so as not to wake their companion.

Chapter 6

"A pity I spent so long dressing myself this morning," said the languid drawl from the doorway, "else I'd be fair tempted to climb into that pile with you."

Edward cracked open an eye instantly at that voice. A soft, warm weight on his chest turned out to be Stillness. She stirred as he struggled to sit, discovering in his travails another warm body alongside him . . . this one rather more unexpected.

"Don't get up. I'm rather famished and will seek my own refreshment, since it's obvious you're unable to serve as host." Cillian tossed off the words with a flick of his glove and a smirk that set Edward's teeth on edge, but he could do naught but agree.

Alaric burrowed deeper into the blankets, and Stillness sat, pushing her hair from her eyes. Thus released, Edward got up, too, well aware of his nakedness but unconcerned. Cillian had seen him in naught but skin many times before.

"My lord, I wasn't expecting you."

"I see that." Cillian let his gaze fall down to Edward's groin, sporting its usual morning pride, and the prince's eyebrows rose. "Don't let me keep you from your just-rising fuck, Edward, though I must say, it's well past the midday hour and I'd have expected you to be up and about already."

The midday hour? Edward ran a hand through his hair and winced. His throat bore a suspicious dryness. Last night's indulgence was slowly returning to his mind, and he looked up at Cillian with as even an expression as he could muster.

"Margera will see to your needs, and I'll be down shortly. I apologize for not being better prepared."

"I told you, Edward, fret not. I'll be in the kitchen scaring your flighty downstairs maid and charming that mannish chatelaine of yours into giving me some of her fresh sugar rolls. I do so adore her sugar rolls."

Edward heard the shuffle of fabric from beside him, and Stillness appeared with his robe, sliding it up his arms and belting it without fanfare. She remained in her skin, her hair falling down over her shoulders and back, and Cillian's gaze took her in with the same flat look a snake gives a mouse before it strikes.

"Handmaiden," Edward said stiffly. "Dress yourself."

She looked up at him, and then at Cillian. "If it pleases you."

She grabbed up her gown from its place on the floor, and he had time to note the unusualness of that—that she had not bothered to fold it as she always did, before she ducked past him and into the bath chamber.

Cillian's tongue slid out along his mouth. "She is most fair."

"She is . . . satisfactory." Edward didn't wish to discuss this with Cillian, whose vivid gaze now flicked back to the bed, where Alaric was still snoring.

"I'll leave you, then," said Cillian. "I'll be in the kitchen."

With that, he swept from the room in a flourish and swirl of his cloak. Edward watched him go, his guts clenching from more than overindulgence. He went to the bathing chamber, and found a basin of icy water already filled. Stillness had dressed and bound back her hair, and held out a damp cloth to him as he entered.

Edward took it and pressed it to his eyes. Her warm hands urged him to sit in the hard-backed chair next to the tub, and she kneaded his shoulders. The touch relieved some of the tension . . . but created as much as it relieved.

She went to her knees before him, taking his hands in hers. "I can bring you tea and some breakfast, and I can step quietly and speak low . . . but I cannot take away the affects of worm and herb."

He looked down at her, meaning to snap, but found himself unable. "I asked you to bed the pair of us?"

"You don't remember?" She let her thumbs trace circles on the insides of his wrists, then pressed firmly to spots next to the tendons.

The pressure made the roiling in his stomach ease, to his surprise. "I was foolish yestereven, with my consumption."

"I did what I thought would please you."

He studied her. "And did it please you, as well?"

She smiled. "Very much."

He thought he might kiss her then, and the impulse startled him, for such a tender gesture it seemed. He was saved from his own foolishness by the stumbling arrival of Alaric, rubbing his face, who went immediately to the wastechair and pissed in such a long, hard stream it rang against the chair's porcelain bowl.

"Morning." Alaric grunted, looking over his shoulder at them. "Sinder's Balls, have I got a headache."

"I'll go brew some tea," said Stillness, getting up. "Enough for both of you."

With one more squeeze to Edward's wrists, she stood and left the room. Alaric finished, shook his cock with two fingers, and then bent to splash his face and neck with the icy water in the basin.

Cursing and blowing, he stood, face dripping. "And how fare you this morn, my friend? If my head hurts, yours must be fair to bursting. Did I hear Cillian?"

Edward nodded. "He's here."

Alaric went to the small window and peered out, then turned back to Edward. "Not alone. It would appear our lord prince has arrived with full retinue."

Edward pushed Alaric aside to look out the window. "To the Void with him!"

"Looks like you're about to host a brannigan."

"You are utterly too jolly for this morning." Edward bent to the basin himself, splashing frigid water all over himself and yelping with it.

Alaric handed him a towel. "Why shouldn't I be, after last night?"

Edward took the towel and looked up. Their gazes met. "Last night is a mite hazy to me, Alaric."

The other man's smile didn't dim in the least, though his gaze flickered a bit. "We both made love with and were made love to by that beautiful woman now brewing us ease for our poor abused pates. Nothing else."

Edward nodded. "If there had been something else. . . ."

Alaric lifted a brow, but said nothing. A first for him, letting a statement like that slide, and Edward understood at once the significance of his friend's silence. Alaric said nothing further, merely shrugged and bent back to the basin.

"If I'm going to be hosting a brannigan, I shall call on your help," he said. "As I'm rather shite with that sort of thing."

"I'll do my best to help you with my remarkable skill with parlor games." Alaric looked out the window again. "Well, fuck me hard behind the stable."

Edward looked up at that, a laugh forcing its way out his reluctant throat. "What?"

"Lady Larissa." Alaric grinned. "She's just stepped out of her carriage."

I t was the wrong season for a brannigan, the weeks-long house party generally thrown in winter when weather made travel difficult and guests and activities helped ease the dullness of short days and long nights. Apparently, Cillian Derouth didn't care for such constrictions on his social life.

"Food and lodging I can easily provide," Edward said that night, slouched in front of the fire while she knelt before him to unlace his boots. "But entertainment I'm sorely lacking."

He took the glass of warmed wine from her and settled back while she put soft slippers on his feet.

"Alaric, I'm certain, could aid you in that." Nessa got up to poke the fire into brighter blaze, then returned to her place at his feet.

"Aye, Alaric."

"So allow him to organize them." It seemed simple enough. "Or perhaps the ladies who've arrived would play hostess, as you've none."

She'd not meant it as reproach, but Edward's eyes told her he took it that way.

"I don't want you to think I'm ashamed of you."

"I know you're not ashamed of me."

It was himself that shamed him, and for that she could do naught.

Edward gestured for her to lay her head upon his thigh, which she did with a contented sigh. His hand passed over her hair in smooth strokes. "Unbind your hair."

He wove his fingers through the braid-kinked strands until they fell across her shoulders and back. Nessa closed her eyes and rubbed her cheek against the soft cloth of his trousers. His hand on her head petted and soothed, as much a pleasure to her as solace to him. She waited, gauging his mood by the tension in his muscles.

Happy people didn't request the services of a Handmaiden. All of her patrons were in some way damaged. As she herself had been damaged. Sometimes, Nessa discovered the source of her patron's pain and was able to dissipate it. For others she never learned what secrets in their past had hurt them, but it didn't matter, for she succeeded in helping them anyway.

Edward was different from all of them, every one she'd ever had. The kind and the cruel, the smart and foolish, the generous and stingy. He'd touched something inside her no other had, and the realization of that was enough to tense her muscles.

Edward was different because . . . she was falling in love with him.

At the infinitesimal tightening of her body against his leg, Edward's hand came once more to rest upon her head. "What disturbs you?"

"It is my place to ask that of you, Edward, not yours to question me."

He urged her with his touch to look up at him. "I would know your secrets."

"I've bared them all to you." She got up on her knees and reached to touch his cheek. "Will you tell me yours?"

He shook his head. He moved her palm over his mouth to kiss it, his lips warm. Nessa got up and settled onto his lap, an arm curving round his neck to put her forehead to his.

"Edward," she whispered. "I want so much to see you happy."

"Because it is your pleasure and your purpose?" He nuzzled her cheek with his lips before looking into her eyes.

"Not only that. No." She kissed his mouth with sweet intent, though the underlying spark of constant passion between them was impossible to ignore.

His hand slipped up to tangle in the hair at the base of her neck. "Will you understand me when I say I want you to fail in your purpose?"

She smiled a little, her throat tight with sudden, nameless emotion. "My expense is too great? You wish to recoup what you've paid to the Order?"

He shook his head. "No. But if you succeed, you'll have to leave. And I don't want you to leave me."

She took a long, slow breath. "If I fail, I would have to leave you, as well."

"Do you always have to leave your patrons, Nessa?"

"I do."

"Have you ever wanted to stay?"

She took his face in her hands and kissed his mouth slowly, and pulled away just enough to breathe against his lips. "Yes, Edward. I have."

With a low groan, he slanted his lips to hers. His hand tightened in her hair, pulling. His tongue dove inside her mouth, stroking her into a gasp of desire.

He pulled back suddenly. "Every time I think I've sated myself with you, I discover I haven't. I'm not sure I ever can."

"I'm happy to serve you—"

"No." He shook his head. "It's more than that. Tell me what it is."

Nessa hesitated. She was never unable to put aside her training, to forget her pleasure and her purpose. Telling him what he wished to hear would surely grant him a moment's peace but in the end might harm more than help. The line was fine, the edge sharp; a false step would slice them both.

His hand in her hair tightened, bringing another gasp from her. "Answer me."

"It pleases me to know that I so please you."

This answer, while the truth, seemed not to satisfy him. He pushed her from his lap, not ungently but without any question as to his intent. "I sent for you because I needed someone who would not play emotional games. A companion who would ease my mind. Make my home a haven and a comfort."

"Have I done so?" She made to go into the Waiting, but his command stopped her.

"Stay on your feet. Yes, Stillness, you have. You have brought light and warmth to these rooms beyond the simple matter of tea and clean floors. And for that, I'm grateful."

"I'm pleased—"

He stood, towering over her. "There's more. You've pleased my mind, but my body, too. An unexpected but welcome gift."

She said nothing, looking up into his face.

"You're here to give me something I think impossible for me to attain."

"Absolute solace. Even a moment of it and my duty is fulfilled."

"And you will do anything I need to achieve that goal. Will you not?"

His voice had gone low and dangerous again. It sent an anticipatory shiver through her. She nodded.

"Yes."

"Then tell me," he said, voice like silk snagged on a rough branch, "that I'm more to you than just another patron."

She wanted to, by the Arrow, she did. But there was no place for love in a Handmaiden's life. Nothing good could come of such a revelation, and her duty wasn't to her heart, but to his.

"I value each of my patrons individually, Edward," Nessa said at last. "Each is unique to me, and each holds a separate but equal place in my heart."

Edward lifted his chin, and when he spoke, ironwood had replaced the silk in his voice. "Then if I'm like all the others, I shall devote myself to the effort of helping you succeed in your task. I shall allow you to grant me solace."

This answer didn't make her happy, said as it was in such a cold tone. "Edward—"

"Take off your gown."

Never before had she had such trouble with obedience. Her hesitation was unintended, the result of the conflict in her mind and heart. Where always in the past she'd been able to set her thoughts to automatic response, now, here, she couldn't seem to manage to find the place within herself that was entirely Handmaiden, and not entirely Nessa.

"I *said* take off your clothes." The command was harsh and startled her into putting her fingers to the buttons at her throat. Edward's gaze glinted. He seemed to grow larger, more intimidating. "Now."

"Yes."

"Yes, sir," he told her.

"Yes, sir." She undid her buttons swiftly and peeled open the gown, stepped out of it and folded it neatly to put on the footstool.

"Hold," he said when she'd begun loosing the laces at the neckline of her shift. "I would see you this way for a moment."

She froze, heart hammering. She searched his face, but of the tender man who'd cradled her on his lap moments ago there was no sign. In his place was the man who used his teeth. The man she knew could be hard but kind in his severity, the one she knew could give her the release she craved, if only he would admit himself capable of it.

She shivered, her nipples peaking and drawing his attention. Between her legs, her clit throbbed once, and as if he could see that, too, his eyes went there.

"With the firelight behind you, your body is outlined in red and gold and shadow. I can see every curve, every line right through the fabric of your shift. Your nipples, begging for my tongue. That sweet slit between your legs, begging for my cock to fill it."

She swallowed hard, her throat tight now with an emotion she *could* name. Lust. Pure, fierce lust. She shifted a bit, legs parting.

"Take off your gown."

She did.

"Move your feet apart. Open your legs."

She did that, too, her breath coming in small jerks as her heart pounded. The heat from the fire caressed her back while the heat from his eyes did the same to her front.

"I want to see your pearl. Show it to me."

Nessa slid her hand between her legs and used her fingers to part her curls and expose herself to his eyes. The touch made her bite her lip and take in a long, deep breath.

"You're wet." Edward sounded satisfied. "This arouses you. Doing as I tell you."

"Yes, sir. It does."

"It will feel good for you to take some of your nectar and rub it on your pearl. Do it."

With a shudder, she did, dipping a finger into her folds and drawing it upward again to slide easily over her clit. Edward hissed at the sight, and Nessa's hips pumped forward, against her hand.

"Your nipples are begging for attention, too. You like them to be pinched, don't you? Twisted. You like that little pain." His voice had grown hoarse. The front of his trousers bulged with an erection Nessa longed to caress.

Again, she nodded. "I do, yes, sir. Yes."

"Because it allows you to forget everything else."

"Yes, sir!"

Her thighs trembled as her clit engorged under her touch. Her nipples grew tighter, too, tingling and throbbing as much as her bead. She let her hand move up to cover a breast, palm against her aching flesh for a moment before her fingers clamped down and both hands moved in tandem, pinching and stroking.

"You could bring yourself off in another moment, couldn't you?" Edward whispered, watching. "You could come like that, with me watching."

She murmured an answer. "If it pleases you."

"It does not," said Edward sharply. "You will be sated when I grant you permission and not before. Do you understand?"

She stopped her stroking, though her body protested. "Yes, sir."

"I have seen full well how much you like to come. Your orgasm will be your reward for pleasing me. Do you understand?"

She nodded, watching him. His eyes had gone half lidded, watching her. He looked toward the cabinet she'd been forbidden to open.

"In that cabinet, on the shelf, is a box. Bring me the small casket inside."

The cabinet doors creaked as she opened them, but inside she found only unlabeled boxes and drawers. Which one? She thought swiftly, opening her mind to him and what she knew of him, and put her hands to the first box in front of her. Within it was the small, carved casket. She brought it to him, Waited at his feet.

"Come here."

She followed him to his desk, wondering at what he held. Edward set the casket on the desk and took out the first piece, a thin, gold chain with a gem dangling from one end and a small loop of gold attached to the other. He lifted an identical piece from the casket and held them up so the gems danced and reflected the firelight.

"Do you know what these are?"

"Earbobs?"

"No." He cupped a hand beneath her left breast and slipped the loop of the piece over her nipple. "Not for your ears."

She gasped as it slid on, the fit snug but not painful. In moments her nipple turned a dusky rose color and tingled deliciously. The dangling gem weighted the chain just enough for her to feel each twist and turn. She gasped again when he slid the other loop onto her right nipple.

"You will wear these as you attend me this evening." Without waiting for an answer, Edward reached into the casket and pulled out another, similar piece. Instead of a loop at the end, however, it had a V-shaped piece of gold and two dangling chains weighted with gems. "Sit on the edge of the desk and open your legs."

Shaking in anticipation, Nessa did. The wood was smooth and cool beneath her rear.

"Grip the edge of the desk with your hands. You will not move them unless I give you permission."

She curled her fingers around the desk's smooth edge and parted her legs wider. Edward moved between them. She waited, breathless, but he looked without touching for some long moments while her clit grew ever harder and hotter beneath his inquisitive gaze.

"Such a lovely cunt you have. It will look even prettier adorned as your nipples are."

He took the third piece of jewelry and placed his thumb and forefinger on each side of her clitoris. She gave a small cry, her hips leaping but her hands staying in place as he'd ordered. Edward gently pinched her arousal between his finger and thumb and stroked it up and down, much as she'd have stroked his cock. Nessa moaned again, her thighs opening wider of their own volition. With his other hand he took the third piece of jewelry and slipped the V-shaped piece over her erect clit. The smooth metal pinched against her engorged flesh and sent a spasm of arousal through her. He took his hand away, yet the metal on her remained, mimicking the sensation his fingers had provided. The chains hanging from it caressed her clit while the gems dangled, tapping her labia gently and sending shivers through her.

Edward looked at her. "This, also, you will wear as you attend me tonight."

"Yes . . ." She swallowed, hard. "Yes, sir."

"And I have two more adornments for you, though they are not as pretty." He reached into the casket and pulled out something that clicked and clattered in his palm. Two sets of what looked like pearls, carved of ironwood, four on each strand. One set was thrice the size of the smaller, the beads of which were no larger than the end of her thumb. She could see no clasp to close the ends of the unusual pieces, and at any rate, neither was long enough to fit around her neck, or even a wrist.

"These are not meant to be worn on the outside," Edward said as though he'd read her mind.

With that, he put a hand beneath her legs and pushed the larger set of pearls inside her quim, slowly, one at time. The last pearl he left outside, tucked up against her opening, where the gem from the chain attached to her clitoris could tap against it. The other three shifted inside her, filled her, and pressed just behind her pubic bone with every motion.

Edward waited until she had stilled herself once again, his hand on her hip. She looked at him, and his smile rewarded her.

"Your response is delightful," he assured her and held up the second set of pearls.

She knew at once where he meant to put those and her body unconsciously tensed. Edward took one last thing from the casket. A small vial, which he uncorked and tipped over his fingers. It released a thick fluid smelling pleasantly of herb. Corking it again, Edward set it aside and rubbed the fluid quickly over the second set of beads.

"Turn around. Hold the desk," he ordered, and though each movement made dozens of tremors run through her, Nessa obeyed.

Edward ran a slick finger down the seam of her buttocks and pressed lightly against her back entrance. The pressure urged a moan from her. With a pleased sound, Edward pushed her flesh. Nessa arched her back in response, lifting her rear. She felt the cool touch of the beads at her back passage and tensed.

"Open for me."

She tried, but when the wooden pearl once more pressed against her, she tensed. This time, Edward reached around and tugged gently on the chain hanging from her clit. A tug, a press of the bead against her. Another tug, another press, until she was positively pushing her rear toward the intrusion.

One pearl slipped inside her, but aided by her arousal and whatever he'd used to lubricate it, she felt no pain, only a delirious pressure that echoed in every pleasure point on her body. Edward tugged the chain again, bringing her closer to climax but not letting her spill over, as he pushed the second bead inside her. Then the third, with the fourth left to press against her on the outside.

Thus filled, Nessa could only tremble and take deep breaths. Her body strained toward the climax so close, but mindful of what he'd said, that her orgasm would be a reward, she didn't seek to force it into happening.

After a moment or two, Edward stepped away. "I've work to do. You shall attend me as usual."

With that, he went to his desk chair and sat, pulling a ledger book toward him and lifting his quill from the inkpot.

Stunned, uncertain, Nessa didn't move until Edward looked up, and in an utterly bored voice, told her, "Get me some tea, Stillness."

She nodded, unable to speak, and stood. Her fingers had

clutched the desk so hard they'd cramped, and she opened and closed them to ease the stiffness. She turned, the motion setting the gems to swaying and the beads inside her rolling a bit. She moaned.

Edward looked up. "Now."

"Yes, sir."

She'd served naked many times, but never so decorated. It took her three steps to get to the back of his leather chair in front of the fire, and once there, she paused to grip the back, thinking she might fall, so deliciously torturous were the sensations running through her.

But Edward had ordered tea, and there could be no hesitating. Not even a swift repetition of the five principles helped much, but they did allow her to gather her breath and make the tea.

For the rest of the evening she served him that way. Every step was scrumptious agony, causing the jewelry to rub and pull and shift against her most sensitive spots, yet never allowing her the relief of orgasm. Edward seemed more fractious than ever before, needier, unable even to get up from his desk to fetch his own books or files when in the past he'd have done so without pause. Tonight, he put her to work harder than he'd ever done in the past, and her body screamed with delight during every moment of it.

Her every sense heightened. Smell, sight, hearing, taste . . . but especially touch. Her entire body, from forehead to the tips of her toes, became as sensitive as her clit and nipples. The breeze created by her movements trailed tickling fingers over her belly, the seam of her buttocks, her nipples. The heat of the flames stoked the fire between her thighs. Every breath she took in brought greater sensation with it, until at last she could do nothing but shake and tremble and await release.

At last Edward got up from the chair and ordered her to attend him once more. "Face the desk and put your hands flat upon it."

She did at once, parting her legs without being told. His touch, one finger tracing her spine, made her whimper. When it reached the crease of her ass, her hips jumped.

"You've been a delightful Handmaiden tonight," he murmured. "You've done everything I asked, without complaint. I do believe it is time for your reward."

Oh, she did adore this. The commands. The torture, the pleasure so intense it had become pain, the small pains that were a pleasure. She loved being told to serve, having the choice taken from her, being dominated in this way. She loved this.

She loved him.

Nessa drew in a deep, sobbing breath. Edward put a hand on the back of her neck, holding her still while his other slipped round to toy with the gems dangling from her nipples. He tugged them gently, and her body jerked.

Edward slipped off first one, then the other, and the relief was so great and at the same time, so disappointing, she cried out. He massaged her nipples gently, tweaking them, and put the chains on the desk. He shifted behind her and she heard the rasp of his buttons being undone. She tensed, waiting, her heart thundering.

His hand still on the back of her neck, holding her still, Edward reached around to tug the chain on her clit. Nessa cried out again, hips pumping forward. Edward gave it another small tug before slipping it off her clit. Again, the release was so great she almost came right then and there. Both her passages convulsed on the beads inside her, and her clit, released from its binding, fluttered. Orgasm hovered, enormous, like a wave curled to strike the shore.

Edward put his hand to the bead resting against her labia, and he eased the second from inside her. She was making a series of shuddering, gasping cries at this point, unable to breathe without making a noise. The next bead slid from inside her, and she bucked her hips helplessly. By the time he slid the final bead from her

quim, Nessa could no longer tell if she were climaxing or only riding one long wave of ecstasy that didn't seem to end. There were no
dips, no valleys, only a series of higher and higher peaks.

Edward shoved his cock inside her, fucking roughly, but she was so
wet, so open, so ready, it only made her push back against him at
once. Her hands slid on the polished wood as he thrust so hard he
moved her entire body. He grunted, fingers pulling her hair again.
Nessa's cries eased as her climax dipped and softened. Only for a
moment, however, as in the next she felt him tug the final adornment.

Edward fucked his prick inside her, hard, even as he pulled out
the first bead. The dual sensation, of being filled and emptied at
the same time, left her too breathless for even a scream. All she
could do was breathe.

Her first climax had overwhelmed her, sent her tumbling. It had
not yet ended when this new sensation sent her soaring again. A
thrust, a tug, and as his thrust became faster, harder, pounding into
her slick passage, he released the final bead and she came again,
moaning and shivering.

Edward let out a shout and thrust once more, so hard he moved
the desk and her hands slid again on the wood. His fingers released
her hair and returned to the back of her neck. He pumped a bit,
slowly, and then bent forward to kiss her shoulder blade.

His shirt felt smooth on her bare skin, and she realized he'd
done no more than open his trousers to take her. For some reason,
this made her smile. Then laugh, the sound hoarse from her abused
vocal chords, but recognizable.

He kissed her shoulder again and withdrew. She let out a murmur of protest. She wasn't sure she could move.

And then, she didn't have to, for Edward put an arm under her
shoulders and one beneath her thighs, and he picked her up and
carried her to bed, where he tucked her between clean, cool sheets,
and she slept.

Chapter 7

Cillian was calmer than Edward had seen him in a very long time. The Prince of Firth reclined on the chaise lounge, his shirt unlaced at the throat, his jacket tossed without ceremony into the corner. He'd unbound his hair and the autumn-leaf waves tumbled over his shoulders and gleamed in the light of the fire. He sighed, sounding so deeply content that Edward chuckled.

Cillian looked up. "I amuse you?"

Edward shook his head. "I'd never have thought to see the day when you, my lord, were worn out from playing cards."

"Not merely cards, dear one." Cillian's lips tipped. "Cards with Lady Larissa. That woman is a harpy."

Edward glanced through the open doors toward the next room, where Ladies Larissa, Marvina, and Sentinell laughed at the antics of Alaric and the other lords Cillian had brought with him.

"James and Persis are amusing them." Edward took a long drink from his mug of spiced hard cider. "And Larissa is laughing quite heartily at Alaric."

Cillian sat up in his chair to follow Edward's gaze. "At least he seems contented in his role, which is more than I can say for you. When are you going to come back to me, Edward? I miss you."

"I haven't gone away, my lord."

Cillian sniffed. "You've known me for how long?"

"Six years in school. Five since then. Eleven total." Edward watched the activity in the other room as James and Persis acted out what he'd have guessed to be the Follies' Uprising, based on the tablecloths they'd thrown over their heads.

"For Kedalya!" Cried Persis, tearing off the makeshift veil and miming stabbing a shocked-looking Alaric. "Rise, sisters, rise!"

This set Larissa and her companions into gales of silly giggles that made Cillian wince. He got up and went to the double pocket doors and slid them closed with a bang.

"Eleven years you have known me. One would imagine that after that time, you would adore me better." Cillian sank back onto the chaise, an arm thrown over the side to pillow his head.

Edward thought carefully before answering. Once he'd cared very much for the man before him. Once, they'd run like young wolves with nothing to stop them. He sipped cider while formulating his reply.

"You have my loyalty and my companionship, my lord prince."

Cillian sighed and rolled his gaze toward Edward. "I used to have your love. Your boon companionship. We ravaged the streets and poetry houses. We were the envy of everyone. You and I and Alaric. Now my father pays you to play nursemaid to me, to keep his abomination of a son from embarrassing him the more."

"You still have my friendship, Cillian." Edward got up to pace in front of the fire. "Just because I don't go whoring with you—"

"You used to be right there with me," Cillian interrupted. "Every step. Every new venture."

"Every vice, you mean." Edward turned to look at him.

Cillian didn't pout. His eyes glittered. "Every *excitement*. Surely you remember that? The thrill of learning a new trick? Some new decadence to taste?"

Edward remembered, though he wanted to forget. "That was a long time ago."

Cillian got to his feet to stalk toward him and take the cup of cider from Edward's hand. He sipped before pushing it back to its place in Edward's palm.

"Not so long ago that you've forgotten, my dear one. I see it in your eyes when you attend me in the playroom. I see it there, now."

Edward knew better than to try to pretend otherwise. He'd never been able to hide anything from either one of them, Alaric or Cillian, his two best friends.

"I remember. Of course I do."

"Is that why you took a Handmaiden?"

Startled, Edward clattered his cup against the stone mantle. "No!"

Cillian smiled. "Are you sure?"

Edward shook his head, though the memory of Stillness, her pretty nipples and quim glittering with jewels, would not leave him. "She's not a whore."

Cillian raised one perfect brow. "I never said she was. But she is a Handmaiden, bound to give you what you desire for the purpose of giving you peace."

"Stillness has nothing to do with the pleasures you enjoy." Edward tossed back the rest of his cider and put the cup back on the table. From the other room, filtered laughter made him turn. "And you have Persis to frolic with. You don't need me."

Cillian's brow remained raised. "Persis is my lover, Edward, not my friend. You and I were something bed partners could never be. I thought you knew that. It's the friendship I miss." Cillian paused, his voice dipping. "You could always make me laugh. Do you know that? Really laugh. You and Alaric were the only two who didn't treat me like my crown was something to be revered. You are the brother of my heart, Edward. What can I do to get that back?"

Edward said nothing, his gut churning at Cillian's speech. He no longer doubted Cillian's sincerity. Yet he could do naught for it but answer with honesty.

"Nothing," said Edward. "It died, along with the girl."

Then he opened up the double doors and rejoined the others, leaving Cillian to stand alone behind him.

Nessa watched from the window for Edward's return. The little party, five men including Edward, and three women, had spent the day picnicking in Edward's far field, where a small, clear pond allowed bathing. She'd already filled the bath for him and laid out his clothes. She hummed to herself as she puttered around his sitting room, thinking of how much she looked forward to this time of day. The time when he returned to her, if only for an hour or so before returning to his guests.

The nights she liked even better, for then she had him for hours on end, and her service to him no longer meant serving tea and running a bath. She smiled. At night it meant a completely other world.

"I see now why he keeps you locked away. You're too lovely to share with the rest of us."

The voice from the doorway made her turn, but Nessa was quick. She bobbed a small curtsy. "My lord prince."

Cillian laughed as he entered the room. "I'm not your prince, Handmaiden. Am I?"

Technically, he wasn't, as she wasn't a citizen of Firth. Nessa smiled anyway. "When in the home of another, obey another's laws."

He moved into the room with fluid grace, each movement almost like a dance step. "You may call me Cillian. I'd prefer it, in fact."

She had to keep turning her body to follow his movement through the room. Cillian pretended interest in the rows of books, the desk, even the windows before finally turning his gaze back to her. He had bright green eyes, the color of summer grass. They were not soft eyes, and she stepped back upon instinct when he speared her with his gaze.

"My lord Edward has not yet returned. I expect him at any moment. Would you like to wait for him, or perhaps I could give him a message?"

Cillian came closer, that sharp gaze studying her closely. Nessa didn't back away, even though he stood close enough for her to feel his breath on her face. He wasn't as tall as Edward, his form slighter, but she had no false beliefs that his lesser stature made him less strong. Cillian Derouth made her wary, but not anxious.

"Cillian," she said steadily. "When in another's house—"

"Obey its laws. This I know." His charming smile was at odds with the calculating gaze. "He has you adorned."

Not a question, and before she could answer he'd reached to run a thumb over the fabric of her gown, just over her nipple. The tight flesh responded at once.

"Here," he murmured, and rubbed the other. "And there. Aye?"

She didn't have to nod. His touch would have told him the answer. On fire with sensation, her nipples poked the front of her gown.

"And one on that sweet slit, too, I daresay."

For one moment she thought he meant to touch her there, too, but Cillian only used his gaze to caress between her legs. Nevertheless, the scrutiny made her acutely aware of the clip on her clitoris, and how the weight of the gem dangling from it tugged with every step.

"And inside you, as well?" He breathed, voice a little hoarse. Cillian's eyes narrowed in speculation and he leaned even closer, to whisper in her ear. "I taught him how to do that."

She had no answer for that, but he seemed to expect none.

Cillian drew back. "You smell good. Is that for him, too?"

"Everything I do is for him," she managed to say.

She couldn't read his expression. After a moment, he gave a small nod, as though he'd expected her answer. He stepped back. Nessa let out the breath she'd been holding.

"Tell Edward it would please me if you were to join us for supper."

Cillian smiled and gave her a half bow, then left the room without waiting for her to answer. But then, she mused, watching him go, he was likely so accustomed to being obeyed he didn't need to hear her agree.

When she told Edward what his prince had requested of him, her patron was rather less than pleased.

"Damn him to the Void," he muttered. "He knows a Handmaiden is not required to serve any but her patron."

"He didn't ask it of me, Edward. He bid me ask it of you."

"Knowing I can hardly refuse him, the bold bastard."

"If it doesn't please you for me to attend the supper, than I shall not." The answer wasn't quite that simple, and she knew it.

Edward cast a glance at her. "And that would grieve my prince, who might take it upon himself to be less than diplomatic in his response to not being obeyed."

"He has no rule over me, but he has over you. And therefore, though it might not please you for me to attend supper at his command, it would surely please you less to make him angry." Calmly, Nessa checked his clothes for stains and tears as she folded or hung them neatly.

"He seeks to plague me. Cillian is a malicious bastard, when he wants to be, which is sadly more often than not."

She put her hand over his wrist, bringing his palm to her lips to kiss it. "It is no trouble for me to serve you at supper, Edward. I don't mind it."

Something worked in his eyes, the expression unreadable. "You're not here to be paraded about like a prize ewe, or to be gawked over like a rare flower, which is why Cillian wants you there."

"He seeks to shame you?"

"No."

Nessa raised a brow.

"Cillian and I were school chums, along with Alaric. We were something of a . . . a pack if you will. Getting into trouble and such. I did things then I was too young and stupid not to understand that they were wrong."

She had an idea of what some of those things were. She passed a hand over her breast, the contact making her nipple thrust forward. "He told me he taught you the use of the adornments."

"Among other things. He wants me to be the lad I was. Not the man I am."

"And your friendship?"

"I'm loyal to my prince. And I fulfill my duties to him as best I can, upon the order of his father, our king. Beyond that, there is nothing."

"That must hurt him a great deal," Nessa said after a moment.

Edward's eyes grew wide before narrowing. "I was ever his friend despite his crown, not because of it. Naught's changed in that. You know naught of what passed between us, Handmaiden. But I assure you, if you did you would not be so quick to jump to Cillian's defense!"

There it was. The damage done. Edward's secret. His reason for needing her. Now was the time to push him a little into revealing it to her, for ripping off the scab so the wound could at last release the poison beneath . . . but Nessa didn't push.

She didn't want him to start healing. For the first time in all her years of service, Nessa wished to fail.

"I plead your mercy," she said in a voice more tremulous than she'd intended and turned her face from his so he wouldn't see the tears in her eyes.

"You will attend me at supper. But not in service. You will sit at the table with us, as any guest would. I can at least balk him in that."

She looked at him. "I will gladly do whatever you want me to do. You know I will. For whatever your reason."

He softened a bit toward her and reached a hand to touch her cheek. "I know. Which is the only reason I will allow it."

Emotion blurred her vision and closed her throat. He embraced her. She felt the point of his chin atop her head and heard him breath in deep against her hair.

But he said nothing, and after a moment Nessa gently broke free and set about laying out his clothes for supper.

A table truly fit for a prince." Alaric lifted his chin toward the spread. "And food fit for all of us, I daresay, and about half a dozen more."

Edward turned to look at his friend. "You've appetite enough, haven't you?"

Alaric grinned wolfishly. "Indeed, I have. A man must keep up his strength for all your brannigan's amusements."

Edward laughed and reached to touch the faint purpling mark upon Alaric's neck, half hidden by his cravat. "I think games of quoites and snap me are not quite so taxing as the other amusements in which you've been partaking."

Alaric laughed and danced out of his reach. "Shall I complain? I dare not. Fate brought my Lady Larissa here, and who am I to argue with Fate?"

"Cillian brought her here," corrected Edward.

"Because he knew she would be pleased to find me part of the party, old man. And a pleased Lady Larissa is one far easier to deal with than a grumpy one."

"And what of a pleased Alaric?" Edward asked, curious.

"Also much easier to deal with." Alaric's ready smile grew soft, his gaze a bit distant, in thought. "I find the lady's company most pleasing, Edward. I'm fair grateful for this chance to prove my . . . loyalties."

Edward grinned and clapped Alaric on the shoulder. "You don't mean to tell me—"

"I do. If she'll have me." Alaric made a half bow. "I'd be glad for you to stand beside me when we wed, if you would."

Alaric, married? And to Lady Larissa, no less? As Edward further congratulated his friend with another clap on the back, he couldn't help feel a faint sense of surprise and disappointment. If even flighty Alaric could wed, did that not mean there could be a chance for Edward, as well?

"Alaric," came the dulcet tones of Lady Larissa from the doorway. She nodded at Edward as graciously as a queen and held out her hand.

Alaric bent over her hand, his lips brushing the back of it, before straightening. "May I escort you to your seat?"

James showed up after that, with a pouting Persis a moment later still. Sentinell and Marvina cooed and fluttered while James paid them both a great deal of attention and Persis slouched in his chair.

"Your mercy, my dear Edward, for our late arrival. But I found this lovely creature hesitating on the stairs and thought to escort her myself." Cillian's languid drawl drew Edward's attention to the doorway, where the prince had appeared with Stillness on his arm.

Edward found only silence at the sight of her. She'd insisted he go down ahead of her, saying she would need time to prepare herself appropriately for a social supper. He'd been expecting to see her clad in the gown of her profession, the high-necked, long-sleeved, floor-length gown that buttoned from throat to hem.

He would never have thought she could look lovelier to his eyes than she had already become, no matter what the gown, but the sight of her literally drew away his breath. The simple dress, unadorned with feathers or ribbon, nevertheless had a fashionable cut. It dipped low, cut square across her chest, and showed a generous amount of décolletage. The high waist bound her just below her breasts and the skirt fell in a straight line to her ankles. She'd pulled her hair up high on her head, revealing the graceful curve of her neck and throat. The sight of a small purple mark at one collarbone, the mark left by his mouth, was enough to stir his cock in memory of when he'd put it there.

"I do believe you've struck him dumb, my dear." Cillian laughed. "And the sight of our dear Edward without words is a rare one, indeed."

Edward gave them both a half bow, Cillian and then Stillness, and when she extended her hand to him he kissed it. His fingers held hers, squeezing gently as he looked into her eyes.

"You look lovely," he told her.

Cillian coughed and held out his hand, too. "And what of me, dear one? Don't I look lovely, too?"

At that, the room erupted into laughter, and Edward took Cillian's hand to shake but not kiss. "As always, my prince."

This made Cillian simper and grin, and they all took their places at the table, Edward at the head with Cillian on one side and Stillness across from him on the other.

This supper ought to have been no different than any other they'd shared since the brannigan had begun, but Edward found the presence of his Handmaiden had changed it greatly. Not from anything she did, of course. Stillness was as cordial and spot-on perfect in her social manners as she was when alone with him. She knew the proper forks to use and how to fold her napkin. She was, in fact, better trained in etiquette than any of them there, and yet he watched her gaze follow the conversations around them and watched as she sipped her wine out of turn and realized she had done so deliberately so as not to embarrass Lady Marvina beside her, whose manners seemed to have been learned rather less than perfectly.

Pride filled him, though he had no right to feel it, for he hadn't trained her. He didn't own her. But watching Stillness make everyone around her feel comfortable with just the right amount of laughter, the perfect responses, by not being better dressed or spoken or mannered . . . yet at the same time being the epitome of a fine lady . . . yes, Edward felt pride.

Edward watched as Alaric gave subtle service to Larissa, making sure her cup was always filled, fetching a wrap for her shoulders without her having to ask. He could have been any devoted suitor, but there was more to it than that when viewed by a knowledgeable eye. Edward wasn't the only one to see it. Cillian noticed, as well.

When the party moved to the library for coffees and cordials, Cillian pulled Edward aside by the elbow. "Yon Alaric is smitten."

Edward looked to where Alaric sat at his lady's feet, looking at her with clear adoration in his eyes. "I think it's a good match for him."

"Do you?"

Cillian's curious tone turned Edward's head. "I do. Don't you? He clearly adores her, and she—"

"She'll chew him up and spit him out again." Cillian spoke fondly, almost in admiration. "She's a vicious witch."

Edward looked at the Lady Larissa as she bent to feed Alaric a bit of something from her dessert plate. Soft affection gleamed in her eyes, and they laughed together as she spilled cacao on his chin. "I must respectfully disagree with you, my lord. The lady and the gentleman appear to be in great accord."

Cillian snorted and pulled his tin of herb from his jacket pocket. He rolled a cheroot as he answered. "You can't convince me you're truly overjoyed for him." He held out his cheroot for Edward to light.

"Of course I am." Edward pulled out his silver matchbox.

Cillian's hand closed over Edward's wrist. "I gave you that matchbox."

"Yes." Edward met his gaze without hesitation. "You did."

Cillian stared into Edward's eyes without blinking, then bent his head toward the lit flame. "She won't share him."

"I wouldn't expect her to." Edward reached for Cillian's tin without asking and rolled a smoke of his own. "But she'll not keep him from his friends."

"She might, if she knows he's in love with you."

Edward looked up at Cillian, who was smiling, and then to Alaric, who was busy with some story that involved a great many hand gestures and much laughter from all watching.

"Don't pretend you never knew it." Cillian's exhaled smoke wafted into Edward's face. "You're far from stupid."

"Don't." Edward shook his head a little. "Leave it alone, Cillian."

Cillian merely gave him a sly grin. "I don't blame him, Edward.

You did save him from his own smart tongue more than once. I'm half in love with you, myself, and you loathe me."

Edward drew in more fragrant smoke and held it in his lungs while he traded stares with Cillian. The argument wasn't worth it. Cillian would have his way, as he always did. As he always had and always would.

Edward let the smoke seep out to hang in the air between them, solid as secrets. "What game are you playing?"

Cillian's gaze cut toward Stillness. He said nothing when he looked back to Edward. More smoke curled from his nose.

"No."

Cillian's brow raised. "You shared her with Alaric."

Edward scowled, wishing he'd had the forethought to lock his doors. "She's not to be shared, Cillian."

Something shifted in Cillian's gaze, a flash of emotion Edward couldn't identify. He'd have thought it might be grief, real pain, if he didn't want to refuse to believe Cillian incapable of such feeling.

"I want her. I want a woman I don't have to fear breaking. And she won't break. I can see it in her. She's been well used, Edward; The chit's got scars."

"She doesn't." Edward's stomach twisted as he looked at her again, his lovely Stillness.

"Not on her skin, perhaps. But then, those aren't the ones that most matter. Are they?"

Edward turned, infuriated by Cillian's languid tone. Their faces but measures apart, he glared into the other man's eyes. He smelled liquor and smoke on his breath and saw triumph in his eyes, and Edward backed off a step.

"Your mercy, my prince," he said coldly. "I overstep."

"You used to overstep all the time," gritted Cillian. "When we were friends."

"I won't share her."

"And when she leaves you and I hire her, how will you feel then?"

"You don't get to choose your Handmaiden," Edward said before he realized Cillian mocked him.

"But she will leave you, Edward. She has to."

Edward shook his head, letting his eyes follow the curves of her face as she laughed across the room. "We're not in school any longer. Why must you always want what I have? She's not a horse or a jacket, Cillian!"

"She's your Handmaiden, dear one." Cillian finished his cheroot and crushed it out in the ashsaucer on the nearby table. "And she also craves what you've been denying her. Doesn't she? She doesn't merely tolerate it. She yearns for it. Am I wrong in thinking so?"

Edward said nothing in his fury. Cillian had ever been able to do this to him, reach inside and twist all the keys that wound him up. He would give him nothing.

"But then, I would wager you haven't tried her out in that manner. Have you?" Cillian's smoke-rasped voice lowered. "You haven't stripped her down, tied her hands. You haven't yet beaten her. Even though the thought of it makes your hands shake and your prick want to burst."

"No." One word, grudgingly given, and Edward cursed himself for even that.

Cillian's low chuckle was like a finger running along the back of his neck, and Edward hunched his shoulders against it.

"I know you want to. You always did adore that. Crossing their flesh with stripes. How many times did we work together, my dear Edward? You behind her and I beneath, tasting her while you fucked her and ran your fingers over the welts you'd given her? How many girls did we share that way?"

It had been too many. And not enough. Edward's throat closed as heat rose in his face and crept down his stomach.

"They loved it, and you did, too. You still love it, dear one. Why don't you give in to what you really want?"

Cillian's breath blew against Edward's face as he stepped up behind him so close his body pressed along Edward's back. The rest of the party dissolved into shouts and cries of laughter, oblivious to the drama taking place in the corner, and Edward was grateful for that.

"She can take what you give her, Edward, or they wouldn't have sent her to you. The Order of Solace doesn't make mistakes."

"What *I* can give her," Edward said, his jaw clenched so tightly each word was painful. "Not you."

Cillian's low laugh blew more scent of herb across Edward's cheek. "I only want to share her, love, not have her all to myself. Maybe it's the closest I'll come to having you back again."

"You are a manipulative, wicked son-of-a-bastard, Cillian." Edward had called him worse, with more affection. Now the words sounded hollow and without effect. He couldn't stop thinking about the picture Cillian had painted of bare flesh, crossed with stripes made by his hand.

"And once you were my friend," Cillian whispered. "And now you're not, and I want it back."

"You can never have it back. I told you that."

Cillian nodded, and again the flash of what couldn't have been genuine sorrow appeared in his gaze. "So let me pretend for a while, Edward. Grant me a boon. For old times' sake."

"No."

Edward had no trouble discerning the emotion in Cillian's eyes this time. "You'll give me what I want, or I'll tell Lady Larissa that her new pet was fucking your Handmaiden in your bed not more than a half day before she arrived for the brannigan. Think you the lady would take kindly to that? Think you she'll still take Alaric's troth, then?" He laughed without humor, lifting his chin. "What? You know I'll do it."

"I know you're vicious enough to, aye. But why hurt Alaric?"

Cillian looked toward the others, still making merry. "Because hurting him hurts you. Because you care more for him than you do me. Because I want what I want, and I have the means to get it."

"Even if I allow this, I will never hold you as the brother of my heart again."

"Stop blaming me because you allowed me to be noble."

Edward wanted to throttle Cillian. To punch that pretty, vicious-speaking mouth and watch the bright blood stream down. And in times past, he'd have done it, but now . . . much had changed.

Cillian's face tightened. "Stop hating me for loving you enough to keep you safe. Tonight. Or else I'll tell Larissa the truth about her lover. I'm no longer noble enough to lie for the sake of friendship."

With that, he stalked off to sit in the corner, joined in a moment by Persis, who offered worm and more herb, which Cillian took.

Edward loosed his cravat a touch and wished for something cool to drink. In the next moment, he had it, the cup pressed into his hand by small, soft fingers. He blinked and looked down at her, Stillness, the woman who had come to give him solace.

"Go to my room," he told her. "And wait for me there."

Because she was obedient she went without the questions another woman would have asked. Edward looked at Cillian. The prince gave him a small nod.

And it was done.

Chapter 8

Stillness didn't know the cause of the tension between Edward and Cillian, but she didn't doubt she'd learn it soon enough. Until then, she readied the room for his return. A roaring fire, scented oils sprinkled on the flames. Herb rolled in paper and set out for smoking. A jug of worm and glasses, as well as whiskey. She'd just put her hand to the kettle, thinking of tea, when the door opened.

He didn't enter alone, and Stillness hung the kettle on its hook when she saw what guest accompanied him. She straightened. Edward, scowling, came forward to take the glass of whiskey she poured.

"My lord Cillian," Stillness greeted. "My lord Edward."

"You don't have to call him your lord, Stillness. He's not." Edward tossed back the whiskey and handed her the glass. "Only I am."

This seemed to amuse Cillian, though he shrugged and nodded in agreement. "Very true."

Stillness looked from one to the other. "Edward?"

He'd closed himself off from her again, gave no hint of his thoughts or emotion. "You are a good Handmaiden."

"Thank you." She looked briefly at Cillian, who lounged in Edward's chair, tapping a finger against his lips as he watched her.

Edward, too, glanced at the prince. "This is a duty to you. Serving your patrons."

"Yes." Stillness didn't understand why he asked her these things, but she could do nothing but reply.

"All of them, the same to you. As any other."

Stillness paused before answering, speaking only when he finally turned his dark eyes toward her. "Each patron is unique to me at the time of my service to them. But the same when all is done. Yes."

His shoulders twitched. She reached for him. He pulled away.

"And tell me again how you like to ease your pain."

At once, looking at him and the man he'd brought with him, Stillness understood the reason for Edward's questions.

"Pain of the flesh helps me to forget the pain in my soul," she said quietly.

Cillian shifted in his chair with a small noise. Edward gripped the mantle, his shoulders hunching. Stillness didn't touch him.

"You want pain." Edward's voice was hoarse, but not with dismay.

And she knew more, then, of how best to serve him and bring him the solace that was her purpose. She knew how to give him what he needed, and as she went to her knees in front of him in the Waiting, her heart ached even as her body roused itself in anticipation. This meant she would have to leave him, at last.

"Yes," she said. "I crave it."

She felt his hand upon her hair, and she shivered.

"Then you shall have it, Handmaiden, for it well pleases me to give you what you want."

In springtime, ice over running water cracks and chips until at last the water that has flowed beneath it all winter can bubble to the top and wash away the rest. That was how Edward seemed to her, once he'd made the decision to give in to his desire. Like a stream that's been warmed by the sun enough to wash away the ice.

He wasn't new to this; she'd seen that in him already. The ability to command. The expectation of obedience. What she had not seen was the extent of his capacity for dominance, and how easily he took control of it.

The thrill of it, the tone of his voice as he told her to take off her clothes, the assessing gleam in his eye as he studied her all thrilled her, and her clit tingled.

Cillian groaned, low, when she revealed the gems dangling from her nipples and her clit. "She is perfection."

Stillness stood as Cillian circled her and Edward watched. Cillian's breath ghosted over her bare shoulder as he leaned in close from behind her. He didn't touch her, and she understood something else. Cillian might be the master in all other places, but not with Edward. Here, now, Edward was the prince.

"She wears the jewelry like a queen, Edward."

She watched her patron's face, heat swirling through her when his mouth tightened into a proud smile. Her clit twitched as the gem dangling from it swung gently.

"She does. Touch her skin."

"Like sateen," murmured Cillian, obeying. His long-fingered hand, smooth, the hand of a man who didn't work, slid over her hip and thigh.

Her nipples grew tauter at that simple, knowing touch. Cillian's hand dipped between her legs to toy with her soft curls, but it was Edward's gaze that touched her. Edward who made her clit throb against the constriction of the metal clip. Cillian had become her patron's hands.

"Do you want to taste her, Cillian?"

"I do, my dear one," Cillian breathed into her ear.

Whatever had happened between him and Cillian in the past, it had been put aside for now. At least most of it had.

"Do it, then." His command brooked no argument, as he loosed his cravat, then his buttons and began to take off his shirt.

Cillian moved her a few steps back until her buttocks hit the edge of the desk, and she leaned against it. He pushed apart her thighs and studied her, exposed. The dual sensation of his eyes on her quim and Edward's gaze upon her face made Stillness giddy.

"Is it the first time a prince has knelt at *your* feet?" Cillian's amused question made her look down.

"No," she said, and he laughed.

Still laughing, he dipped his red-gold head between her thighs and licked her. Stillness drew in a deep, gasping breath when his tongue flickered along the tiny chain, then across the metal clip. The sensation was enchanting and agonizing too, but in the next moment he'd slipped the bauble from her skin. She cried out at the release and her hips leaped forward, pressing her to his ready tongue. Cillian laved and licked her, using a finger to press inside her. Edward watched them as he got undressed.

"Stillness. Come here."

Cillian moved aside, and she went to Edward with slow steps, her legs atremble with the passion Cillian's mouth had aroused in her.

"Go to that wall. Put your hands flat upon it, just past the width of your shoulders. Your fingers will be spread wide. You will close them together should you need relief. Do you understand?"

She nodded. Few of her patrons had understood the need for such signals, and again her nerves tingled with arousal at Edward's skill. The plastered wall felt cool beneath her hands. She leaned toward it, the gems still attached to her nipples swinging freely. She waited, tension building with every moment.

She heard the open and close of his cabinet.

"You're not going to bind her?"

"No." Edward's sharp voice made Stillness twitch, though not with fear. "She needs no binding. She'll obey."

She heard the sound of leather drawn through hands. The rustle of clothing. Her mind slipped open and down, finding the beginnings of her own solace.

"Very nice," came Cillian's next words, admiring. "I remember that one."

Two men, discussing their tools as if they were blacksmiths talking about hammers and vises rather than crops and cat-o'-nine-tails. What would he use on her? The sting of thin leather straps or the different burn of the crop?

Slick moisture slid down her thighs in readiness. Stillness waited. Her breathing slowed.

"You are beautiful."

She wanted to thank him but couldn't find the words.

"Are you ready?"

She nodded.

"You will count. Do you understand? I will give you ten, to start."

"Yes, sir." She found her voice to say.

Every muscle twitched with anticipation, the tension of which was more difficult to bear than the pain would ever be. She took in a slow, long breath in preparation, making a conscious effort to relax, but it had been so long since she'd had this. So long since anyone had understood how to give her what she needed—not the back of a hand to her cheek in anger. Nothing in anger, but careful, perfect punishment administered with consideration . . . and love.

He gave her no warning before he laid the first stripes across her shoulders. Pain bloomed like some dark flower, spreading out from the point of contact and through the rest of her body. By the time it reached her quim, the sting had become sweetness. She drew in a breath, "One, sir," and he struck her again. *A flogger*, she thought as her flesh welted. Wielded with a masterful hand, the second stripes laid below the first.

"Two, sir."

"She takes it without a shout." Cillian's murmur tickled her ears, though he was out of her range of vision. "Make her cry out."

"In good time."

She braced unconsciously for the third strike, and it stung all the more for that tightening of her muscles. Not enough to loose more than a whimper from her throat. It was exquisite. Her clit pulsed and her hips moved forward of their own, seeking and not finding something against which to rub her swollen flesh.

The flogger fell again and again until her entire back was on fire. She hadn't moved her fingers. She counted each one aloud. By the time he reached ten she was sobbing the words. He'd stopped before reaching her tender buttocks.

"She's not even close to having enough," said Cillian authoritatively. "Edward. She can take more."

She felt heat on her already burning skin, and a hand slid between her legs from behind. She moaned, pushing back against it. Fingers stroked her, found the bead of her clit and pinched it gently so her entire body jumped. Breath caressed her cheek.

"This arouses you," Edward whispered. "You are so wet, I could slide inside you without any effort, all the way to your womb."

He demonstrated with his fingers, thrusting gently in and out. Nessa shook in waves of pre-orgasmic pleasure. She would come in another moment, if he moved a finger over the ripe bud of her clitoris, but Edward knew how to hold her off.

"Cillian thinks you can take more. Can you, Stillness? Can you take more from me?"

Eyes closed, she ran her tongue across her lips before answering. "I can give you more, Edward."

Tenderly, he smoothed her hair and rearranged it so the heavy braid hung over her shoulder and across her breasts. Then he moved away from her, and chill air replaced the warmth of his breath.

She did cry out at the next blow; her body had had time to acclimate to the pain it had already absorbed. This fresh insult overtop the previous stripes was more excruciating and all the more exquisite for it. She tasted the tang of salt, tears and sweat, and pain exploded on her back and ecstasy burst inside her womb as he laid another series of stripes over the first.

Oblivion beckoned, and she embraced the stillness for which she'd been so appropriately named. Everything went away but for the hiss of leather in the air, the slap of it on her skin, the smooth workings of her inner muscles as her body responded. She heard Edward's grunt, and Cillian's low murmurs of approval. She heard them talking about her, admiring, praising, two voices rising and falling as the crop rose and fell, but she didn't pay attention to what they said. She was aware she counted, as she'd been ordered, but couldn't be sure if her voice cracked or whispered, only that each time a new line of pain seared her, she saw Edward's face.

Her orgasm surged and retreated, flaring with every strike.

Her fingers didn't move.

She was coming, over and over, deep in that place where everything had become pleasure.

She heard the low rumble of laughter, sated, and smelled the musky scent of semen. Not Edward. Cillian, then, had finished, and she moaned, waiting for Edward to fill her as he'd promised to do.

"You've beaten the breath fair out of her." Cillian sounded amused. "Fuck the cunna before she passes out, Edward—"

And then it all went bad.

This time the crack of leather on flesh didn't result in pain. The cry wasn't hers. Edward shouted something, voice tight with fury, and Cillian replied. Stillness heard the crunch of fists on bodies, and she whirled in alarm.

Edward, bare chest agleam with the sweat of his exertions, had knocked Cillian to the floor. He'd fisted his hand in the other man's collar, holding him still while he punched at his face. Bright blood streamed from the prince's lip, and she saw the red slash of a flogger's kiss on his cheek.

"Edward!" she cried.

He didn't turn. Cillian, quite capable of defending himself, yanked Edward down with a calculated move. The men, punching and shouting, rolled on the floor. She thought they might be trying to kill each other

"It's your breath that should be stoppered, you foul-mouthed prick!" Edward shouted, punching. "You won't speak of her that way!"

Cillian wasted none of his apparently ill-deserved breath in insults. He dodged Edward's punches and landed a few of his own. Stillness shouted at them both again, but neither paid her any mind. Leaving the fracas, she went to Edward's privy chamber and brought a basin of water, which she threw over both of them.

They flew apart, cursing and dripping. She tossed the basin to the floor, where it clattered loudly. Then the world tilted a bit again, and she reached for the support of the back of Edward's chair.

Both men got to their feet, glaring, fists clenched, but well apart from one another.

Cillian drew the back of his hand across his mouth, smearing crimson upon his lips like an overabundant application of cosmetic. "Your mercy, Edward. I didn't know—"

But Edward wasn't appeased. "No more, Cillian! No more of this! No more serving you, no more pandering, no more living my life beneath the shadow! I won't have it!"

"I never asked it of you!" Cillian's cry was sharp as a blade. "I only ever wanted your companionship, Edward, for things to be the way they were before—"

"They can never be! Don't you understand? We can't go back! And I won't go on with this lie, yielding to your whims, doing whatever pleases you out of fear!"

"I don't want you to be afraid of me!" In the silence left behind after the shout, the sound of dripping water seemed very loud. "I never did. It was my father who bade you attend me, my father who threatened you. I lied for you, Edward, because you were the brother of my heart, and I loved you. And you have ever hated me since."

Stillness didn't know what to do. She looked from the prince to her patron and back again, but Edward's fierce pose prevented her from going to him. Wherever he was, it was a place she couldn't go.

Cillian reached a hand toward him, but Edward turned away. Cillian turned toward Stillness, his vivid green gaze bloodshot. The blood from his mouth had drawn a line down his throat and stained the pristine collar of his fine shirt. The welt on his cheek was already going purple.

"Your mercy, lady," said Cillian. "Serve him well, for he is in sore need of what you are bound to provide."

Helplessly, Stillness watched as Cillian left the room, not looking back. Edward's shoulders hunched, and she watched, horrified, as he went to his knees, head cradled in his hands, and began to weep.

She went to him, and took him to her bosom, heedless of the agony in her back when he clutched her with the desperation of a man who has no hope of ever finding peace.

"Hush," she soothed, stroking his hair over and over. "It will be all right."

W e were boys," Edward told her as they lay together in his bed. "Alaric and I the sons of merchants aspiring to nobility and friends since boyhood, but Cillian, of course, the son of a king. I saw Cillian right away, for how could anyone miss him. That hair, the swagger, his sense of innate right to the best of everything." Edward smiled at the memory. "He was instantly loathed by most of the other lads, though none dared balk him. There were other rich boys there, but no other princes. He had many admirers."

"But no friends," she murmured. "Until you."

"The day I found him as part of a group teasing Alaric about the shabby condition of his best cloak, I punched him in the face for being a snotty bastard."

Her chuckle sent warm breath over him. "And that's how you became friends?"

"Nobody had dared stand up to him before that. At any rate, the day I bloodied his nose, Cillian declared me his boon companion, along with Alaric. And the three of us discovered we had much in common besides our nationality."

"Your inclinations." Her hand smoothed and stroked, smoothed and stroked.

"Yes. By the time we were ten and eight, we'd discovered the lure of doxies to be had for a few coins and eager to serve those such as us. We took them together, sometimes. The one who introduced us to it called herself Lady Gentia, and I think we were all mostly in love with her. Or at least in awe, for she was easily twice as broad as any of us and more than a head taller."

This made her giggle again.

"She took the crop to Alaric's back when he displeased her. Then to each of ours."

"But you enjoyed employing the punishment rather than receiving it."

Even now, his balls tightened at the memory of how it had felt, that first time. Watching the skin turn color and grow warm beneath his hand. Hearing the woman cry out, but not begging him to stop. Begging for more. How she'd tasted, like sweet honey, as she writhed beneath him.

"Cillian and Alaric had become the brothers of my heart, but Cillian was the one who knew best how I felt. Alaric joined our escapades but he cared less for them than we did. And his schoolwork called him, for though Alaric is clever of wit, he struggled with lessons.

"Cillian was the one who urged us to greater adventures, but I was more than willing to follow. Nothing seemed too debauched to try, not when Lady Gentia's girls were all well trained and eager for it."

His heart skipped at the memories of how it had been. Nights of sexual excess, of slick bodies, hot mouths, tight, wet cunts. How he'd spent himself inside one after the other, Cillian often at his side while they rode whore after whore.

"It was Cillian who bound her and he who put the ribbon round her throat, but I was the one who rode her when she suffocated and died."

He closed his eyes at the memory. "She had told us how stifling the breath led to greater orgasms. She gave us the ribbon and bade us put it around her throat, told Cillian to pull it tighter as I fucked her. We thought she was just . . ." He faltered, cold sweat washing over him at the recollection. "We didn't know it had gone too far until it was too late. We never even knew her name."

He shuddered, and Stillness's hands were there again, rubbing his skin.

"We thought we were men. But we weren't. There was to be an investigation. The penalty for murder, even accidental, is death by hanging."

She murmured against him and kissed his neck. He stroked her hair, drawing strength from her.

"Cillian said he'd been the one to do it. That I had naught to do with it. He said I'd drunk too much worm and passed out. He took the blame for me, entirely, and I was released from responsibility."

"But he wasn't hanged."

"No. He was sent to an asylum. His father had enough influence and money to do that for him." He laughed, bitterly and ashamedly. "He lied for me, and I let him. I finished my schooling and came back to take my place in society while Cillian went to a house for madmen. And he came out more than a little mad, himself. His father, who perhaps knew more of the situation than he'd ever let on, made a place for me in his court. I would be Cillian's watchdog, guarding him against future accidents. He was my responsibility. My burden. My reminder of what happened when desire was left to run unchecked."

She propped herself up to look into his face. "But you blamed yourself."

"For the girl's death, aye. For his madness, certainly. And yet I could do nothing but be what his father had bade me become, his hovering angel. His restraint. I couldn't look at him without remembering what had happened, nor what he'd done for me. There are rumors he'll not be allowed to take the throne because of his madness. That no good monarch will troth his daughter to him, for fear of gaining insane grandchildren."

"Do you think he blames you for that?" Her soft words made him shake his head.

"No, the bastard never did." He smiled, looking up into her face. "He has ever been the Cillian of our youth, impetuous, smart, and just this side of dangerous. It was I who changed."

She bent to kiss his mouth, softly. "Your sorrow has faded, but you can never stop grieving."

He nodded, relieved to have found someone at last who understood. She took his hand and put it on her breast, where the nipple immediately sprang to life. Her next kiss was deeper, urging his lips to part.

"We are lock and key," she whispered against him. "I need what you give. You need never hold back with me, Edward, for I can take what you give."

She reached between them and took his cock, stroking it to life. He echoed her sigh as she straddled him and pushed him inside her. She kissed him again, harder, with lips and teeth and tongue. He breathed in. She breathed out.

She rode him slowly at first, leaning over to kiss him, or to allow him to suckle her nipples. Edward pressed his thumb to her clit, rubbing as she rode him. At last she sat up straight, head thrown back in ecstasy, and the glory of her hair tumbled down all around them. He lost himself in her. The sight, the touch, the smell, and something deeper. Something that couldn't be touched or seen or smelled, but something inside him. It broke him open, and he gasped with it, at the sudden pretty pain of realization.

"I love you," he gasped as their bodies joined their release.

Stillness looked down at him, her dark eyes wide and her lips curved in joy. "I love you, too."

And there it was. The moment of utter, perfect solace. He had found it with her, and he cried her name as she answered with his, and together they found a place where the thorns of grief had no room to prick them.

S he didn't have much to pack. A small case of clothes and personal items. The letters of finance that would assure the transfer of her personal monies to her new residence. It took her only moments to gather it all, and Stillness looked around the room that had been her home with a small sigh at the thought of the journey ahead.

"Are you ready?"

The voice from the doorway made her turn, and she smiled. "Yes, Edward. I'm ready."

The man she loved smiled, too, and held out a hand. "The carriage is waiting."

She went to him and took the hand he offered, laughing when it pulled her close for a kiss.

"Will you regret leaving?" he asked her, pulling away to gaze at her with serious eyes.

Stillness looked once more around the room the Order had assigned her. She turned back to kiss him again. "No," she said when she pulled away. "No, my love, I don't regret leaving here. Not when it means going home with you."

"Come then," said Edward. "Let's go home."

"If it pleases you," Stillness said.

Edward reached to cup her cheek. "It pleases me greatly."

Indeed, it pleased them both, she thought as they left the room without bothering to close the door behind them. And that was the best sort of solace to be had at any time.

Honesty

Chapter 9

The lamps had been lit, the fire stoked, the wine poured. Cillian had tied fresh lace at his wrists and throat and worn his finest waistcoat. Now all he had to do was wait.

"Sinder's Blessed Balls," Cillian gritted out, pacing. "Where is she?"

Alaric looked up from the chair in which he lounged, wine in hand and feet propped carelessly on the ottoman. "I'm sure she's on her way. Perhaps a delay at the station—"

"I had my man posted at the bedamned station. If there was a delay with any of the trains, I'd have been informed as swift as that." Cillian snapped his fingers to demonstrate his utter power.

Alaric raised a brow, too foolish even to make a pretense of being impressed. That was, Cillian reflected sourly, the bane of having a bosom companion who knew you too well. Alaric thought he didn't need to fawn. Thank the Holy Family, Cillian had plenty who did, else he'd have been put even more sorely out of sorts.

Alaric got up, set his wine aside, and embraced Cillian to rub the back of his neck beneath the clubbed braid. "Hush. She'll be here."

Cillian relaxed only a moment into the touch before shrugging it off. Every muscle tensed, every inch of his skin prickled with the thorns of his anticipation. It had been weeks already since he'd been granted the word his application for a Handmaiden had been approved. A full fortnight since he'd had the letter stating she'd arrive on this evening's last train to Pevensie Station. He should've ordered another train. He would've, had he the power to do so, but even his father the king would've been hard-pressed to change the running of the trains.

"She's late," he said flatly. "I'm most displeased."

Alaric, for all he was a fool, was also a very good friend. He crept close again, this time to rub Cillian's shoulders. Cillian allowed Alaric to push him into a chair and hand him a glass of sweet red wine before he dug again into the knots in Cillian's neck and back.

"She'll be here. The Order said she'd come. They don't lie."

Cillian groaned, tilting his head to allow Alaric to get at the sorest spots. "By the Void, Alaric, I'm half mad with the waiting."

Alaric chuckled low, and bent to kiss the top of Cillian's head before taking his own chair and cup again. "You're half mad from many things, my prince. You can't blame the waiting."

"I could have you thrown in gaol for saying so."

Alaric's eyes gleamed, and Cillian's jaw tightened again at the sight of his friend's unflappable good humor. But he couldn't stay angry with Alaric for long, not when the fool was Cillian's dear friend. His only dear friend, since Edward had refused even the king's command to come to court. He'd abandoned Cillian entirely this past sixmonth.

"She'll be here, Cilly."

"Don't call me that. That prat Persis thought to make a pet of me with that name."

Alaric understood him only half as well as Edward ever had, but it proved to be enough. "And you are nobody's pet."

"Indeed. More wine."

Cillian held out his cup, and Alaric filled it, and together they drank in silence, each taken up with the importance of his own thoughts until Cillian could take it no longer and leaped to his feet once more. He drained his glass, and in a fit, tossed it into the fire where it didn't have the grace to shatter nicely but cracked and scattered the drops to make the fire sizzle. Even that would insist on balking him?

"My lord prince." Bertram, Cillian's man, shifted from foot to foot in the doorway. "Pleading your mercy, m'lord, but I've been to the train, wot she weren't on it."

Cillian meant to fair rend the air with his curses, but naught would come from his lips. Instead, he found himself on his knees on the cold, hard floor, face cradled in his hands. She had not come. Again, she had not come.

"Go back and wait for her, idiot," Alaric said quietly to Bertram before kneeling by Cillian's side. "Let me put you to bed."

"No." Cillian shook his head. "I'm not overdrunk on wine, Alaric. I'm merely . . . I . . ."

"I know." Alaric put a strong hand around his shoulders and gave a squeeze. "You want. I know."

Cillian raised his head and gave his friend a steady glare. "You presume to know what I want?"

"I presume to know *you*." Alaric let go and got to his feet, offering Cillian a hand he took to get up. "And I know a bit about wanting."

"But you have what you want. I lack for nothing, and yet I remain unsatisfied." Cillian swallowed against the dreadful lump in his throat and tried in vain to shake off his disappointment.

Weeks and days he'd been waiting, certain his torment would ease as soon as his Handmaiden arrived. He'd forgone his daily visits to the playroom in anticipation of her. And yet, though he'd been promised her solace, he had yet another day to wait for it. It was not to be borne!

"Go away, Alaric. Go seek your lady's bed, lest she find it cold and choose to warm it with another. Leave me alone."

Alaric sighed and gave Cillian a half bow that wasn't even mocking. "My lady has bid me leave to stay until you have no more need of me."

This raised Cillian's brow. Lady Larissa did not grant her favors easily, but once granted, she did not release them. "Larissa has bid you serve me instead of her?"

Alaric, with his fair hair and coloring, could do little to hide the heat in his cheeks. "Not . . . to serve you, Cillian. Not that way."

Cillian's brow inched higher and he crossed his arms over his chest. "Indeed? And what if that's the sort of service I should require?"

Alaric blushed, but now recovering quickly, he gave Cillian a shameless, provoking grin. "I'm not your flavor, and you know it."

Cillian sniffed. "You have no rein to poke at me just because you're my boon companion."

"I'm not poking, truly." Alaric looked contrite. "It's only that . . . well. Since Edward has taken his leave—"

"Speak not his name to me." Cillian put a hand over his heart, where the pain sliced deepest. "I am the Prince of Firth. I command whom I please. It's not my pleasure to force Lord Delaw into my presence if he wishes not to be in it."

Alaric nodded and made another half bow. "I know."

"You claim to know too much!" Cillian snapped and turned on his heel, already unbuttoning his wasted waistcoat and ringing for his fetchencarry. "Go home to your mistress or to your own hand for all I care, Alaric. Just go."

Alaric left without another word.

Cillian paced, muttering curses for every moment it took

Renzell to arrive. The man would insist upon taking his bedamned time, no matter the consequences. It came from being too soft on him, Cillian thought with a curl of his lip. Mayhaps the man would leap more quickly to his master's command if he'd felt the strap once or twice.

Even the prospect of that didn't please him, and Cillian satisfied himself with breaking glass after glass in the fire, where the shards glittered and gleamed and refused to melt. He'd raised the last glass when Renzell at last bustled in.

"M'lord," Renzell said. "She's not arrived yet, eh? Late? Would m'lord like me to lay out his nightclothes, then, m'lord?"

At the man's inane and cheerful rush of words, Cillian drew in a breath, and then another, and put aside further thoughts of beating the idiot into some semblance of submission. He would own being irritable, tempestuous. Even difficult. But he refused to become the monster Edward accused him of being.

"Lay out my oxenhide trousers. I'll be in my playroom for the next few hours."

Renzell nodded and bustled around while Cillian resisted pacing in front of the fire. The man was fast but not efficient, taking many steps when one would suffice, but at last he'd laid out the clothes Cillian required and helped him out of the ones he'd worn to greet the Handmaiden.

"Would m'lord like the maids to draw a bath for him, later?"

Cillian closed his eyes, briefly, and bit back a harsh reply. "Of course."

What he wanted more than anything was not to need to tell anyone what he wanted. To come back from taking his pleasure in the playroom and find all he wanted in readiness for him. What he yearned for, indeed, what he craved, was to have someone who knew his every wish before he made it, and one who'd do her best to grant it.

"And a meal, m'lord?"

Renzell was not the brightest burning taper in the candelabra, but again, Cillian forced back a sharp retort. Edward was not there to see his efforts or appreciate them, but . . . Cillian tried anyway. "Yes, Renzell. A meal. I'm sure I'll be fair famished."

Renzell offered a bright, cheery, and utterly loathsome grin. "Anything else, m'lord prince?"

Cillian remained stripped to the waist but pulled on his black trousers. Velvet-soft oxenhide, treated against moisture and stains, they were one of the few garments he owned for practicality, he thought, for once not overproud of his frivolity, but half disgusted with his own excess.

"That will be sufficient, Renzell."

He didn't wait for more inane babbling. The fetchencarry would go on, if allowed. No matter how many times Cillian had screamed at him or threatened to take a crop to his back, the man simply never broke. It would have been more inconvenient if Cillian hadn't been too lazy to train a new body servant every other fortnight. As it was, he'd had to holler himself hoarse enough to need honeyed tea at least thrice a week, and Renzell continued his service without changing the manner in which he provided it.

The playroom would have to soothe him, since there was no Handmaiden to do it, and after so many days without that release, his blood thrummed in fierce anticipation. Cillian took the back stairs, bare and wooden and without decoration. A servant's staircase, meant for the passage of staff to keep them from the eyes of nobles who wished not to be bothered with mundanities such as who did their laundry and emptied their chamber pots. These stairs weren't meant for princely feet, and Cillian took great pleasure in using them. The old man would have a fit should he learn his only son was traipsing about the servants' corridor, but then again, he pretended he didn't know about the playroom. Both facts would cancel out the other.

The door flung open on well-greased hinges, and inside, the women Cillian had procured looked up from their various activities. He gave them anything they needed to occupy themselves whilst he was not here. Embroidery, cards, paper-folding. Ladies' pastimes with which most of them had never occupied themselves before his employ. Female all of them, but ladies none.

A sweet, chirping chorus of "my lord prince" greeted him and sought to tug a smile to his lips. The door closed behind him, and Cillian breathed in deep and long. The scents of ironwood, rose oil, and the salves his women used mingled with the odor of desire created a pungent miasma he lifted his head to capture as deeply as he could.

Here he was the master, and not for the crown upon his head but for the rod he wielded. Here he was given everything without being asked for anything in return. Here, in this place, with these women, Cillian need not curb his temper, bite his tongue, rein his hand. Every one of them had been chosen not for their physical perfections, for indeed many of Cillian's hareem women wore the evidence of hard living on their faces and bodies, but for something more lovely to him. Their desire to serve him in any way he deemed fit, and their utter and unrelenting pleasure in doing so.

Here he need be nothing more than a man, no matter how much a prince they made him with their obedience.

"Beauties," Cillian said and opened his arms to embrace them all at once. "Who is first?"

The train was more than late, it did not arrive at all. Ten miles out of Pevensie station, the cars shuddered to a halt, the metal wheels shrieking. The scent of burning hair filled the cabin in which Honesty had been riding, and the people around her shook their heads, muttering when she covered her nose with her sleeve.

"It's an odenbeast," said one elderly gentleman with a sigh and a shake of his newsprint. "They've gone wild in this part of Firth since the prince declared their hides are no longer in fashion. Nobody hunts them any longer. They get on the tracks, the bloody great stupid things. The train's hit it."

Honesty had never heard of such a thing, even from the most backward of provinces. In her home province of Bellora the train system had been elevated, in fact, to prevent such mishaps, but she didn't point that out. She hadn't been to Bellora in a long time.

The odenbeast on the tracks had necessitated an entire removal crew to come out from the station, and they seemed in no rush. Nobody on the train seemed to find this a matter of consequence. Honesty, however, had been traveling for several days nonstop. She hadn't eaten a full meal since luncheon the day before and that had been a pocket tart grabbed hastily as she ran from one train to the next.

"No sense in fidgeting," the old man told her from over the edge of his paper. "Wherever you're going will still be there when you get there, I'm sure."

That was true enough, as well as discouraging. Honesty concentrated on reciting the mantras of the Order in her head, trying to ignore the smell of singed odenbeast and the curious glances her gown garnered. No matter where she went it seemed there were always those who hadn't seen a Handmaiden in the flesh, and who didn't believe she was as human as the rest of them.

As the hours melted into one another and her stomach grew emptier, it had never been so difficult to convince herself that true patience was its own reward. By the time the train, cleaned of its unexpected passenger, rolled into the station, so many hours had passed beyond her estimated arrival that Honesty doubted there'd be anybody to meet her. She knew all too well how impatient princes were. So when the man, head bent to his chest and shadowed by the brim of his hat, stirred at the sound of the train and got to his feet, Honesty didn't expect him to greet her.

"Miz?"

She clutched her hand-trunk to her side, wary. Handmaidens were under the protection and long-reaching arm of the Order of Solace, but that didn't stop every idiot from believing he might be the first to get away with taking what other men needed to pay for.

"You waiting for a ride?" he asked when Honesty didn't answer.

The man turned out not to be some randy scouse git with an aim at mischief, but the Prince of Firth's own man, sent to fetch her from the station. He firmly ensconced Honesty in a carriage so finely made it was like riding in a jewel-case. And she the jewel, she mused, settling onto the black velvet seats with a spread of her skirts.

She didn't mean to sleep, but weariness overtook her. She'd had a hard few days of travel. Though all Handmaidens had personal rooms within the main Motherhouse in Neaku, the Order of Solace had sister-houses in many of the provinces. She'd most recently come from one of them, fresh from her last assignment without even a trip home before beginning the next.

She woke when the carriage halted and Bertram opened the door to let in a breath of fresh night air that smelled of rain. The sky held no hint of moon or stars and though she couldn't see them, Honesty felt the weight of the clouds like a mantle over her shoulders when she stepped out with Bertram's hand to assist her.

She lifted her face to breathe in the wet-thick breeze. "Storms are coming."

"Oh, aye."

As if at her word, thunder rumbled. She laughed gently at Bertram's assessing face. "I like the rain."

"So do the fields, Miz." Bertram grinned, showing straight

white teeth set in sharp contrast to his shadowed face. "We'd best get you inside."

Night hid the palace, which was just as well. Honesty didn't need to count the number of towers or judge the quality of the brick and marble. She wasn't here for that. Her interest lay inside with the prince who'd called for her. Everything else was merely the cream on the custard.

At this time of night, only sentries roamed the halls. *Sentries and drunkards*, she thought as they passed a thick wooden door half cracked to show a party of young lords inside. The sounds of their revelry and the scent of herb reached even to the hall, and Honesty paused, assuming her prince might be amongst the merrymakers, but Bertram only shook his head and motioned with one thick finger for her to follow down another set of corridors, more plainly dressed, and around the corner to a dusty, unkempt hall.

"He's down here." He pointed to a door at the end of the hall.

She waited, but clearly he wasn't going to take her farther. Honesty blinked, stifling a yawn. Bertram nodded and stood aside. There was no sense in waiting, she saw.

Honesty went through the door.

A short flight of stone steps took her to another door, the wood of this one outlined in scrolled black metal ornamentation. The gas lamps had been dimmed to dusk here, and she blinked again to clear her vision of the dust motes dancing. She pushed the door open.

She'd been trained to expect anything from her patrons. To withstand much and look past more. Even so, Honesty recoiled at the thick, rolling scent of sweat and sex and blood that assaulted her the moment she walked through the door.

She saw a girl bound by her wrists to a cross of ironwood, naked, her back crisscrossed with welts. Her head hung down and her tawny flesh gleamed with sweat. Her shoulders rose and fell with each breath. There were other girls, too, most naked though a few wore sheer night rails that hid nothing. Had Bertram sent her to the wrong room?

Tendrils of red fog edged her vision like lace. Hunger and exhaustion assaulted her, along with the heat and miasma in the room. Honesty drew in a breath, lip curling at the taste of the air. It gave her no respite. If anything, every breath she drew made the buzz in her ears and her sudden unsteadiness worse.

Then she noticed the man. Stripped to the waist, he stood with his back to her. Long, thick hair tumbled over his shoulders and down to the center of his back in the colors of ferlafruits. Amber, russet, glints of gold that caught in the gaslight. His hair was enough to make her throat close tight on a breath meaning to escape as a sigh, but when he turned to face her . . . oh, Invisible Mother.

He was beautiful.

His upraised hand gripped the handle of a flogger, leather tails dangling. Sweat ran down his face and across his lips, and his tongue darted out to swipe it away. He dropped the flogger to his side.

"Who are you?"

His voice, fluid and melodious, reminded her of the stream in her father's orchard as much as his hair had called to mind the fruits. Honesty, shaken by memory, took a step back, her hand over her heart. She didn't answer.

"Invisible Mother," whispered the Prince of Firth. He dropped the flogger and stepped over it, unheeded, toward her. "You're her."

And then she fell.

I've had fluttering eyelashes and curtsies directed my way," Cillian murmured, "but I must say until today I've never had a woman faint dead away at the sight of me."

Consternation flooded her, and Honesty struggled to sit. The blankets that had been tucked so tightly around her waist tugged at her as she moved, and the prince, for there was no question he could be anything else, shifted his chair a bit away from the bed so she had space to move.

"I plead your mercy," Honesty said, her voice rough.

The prince poured a cup of water from a pitcher and handed it to her. "Bertram was under orders to bring you directly to me. If I'd known you weren't able to handle the sight, I'd have given him different instructions."

Honesty sipped, the cool water sliding down her throat slowly enough to give her time to answer. She hadn't fainted in months, though she was prone to dizziness when she went too long without a meal, and she was still a little disoriented. If given her choice, she'd have put her head back on the pillow, but the prince was staring at her with such expectation she knew that wouldn't suit him. It didn't matter what she wanted. *Selfish is the heart that thinks first of itself.* The mantra rose easily enough in her mind, even if it settled less certainly in her heart.

He had green eyes, like grass, but spangled with white, like the sea flecked with foam. This, too, reminded her of the home of her childhood. Honesty made to speak again, but thoughts of her life before still crowded her tongue, and they had no place here. No purpose. They would bring no pleasure—not to him and certainly not to herself.

Prince Cillian, Prince of Firth, her patron, leaned forward curiously in his chair to capture her gaze with his. Looking into his eyes was much the same as staring into the sea had always been. She thought she might drown in that gaze, should she allow it.

Honesty looked away. "I plead your mercy. I was overcome from my journey, not the sight of you. I ought to have demonstrated more appropriate control."

His hand lifted, whether to strike or caress her, Honesty couldn't tell. He withdrew his touch at the last moment. The prince stood, still shirtless. His finely cut oxenhide trousers clung to him as though they'd been made of ink poured over his legs.

"The Order promised me a Handmaiden, and yet here I sit, bathing your wrists and head as though I were the maid instead of you. Tell me," Cillian said in a voice low but nowhere near soft, "is this the way your Order trains you to behave?"

"No. I plead your mercy, as I said." Honesty pushed back the covers. She was in the prince's bed, if the sheets were anything to judge it by. Someone had removed her shoes and stockings, and her bare feet reproached her further. She swung them over the edge of the bed and tested her equilibrium before she stood.

He was not a tall man, and she didn't have to tilt her head to look at his face. She spoke softly as a matter of training, not because she was by nature soft. "Your mercy, sir. I was remiss. I should've made certain to eat and drink and sleep properly, so that I might adequately serve you upon my arrival. I regret I didn't do so."

Not that she'd had the chance to do so, not with so little time between leaving her last house and being summoned here. It was unusual, if not unheard of, for a Handmaiden to be assigned a new patron within hours of being released from the last, but Lady Valennda hadn't yet been wound into her shroud before Honesty had received the summons to move on. She hadn't been given time to protest.

"Regret doesn't give me solace." Cillian's voice edged along her skin, rough as brambles.

"No, I daresay it doesn't." She tilted her head to offer him a smile he didn't return.

"You're not what I was expecting."

"I rarely am." Honesty's smile gave away none of her desire to turn his face with a slap at his tone. Once she'd been in his place. It had taken her years of training to learn her craft. "But since no matter what the Order tells anyone in advance, they never know what to expect, I'm used to that."

This raised his eyebrow, and he put his hands on his hips to rake her with his gaze. He would say he thought she'd be prettier, Honesty thought, and braced herself not to react. With no food in her belly and not enough sleep to gentle her emotions, it would be harder for her to play at sweetness. It had been difficult for a long time.

"That seems ridiculous and inefficient. They told you all about me, did they not?"

She nodded. Pages and pages of documents she'd meant to read on the train but which had remained in the bottom of her hand-trunk. "Of course."

"Am I what you expected?"

"Yes," Honesty answered at once, though truth be told, she hadn't thought of him at all beyond the fact he'd been born to a crown and depended on someone else for his happiness.

"What's your name?"

"Honesty."

The corner of his mouth quirked. "You only have the one?"

She had another name, but didn't use it with her patrons. It raised too many questions about her ancestry. "*Honesty* is all you need."

Her empty stomach had been only partially satisfied with the drink. Now it rumbled and she put a hand over it to quell the noise. "Might I beg something to eat? I've come a long way in the past few days, and while I do plead your mercy for not being ready to serve you at once, I'll be far better able to begin once I'm fed."

His pale cheeks colored. "It's not enough for me to nurse you, now I'm to be your kitchen drab, as well?"

Honesty bit back the retort threatening to spill from her lips and offered a gentle smile and inclination of her head. "I would imagine a man of your stature would hardly need to serve. Surely you could ring for someone to bring me some fruit and cheese, perhaps a biscuit?"

He stared for so long she thought he would refuse, which would make this the shortest assignment she'd ever taken. She hadn't arrived quite ready to serve, that was true, but he was still required to provide her with food, shelter, and clothing appropriate for the seasons and activities. If he refused to feed her, she would walk out without another look behind her. She tensed, half hoping he'd give her reason to do just that.

Cillian nodded sharply, instead. "Indeed. The hour grows late, nearly the first chime. Fare will be limited."

Honesty looked at him through lowered lashes. Deference was simple to feign and always well received. "Whatever your kitchen can provide its prince at this late hour will certainly suffice."

She waited the span of four, five, six heartbeats before he began to laugh. He'd been gorgeous in disapproval, but in mirth his face lit up from within and turned his countenance into a sun from which she had to avert her eyes.

"You are clever," he said. "I do like that."

"I'm happy to please you," Honesty said, and if her response was made with less than what her name claimed her to be, nobody knew it but herself.

S he'd made use of his bath chamber while they waited for the food and now sat before him with her hair damp and skin gleaming. She smelled of his soap, a scent that had never aroused him on his own flesh but clung to hers in such a manner he fought the urge to lean forward and sniff her as though he were a hound. She wore one of the simple linen gowns he'd given her, cut in the same style as the one she'd worn upon her arrival but in sheer rose instead of dark blue. The material clung to every curve and showed the dusky circles of her aureoles and the triangle between her legs, but Honesty didn't seem to notice she was as good as naked before him. Or perhaps she didn't care.

She had the manners of a noblewoman, Cillian noted as Honesty used her knife to push a mouthful of tumbleberry jam onto her spoon before she tucked it between her lips. And yet in the next moment she used her fingers like a peasant to lift a slice of cold duck. She ate swiftly, efficiently, without lingering or sighing over the food, which was the best his cook could prepare at this hour. Cillian had taken her comment about his kitchen to heart, and though he rarely called for a meal past the ten chime, he'd wanted to see just what would happen if he did.

Consequently, the table in his chambers had been set with fine linens and porcelain and silver utensils. Wine poured, butter served in its own small crock, platters of artfully arranged delicacies provided. The effort deserved to make an impression.

The Handmaiden sipped once more from her wine and wiped her mouth with a napkin made of finer lace than graced most of his courtiers' cuffs. "Delicious."

"You ate it like a peasant in the field." It wasn't true. She'd eaten with gusto, but daintily.

Emotion flashed in her dark eyes. "I was hungry."

Such a simple statement, devoid of pretense, but it set him back more surely than if she'd woven an elaborate tale that failed to convince him. "You were . . . hungry."

"Oh, certainly." She gave him that bedamned smile again, and again he caught a flash of something in her gaze. "I thank you for the meal. If you could show me to where I might sleep, I'm certain we'd both like to go to bed. The hour, as you said, is late."

The chit knocked him fair to speechless. Show her to her bed? As though she were a common houseguest, a visitor? And he the chambermaid?

"Madame," Cillian said as he rose from the table to tower over her, "I believe you overstep."

And did the woman cower in front of him? Did she drop to her knees? She did not, but instead merely stared up at him with another of those half smiles that quirked a dimple in her cheek.

"I plead your mercy," she said calmly. "It will take me some time to learn what you like and how best to serve you. I thought it might be best to start in the morn, when we've both had time to rest."

Cillian had taken his hand to many women before this one, though never in anger. Others might believe it of him, might accuse him of being quick with his fists, and he didn't disabuse them. People believed what they would. But now, watching her small smile, Cillian wanted to shake her until her teeth rattled.

"Is this a Handmaiden's task? To put me off with request after bedamned request and provide me with nothing? I thought your purpose was to provide me with solace," Cillian bit out. "And I am not soothed!"

Honesty had risen and taken his hand with her soft and warm fingers before he knew to pull it away. "Then please, sir, allow me to assist you."

She drew him from the table toward an upholstered chair. With those small, soft hands she urged him to sit, and to his surprise but not, perhaps, to hers, Cillian did.

"Your hair," Honesty murmured, "is in atrocious condition."

Her words, each a thorn, pricked him. "There are perhaps three

men who could say such a thing to me with immunity, and not a
woman alive who would dare."

"Apparently there is at least one, for I've just said it." Her nimble fingers ran through the length of his hair and snagged in it,
pulling.

Cillian had neither Edward's bulk nor Alaric's height, and it had
deceived many into thinking him weak. When his fingers clamped
onto her wrist, Honesty could have no such misconception. His
squeeze arrested her hand, and yet she didn't flinch.

"Your hair," she murmured, "is tangled and doesn't befit you.
Let me brush it."

Cillian caught his reflection in a looking glass across the room,
and his lip curled. He'd allowed his hair to grow overlong in a direct
thumb-bite at the Council of Fashion, over which his father insisted
he preside. The length made it more difficult to manage, and the
time in his playroom had worked it through with sweat. He'd pushed
most of it off his face, but tendrils had escape and floated, careless.
He looked disheveled, at the least. *Atrocious*, as she'd said.

Honesty had already gone to his dressing table and found the
brush. "See how much nicer this will be, and then you'll sleep."

She took a handful of his hair and brushed it, working slowly
from the ends to the roots. Only when she could run the brush
through the entire length did she move to the next section. She
worked as efficiently at his hair as she had her dinner.

By the fourth section, Cillian had begun to lean into her touch.
He'd had lovers aplenty over the past few years, between his hareem
and those who sought favor in his bed. But none had touched him
this way. He wouldn't have allowed it.

He closed his eyes as she worked and lost himself in the tenderness of her care.

"There," Honesty said at last and patted his shoulder. "Much
better."

Cillian opened his eyes and ran his hand over his hair, now smooth and free of knots. She'd braided it and tied it at his nape with a length of soft cord. Her hand still rested on his shoulder. She was smiling.

"Now," she said. "To bed."

Chapter 10

I t could take her an hour to know a patron. It could take her a day, a week, a month. Never longer than that. Honesty didn't know Cillian yet, but she had no doubts she would. He didn't impress her as being difficult to know.

Blaming her weariness, she gave in to foolishness for a moment and passed her hand down the beautiful fall of his hair. Even tangled and dirty it was like spidersilk between her fingers. How would it feel against her face, over her body?

"Bed," he said in a thick voice, the sound of which she knew well.

If the gown he'd provided hadn't shown her at least part of what he expected her to be, the look in his eyes did. Surprising heat flared in her belly, and Honesty embraced it. Its source might well be that gorgeous hair, those eyes, his firm, lithe body. She hadn't made love in over a year. If the prince required service in his bed to bring him solace, at least he was physically appealing, and at least it was an act she knew well how to perform without any necessary thought.

"Where would you have me sleep?" she asked.

He didn't stand so much as he unfolded himself from the chair. "I thought you might anticipate my every need."

True patience, she reminded herself. *True patience is its own reward.*

"In time, my lord. I'll do my best, at least. But in order to know you, I need to ask. I can't read your mind."

Cillian reached for the braid hanging over her shoulder and wrapped his fist in it to pull her closer. His breath, sweeter than she expected, caressed her face. His heat pressed her through the thin fabric of the gown he'd given her.

"I'd thought you'd share my bed."

"If it pleases you."

Cillian didn't tower over her. If he pulled her closer, her cheek would fit just right against the curve of his neck. "I suppose we'll find out, won't we?"

She ought to offer him a bath before bed, but by now all Honesty could think of was sleep. The meal had replenished her, but she still needed to rest. He did, too, by the looks of him, gray shadows under his eyes. When she yawned, so did he.

"Come, then." She put her hand over the one tangled in her braid and loosed it gently. "To bed, before we both fall asleep on our feet. Have you a night rail?"

"I sleep in my skin."

Then she would, too. Honesty stripped out of her gown and put it aside neatly on the chair, then unlaced his trousers with swift fingers as she bit back another yawn. The prince didn't help her, but he didn't resist, either. She helped him out of the trousers and found him bare beneath. His cock, surrounded by a thick nest of curls slightly darker than on his head, stirred at her touch, but Honesty pretended not to notice.

When she looked up at him, his look of undisguised confusion set her back a step. It passed in a moment, replaced by the look of discontent she'd already grown used to. She waited for him to comment on her lack of attention to his prick, but when he didn't, Honesty took him by the hand and led him to the bed, where she slid between the sheets first with a sigh of irrepressible relief.

"The bed pleases you?" There was no hint of irony in his question.

Honesty reached out a hand to him. "In my last house I was given a straw pallet to sleep on, and I've spent the last two days sleeping upright on a train. This bed is like the Land Above. Come to bed, and let us both find pleasure in it."

She watched the flicker of contrasting emotions cross his face. Then he took her outstretched hand and slid into bed next to her. She arranged the covers over both of them and turned on her side to allow him to seek whatever position he found most comfortable.

"Sleep right," she murmured, already dozing.

The bed shifted as he moved and she waited for him to nestle against her backside, the cup of his hand on her breast. Though she felt the warmth of his body close to hers, Cillian didn't touch her. Yawning into the pillow, Honesty could wait no longer. She fell asleep.

Cillian did not sleep.

The low, soft breathing of the woman beside him should've soothed him toward dreams, but it had been so long since he'd shared a bed with anyone, the presence of another body beside his kept him staring at the ceiling long after she'd fallen asleep. She didn't roll around or snore. She lay silent as a stone beside him. She slept, and he did not.

None of this had gone as expected. She hadn't arrived when anticipated. She hadn't seen him in his finery, or the proof of his generosity laid out for her in the clothes and jewels he'd intended to give her. No, she'd met him in his playroom, stinking of sweat and other women, and she'd fainted dead away at the sight of it.

She was nothing like Edward's Handmaiden Stillness, who craved the kiss of the lash as fiercely as his friend yearned to wield it. Cillian had expected . . . well, by the Blessed Balls, what had he expected?

In his mind his Handmaiden would arrive and within an hour strip herself bare and take the flogger until she screamed in ecstasy. Then he'd fuck her until they both spent themselves, and then . . . and then, by the Void, she would love him. The way Stillness loved Edward.

And then what?

Cillian, scowling, got out of bed and paced the length of the room. It was cold, the fire gone out, and strewn with clothes and books and packages of trinkets sent by the fabric merchants seeking to gain his favor so that he might promote one over the other. Thinking of how it would be with his Handmaiden, he'd sent away the maids weeks ago. The room was a mess, and he stubbed his toe and set to hopping with a curse. This was nothing like Edward's immaculate rooms with the scent of good tea and quickbread, a crackling fire, and a woman on her knees, ready to serve his every whim.

She hadn't even bathed him, by the Void!

He went himself to the bathing chamber and sponged himself clean with cold water, too impatient to wait for it to heat. He threw on a robe of soft, thick fleece. She still slept when he came out of the bath chamber. Slept when he knelt in the ashes himself to raise the fire. Slept as he served himself a plate of her leftovers and ate them without joy. And she slept when he arranged himself in his chair by the fire, disgruntled and dissatisfied and determined to stay awake all night.

He closed his eyes on darkness and woke to golden light shining through the tall windows. Honesty had pulled back the curtains, and Cillian flung up a hand to cover his eyes.

"You're awake," she said pleasantly.

"Can one wake when one hasn't slept?"

"You slept," she pointed out serenely, unaware of how close he was to losing his temper. "Though not well, I'd wager."

"Not well . . . not . . ." Cillian got to his feet and groaned at the kinks and knots in every muscle he'd ever known he had and a few he hadn't. "What, by the Void, makes you think I could possibly have slept well?"

Honesty had dressed already and looked impossibly fresh in another of the gowns he'd provided. "I daresay I don't think you could in that chair. You should've stayed in the bed."

Cillian was not, at the best of times, accustomed to controlling his temper. He well knew its fierceness, knew it struck fear into many, and he'd never cared. There were few in his world whose rank demanded his obeisance, and fewer he loved enough to give homage.

"I applied for a Handmaiden, not a fumble-fingered maid of ill constitution," he told her flatly. "Not a failure."

Honesty listened to his speech with wide, unblinking eyes. When he'd finished, she drew herself up, rigid, her chin lifted in a defiance Cillian couldn't believe she dared. "I've not failed you."

"You have!" He flung his arms wide. "This is not what I want! How do you expect to bring me utter solace when you can't do something as simple as give me what I want?"

She didn't flinch from his words, and admiration at her courage crept through his anger. Honesty even dared to step closer to him, well within reach of his hand should he decide to strike her. She looked him up and down, and the assessment in her gaze further fueled his rage.

"I told you to let me know what you want," she said.

Which wasn't what he wanted, at all. Where was the woman who got on her knees and gazed adoringly up at him? The one who knew just how to please him without him having to ask? Cillian's head pounded from the ache in his neck and shoulders, and his temper flared higher.

"I want . . . tea."

"I can make you tea."

She went to the fire but of course, no kettle hung there. He didn't even like tea. She glanced at him over her shoulder, the heavy weight of her dark braid swinging. Then she straightened and shrugged with another of those beatific smiles that scraped him.

Honesty gestured. "If you'd like me to make tea for you, you might provide me with the means."

She made it sound so simple, and of course it was. Cillian, sore and out of sorts, crossed his arms over his chest and did his best to glare her into submission, but unlike the women of his hareem, who trembled and threw themselves to the ground at his feet with no more than a glance, this woman only stared.

"You haven't yet told me what you'd like me to call you." Honesty dusted her hands from the slight bit of soot on the palms, then moved to the wall to yank the bell cord. "And you might tell me what you'd like for your morning meal, so I can tell the maid when she comes."

None of this was going how he'd imagined, and anger swelled up from his gut, strangling him to silence. She looked at him again, curious, and her mouth thinned for so brief a moment he was sure he'd mistaken the sight.

"I could tell the maid myself," he said coldly. "But when I've laid out the cost of Handmaiden, I expect more than having to make it so."

At this, Honesty let her gaze roam him up and down, and once again Cillian had the odd and distinctly uncomfortable feeling she was judging him. "Did you send for me to be your maid? Or perhaps you sent for me to be your whore? I might imagine you'd have both aplenty, for half the cost, though I'm certain you can well afford it."

The cost didn't matter to him. Firth had coffers overflowing with riches, and his father had granted him a more than generous allowance. His mother had left him lands and estates that brought him income of his own, too.

"It's not the cost." If the chit thought it was the cost of her keeping that was slicing at his nerves, she was stupid.

She moved toward him with that same look of assessment. "So what is it then? If I'm to be your maid or your whore, I still need to know what it is you like before I can grant it. And you have to give me the tools to provide it."

He loosed the knot at his waist and opened the robe, then flung it off so he stood naked before her. His cock, already half hard as was usual upon rising, thickened under her gaze. Cillian swept his hands down his body.

"Here's the tool you can use if you're to act as my whore."

"Very nice," Honesty murmured.

Her response took the steam from his engine. When she undid the row of buttons at her throat to her waist with quick, practiced fingers and shrugged out of her gown and shift to stand naked before him, his mouth dried. He'd paid little thought to what she would look like, his imaginary Handmaiden, only of what she would do for him. Forced now to look upon her full, rounded breasts, her luscious curving backside, he had to admit she was perfection.

"Do you like what you see?" Her words oozed over him as low and liquid as molten sugar.

"No. I don't."

She dared to grin at him as she sank to her knees. She untied the cord holding the end of her braid and finger-combed her hair until it fell over her shoulders, those creamy, pink-tipped breasts, and down her back to tickle the underside of her sweetly curving ass. "Now?"

Muscles clenched deep in his groin as heat surged in his gut. She slid her knees apart a little, enough to show him a hint of her pink slit beneath her dark pubic curls. Her nipples, Void take her, had gone tight and begged for his mouth on them.

"I want you to go," he managed, but his cock betrayed him by rising. "Get out."

"You don't want me to go," Honesty said.

Then she took him into her mouth, and Cillian was lost.

What had she learned thus far but that he was a man consumed with fury? A man whose position granted him whatever he pleased and whenever it pleased him, and yet the smallest balk could send him into a rage. Leading him to solace would be like putting a recalcitrant horse into harness. It would take a great deal of effort and mayhap a long time.

Honesty had suffered long assignments in the past, but now . . . now things had changed for her, and all she could think of was how fast she could bring this cranky man to some semblance of peace, no matter how brief, so that she might return to the Motherhouse.

The Order taught them every patron was unique, but Honesty had dealt with men like Cillian before. They could be assuaged with submission, soothed with pleasure. Sometimes, it was the only way to distract them from their greater anger.

But that wasn't why she put his cock into her mouth. Honesty had a simpler reason than that. She wanted to taste him. She wanted to hear him cry out, feel his thighs tremble, feel his hands tangle in her hair as he jetted his pleasure into her mouth.

She wanted to prove to him she was not a thing, she was a person. *Women we begin and women we shall end* was the Order's fifth principle, and just then, Honesty was all woman.

He groaned when she sank his cock so deep it nudged the back of her throat. She hummed as she withdrew, pausing at the head of his prick to suck and lick before sliding down again. The thick carpet under her knees cradled them so she could do this for an hour, should he last that long.

"By the Arrow, your mouth is a delight," he said in a low, strained voice.

Honesty gripped his cock at the base and stroked upward along his hot flesh, slick from her mouth. His chair was close, and he might need it. "Sit, and I'll do even better."

He sat and she knelt between his legs to take him in her mouth again. Cillian thrust upward as his hands gripped the chair. His harsh, panting breaths were music to her, as was the creak of leather and wood as the chair moved under him when he moved to meet every suck and lick she provided.

This was for him, but oh, by the Arrow, it was for her, too, and Honesty let herself fall into the sweet oblivion of giving pleasure. It had been so long she feared she might have forgotten how, but just as her hand crept unerringly to her lap to twist and stroke, so did her mouth recall just how to move.

Cillian cried out, hoarse. His prick pulsed against her tongue. Honesty, circling with a fingertip, shuddered on the cusp of her own climax as she eased off from granting his. Cillian muttered a curse and thrust harder, but Honesty used her free hand to grip and hold him still.

Panting, Cillian glared down at her as she fought to catch her breath. "Don't stop!"

"I would make this last," she said. Her finger slowed against her flesh and she dipped it inside her well to withdraw it, glistening.

She painted his cock with the evidence of her arousal, and Cillian gave a low, short groan at the sight.

His hands dented the soft leather arms of the chair, and he cursed again. She made a tunnel of her fist for him to fuck into while she laved his sensitive balls and used her other hand to bring herself to the edge over and over without giving in to sweet orgasm. Taking him once more into her mouth, she juggled their individual pleasures until at last she could no longer keep herself from tipping into a climax so fierce it shook her entire body.

Cillian came in silence. He flooded her with his ecstasy, and the chair fair shook to pieces with the force of their rocking, but he climaxed without a sound. Still shaken from her own orgasm, Honesty could only be a bit disappointed she hadn't moved him to a shout.

She sat back, well satisfied with his taste clinging to her tongue. Cillian had thrown back his head, eyes closed. He opened them to look at her.

Honesty stood and took no small enjoyment in the way his gaze traveled over her body before focusing on her face. Naked, she went to the table and poured them both cups of cool water and pressed one into his hand before drinking her own. Cillian drained his and let the cup drop to the floor, where it bounced on the thick rug. He swiped his lips with the back of his hand and straightened in the chair.

He didn't look angry anymore.

"You're smiling," he said. "Is that because you've pleased me, or because you pleased yourself?"

Honesty finished her water and set down the cup, then retrieved her shift and tugged it over her head. She braided her hair as she answered him. "Both."

She bent to grab up his robe and handed it to him. "I'll draw you a bath."

She felt him watching her as she left the room, and another smile tugged her lips. She was learning him, but he would need to learn her, as well. She filled the tub with hot, clear water and gathered the soap, soft cloth, and rinsing bucket from their places in one of the cabinets. By the time she'd finished, Cillian stood in the doorway.

"You'll wash me?" He sounded wary.

"Would you like me to?"

"I have to tell you?"

She studied him, knowing what he'd expected and what she would be able to grant him would likely be quite different. "Only once. Because after that, I'll know."

"And if you forget?" He dropped the robe, careless of where it went, and sat on the low bathing stool over the drain.

Honesty dipped the cloth into the water and rubbed the soap to lather. "I'm fair certain I won't forget."

"But if you do," he said in a low voice as she moved the cloth over his body with smooth unhesitating strokes, "might I punish you?"

She thought of the playroom, and her hand stopped its journey along his body for the time it took to blink. "Would it please you to punish me?"

"It might."

She moved the cloth lower, over his legs and down to his feet. She lifted one, then the other, and washed them. His foot jerked in her hand, and she bit back a smile. Ticklish.

"You find that amusing?"

She looked up to see his brow once more creased in irritation and sent up a prayer. *Invisible Mother. I know true patience is its own reward, but I could surely use some help with this one.*

"Certainly I do not."

His hand on her wrist arrested her, and she sat back on her heels to stare up at him.

"You don't speak to me as I thought you would."

"You expected a bowed head?" Honesty watched his face for signs she was correct. "A bent back?"

She reached for the rinse bucket and emptied it over all the parts she'd soaped. Now she stood while he sat, looking up. She poured warm water over his skin and sluiced away the soap, then stood back to allow him to get into the tub.

She thought of the girl tied to the cross and the flogger that had been in his hand. The Mother-in-Service who'd told her of this assignment had said nothing about the prince's proclivities. Honesty thought of the documents, unread, in her hand-trunk. "If I felt it was to provide you with solace, I would offer my back to you. But I know for a fact you have a bevy of women better suited than I to such a task."

"So you won't allow me to bind your wrists? To beat you?" He shifted on the stool but made no motion to hide his nakedness.

"I'm here to lead you to absolute solace. Not to serve as your whipping boy." Honesty knew some of her Sisters served in such a manner, but she'd never been assigned to any patron who required it. She'd never expected to be.

This didn't please him. "My friend Edward was granted a Handmaiden who suffers his every whim, and tidies his quarters, besides!"

Petulance was one of Honesty's least favorite expressions. "I'm not your friend Edward's Handmaiden, I'm yours. We're not all cast from the same mold. And I'm not some genie from a bottle. Nor a member of your hareem."

Cillian didn't move. "Then what was that out there? You seemed happy enough with my cock down your throat while you frigged yourself. You seemed to like being on your knees."

Ah, so many had made the same assumptions, and so many times Honesty had bitten her tongue and forced a smile to appease.

It should have been no great hardship to do it again, but for the fact she'd grown weary of placating. *Sinder's Quiver be damned*, she thought as she watched the spoiled prince pout in front of her. *Let someone else fill it.*

"Just because I choose to get on my knees for you doesn't mean you own me," she told him. "It doesn't work that way, no matter what you've been told."

Cillian still hadn't shifted from his place on the stool, though the water in the tub had ceased to steam. "When I applied at the Order, they told me you would grant me what I needed. This is not what I want. Not at all!"

Honesty sighed, not caring about his bloodline or how much money was in his treasury or how rich his attire. Just now he was a naked man on a stool, like all the other naked men she had ever served. Disgruntled when they didn't get their way.

"What you needed, aye," she said coolly, with lifted chin and raised brow. "But what you seem not to understand is that I'm not here to be your plaything or your nursemaid. I'm here to give you what you need. It might not be the same as what you want."

And with that piece of advice she knew he still wouldn't understand if she wrote it out for him on parchment or tattooed it into his skin with ink, Honesty swept out of the room and left him to take his own bath.

Chapter 11

So, old man, you're looking well taken in hand." Alaric reached to flick the fall of lace at Cillian's throat.

Cillian knocked his hand away. It had been four days since he'd seen his friend, and that long since his Handmaiden had arrived to disappoint him. He'd been in a fever of a bad mood ever since, one not even nightly visits to his playroom had been able to ease.

"Well, how is she?" Alaric was too full of sunshine to suit Cillian, but at least with Alaric, Cillian could be himself without fear his friend would run with tales to his father or his father's ministers.

"She is . . ." Cillian paused on the string of words he might use to describe Honesty, but settled on one. "Honest."

"Honest? That sounds good."

Cillian shook his head. "No. I wanted what Edward has. Honesty is not what Edward has."

Alaric settled into the couch and propped his feet up on the low table. The library was empty, as it usually was, for Cillian's were not the only lords who preferred billiards to books. His father's retinue had little use for this room, which was what made it the perfect spot for Cillian to smoke a bowl of herb with Alaric and not have to worry about any of them showing up.

"She is too honest," he said as Alaric lit the match to start the bowl smoking. "She tells me exactly what she feels I need to hear. Not what I want to hear," he added. "What I need to hear."

Alaric made a face. "I can imagine you don't take to that very well."

Cillian paused in drawing a lungful of smoke to frown. "No need for you to add your insult to this situation."

"Your mercy, my prince," Alaric said with only the slightest trace of mockery. "Pray, tell me more."

"She tidies the room but not even as neatly as a maid. She makes tea but only when she wishes also to drink it. She reads my books and offers them to me—"

"Books? Sinder forbid," Alaric said.

Cillian threw the pouch of herb at him. It bounced off Alaric's chest and hit the floor. Alaric looked at it, then at Cillian.

"I'm sorry she's not to your liking. Maybe you should send her away."

The thought had crossed his mind every day since her arrival, and yet . . . "She says she will go if I want her to."

Alaric raised a brow. "So? If she doesn't please you, won't they send another, if you complain?"

Cillian had spent hours filling out the application for the Order of Solace. A full medical history, essays on his childhood, questions on his tastes in food, drink. A complete sexual history. He'd stinted on nothing, lied about nothing. Held nothing back. He'd been . . . honest.

And they'd sent him this woman. Of all those in service to the Order, they'd chosen Honesty. If she couldn't bring him solace, Cillian was certain nobody ever could.

"I can't send her away. She would go. And I don't want another."

"By the Blood, Cillian, why not? If she doesn't make you happy?"

"Maybe she isn't supposed to make me happy," Cillian muttered.

Alaric had cotton in his ears when it suited, but he'd heard that. For once he made no jest, just clapped Cillian on the shoulder and gave it a gentle squeeze. "She's not your only chance."

Cillian shrugged off the touch and strode to the window to look out to the sunshine beyond. He'd learned to walk on that grass. As a child he'd played on those lawns. Run through the fountain naked and splashing, his nannies in tow. He'd lost his cherry to a kitchen maid out there in that grass one moonlit summer night.

All of that seemed very long ago, and as though it had happened to someone else. Not the man he'd become. Cillian turned back to his friend.

"How many chances does one person have, Alaric?"

"You ask the wrong man. You know I don't believe in filling Sinder's Quiver. Frankly, my friend, I didn't think you did, either."

Cillian had been anointed in the Temple at birth and not set foot inside since. "I don't suppose it matters. She'll still try?"

"Of course she will. It's her duty. But from how you make it sound, she's not very good at it."

"Yet she's the one they sent me. What do you suppose that means?" Cillian went back to the table and snagged the bowl of herb, which had gone out. He relit and drew it in deep, holding it before letting the smoke seep in burning tendrils from his nostrils.

Alaric looked impressed. "I always loved that trick."

"Is that what I am? A trick?"

He hadn't meant it to sound quite so harsh, but Alaric didn't seem to mind.

"Of course not."

It was how he felt, though. Like a puppet master making the life-size Prince Cillian dance without strings. Playing the part he'd been born for, but without a script to memorize. A show without direction.

"Cillian. You know you can talk to me. About anything." Alaric paused. "I know I'm not Edward, but I am your friend as much as he ever was."

Not like Edward. Edward had been Cillian's brother of the heart, and Alaric loved Edward as somewhat more than that; they had made a triangle with Edward their point in common. Alaric would ever be Cillian's friend, but it would never be the same for either of them with each other as it was with each of them and Edward.

"I don't want to send her away if she'd not care," Cillian said. "I only wish to send her back if it would pain her to go."

Alaric raised a brow but made no other comment. Cillian drew in another breath of herb, but it granted him no joy. It settled in his lungs until he coughed it out and then he set down the bowl.

"Ah, Prince Cillian." The man in the doorway swept in on a cloud of perfume covering the underlying stench of body odor. His hair, pomaded to slick brilliance, hung in lank curls to his shoulders, and his skin gleamed with sweat. Several pox marks scored his lean face, and other blemishes sprouted along his hairline.

Alaric turned his back and grimaced, then rolled his eyes at Cillian. "And I must be off. Lady Larissa is expecting me."

That Alaric would abandon him to Lord Devain's blatherings didn't surprise Cillian, but he shot his friend a glare anyway. Alaric grinned and gave Cillian an entirely insincere half bow, turned on his heel and provided the same to Lord Devain, who ignored him. Devain had no time for the sons of merchant farmers, no matter how high they'd risen.

"Prince Cillian. About this matter of the trade routes," Devain began without preamble, but Cillian held up a hand.

"I discuss such matters when it's time. It's not time now."

Devain had become one of the king's appointed ministers while Cillian had been what his father referred to as "recuperating," though Cillian had never been ill. Devain had been a magistrate of the province where Cillian had attended school, one of those called to decide the prince's fate after the prostitute's death. He'd been one who ruled Cillian should enter the asylum instead of hanging.

Cillian supposed he ought to be grateful.

Devain supposed so, too.

Devain looked around the empty room, then gave a pointed glance to the herb bowl. "You're too busy, now?"

Cillian swallowed the retort that rose instantly to his lips. This man had been there when they took Cillian to his cell. When they'd shorn his head and dressed him in rags. And when the board of medicuses had met to determine if the Prince of Firth, the king's only son, could be allowed to return to society, Devain had been there, too. Devain had been the one to ask the most pointed questions about Cillian's progress, to make the medicuses doubt. And when Cillian had at last come home after near two years in that pit, he found Devain sitting at his father's side and whispering in his ear.

"I didn't say I was too busy. I said now was not the time." Cillian kept his voice steady, and also his gaze. Devain, like a jackal, could sense weakness. "If you wish to meet with me, you can take an appointment at court, the way the others do."

Devain's smile crept into his eyes and yet was devoid of any humor. "As you wish. I merely thought it might behoove you to take the time to listen to my proposal without the jabber of all those others to distract you."

"You meant you want me to put your interests over those of

others, and you believe yourself above the protocol they're all required to follow."

Devain drew himself up to his full height, head and shoulders
above Cillian, who didn't give the other man the honor of tilting
his head to look at his face. Devain let out a slow, hissing breath.

"One might forget how one was once in a madman's rags, sitting in his own filth," he said in a voice meant to bring blood.

Cillian had bent and been broken for love and would do it
again for no less than that. He surely, by the Void, wouldn't do
it for Devain. His fingers twitched into fists for but a moment before he straightened them, but Devain saw it, and smiled.

"No, my lord," said Cillian in a voice as sickly sweet as joba
syrup. "One might remember."

F our days into this assignment, and Honesty was sure Cillian
would send her away. That wouldn't please the Mothers-in-
Service, but it would make Honesty happy. If he sent her away, she
wouldn't have to abandon him.

She'd expected to feel more guilt about her lack of enthusiasm
for this assignment. After all, she was failing not only the prince,
but the Order and the Holy Family. Herself, too, if she wanted to
admit it. She'd taken a vow to do her best to serve her patrons, and
this was not her best.

Her sigh began in her toes. Honesty stared out the window.
She'd been a veritable captive in these chambers, since it hadn't
pleased her patron to take her out of them. Four days since her arrival, and he'd left her every morning after the first without a word
of explanation about where he was going or when he'd be back.

The nights had been interesting. Cillian slept on the chair in
front of the fire and every night she fell into sleep waiting for him
to join her. After that first night, he never had. She'd woken each

morning before him but had forced herself to stay abed until he rose, often with a groan of protest at what must have been screaming muscles. He bathed and dressed and left, every morning, and left her there. Alone.

No patron had ever ignored her. Especially not after she'd used her mouth on him. She might have made a mistake with that, she mused, though it had been delicious. He might not be the sweetest tempered man she'd ever met, but he was beautiful. Even so, it seemed she'd misjudged him, and despite her desire to quit this place and this career, she couldn't help but be a little ashamed.

His abandonment had done one thing for her. Convinced her the apathy for her chosen field was no passing thing, that she was, indeed, no longer a Handmaiden in her heart. Oh, she'd been playing the role for so long she wore it like a costume, her smile a mask and her words of comfort dialogue in a play she'd memorized so long ago she no longer had to think about the plot.

She knew the truth, now, no matter how much she'd like to pretend she didn't. She wanted to go home, and not to the Motherhouse. Not to await her next assignment. Not to attend any more people so caught in their webs of sorrow and discontent they couldn't see clearly for even the single moment required to pass as solace. She wanted to go home, to Bellora, where she could sit in her father's orchards and smell the tart-sweet scent of ferlafruits and let the wind tug tangles into her hair.

She wanted to return to the place that would not, in any likelihood, welcome her.

She couldn't go anywhere without first finishing this assignment. Not unless she wished to run away, and she owed the Order the debt of her consideration, at least. She could flee her duties, but never her obligation.

With nothing else to pass the time, she'd done a bit of tidying. And, since Cillian had apparently sent away all his maids, she was left to straighten the bedcovers and sweep up the dust and stoke the fire. She could and did ring for meals when she was hungry and had someone come to take away the dishes, but the rest of every long day she'd spent reading and looking out the window. She'd devoured all but three of the books on his shelves and memorized every blade of grass on the lawn outside.

If this kept up, she'd have to go in search of him. She couldn't bring him to solace if he was never with her, nor could he send her away. And if he didn't send her away or give her the chance to give him what he needed, she'd have to decide to leave.

She wasn't ready to decide it. Better, if more cowardly, to have him make the choice for her. Failure here would mean she'd have good reason to go to the Mothers-in-Service and tell them she was finished. Nobody would fault her for leaving if it was clear she was no good. No, she had to do what he'd already accused her of doing. She had to fail here.

But, damn him to the Void, she couldn't fail him if he wouldn't give her the chance.

Honesty had turned, deciding to grip the horse by the reins when the door flew open hard enough to slam into the wall and shake the pictures. Cillian kicked the door shut behind him. He stood there, seething, his eyes like storms in a face gone pale with fury.

He looked at her, his mouth parted, but if he meant to speak, he bit back the words and looked away from her. That stung more than she'd have thought it could from a man she didn't even know. He strode to the table next to the fireplace and poured himself a cut-crystal glass full of whiskey and tossed it down his throat before taking another. Then he stood, shoulders slumped, and held the glass in his hand as though it were too heavy even to lift.

Now was the time for her to succeed with failure.

Witty words rose to her lips, a taunt designed to prick him to anger, but died there when he turned. She'd found him pleasing to the eye upon first sight, beautiful in laughter and arousing in his desire. Looking at him now, the bleak gaze, lips drawn to tight whiteness, Cillian broke her heart.

"Tell me what happened," she said softly.

Countless other men had taken what she offered, but Cillian did not. Indeed, he stepped back as though her touch were poison. He sipped slowly and set the glass down half empty. He shook his head and pushed past her without a word. He went into the bedchamber and shut the door.

He didn't want her. Honesty gripped the back of the chair to steady herself. From inside the bedchamber came the sound of a single, strangled . . . sob?

This had naught to do with her. Whatever wounds festered in the Prince of Firth, she wasn't meant to heal them. She didn't have it in her any longer to be what someone needed before they knew they needed it. To be someone's comfort. She had nothing left for anyone; she barely had enough for herself.

Her feet moved anyway, soft steps cushioned by the thick rugs and the lovely slippers he'd provided. He'd been generous in that respect, clothing her in garments fit for a . . . well, perhaps not quite a princess, but a prince's consort, at the least. They were the finest she'd owned in a long time, the fabrics rich and soft and of a flattering cut. If nothing else she owed him a thank-you.

She could try to fool herself into thinking that was what she meant to offer when she rapped on the door and waited for him to speak, but Honesty knew herself too well to be convinced. She couldn't ignore or resist the look in his eyes. The man needed something with the desperation of the haunted. He needed her.

She knocked again and when he didn't answer, she pressed the latch. Inside the prince crouched, still half dressed, on the floor. That rich auburn hair had tangled again, tumbling over his shoulders and bare skin. He'd taken off his shirt but left the trousers on, and he clutched his knees to press his face against them. She heard the hoarse, strangled rasp from deep in his throat.

So caught in his own despair, he hadn't noticed her entry. She could turn and walk away, leave him to his misery. Instead, she knelt next to him.

He startled when she touched his shoulder; the jerk of a man expecting a blow. When he looked up at her with red-rimmed eyes, seeing but not knowing her, she touched him again the way she'd have gentled a horse. Slow and easy, she stroked her fingertips down the length of his bare arm and ended at his hand. It clenched, but he didn't pull it away.

"Leave me," he said.

"No."

"I want you to leave me," he insisted.

The grief in his voice pricked her fiercely as a pin. Honesty curled her fingers around the lump of his fist. "No."

Another strangled sob lurched from his throat and he buried his face against his knees again. "Did they send you here to torment me?"

"No. I don't think so." Guilt poked at her. It wasn't his fault he'd had the misfortune to be assigned a Handmaiden who wanted to leave the service. "I'm sure they thought I'd be the best suited to you. Tell me what troubles you."

He shook his head. "No. You can't help."

Though the scent of herb clung to him, Honesty didn't think he was intoxicated. She squeezed his hand. "I can try."

He looked at her, then, his expression so bleak she wanted to weep. A shudder ran through him, and at first she thought it was the jerking of his muscles that shifted her toward him, so subtle was the gesture. But then he moved again, no closer than the thickness of a thread.

He needed her, and Honesty found she couldn't deny him. "Come here."

She opened her arms and he slid into her embrace with a groan. With both of them on their knees, his face fit perfectly into the curve of her shoulder. His back was hot beneath her palms as she pulled him close. His breath, hot, too, against her throat. She held him in silence until the small tremblings in him ceased and then she stroked a hand down his hair. She kissed the top of his head and his arms tightened around her.

After so many years in service, she didn't think she could be surprised by anything a patron did, but in that moment Honesty learned she could surprise herself. She took his chin in her hand and lifted his face to hers. She kissed him.

Cillian turned his face at the last second, so her lips landed at the corner of his mouth and not full upon it. "You don't have to do this."

An odd statement from a man whose cock she'd already had down her throat. "I know."

"I don't . . . I haven't . . ." He shook his head and tried to move away, but Honesty stopped him with her hands on his shoulders. He wouldn't look at her.

"Shhh. You don't have to say anything." She kissed him again.

His lips parted. She cupped the base of his neck. She tasted his earlier indulgences, but his mouth was sweet for all that. She stroked his tongue with hers and he shivered. He kissed with his eyes closed, she saw, and as simply as that he endeared himself to her.

With the bed so close there was no need for them to stretch out on the floor, but it was no hardship to rest on thick carpets. Honesty pushed him onto his back, an arm cradled beneath him. For a moment he simply let her push him, but in the next he'd pulled her down on top of him. Chest to chest, their legs tangled. His kisses grew urgent. Harder. The sudden passion in them heated hers, and she moaned softly into his mouth.

Cillian stopped at the sound and pulled back to look at her face. "I said you need not do this."

"I know." She bent to kiss him again, but he turned his face once more. This time, her kiss didn't even reach his skin. Honesty stilled, the position awkward but the tension between them worse. "Is it so difficult for you to believe I'd like to?"

Gently but firmly he circled her upper arms and pushed her to the side so they could both sit. When he got up to pace, Honesty stayed on the floor to watch him. At least he no longer looked as though he were staring into the Void and thinking of jumping.

"You said yourself, you're not a whore." His voiced stayed low.

"I'm not, that's true enough." As he paced, she got to her feet, too. "But does that matter? A whore sells herself. I'm offering."

He shuddered again and went to the window to stare out. He pressed his fingertips to the glass, then the whole of his palm. At last he leaned to rest his forehead there, his eyes closed. He took in breath after breath, each deliberate and slower than the one before it.

Giving comfort sprang from intuition. Sometimes, many times, from utter guesswork. It meant she'd been wrong upon occasion, though never grievously. People were people, some more damaged than others, but most the same at heart.

"Cillian," she murmured, and he twitched but looked at her.

"That's the first time you've used my name."

She'd thought of him by name since her arrival, but he was right. "We haven't had much chance for conversation."

"I've been avoiding you."

Honesty tried to tempt him with a smile he didn't return. "I noticed."

"I don't want you to want to leave." The man speaking to her now didn't sound like a prince . . . but weren't all princes men beneath the crown?

"Is that why you've been avoiding me?" She moved closer, and he didn't move away.

Cillian took in another low, slow, and deep breath and turned from the window. "You said you'd give me what I need. Not what I want."

"That is my purpose, yes." She watched him carefully.

"But not your pleasure?" The hint of a smile quirked his lips but faded fast. "You can't say that and live up to your name."

"It has ever been my pleasure to serve my patrons." It was not a lie, and yet untruth clung to her tongue and stifled her from further speech.

His eyes closed again, the dark lashes in such contrast to his bright hair sweeping shadows on pale cheeks. His mouth thinned, and he swallowed hard. He put a hand over his heart. Alarmed, Honesty grabbed his arm, feverish hot beneath her fingers. He looked at her then, those green eyes swimming with a depth of emotion she couldn't refuse.

But when she tried to kiss him, again he turned his head. She'd gone on tiptoe to reach his mouth and her lips hovered over his cheek. She pressed them instead to the beard-prickled roughness of his throat, warm as his arm had been. She put her arms around him, his chest hot against her through her gown. He was burning up with something inside him that didn't feel like illness.

"You don't want to help me," Cillian said.

It wasn't a matter of want, but she didn't tell him so. There were many ways to provide the comforts that led to solace, and thus far she'd failed him in most. But this, the most basic, she already knew he'd respond to. Her hand slid to the laces at the front of his trousers. "I can try."

Cillian shook his head and put a hand over hers. She kissed his throat again, then his shoulder, then his chest. When she licked his collarbone, Cillian hissed. His hand clamped, hard, on hers but he didn't pull it away. When she moved her mouth lower over his salt-sweet flavored skin to tug his nipple between her lips, his groan swept over her in a rush of heat.

"You taste good," she whispered and looked up at him.

He opened his eyes, ablaze with desire. Under her hand his cock filled and pressed against his trousers. His heart thundered beneath her mouth and when she bared her teeth to press his skin, it humped at once into gooseflesh as he shivered.

"This won't solve anything," he gritted out.

She licked him again, this time moving over his ribs. "Shhh."

When she got on her knees and unlaced his trousers, Cillian stopped protesting. When she pulled the material over his thighs and down his strong, muscled calves, he stepped out of them to stand naked before her. When Honesty cupped his testicles in her palm and nuzzled his cock before licking it from base to crown, he curled his fingers into her hair.

She took him in her mouth, but only for a few strokes of her tongue before she moved up his body again with her mouth. She didn't try to kiss his lips again, but stepped back to undo the buttons on her gown and shrug out of it.

His gaze flickered, then dropped to caress her body. He licked his mouth when she pulled the shift over her head and tossed it to join the gown. His prick lifted, and Honesty's breath quickened at the sight of his response. He might not believe she took as much pleasure in this as he would, but she had no doubts.

She cupped her breasts, offering them, but though the heat in his eyes flared, he didn't move. His cock spoke for him, thickening further, but he stayed still as stone even when she licked her fingertips and tweaked her nipples tight. Nor did he move when she again sucked a fingertip and slid it down her belly to part her curls and circle her clitoris. His chest heaved and his tongue swept over his lips again, his fists clenched at his sides, but Cillian wouldn't move.

Honesty stepped backward to the bed and lay back with a crook of her finger. "Cillian. Come here."

He took a step and stopped. Then another. One more. Two more would bring him to her, but he stopped, and she was reminded again of the effort it took to gentle a horse. Honesty didn't push. She ran her hands over her body, finding all the places that felt good. She lifted her hips off the bed to give herself better access to her cunt, now slick with desire. She slid a finger inside herself and drew it up to rub her clit again. The sigh slipped out of her and she did nothing to hold it back.

"Cillian," Honesty murmured, and watched how his gaze flared at the sound of his name on her tongue. She said no more, gave him no words to resist. Only the sight of her.

Cillian watched her, and at last his hand went to his cock to squeeze just behind the head. His lips thinned, but his throat worked to hold back the moan she heard anyway. It urged one in response from her, and Honesty made no pretense at holding it back.

"I might believe you want me," he said.

"Come and let me show you that I do."

It was a courtship as coy and stifled as any she'd ever witnessed, made ridiculous by the fact they were both naked. Yet if either of them felt the fool, Honesty couldn't tell it. They might have been sitting in a garden full of roses, her invitation made from behind a fan and his love-gift to her a posy, not his prick.

And at last he moved toward her, step by step, until the bed dipped under his weight. Behind the blaze of lust, Honesty glimpsed

a slew of other emotions, fleeting, in his eyes. Cillian licked his
mouth again and ran a hand along her calf. He stopped at her
knee, fingers curled lightly over her skin.

He kissed it.

She twitched at the soft, unexpected press of his lips to flesh
unused to caresses. His name slipped out of her unbidden this
time. Cillian nuzzled the fine hairs on her thigh and moved higher
as Honesty's legs opened wider to accept him.

On hands and knees he crouched between her legs, his mouth a
scant breath from touching her. She tensed, waiting for him to kiss
her again. Or to lick her. Even to touch her with more than the
gust of air seeping from his lips.

Her last lover had been a worker from the fields outside the
Motherhouse. She'd seen him from her window, bare-backed and
sweating in the last summer sunshine as he pulled the weeds from a
crop of joba melons. He'd worn his hair too short for fashion, and it
had stuck up crazily when he swept dirty hands through it. She'd
gone down to watch him work, and he'd handed her a melon fresh
off the vine, tart enough to pucker her mouth. He'd taken her hand
and gone behind the toolshed where they'd lain on a bed of seed sacks.
He'd been the last man to put his mouth on her cunt, and he'd
tongued her only long enough to make her wet enough to fuck.

Cillian took his time. His hands slid beneath her bottom to
hold her to his mouth when at last he touched his lips to her clit.
She cried out at the flicker of his tongue. He smoothed the flat of it
over her, and her hips bucked until he held her still.

"Please," she said.

He looked up at her, even the lust in his eyes dimmed behind a
veil of inscrutability. Slowly, deliberately, he slid his tongue over her
heated flesh and down to press inside. Then again, the same motion in reverse, while Honesty arched and writhed as best she could
against the bonds of his grip.

Time slowed for her beneath his touch, and Honesty gave herself up to it, utterly. Pleasure washed over her in slow, rolling waves. She found the softness of his hair with her fingers and twined them deep in the silken depths as her climax burst through her.

Trembling, she fell back onto the pillows with a low cry. It took her some moments to realize he'd moved away from her, but when she opened her eyes to find him, Cillian was staring at her. He didn't move away from her when she sat and drew him close for a kiss. She was the one who hesitated this time, and he the one who captured her mouth. The taste of her pleasure on his tongue sent another surge of desire through her.

Still kissing him, Honesty lay back again and Cillian followed. He braced himself to keep from putting all his weight down, but Honesty would have none of that. One orgasm was not enough to sate her. She needed more, and one from him, as well.

Somewhere along the way she'd lost sight of her reasons for this, whether her selfish heart thought only of itself or if woman she began and ended. All she knew was that his mouth was too sweet to deny, and the heat of his prick on her belly parted her legs. She wanted him on top of her, inside her, no matter if it was for her comfort or for his.

"Make love to me," she murmured into his ear, and Cillian shuddered against her neck.

His cock nudged her gate and she opened for him. She wrapped her legs around his waist to draw him closer. Her fingernails raked his back when he thrust deep with a groan. When he nipped at her neck, she cried out and lifted her hips.

Cillian was as skilled with lovemaking as he'd been with cunnilingus. In moments she surged to the edge again. Honesty cried out her ecstasy and drove him harder with her heels and fingernails. Her body convulsed around him and Cillian thrust again, voicing his ecstasy in a hoarse shout.

They clung to each other for the span of a heartbeat or two, a few breaths, and then he rolled off her. His hair spilled out over her shoulder, his head on the same pillow. Still languid in the aftermath, Honesty turned on her side to face him and stroked a hand over it.

"You have such lovely hair."

He laughed, a sound as unexpected as the kiss to her knee had been. He didn't look at her, but he laughed. Then he covered his eyes with a hand and his laugh faded into something more like a sob.

Words were not always the best choice. Honesty reached to draw the blankets over both of them, for although touching him earlier had been like caressing flames, now they were both chilled. Yawning, she tucked herself up beside him and waited for him to push her away and get out of bed. Moment by moment, he softened beneath her until the hushed sound of his breathing told her he slept.

It took her a very long time to join him.

Chapter 12

This fountain is lovely." Honesty pointed with the hand not nestled in Cillian's. She'd taken his hand as they walked and noted how he'd tensed at the touch before relaxing. "What is the statuary representing?"

"I don't know. I never asked."

Though he wasn't much taller, his stride was longer. He'd shortened it to accommodate her. In the sunshine, his hair shone like flames. She'd tied it down his back with a dark green ribbon interwoven in the braid, but the sedate hairstyle couldn't hide its beauty. She wanted to touch his hair, and so she did.

Cillian shot her a glance at the touch. "I could find out for you."

"It's not important." She didn't really care. Once she was gone she'd never come back here to marvel at the carved stone angels with water shooting from their mouths. "Let's go into the hedge maze."

Cillian grimaced. "That place? Why?"

How much had changed since she'd taken him to bed, she

mused with a small smile and a tug of his hand. He was still not the smoothest tempered of men, but seemed less inclined to instant rage or contempt. If modesty had been one of the five principles she'd surely have failed at maintaining it, because Honesty took no small amount of pride in how he'd changed in just the past few days because of her.

For a moment, unease twitched in her gut. She'd made a marked difference in him without even trying. She could ease him into great changes, should she make an effort . . . but no. It didn't matter that his hands and mouth brought her such fierce pleasure. She ought to have told him the truth. She was no longer of a heart sufficient to serve. She might bring him some small comfort, but solace would be out of reach if he relied upon her to lead him to it. She ought to have left already, except she still hadn't gathered the courage to make that choice.

"Because it would be most merry to see how long it takes us to find the center, and because I fancy finding out how private such a place might be." Forcing away her dark thoughts, she grinned at him, then dropped a slow wink.

Cillian, for all his swaggering and his private room full of naked women, blushed. The color rose high on his cheeks and sent heat swirling throughout her body at the sight. This man . . . oh, this man was not at all what she'd expected.

"I haven't been to the center," Cillian said, but followed.

Like lovers, they strolled through the gate of woven vines laced with bits of ribbon and beads. Honesty paused to set one strand to swinging. "What are these?"

He laughed. "They're called braggart's laces."

Honesty stroked along another length of satin with a glass bead dangling from the end. "And what do they do?"

"They're left by those who've visited the maze. If a couple has been . . . intimate . . . whilst inside, the gentleman begs a bit of lace or ribbon and a bead from the lady, and they string it there."

"How unfortunate I don't have any extra beads with me, then." She watched him, curious at how he reacted to her gentle teasing, and when he hesitated under the gate, she stopped to tip her face to his. "At home, we had a gate much like this leading into my father's orchards. But nobody hung beads and ribbon. We called it the kissing gate, though. Because every time you passed beneath, you were supposed to kiss your fingertips and press them to the vines. For luck. And if you happened beneath the gate at the same time as another . . ."

"You kissed them?" Cillian laughed.

Honesty tipped her face farther, lips pursed. He didn't bend to kiss her. He looked around as though checking to see if they would be seen, and Honesty tucked this observation away the way she'd done with everything else over the past few days. He was a puzzle she couldn't stop herself from wishing to solve.

"You kissed them," she said. "For luck."

"Let it never be said I've too much luck to throw away the chance for more." Cillian angled his mouth above hers.

The kiss was brief and almost chaste, but it was enough to satisfy her for the moment. She tugged his hand and drew him into the maze, which was well plotted, with dead ends aplenty and many alcoves perfectly suited for intimacies. She took advantage of the ones they discovered, finding that each time she kissed him or urged him to kiss her, the prince softened a bit more until by the time they discovered the maze's center, they both were breathing fast and grinning. She moved to the low stone bench set in front of a small ornamental pond.

Cillian didn't follow at first, even when Honesty leaned back to give him room beside her. He swiped a hand across the back of his mouth and then over his hair, which had begun to come loose from the braid she'd tied in it earlier. He went to the pond and knelt to peer into the water.

"It's lovely here," he said.

"It is. You've never been?" Honesty watched as Cillian dipped his fingertips in the water and then wiped them without concern on his trouser leg. She'd not have imagined him to ever be so careless with his clothes.

He shook his head. "No. This is a place for lovers."

"But you've had—" His expression stilled her tongue. "You've had lovers, Cillian."

He shrugged and looked away. "No. Not the sort one brings to a garden maze."

"I find that difficult to believe."

He shrugged again. "Do you, truly? When you know all about me?"

She'd yet to read the documents about him, her reluctance ridiculous now as well as shameful. She couldn't tell him she hadn't thought him worth the effort at first. "You've brought me here, now."

He laughed and shook his head. "I believe you've brought me, Honesty. Not the other way 'round."

"Very well. So I've brought you here to the center of this maze. Shall you have your wicked way with me?" She gestured again for him to sit beside her, and this time, he did.

She stroked a tendril of hair from his cheek. "Cillian. I have no ribbons or beads, but I think I'd like to give you something to brag upon."

"Is that what I need? To make love to you on the grass in front of that pond?" He turned his head to kiss the hand stroking his hair. "How do you know me, Honesty, that you might decide what my soul needs, truly?"

He wasn't the first to ask her, and she answered him as she did everyone else. "Not everything I do is based on some grand cosmic scheme."

He kissed her hand again and captured it between his. "I thought everything you did was designed to send me toward solace. I thought you did nothing else but work toward that goal. So you could leave."

"I . . ." Words failed her, for to speak anything but agreement would be a lie.

"I know it's the truth. I was a fool to believe there could be anything different about a Handmaiden than any other woman. I was . . . well, I was a madman." Cillian pressed the flat of her hand to his cheek. "But I thank you for staying. I do feel more at peace with you at my side."

A blithe reply rose to her lips and hovered there without leaping free. The first time she'd seen him he'd been flogging a woman tied to an ironwood cross with a group of naked women waiting for his attentions, and she'd assumed he'd be easy to put aside. Honesty swallowed guilt, the taste bitter on her tongue. She'd set out to fail him, and she'd nearly managed.

She couldn't do it.

Honesty swallowed the pretty speech that would do everything to make him happy and yet would still be false. "I wanted to fail you."

He didn't even give her a curious look. "Of course you did. You arrived to find me in my playroom . . . and my temper . . . I am impossible, as I've been so often told. I'm more than you should have been given. I understand."

Honesty shook her head. "No, Cillian. You don't understand. My desire to leave had nothing to do with you. I didn't even know you."

She shifted closer, and he put their hands, fingers tangled, into his lap. When he didn't answer, Honesty took a deep breath and gave him the truth. "I've long felt I was no longer suited to this vocation. Each time I helped a patron toward solace I was left a bit emptier. My last patron . . . she was very ill. I thought it would be a few weeks before she passed into the Land Above, yet she lingered for months. Nothing I did could possibly bring her any comfort, other than the most basic of physical, and I'm a Handmaiden, not a medicus. I could do nothing for her, but leaving meant being assigned a new patron. One who'd demand rather more of me than I'd grown accustomed to providing."

"A patron such as I."

"Yes. Just like you." She leaned to kiss his mouth, but tenderly. "One who truly needed me."

Cillian said nothing.

Honesty sat back but didn't let go of his hands. "I knew I couldn't possibly provide you with what you needed any more than I could have done it for my last patron. Only unlike her, the failure to serve would have come from inside me, not circumstances I couldn't control. And for the first time since joining the Order, I didn't care. I plead your mercy. I shouldn't have taken this assignment."

"But you did. And you stayed."

She ducked her head and chuckled. "I haven't had a bed partner in a long time. I . . . was weak."

Cillian made a soft noise. "I thought they would send me someone who would change everything."

Honesty didn't let go of his hands, a decision rising from inside her. "You've not found it to be so. I plead your mercy. There's still time."

Cillian's laugh had little humor to it. "One always imagines it would be so, yes?"

"I would make it so." She watched him while he pulled his

hands gently from hers and got off the bench to stare again at the pond.

"I've never courted a woman, Honesty. Nor a man, for that matter. I have never pinned a posy on anyone during the Feast of Sinder, and I haven't ever walked hand-in-hand or whispered love poetry. I had ever thought when I was a lad there would be time for me to do such things, that I would, one day, wed and have children and take the throne from my father."

"And why should you not expect that to happen now?" Curious, she watched him pace, his fine boots scuffing the neatly trimmed grass.

"With whom? With you?"

Honesty watched him in silence for a few minutes before replying. "Perhaps not from me. But after me. If I do the work I was sent to do."

He laughed, low. "I shouldn't have sent for you. I should send you away, but I find myself unable."

Her heart stuttered at his words. She reached for his hand. "Then I shall find myself unable to go."

Cillian had long known he was a coward. If he were not, he'd have put Lord Devain in his place some time ago. Instead he'd watched the son-of-a-bastard seek to replace him in the king's affections. It hadn't been difficult. King Allwyn had ever looked at his son and seen his dead wife's face, and while any amount of prancing ponies and sweets had convinced the king he loved his boy, it had never done much to convince Cillian.

Now he watched Devain whisper into the king's ear. Something snide, by the way Cillian's father chortled and gestured for another platter of pastries to be brought from the long buffet table set for the court to enjoy.

He had his own plate of food brought to him by Honesty, who'd filled it with all his favorites without asking what he liked. He didn't know if she'd guessed or if she'd remembered a list from something he'd filled out and sent to the Order, but it didn't matter. She'd brought it to him without him having to ask.

Now she sat with a book in the chair behind him. Not at his side, for that would be inappropriate, but nor was she hidden away. Nobody had commented when they arrived, though her presence on his arm had earned a few curious looks. He hadn't presented her to his father. She wasn't his betrothed.

But she was special, he thought, watching her flip through the pages of a text he'd found so deadly dull he'd never read past the first few chapters. She glanced up and saw him looking and gave him a smile he returned. She did know what he needed.

Only a few days had passed since the conversation in the garden maze, but everything had changed for the better since then. He wasn't foolish enough to believe sex had caused the difference, but what it was, exactly, Cillian didn't know. She'd warmed to him, somehow, and he'd . . . well . . .

He trusted her.

The Order had sent her because she was best suited to him. She would do her best for him, and not only because it was her purpose. He believed it would be her pleasure, too. She was no Stillness, not what his dear Edward had found, but then he wasn't Edward and would never be.

He'd asked her to come with him today because he found with Honesty at his side, nothing seemed to urge him into a temper the way most everything did without her. Though she hadn't taken over his every whim—the tea had gone unboiled and the tidying had been left to the maid she'd reinstated, but more often than not it was the simple, quiet touch of her hand or her smile that led him toward peace when he felt himself leaning toward rage. She walked with him in the gardens and listened to him talk as though every word he said made utter sense, and she urged him to laughter with her gentle jests. She slept beside him and rose beside him, and the day only truly began at the moment he first saw her smile.

The men waiting to speak with him were impatient, but he made them wait as he took his seat at the table on the dais where they would come to plead for what they wanted. As head of the Council of Fashion, he didn't have much of import or interest to decide. Setting the length of trousers and dip of décolletage, determining which jewels were in style and which wouldn't be seen on any noble of worth had little value to him other than it gave him control over those who sneered behind their hands at him. More than once Cillian had deliberately set a style that wouldn't flatter someone who'd irritated him, which had been most of his father's court at one time or another.

Now he listened to all those who'd come to make requests. Velvet merchants, gemists, leather makers. And through every boon granted and every one turned away, Cillian watched Devain court his father.

Devain saw him watching, even if the king didn't, and when the last merchant had gone, he left Allwyn's side and made his way toward Cillian. "Is now the time?"

"I've just finished." Cillian affected a disinterested tone that fooled neither of them.

Devain put a foot on the dais and an elbow on his knee, his chin in his hand, to stare upward. He flicked a glance toward the king Cillian couldn't miss. "I think you'll have time to listen to me. Won't you? It's about a new shipment of Alyrian lace I'm expecting."

"Alyrian lace is heavily taxed." By long custom, not Cillian's choice, but one he'd never changed.

"That's what I want to speak to you about."

Cillian had imagined as much. It was impossible to keep the curl from his lip. "I'm in no mood to favor changing a long-structured tax, Devain. That tax provides a tidy source of income."

Devain raised a brow. "Indeed I know it, for I've paid it often enough. But surely you can see the . . . advantages . . . to granting an exemption."

"To you? And not to anyone else?"

Devain inclined his head in a manner meant to be graceful. "There would be advantages, as I said, in your granting exemptions for certain businesses. There would be disadvantages to denying them, I think."

Cillian's stomach churned. Devain had never asked him for a boon. His dabbling in the fashion industry had begun only recently. Rumor had it his home estates had been mismanaged. Some said it was because Devain's wife had let the field manager she was fucking woo her into making bad decisions with the crops. Rumor had it Devain was more inflamed by her lack of judgment in the management of their finances than in who she let into their marriage bed, and Cillian had no trouble believing this was true.

Even so, until now Devain had kept his financial interests far from anything to which Cillian could provide benefit. His courting of the king had been a subtle insult all noted but none spoke on, unless the rumors had been so well kept from Cillian he'd not heard them, and he had no trouble believing that to be true, as well.

"Why not ask my father? You've become quite the chums." He couldn't quite manage to keep the derision from his tone, but if it offended Devain, he didn't show it.

"Your lord father," the man said smoothly, "has made it clear he wishes to have naught to do with your business. He feels, and rightly so, his son and heir should have at least one responsibility for which the king himself is not held accountable."

Perhaps Devain wasn't as close to the king as he'd hoped. Cillian smiled and leaned back in his chair, though the seat of it had long grown uncomfortable and he longed to rise and stretch his legs. "What sort of prince would I be, to take the interests of one over many?"

Devain looked toward the king, who'd moved on from the pastries to the plate of candied fruits. When he looked back at Cillian, his smile was a snake on his lips. "One who remains in line for a throne instead of a set of shackles and a binding jacket, perhaps?"

Cillian bit down on his tongue hard enough to taste bitter blood. Deep in Devain's gaze writhed a threat belied by the smile he showed the rest of the world. "Do you threaten me?"

"You? My lord prince, never." Devain's half bow was clumsily executed, and when he rose his gaze went past Cillian's shoulder to something beyond it. "Never."

Cillian turned to see what had so captured Devain's attention. His heart leaped at the sight of a familiar dark head, hair clubbed at the neck with a bit of bright ribbon. Edward would never have worn blue in his hair before taking a wife who made sure to dress him top to toe. And there she was beside him, the front of her gown tenting over the belly swelled with Edward's child.

Cillian's breath left him, making it impossible to speak. It had been too long since Edward had deigned visit court, and he'd never brought Stillness with him. She looked different, clothed in the dress of a lady wife and not a Handmaiden. Envy slanted over him at the way Edward's hand rested so solicitously on the small of her back as he guided her through the maze of lords toward the king.

Too late, Devain had seen the look on Cillian's face. "As I said, my prince. Advantages and disadvantages."

Cillian said nothing. Devain made a leg and turned. He left the room, and if he paused to speak with anyone else Cillian didn't notice, so caught was his attention by his friend. Honesty's presence beside him didn't turn his gaze from the sight of Edward approaching the king and introducing Stillness to him.

"Who's that?"

"That," Cillian said in a voice steadier than he'd believed possible, "is my dear friend Edward Delaw. And his wife, Stillness."

"What are they doing?"

"He's introducing her to my father."

"They haven't met?"

"No." Cillian swallowed against the pain like shards of glass. "Edward was granted permission to wed at his home and had no court wedding. This is the first time he's brought her here."

She couldn't know how seeing Edward, his dear one no longer so dear, affected him, but Honesty nonetheless kept her hand tight in his. She moved closer, naught improper about her stance, but he felt it all along him just the same. She knew him better than she had even a few days ago.

"Why do you suppose he's done so, now?"

Cillian watched as Edward laughed at something the king said, and as Stillness made the most graceful of curtsies. He could too well remember the taste of her, and wished he hadn't been such a fool to insist on finding out. He'd thought it would bring them closer, he and Edward. Instead it had only cleaved the final thread between them. "He is presenting her to my father because she's going to have a child, and Edward would like it to carry his title."

"Would the babe not automatically carry the title of the father?"

"Edward's father was a spice merchant who worked his way into my grandfather's favor and gained a title. They're not blood nobility. Edward took the title his father earned, but since Edward himself has done naught to earn such a boon title for himself, he must petition the king for the right to grant his son the same privilege. Or maybe he's going to start pandering in order to be given his own boon title," Cillian added with a small shake of his head. "But knowing Edward, he cares much for the fate of his child and little enough for his own."

They both watched, silent, until Honesty said, "He was your friend."

She hadn't made it a question. "Yes. He was, once."

From anyone else the sympathetic noise would have earned a scornful glare, but Cillian only gave her a smile and brought her knuckles to his lips for a kiss.

The business of the court finished for the day and the entertainments begun, the noises of the dancers and musicians made their conversation private. Honesty smiled into his eyes. Cillian kissed her hand again, for no other reason than it pleased him.

"That man Devain," she said quietly. "He was threatening Edward to get to you?"

"Devain was unwise to speak so freely in front of you."

"Men like Devain never see women like me unless seeking to use us for their own purposes."

"Devain would see himself set in my place, I think," Cillian said.

"And your father doesn't care?"

"My father." He had to stop and swallow again against the rise of sharp pain in his throat. "My father sees what he wishes, and most often it's not me."

"You're his son."

"And his heir. It doesn't matter." He shook his head. She knew all about him and yet her surprise on his behalf sent warmth circulating all through him.

His father, surrounded by a bunch of cooing and posturing lords and ministers, swept from the court without even a glance toward them. Cillian watched him go. Edward and Stillness waited until the king had gone before Edward urged her toward a padded chair and went to the sideboard to fill a plate for her.

"Look how things change," he murmured. "Edward was never a man to serve."

Honesty followed his gaze with hers. "He looks to be a man deeply in love with his wife and concerned for her."

Cillian shrugged, feigning disinterest, but Honesty wouldn't let him get away with it. She slipped her hand into his and rested her head lightly on his shoulder. Cillian, too, was not a man to serve, but with Honesty's fingers entwined in his, he thought he could understand the inclination.

"Come." She tugged him, and he resisted.

"What?"

She tugged again and Cillian took a reluctant step toward his former best friend. "Come. This is ridiculous. You're staring at him as though he were made of pastry and you hadn't eaten in a fortnight. Go talk to him."

"No." He dug in his heels, his reply loud enough to turn a few incautious heads.

Edward didn't look up, but Stillness did. Honesty didn't stop pulling, though she managed to do it discreetly. Cillian couldn't continue to resist her without making a scene—and he'd made many a scene before, so it wasn't as though he didn't know how.

"No," he repeated. "Not even if you think it's what I need."

The expanse of the long room stretched between them, but it wasn't long enough. Edward, at last, turned his head and saw Cillian. He didn't blink. Didn't smile or frown. His gaze slid over Cillian as though he didn't exist, and that was worse than a sneer.

Stillness got to her feet and waved away the plate her husband had brought her. She shook out the folds of her gown and moved forward. Only then did Edward change his expression and reach a hand to grab her back, but with his hands full of food he could do nothing to catch her. Stillness, face serene, drifted toward Cillian on silent feet, ignoring all the looks following her.

"My prince," she said easily, with a curtsy. "How nice to see you."

In his hand, Honesty's fingers twisted. Cillian spared her a glance, but her expression had gone as smooth as her Sister's. "And you as well."

"Stillness." Edward's tone brooked no argument, but his lady wife merely smiled at him before turning her attention back to Cillian.

"My prince, it has been sadly overlong since we've seen you," she said. She looked at Honesty, then held out a slim-fingered hand. "Hello. I'm Nessa Delaw."

"Honesty."

The women shook hands as men did. Edward stopped sharply behind his wife and glared at Cillian, which was by far better than being ignored. Edward put a hand on Nessa's shoulder, and she covered it with hers.

"Stillness, come. It's time for us to leave."

"In a moment, love." Stillness gestured at Cillian and Honesty. "I'm speaking to our prince and his companion. Surely you don't wish me to be rude?"

"No. Of course not." It would have been merry to see the way Edward about-faced, had it not hurt Cillian's heart so to see it. Edward made a leg, but didn't look at Cillian's face.

Stillness sighed so loud and long and with such dramatic emphasis there could be no pretending he couldn't hear it. She looked at Honesty. "I would dearly love to hear news of the Motherhouse and the Order. Would you do us the honor of dining at our home tomorrow evening?"

"No!" Edward shouted.

Cillian yanked his hand from Honesty's and gave Stillness a glare meant to put her cowering in her place. He hadn't forgotten how she'd taken the lash from Edward, though. Not even a look from a prince could compare to such as that.

Edward growled from deep in his throat. "No. By the Void, no."

Stillness turned a cool gaze upon Cillian. "What say you, my lord prince? Would you sup with us?"

Cillian's mouth twisted on his angry retort, but before he could speak, Honesty did.

"We'd be happy to, of course."

Both men turned to stare at her. Both women smiled at each other. Cillian jerked his hand from Honesty's grip so hard her entire body moved.

"You don't speak for me," he said.

"Fine." She turned to face Stillness. "I would be happy to have dinner as your guest."

"No!" Edward and Cillian both shouted at the same time.

Edward gave Cillian a look he thought he'd never see again on his friend's face—amusement.

"It would seem we are at odds," Edward said. "It would seem my lady wife is not as well taken in hand as I thought."

"You might have to punish me," Stillness said serenely, as though the idea bothered her not at all.

"I'm not Cillian's lady wife," said Honesty. "And I don't believe I'm bound to obey him without question."

"Maybe you should marry him," suggested Stillness.

Cillian's heart dropped into his gut and he choked on a swell of emotion. "Edward, your wife oversteps herself."

"She does," Edward said with a sigh. "I plead your mercy."

In the past Cillian would have thought nothing of raging at the woman. And his friend. He'd have spared no second thought at tearing the place apart in a fit of fury. But now . . . now he merely blew out a long, slow breath and crossed his arms over his chest. The hint, bare though it was, of Edward's smile had appeased him. At his side, Honesty turned to face him.

"Cillian. Say yes."

Cillian looked at Edward, who for once in a very long time didn't look away. "I won't force my presence on anyone who doesn't want me."

"Nonsense," said Stillness. "We want you."

"Nonsense," said Edward after a pause. "You force your presence on anyone you wish, you always have. And I daresay, you always will."

It was an insult, and Cillian was again reminded of the abuse he was willing to take from those he loved. "Marriage seems to have agreed with you, Edward."

Edward gave Stillness a look of such fondness it was fair embarrassing. "Aye. I would agree."

"Tomorrow, then," Stillness said with a look to Honesty Cillian didn't try to discern.

As simply as that, it was done.

Chapter 13

She'd brought no formal gowns with her, nothing suitable for taking dinner as a guest in a nobleman's home, but Honesty didn't fear. Cillian had provided a wealth of gowns for her use, all tailored to fit her exactly. A hot, scented bath and sweet lotions to perfume her had already set the mood, and now she sifted through the pile of pretty dresses, comparing them one to another to see which would best suit her.

She held up the green, which would look striking next to Cillian should he wear the same shade. And, she decided, she'd insist upon it. She nodded at her reflection, turning her face to look at the lines and angles to which she so rarely paid attention.

She was dressing for him, she realized, and the dress fell from her suddenly nerveless grasp to puddle at her feet. She'd sent away the lady's maid, used to and preferring to take care of herself, and so there was nobody else to smooth the wrinkles from the fabric. Nor anyone to help her to a chair or pour her a glass of cool water from the pitcher, so she sank instead to the floor along with the dress.

From her place there she could see the ceiling, the pattern of stamped metal and the painted designs depicting the Fall of Sinder. It was perhaps meant to be an erotic scene, something to tantalize the bedchamber's inhabitants as they lay abed, but to Honesty the scene was anything but sensual. Sinder had come out of the Void and created the world, and he'd come across Kedalya in the wood, and he'd fallen in love with her.

He'd fallen.

A week was not long enough to lose a heart, she thought, and knew that to be a lie. A heart could be lost in a day. An hour. A minute. With one glance, a sigh. A breath.

"I don't love him," she whispered. "I do not love him."

Perhaps not, but something stirred within her, and it was more than the normal emotion she carried for every patron. Honesty sat amongst the tangles of ribbon ties and lace hems. When had it begun? The first time she took him into her mouth, maybe. Or when he'd allowed her to take his hand, or when he'd smiled instead of losing his temper. When he'd tried to refuse her, she thought, and when she'd realized how much difference she could make in his life, and how much he deserved to have such a difference made.

She knew the sting and bite of love, knew the power of it. How it could send a strong man to his knees and pull a weak woman off hers. What she felt for the Prince of Firth wasn't love, but it was something well on its way.

"Your mercy!" The low male voice from the doorway startled her into getting to her feet.

Honesty clutched the robe about her; the gown remained crumpled at her feet. "Who are you?"

"Your mercy, lady. I'm Alaric. Cillian's friend. I came to see if he were here."

The man in the doorway looked sore in need of caretaking. His hair, the color of butter, hung in lank curls to his shoulders. An angry red line marred his throat, and a few days' growth of beard shadowed his jaw. He looked nothing like a prince's friend.

Honesty drew the fabric of her gown tighter around her. "He's not here. He had some business to attend in a warehouse or some such thing. He said he didn't need me to go with him."

"You're the Handmaiden." The words sounded assessing but the man himself gave her no more than a cursory glance. "Warehouse? Not the playroom?"

This lifted her chin for a reason she didn't want to dissect. "No. His warehouse. Where the fabrics are kept."

"Ah. Your mercy," Alaric repeated. "I'm overweary at the moment and not thinking straight. My tongue leaps ahead of my mind. Of course he wouldn't be going to his playroom . . ."

"Sit down," Honesty said as she watched him sway. "Before you fall. Are you ill, sir?"

"No." He shook his head and put a hand over his heart. "Not with anything a medicus can cure, at any rate. Please tell Cillian I stopped by and please tell him . . . simply tell him . . . I am . . . uncollared."

"You should sit," she told him again, but he waved her off.

"No. I can't, really. I can't stay. Not with you here. No offense meant," he added as an afterthought, which meant she probably should be offended.

"I'll tell him you were here."

Alaric, who might have been handsome without the dark rings beneath his eyes and pallor of his skin, bared his teeth in a smile that set her back a step. His gaze skittered over the piles of clothes on the floor, then up over her body. She'd had men look her over many times, but never one whose eyes traveled over her from head to toe without pausing to assess her. Alaric looked at her, but he didn't see her. He didn't seem to see anything.

"Thank you," he said and gave a clumsy bow as he backed toward the door.

"Wait—" But he was already gone, and Honesty went to the door to stare after him.

He walked as though the hall were on a ship, listing to the left and right, and his hand went out to the wall to steady himself. She watched him until he'd rounded the corner and then she went inside and shut the door. It was easy for her to see when someone needed succor, and it was as easy for her to accept she might not be the one to provide it. But she did make note to tell Cillian of his friend's all too apparent distress.

The blue gown instead of the green, she thought, staring at the floor. It would go with her eyes and make her lovely in Cillian's gaze. And she wanted to look so, to be more than the Handmaiden he'd paid for. She wanted to be a woman to him tonight, and in that gown she just might be.

She'd put on the dress and fixed her hair to let it fall about her shoulders in soft, loose curls instead of the tight braid she most often wore. She'd applied cosmetic to her lips and eyes. She had no jewelry and made due with a flower plucked from a bouquet in a vase from the hall.

And, she Waited.

On her knees, one hand cradled in the palm of the other. She could and had held that position for hours in the past, as comfortable to her as sleep, but that wasn't why she did it. She knew it would please him to see her on her knees for him. She hadn't forgotten the playroom. Cillian had never asked her to visit it and as far as she knew, he'd been absent from it for a while, as well. But that didn't mean he didn't want what went on inside it, so even though she couldn't bring herself to offer herself in that manner, she could do this.

The look he gave her when he returned was worth every effort, and Honesty found her heart beating faster at the way Cillian's mouth parted with words unspoken. He gestured at her to rise.

She did, twirling slowly to allow the hem of her gown to float around her ankles. "You approve?"

"Of course I approve. I bought that fabric and had that gown made, just for you."

"And to think, knowing exactly what another needs is supposed to be my duty," she teased.

Cillian's gaze brightened and his tongue slid along his lower lip. "I didn't know it would suit you so well, but I'm pleased it does."

"And if it hadn't?" She asked, curious.

He looked away for a moment before bringing the intensity of his gaze back to hers. "You'd have worn it anyway, should I have deemed it appropriate. Yes?"

"Yes, of course. If I'd deemed it necessary to appease you." Honesty tilted her head to look him up and down. "But that's not what you mean. Is it?"

"No." He shook his head.

She stood on her toes to bring her eyes, and her mouth, level with his. "Fortunately for us both, it suits me perfectly."

He put his hands on her hips tight enough to keep her still but not hard enough to wrinkle the dress. "Is this what you think I need?"

She brushed her lips over his and stepped back. "Everyone needs affection. It would seem to me you lack it, Cillian, despite your hareem."

He laughed derisively. "Which I've not visited in near two weeks, because of you."

Honesty dimpled. "Am I to blame if you're kept so busy in your own bed you don't need to seek the company of those other women? After all, it's not my sole function but one I am willing to provide. And enjoy."

She watched him carefully, aware her tone had been light and teasing but the emotion behind it deeper. But Cillian couldn't know that and wouldn't know that, if she could help it. He didn't need to know she had any motivation beyond duty.

His hand cupped her neck and brought her closer, his mouth slanting over hers but not kissing. Her breath quickened at the suddenness of his action, more forceful than he'd been with her. Cillian drew her closer, body to body.

"You wouldn't enjoy the games I crave, Honesty."

Her breath hitched and her eyes fluttered closed. "I told you before, if I have to offer my back to you—"

"If you believe I need it for solace. As part of your duty, yes. But not because you want it. Not because the sting of my palm on your skin gets you wet."

"And yet you come to your bed each night and make love to me, nevertheless. You've not been to your playroom for days and days." Some time ago she might have kept the triumph from her voice but couldn't, now. "Perhaps the games you crave are not as necessary as you thought."

His fingertips twitched against her skin, and he withdrew with a small smile. "Some are born to a taste they might acquire only later, Honesty. Some can be led to it."

Her heart trip-trapped in her breast at the thought of the iron-wood cross. "Some never learn to crave those sorts of games."

"I know it." He reached to tug the curl hanging over her shoulder. "Which is why I haven't made you go to the playroom. The women of my hareem were chosen, as you said in the beginning, to serve me that way. But you are not. I take no pleasure in forcing a lover to a different sort of kiss, no matter what might be said of me. I've never forced anyone."

"I didn't believe it of you," she said quietly, and noted the speculative look he gave her.

Tension spiraled between them as tightly as a ribbon wound upon a finger. Clothed, they might well have been naked, so fiercely did her body feel every brush of his against hers. Lust she'd felt aplenty, but this went beyond that. This was different, no matter how she might resist it.

"When I was young," she told him as she took his hand between hers, "I was betrothed to a man much older than I. It was for the benefit of my father, not myself, but that was no more than I had been raised to expect."

Cillian's fingers squeezed hers. "I knew it. I knew you were of noble birth."

Not merely noble, but Honesty didn't correct him. "I didn't want to wed him, though it displeased my father for me to say so. My father loved me, but he needed me to obey him without question. My betrothed was a man much the same but without a loving hand to temper the desire."

His breath hitched and a flash of excitement lit his eyes, a gleam she didn't miss. "Did he beat you?"

"No, my prince, no matter how the thought might excite you. He didn't raise a hand to me in anger. Nor in pleasure," she added. "Though he would have had me on my knees, his was a cleric's cock. How he hoped to get a child on me, I don't know. The marriage seemed without worth to me. To be wedded and never bedded, or at least bedded unsatisfactorily?"

Cillian's thumb passed along her palm and she shivered at the soft touch. "Indeed."

"Anyway, my story, unlike my betrothal, does have a point." Honesty swallowed and licked her mouth, suddenly dry. She looked into his eyes and marveled at how clear such a gaze could be between two who barely knew each other's heart. "My point is that though that man tried his best to subdue me, I would not bend to him. However, had he tried to know even the least small piece of me, I'd have done my best to learn what brought him pleasure."

"Had you wed him."

"Yes."

"Even though you didn't love him."

She shook her head. "I did not love him, no. But I knew what was best for my father might well be best for me. And I couldn't have waited for love, in any case. I had to be married."

He blinked and stepped away from her, leaving her hands chill in the absence of his heat. "Surely it didn't mean so much."

It had meant everything, but telling him she'd once worn a crown richer than his own would serve her no purpose. "You're not listening to my tale, Cillian. You hear my words but you misunderstand me."

He turned from the window, an eyebrow raised. "Do I? Perhaps you should be clearer."

"I would have done what pleased him, and I wasn't a Handmaiden then, bound to serve. If he'd only tried to know me, I'd have tried to know him, too."

"You would bend your back to my pleasure, you've said so," Cillian murmured, coming closer. "But what say you now?"

"I might be unable to learn to love the touch of a lash, but that doesn't mean I couldn't learn to play your games. There are more versions than just that one." She paused. "I've seen much in my time of service. And no, I wouldn't seek an ironwood cross and the back of your hand. But there are other pleasures. You would know them better than I."

"And again it is I who must serve you. Is that the way this is to go?" He paused, voice not risen in anger though his words might sound cross. "Is that what I need, Honesty?"

She lifted her chin and slicked her lips again, conscious of the way his gaze followed the movement. "I think so, yes. I can give you what you want before you want it, but if you don't feel worthy when you have it, my effort is wasted. You should woo me a little, Cillian. Convince me."

He took a step back, almost a stumble. The window seat caught the back of his knees and he sat, hard. One hand came up to cover his eyes. "You would have me love you, in the end. And then what? Then you leave me, yes?"

Her heart leaped but she kept her voice steady. "It seems to me you might benefit from loving."

"All I have ever done is love, over and over, and been turned aside," Cillian told her. "I am of little mind to try again."

She moved closer. "I didn't want to marry that man, so I did what I should never have done. I took a lover. I disgraced my family and my father's name. I bore a son my betrothed claimed as his own so as not to break the tie that would bind him to my family, and I was banished from my home as though I'd died. I do believe I know the penalties of love."

"You did love him? The father of your child?"

"Oh, yes. In the way a young women does with the first man to hold her heart in his hand. I loved him enough to bear his child rather than ending it in my womb. And I loved him enough not to insist on naming him the father, though everyone knew it was him and my so doing might have saved me even as it ruined him."

"So you went to the Order instead."

"Oh, yes." She smiled, stepping closer. "And there I served well, for a time. A longer time than ever I'd have thought I could find within myself. But now . . . I'm tired, Cillian. I would go home. See my child, who won't know me as his mother. I would finish my service to you, if you'll allow it, and not by failure."

It was his turn to swallow and he looked away from her, to the floor. "Honesty. I would have you grant me solace, I swear by the Arrow, I want it. I sent for you hoping . . . well, hoping you'd give it to me. But what you ask, I'm uncertain I can grant it. I crave what I crave, as I have ever done, but knowing you don't want to bend to me in that manner does nothing to fulfill me. And all the rest you provide, your good humor, the touch of your hand, the pleasure of your body—"

"You are too empty a man to be filled by any one person, I'd wager," Honesty broke in before he could say more. "But let me try. You will get what you need and I will, too."

"What shall I do, then?" He quirked a grin at her that set her more at ease.

"As I said, there are other variations." She grinned, too. "I think it would not please you for me to be the one to name them."

"And how should I know if you approve?"

"We shall have to learn together," Honesty told him. "Tell me about the playroom."

"No." He shook his head again, but when he tried to pull away, her hand caught him.

"Tell me. You might think you can shock me, or disgust me. But you can't, Cillian. Believe me, I've seen and done more than you can imagine."

"I can imagine a great deal, Honesty."

She drew him closer with a gentle hand. "It would seem we are well matched."

He let her move him until they stood, bodies touching. The caress of his breath passed over her cheek and he took her into his arms. His face found the curve of her shoulder. His lips pressed her flesh, warmth on warmth.

"It helps," he whispered. "It helps me forget."

She put her arms around him to hold him closer. "Forget what?"

"All they would have me remember." Cillian closed his eyes but opened them in a moment to look deeply into hers.

"Then if what you need is to forget, I'll help you do it." She pressed his fingertips to her lips.

"Well," Cillian said with a tilting, shifting smile, "you can try."

S top squirming." Honesty made to adjust Cillian's cravat, but he pushed away her hand. "Fine. Do it yourself."

He stared into the mirror with a scowl and tugged the fabric looser at his throat. "A man should know how to dress himself properly, not rely on anyone to do it for him even if he has the means to have someone attend him so."

"I don't disagree with you." She settled against the edge of the window seat and watched him. "But you've fumble fingers, and I was only trying to help."

"Will helping me with my clothes get another Arrow in the Quiver?" He sounded snide and had meant to, but if Honesty took umbrage she showed no sign.

"It might help us get to dinner sooner rather than later, and since my stomach is empty, that's more important at the moment."

She had such a way of diffusing him. The only thing that had done so previously was time spent in his playroom with a flogger in his fist and a sweet, honey-skinned cunna begging for its kiss. He hadn't been there in weeks, though even now the thought of a sweat-slick leather handle in his palm had his cock to twitching. He'd spent longer periods of time away from the pleasures of his hareem, but not in recent memory.

Cillian fussed with the soft fabric and jerked it free, then tossed it to the floor. He'd go without. Likewise with the lace at his cuffs, which bound them too much like shackles for his taste tonight.

"Cillian, you're as skittish as a colt. Stop and take a breath. Surely you're not overanxious about taking dinner with your friend?

No matter what might have happened in the past, it must be time to put that all aside."

He wouldn't take a breath, if only because she'd said to do so. He stared at his face in the mirror and wondered if the man he saw there would ever be the one he'd imagined himself as becoming when he was a lad.

"Cillian. A disagreement is nothing to friends such as your-selves."

He wasn't the one who'd held on to the past as an excuse to keep Edward distant from him. He'd clung to it as proof of his love, and look what it had gained him. Naught but a cold cell and his father's disdain and the taint of madness overhanging him. And yet he still loved Edward for the boy he'd been and the man he'd become, even if Cillian hadn't joined him.

He looked again into the mirror and gestured at the fallen lace for her to aid him. She fussed with it, arranging the fall at his throat with expert fingers and stepping back to admire her work. At her low murmur of approval, he looked at her face.

"I love him. I have ever loved him, from the first moment he thrashed me for picking on Alaric."

She nodded. "Sometimes our best friends are the ones we meet as children."

"We weren't children."

"Boys, then." She stepped back to look him over. "There. Lovely. You are fair gorgeous, Cillian, but you know that."

"The mirror has said so as well as many others." There was no sense in denying it. He'd been patched together of his parents' best features and had had the benefit of good food and a medicus on call for any ailment. Not even a pit marked any of his teeth.

"Well, I say it now." Honesty turned him to face her and smoothed the fabric at his throat once more.

She stood on her toes to reach his mouth. Her kiss barely brushed him, but he pulled her closer. Her warmth filled his arms. He traced the outline of her breast through her gown.

She shuddered, eyes fluttering closed again, and he smiled. "You don't lie."

"No." She shook her head.

The door opened to admit Bertram. "My lord. The carriage is ready."

Cillian looked down at the woman in his arms and released her to offer her an elbow. "Lady? Might I escort you to dinner?"

Her smile gave him the answer.

Chapter 14

Edward Delaw served the meal in low style, which meant they didn't need to keep court manners, and that was fine with Honesty. The meal was casual but delicious and served intimately in the parlor rather than a formal room, and the wine flowed freely. Cillian had given Edward the head of the table, which seemed to surprise the other man though he'd made no comment.

Edward's wife had been the one to start and keep the conversation moving with gentle anecdotes about life on their estate and the weather as well as commentary on the recipes the cook had used. All soft topics. Honesty knew at once what her Sister-in-Service was doing, for she'd have done the same had she been the mistress of the table and not a guest. The men, for their part, kept tight mouths at first, each speaking to the women and ignoring the other until at last Stillness pushed back from the table with sigh and patted her rounded belly.

"My goodness, if I eat another bite, I fear I'll explode."

Edward frowned and leaned toward his wife. "Do you need to lay down, sweetness?"

Stillness threw him a fond glance but gave Honesty a knowing look. "No, husband. I'm merely overfull and would seek something entertaining to keep me from forcing another bite of this delicious dessert. I want more, you know."

He laughed, though the crease in his brow didn't ease. He would be an interesting man to serve, Honesty thought, watching him get up from the table. Different from Cillian and yet very much alike, though she doubted either would admit to it.

Well, perhaps Cillian would, she amended, seeing the way her patron watched Edward with a burning gaze when he thought the other man couldn't see. Cillian would have them be as brothers, she thought, not even mere brothers of the heart but as close as brothers of blood. The prince blinked and studied his glass of wine when Edward looked up. Emotion twinged deep inside her at the sight of her patron's thinned mouth and clenched fingers. Cillian was hurting, and for this she had no solace.

"My wife needs to leave the table. Thank you for coming," Edward said stiffly to Cillian. To Honesty he gave a softer smile. "And you, lady."

"Edward!" Stillness looked stunned. "Surely you're not sending our guests away now?"

"I'd thought—"

"We can go, if Edward wishes." Cillian spoke quietly, his eyes lifting now to seek Edward's own. "We don't wish to overstay our welcome."

For the first time since their arrival, Edward really looked at Cillian. For the span of several heartbeats the men stared at one another until Edward nodded once, stiffly. His gaze went from Cillian to Stillness and back again, then briefly to Honesty, where it hung for another long moment before returning to his old friend.

"If my lady wife wishes you to stay on for some after dinner en-

tertainment, far be it from me to counter her desires. Stay, Cillian.
If you like."

Honesty had watched the silent exchange and now listened to
Edward's tone. She, too, looked at Stillness who, despite her earlier
nonchalance, had sat on the edge of her chair with her back stiff as
though she expected her husband to do just as he'd said he would
not. Honesty, watching them all, understood what they all had
known and she hadn't.

Cillian had been with Stillness.

"My love, I've had Margera lay in a supply of that fine Alyrian
brandy you so enjoy. Take our prince to the library and lay out the
cards. I would speak to my Sister-in-Service alone for a bit." Stillness tempered the words, which could easily have been read as a
command, with a gentle smile that had Edward fair twitching to
leap to do her bidding.

He shot Cillian an assessing glance but gestured. "C'mon then.
My lady wife wishes to be alone with your Handmaiden. We'll let
the women talk. And . . . I think we have much to speak on, ourselves."

Relief skittered swiftly across Cillian's face, so swift any who
didn't know him well might have mistaken it for something else.
Edward saw it, Honesty could tell. Stillness saw it, too. For the first
time, Honesty wondered if what she thought she knew about Edward's reasons for abandoning his friend was the entire reason behind their falling out.

Stillness waited until the men had left before sitting back again
in her chair with a heavy sigh. She reached for the laces at the front
of her gown and tugged them open until the bounty of her breasts
and belly, still covered by the shift beneath her gown, surged forth.
She ran her hands over them and sighed again.

"My husband would be certain I remain modestly covered in

front of our guests, but I swear I'm fair to bursting in this gown. This babe's not due to arrive for another few months but I swear soon I'll be forced to go 'round in naught but my shift the whole day." She laughed.

Honesty sipped a final mouthful of dessert wine and sat back herself. "He fears for your health."

Stillness's smile faded. "Aye. He does."

"While you fear for the babe itself and care less for your own well-being." Honesty ran a fork through the remains of the fruit crumble, decided she couldn't resist the last bite, and took it.

Stillness nodded. "You are well named."

Honesty shrugged. "Have you ever known one of us to be anything less?"

The women stared at each other in silence that needed no words. No matter how long out of service a Handmaiden might be, or how short a time she served, nobody else could understand what it was like to be bound to the Order except another who'd done the same.

"I would have news, if you have it. I haven't been to the Motherhouse in a long time."

"Nor I." Honesty described her last assignment and the swift rush to place her with the Prince of Firth.

Stillness looked surprised. "Unusual but not unheard of, I suppose. To place you so quickly into another's service means the patron is in great need."

"Or has great wealth," Honesty said.

"The Order has threads in many tapestries," Stillness replied after a moment. She looked toward the double sliding doors through which the men had gone, her head tilted as if to listen for laughter . . . or shouts. "Our prince is not part of an intrigue, as best I know. He's ever avoided such pastimes, so far as Edward has ever said."

Honesty had heard tales of the Order's political influence, but they'd been rumors and whispers only. She'd never had reason to believe the Order of Solace had any intentions beyond the faith. "I haven't been with him long enough to know, but I've seen no evidence of his interest in politics beyond what his position requires."

Stillness sighed and leaned forward over the mound of her stomach to scrape the plate clean of syrup with her spoon. She tucked it into her mouth with a happy sound. "Even so, you've done him good."

"You know him well enough to see a difference?" Her answer came sharper than she'd meant it, but Stillness didn't seem to take offense.

Stillness licked her spoon and contemplated it a minute before setting it down. "I don't. But I know Edward, and he's seen a change. He wouldn't have agreed to this dinner otherwise. He wouldn't be in that room with Cillian now if he hadn't."

Still no sound of male voices raised in laughter came from the library, but at least neither had they erupted into a fight—unless it was the silent sort, and Honesty didn't imagine either of them to be the kind to argue in whispers.

"What happened between them?"

The other woman's brow furrowed briefly. "You don't know?"

"I know he and Edward were schoolmates. I know they were great friends. I know Cillian loved him. Did . . . was it improper in Edward's eyes? Did Cillian make an offer to him that Edward couldn't accept?"

Stillness laughed softly. "Do you mean did our prince try to make love to my husband and was rejected?"

"It's ruined friendships aplenty," Honesty said.

Stillness looked at her plate and traced a design in the remains of her dessert with her fork before looking up at Honesty again. "Were you not informed of your patron's history before being sent to him? I can't imagine the Order sending you to him without some sort of . . . warning."

That sounded more ominous than she'd expected. Unusual heat crept up the column of Honesty's throat to warm her face as she thought of her hand-trunk and the sheaf of documents, ignored, within. "I was given only the barest information by the Mother-in-Service who told me of the assignment. I was given his materials, but . . ." There was no sense in lying. "I didn't read them."

Stillness's jaw dropped, just a fraction, before she recovered. "Oh. Well. Sister, I would like to share with you all I know but it's not my place to tell his tale. You must ask Cillian himself. Or read what you were given. I can't think . . . Sister, how did you hope to grant him solace if you didn't know about his reasons for needing you?"

Honesty sighed. "I didn't want to. I'm tired. I wanted simply to . . . go home. And when I decided to stay, it seemed I already knew him well enough without a bunch of papers that could tell me his every visit to the medicus and nothing about who he really is."

Stillness nodded after a moment, as though she understood. "Even so, you haven't left him. And you've been good for him. You changed your mind, at least enough."

"I did." At last from inside the library came a burst of laughter, muted and hesitant, but more reassuring than the silence had been. Honesty looked at Stillness. "So their estrangement had nothing to do with you?"

Stillness laughed again with a duck of her head. "Oh, my. Well, I suppose that might have been part of it. Edward and Cillian had long been parted, though Edward had taken on an assignment from the king to watch over him."

"As though he were a child?" Honesty frowned. "Cillian is willful, but he's never seemed to need taking care of, to me."

There'd been a man in her father's house who'd been kicked in the head by a horse. Though his body had aged, his mind never had, and though to anyone who didn't know him he seemed fine, the briefest conversation revealed him to be damaged. "Was he in an accident? Is that the reason for his mood swings and the anger?"

"Sister," Stillness said after a pause, "you should read what the Order gave you or ask him yourself."

Of course she must, and it was long overdue. Honesty nodded and got up from the table. "I thank you for your hospitality. Your home is lovely. Best wishes on the child."

Stillness sighed, her hands on her belly. "Thank you. There are days the birth can't come soon enough. And others I wish to stay this way forever, if only so that I need not worry about what might happen after the babe is born."

Honesty had often wondered what had become of her own child, raised as another man's son and never as her own. "I'm going to see what's happening in the library. Will you come?"

"In a moment. I need to relace." Stillness indicated the front of her gown. "And it will take me long enough to heave my weight from the chair. You go. I'm sure all is well, Honesty. They only needed a reason to forgive one another."

Honesty hoped the other woman was right. From what she'd seen on Edward's face it would have been more difficult than that to reconcile them, but when another soft burst of laughter floated out to her, she smiled and went to the door. Inside the library, the men sat in facing chairs, identical glasses in their hands. Though an herb bowl rested on the table between them, no hint of the pungent smoke reached her nose.

Cillian had laughed with her. He'd been soft with her, too, though briefly. But she'd never seen him look at her the way he was now staring at Edward, his eyes alight with something akin to joy. Envy ripped through her, fierce enough to buckle her knees and force her hand to the back of a chair in order to keep herself from stumbling.

Spoiled, she was. Spoiled by her years in Service, bringing people to peace. She didn't deserve such a look from Cillian, for she'd done little enough to create it. Watching him gaze with such pleasure upon his friend, Honesty found herself wishing for the prince to turn such a gaze upon her.

It was foolishness of the worst sort. She'd mocked the tales of Handmaidens who'd fallen in love with their patrons only to be turned aside when solace was granted and the assignment ended. Not many ended up wedding them the way Stillness had. Honesty had never yearned for such a thing, herself, a marriage based on only the best of what a relationship might be and naught of the worst.

"Cillian," she said, her voice too loud.

He turned to her but it took some seconds for him to pull his gaze from his friend's face. "Honesty. Come. Edward was telling me of his plans for the estate. He wants to plant an orchard. Can you imagine?"

She could, having loved her father's orchard so. "An orchard? For profit?"

Edward shook his head. "I expect it to be a labor of love at the first. A specialty crop. Perhaps enough to sell at a market, or provide to friends. Nothing much more than that."

"He'll be brilliant with it, I'm sure. The king will be certain to grant you a land boon, Edward, and a tax boon, too. I'm sure of it." Cillian sounded eager, and both Edward and Honesty looked at him.

Things were not perfect between them. Edward still watched Cillian a tad too warily, and Cillian, despite his obvious joy, was still a little too stiff. It was better than it had been and over her envy washed relief for Cillian's sake.

"Come," Cillian said with a gesture. "Sit by me."

Edward was already looking toward the door, a question in his eyes, when Stillness appeared in the doorway. Her laces had been done up but her hair had come loose round her face in frazzled tendrils. Her eyes, wide, swept from her husband to the prince and back.

"Edward—"

"What is it?" Edward was already at her side, gripping her waist. "Is it the babe?"

"No, love. Something else—"

Before she could finish a figure loomed behind her. Broad-shouldered and in shadow, the sight must have startled Edward for he pulled his wife away and stepped between her and the visitor with a cry.

"Hold!" Cillian said. "Stand down, Edward, it's my man Bertram."

Bertram stepped through the doorway without a second glance at Stillness and only the most cursory for Edward. "My lord prince. Your father has fallen."

The room surged into silence, broken then by Cillian's reply. "When?"

"An hour past. Fell ill at his supper and was taken to his chambers. He's not expected to make it. But you must hurry," Bertram said, moving closer. "They're coming for you."

Cillian straightened, got taller, his shoulders square. "I'm ready."

"No, my prince," said Bertram. "They're not coming to have you replace your lord father on his throne."

"What then?" Edward asked.

Bertram gave a low noise of distaste and slid his gaze from Cillian's. "They're coming to arrest you."

Coward he was no longer. Cillian met Devain and his men at Edward's front door. They hesitated at the sight of him standing straight and strong, not cowering, and he remembered how not so long ago some of those men had been the ones to guard him in his cradle. Devain had risen fast but he'd not known these men as long as they'd known their prince, even with all his faults.

"Devain," Cillian said.

Devain hesitated, too, his foot on the gravel path leading to the porch where Cillian waited. "Your father is dying."

"And what a party you bring to escort me," Cillian said with a smile designed to set Devain's teeth to gritting. "I don't need the pomp. I can attend my father without it."

"Your mercy, my . . . sir." Gentian, a king's man since the king himself was a prince, stepped forward. "We've come to fetch you."

Behind him, Cillian felt the press of Honesty's body against his back and the chill of her fingers as she entwined them with his. He took them from her grasp and stepped forward, not looking at her. He'd give Devain nothing with which to bargain. Naught to hold over his head.

"Have you brought chains?" he asked Devain and was pleased when his voice trembled not in either rage or fear. Indeed, only coldness swept over him, encasing him in ice. His father was dying and had not sent for him; his father was dying and Devain was making his play for the throne. He must have a strong enough case for it to have garnered the loyalty of his father's men.

"But of course." Devain showed his teeth. "I am hoping not to need them, but I would have been a fool not to prepare myself, considering your . . . history."

"You speak to the Prince of Firth," Edward broke in. "Have a care how you address your next king."

Beside him, Edward's warmth did little to chase away the chill, and Cillian didn't dare give his friend more than a small, shifting glance. Devain already had made it known he would gladly see harm come to Edward and his family. Cillian had borne much upon his conscience, but he refused to bear that.

"You won't need them," he said and stepped forward.

"Cillian, no!" Edward stepped, too, but stopped when Cillian turned.

He forced his voice to the same sly tones he'd so often affected. "Don't play the part of my fetchencarry, Edward. It doesn't flatter you."

Edward's gaze shuttered at once and he stepped back. "As you wish."

Cillian faced Devain with his chin lifted and contempt in every word. "What are the terms of my arrest?"

"Debauchery. Lewdness. Coercion. Perversion. Insanity." Devain grinned at the last and made a mocking bow. "And treachery. Cillian Derouth, you are charged with failure to comply with the requirements of your position and judged unfit to rule."

Cillian didn't miss the grumbling, faint as it was, from more than a few of his father's men at Devain's words. Though inside he was still ice, he stood even straighter and fixed Devain with an unwavering look. "Charged but not judged, Devain. Not even you have the power to set me aside without the chance to redeem myself."

Devain's grin thinned at the truth of this, and he stood upright. "We shall see. Won't we?"

"He can't take you, can he?" Honesty spoke at last and grabbed at Cillian's arm. "Not just like that? What's he talking about?"

Cillian kept his gaze on Devain's. "Naught I've ever done in my playroom was ever done against the will of any who served in it. And yours were the mediatuses that deemed me fit to leave the asylum, so your argument is faulty there as well. I have committed no treachery against my father, against my country or the people in it. And as for the requirements of my position, I have ever obeyed my lord father in all he would have me do."

"Not all," Devain said. "Come now. It's time."

Behind him, Cillian heard Honesty's soft, indrawn breath. "I don't understand."

Cillian wouldn't have taken his eyes from a snake about to strike, and he kept his gaze on Devain the same way. "Devain is claiming me as a perverted madman, unfit for the throne."

Again, a grumble wafted through the ranks of men at Devain's back. Cillian heard it. From the way Edward grunted low in his throat, he must have heard it, too. Devain, if he heard the small sound of dissent, ignored it.

Edward looked at him. "None of that matters, Cillian, and you know it. You were born to the throne and have ever been prepared to take it. Nothing of the past can change that, and Devain knows it. Why else would he have had to so fiercely court your father and yet still not be named in line for successor?"

"Come," Devain said again. "There's no point in delaying this."

Honesty reached again for Cillian's hand and this time, he let her take it, even if he didn't look at her. "How can he say such things?"

Now he looked at her and saw the confusion in her eyes. "Because they are true."

Honesty blinked and stepped back. Edward muttered and stepped forward to make a rude gesture at Devain, who ignored him and crossed his arms, foot tapping. As far as dramatic arrests went, the man's sense of show must be fair disappointed.

Honesty shook her head slowly, lips parting but on air only and not words. She hadn't known, he saw that now. All these weeks at his side, her calming words and soothing touches, the lovemaking . . . Of all of those assembled, she'd known him the least amount of time and yet knew his heart the best. And yet she hadn't known him at all.

Cillian took his hand from hers for the second time. "You are dismissed."

"What? No—" She stepped forward but stopped short of reaching him.

"Go home, Honesty," Cillian said in a voice as cold as the ice in his throat trying to strangle him. "Get you gone from my sight. You are dismissed. I have no need of you now."

"You have more need of me now than ever," she declared with that same stubborn tilt to her mouth he'd come to know so well.

He'd been a fool to think he could buy affection. Purchase peace. She didn't know him and never had, and now he hoped she never would. He would have that, at least. The memory of how she'd taken his hand and thought him an entirely different man.

She stared up at him with eyes softer than any she'd ever given him. Cillian didn't want her pity. He willed the lie to his lips and into his eyes and forced himself to believe it so she would, too.

"Perhaps I do," he told her. "But I no longer want you."

The king had not yet died, the prince had been put into custody, and Honesty had been escorted from the palace with only the clothes on her back and the hand-trunk she'd brought with her. She hadn't been allowed to see him, but caught a glimpse of that fine fall of red-gold hair from a distance as he'd been hustled down a far-off hallway.

"They can't put him in gaol," she said as Bertram opened the carriage door for her. "He's a prince! And he's committed no crime, he can't be treated like a common criminal!"

It might have pained the man to have to treat her with so little compassion, but his orders had come directly from that insufferable idiot, Devain. Bertram, his fingers clutched uncomfortably tight on her upper arm, shook his head. "He's not only having to face the Council of the Book about whether he's fit to succeed his father, he's having to face the Temple priests now, too."

The glare he gave her meant this was somehow her fault, and though she knew she couldn't be held accountable, her stomach dropped. She shook off his grip and clutched her hand-trunk closer to her. He'd already searched it, the humiliation of having to prove she wasn't a thief was nothing compared to what Cillian must feel having to fight for his rightful place. Bertram had the grace to look discomfited.

"The priests? Why?"

Bertram shrugged, looking down, and gestured at the carriage. "Please, get in. I'm to take you to the train, lady. Please just get in."

"No. You tell me what's going on. It's obvious Devain has had it out for him for a long time and can do this only because the king fell so suddenly ill. If the king had named another his heir it would have had to go through the council, yes? Before now? So Devain is merely using the king's illness to throw everyone into confusion. He's been plotting this for a long time."

Bertram cleared his throat. "Lady, it's not for me to say."

It had been a long time since Honesty had played these kinds of games, though she'd learned them at her father's knee. A long time since she'd had to stretch her mind in so many directions to imagine what might be done and how it might affect an entire situation. She'd been focused for so long, her duties to one person at a time, so now she struggled to put into place all the pieces she could grasp.

She was missing too many. "Why is he being questioned by the priests, Bertram? Firth is of the faith but not strongly so. I've never even heard the Temple chimes once since I've been here."

Bertram sighed heavily. "It's not enough for Devain to prove the prince's lack of ability, he's now got more against him than madness and debauchery and whatever else he's thrown out. Since you failed—"

Guilt slashed at her. "I didn't fail him."

The man looked at her. "Since our prince sent you away, since he declared his Handmaiden of no use to him, Devain is contending the prince is incapable of solace. He's incapable of anything but what he's known to be, and therefore, unfit to rule. Devain has a strong and solid case, the documented support of the king himself, and the support of many of the lords of the court. He's been stoking this fire for some time while, forgive me for saying it, our prince has been playing at everything but what he was meant for. It's no wonder Devain's been able to topple him from his place."

"He's not toppled yet," Honesty said.

"No. But he will be," Bertram said. "There is no way around it, lady. You can't take away what he done in the past or what has happened since, and you can't take away the fact he's not done what's required of all our princes before they become kings."

"Which is what?" she cried, wishing more than ever she'd read the papers in her hand-trunk when she was meant to. "What, by the Arrow, could he have needed to do that would keep him from taking his place?"

Bertram sighed, apparently accepting she wouldn't do as she was told until he gave her what she wanted. "He's not married, lady. Nor betrothed, nor has he ever been and nor will anyone send their daughter to him."

This struck her back a step. "The prince must be wed before he becomes king?"

"Or promised in some fashion. How else can he get an heir?" Bertram shrugged and rubbed his forehead. "The king has sent his requests to many with whom he'd like to make an alliance. Because of what happened, none will take it."

"What happened, what happened," she cried, irritated. "Everyone says it's because of what happened, but I scarce can think of anything that he might have done that would be so terrible years later!"

"He killed someone, lady, and went to the madhouse for it." Bertram's low voice held shame, but truth.

Honesty's stomach turned again, twisting. "He's not insane."

Bertram looked pointedly at the open door. "You would be one of the few to think so."

"He's not . . . I would know. He's not crazy, Bertram." Honesty got up into the carriage and arranged her skirts out of the way of the door.

"There's all kinds of crazy, lady," Bertram replied and closed the door so firmly there was no way he could hear anything she said after that.

In moments the carriage began its rocking and a short time after that Honesty was on the train, moving out of the station and away from Firth. She hadn't even asked where they were sending her but assumed it was back to the Motherhouse. She stared out the window as night fell and the countryside changed. She stared through darkness and until the light again filled the sky.

Then she pulled open her hand-trunk and began to read.

Chapter 15

The plate of food stood untouched on the table, drawing flies, but Cillian didn't bother even to wave them away. Devain hadn't been so foolish as to try and hold the king's son as he would have a man of lesser status, but even if the room was decently appointed it was still a cell, and though the food was as fine as any that had ever graced Cillian's table it was still a prisoner's fare. It turned his stomach to take even a mouthful. He hadn't even taken any of the small ale Devain had ordered for him.

What he wanted was a bath and some sleep, but the former had been denied him these five days past and the latter he dared not take. They kept you from bathing to demoralize you and put you closer to the beast they claimed you to be, but sleep was when they came to hurt you. Lessons well learned and not forgotten. Devain would know that and would be watching Cillian for signs of it breaking him, but Cillian refused to give the bastard even a hint that this treatment had affected him. He wore his soiled, five-days-worn clothes as though attired for a formal ball, and he stretched out on the thin mattress of the cot and closed his eyes for hours at a time, though he didn't sleep.

He'd had visitors aplenty, for Devain couldn't dare deny him that, either. Cillian greeted them as though holding court, even as he knew sluts like Persis Denviel were coming so as to brag on his closeness with the prince rather than true concern. Alaric had come, looking worse than Cillian, his blond hair dulled and tangled and shadows on his face but bringing a bowl of herb to share and news of what was being said, mostly about the king's health and what had brought him low, speculation it was something other than his long habit of overindulgence. Rumors of if the king had indeed officially named Devain as his heir and denounced Cillian, and if he had the right to do so. Nonsense, mostly, but satisfying nonetheless. The country might have shaken its collective head at Cillian's recent exploits, but most of them couldn't also forget he was the son of Queen Ingrid, their beloved, that he bore her features and the color of her hair, and how they'd celebrated his birth and first steps as though he were their own dear boy and not only the king and queen's.

Edward came, too, grim-faced but determined, revealing what was being said in the court amongst the lords who'd judge him when the time came. Devain had been hasty, acting as soon as the king fell, and people panicked about who'd take his seat. It had been easy to garner enough signatures to arrest Cillian on the charges Devain had provided, but it was taking him longer than he'd thought to get enough men to agree to bring Cillian to trial.

"And yet he can hold you here," Edward said through gritted teeth, his fists clenched at his sides as he paced. "For your safety, he says. Lest there be an uprising."

Cillian found a laugh, made easier by Edward's presence. "So he holds me for a few more days. So he brings me to trial, Edward, what then? What will he prove? I am my father's son, and there is none who will deny that. All the rest is detail."

Edward turned with a shake of his head. "Devain has his heart set on your seat, Cillian. He wants it and he'll stoop as low as he must to get it. There have been pantomimes in the public square called 'The Mad Prince.' Think you Devain doesn't encourage them? He has the truth behind him."

"And I'll not deny it," Cillian said quietly. "But you and I both know the worst I've ever done is better than some of the kings this country has seen."

Edward's smile came slowly, but warmed the room when it did. "He's trotting out that ancient ruling about being wed."

Cillian's man had brought him the old texts laying out the lines of succession. "I have a year after taking the crown to marry. Perhaps no father has wished to send his daughter to a prince of questionable person, but I'm fair certain, my dear one, that a king's crown and castle are of sufficient sweetness to lure at least one princess to overlook the fact of madness. And I'd only need one."

Edward looked doubtful. "He's going to make you face the priests, as well."

They would be more difficult to sway. "I shall have to put my trust in Sinder, then. I know my holy texts, even if I'm not a Temple-goer. I can quote them to please the priests. I can promise them money, if that's what it takes. Who knows. Maybe I can even find some true faith, if I have to. More than one condemned man has found his way to the light."

"You have an answer for everything." Edward came closer and put his hand on Cillian's shoulder. "But then, you always have."

The muscles beneath Edward's hand leaped and tensed, and the face Cillian had maintained to keep Devain and any who watched on his behalf at bay cracked. Edward saw it or felt it, he had to.

He'd known Cillian too long not to notice. His fingers curled squeezing, and then Edward had both his arms around him.

Cillian pressed his face into the familiar scent of Edward and gave in to his dear friend's comfort. He closed his eyes and pretended they were lads again, running and snapping at each others' heels. He pretended they were young and nothing had yet come between them, not jealousy, not fury, not hate. Not love.

"I can help you." Edward's lips tickled Cillian's ear. "There are many who would see Devain encounter an accident and be happy of it."

Reality snapped into Cillian, and he stepped back to stare into Edward's eyes. "No."

"Cillian—"

Another step back took him farther from Edward's embrace. "No, Edward. You have your lady wife and child to think of. What you say is too dangerous. I won't allow it. There are many who support him who'd look first to you should something happen. I won't have it. I won't have you risk your entire life."

Emotions struggled on Edward's face. A flash of anger, of guilt. Cillian had put himself forward years ago to save Edward, and now the man, damn him, felt he should do the same.

"I was a prince," Cillian said in a low voice, eyes never leaving his friend's. "With naught to risk but myself. And I loved you."

Edward's jaw clenched and loosened. "I know you did."

"And I still do." His heart swelled into his throat, threatening to choke him. "As I ever have. But you will not do that. If harm comes to Devain, you'll be the first blamed, and I won't be able to save you from this cell."

"You would be king," Edward pointed out.

"And what you did would still be wrong," Cillian told him.

Silence. Edward's chest heaved and he blew out a long breath, then turned away. Cillian swallowed hard and sat, his legs gone weak from lack of sleep and anxiety. His heart pounded, choking him further, and he loosed his collar.

"It would be wrong," he murmured to Edward's back. "I can't let you make yourself what you are not for my sake."

"What I'm not?" Edward sounded strangled. "But I am, Cillian, have you forgotten?"

"An accident caused by passion's heat is not the same as a premeditated one." He didn't say murder aloud, aware that Devain's guards could be bought off but the word would raise the price.

Though he had at times imagined what it might be like to have Edward at his feet, Cillian had never truly expected to find him there. Edward crossed the room in three long strides and knelt, his hands on Cillian's knees and his forehead pressed to the backs of his hands. Cillian felt their heat even through the heavy velvet of his trousers, but was too surprised to do anything except place his hand on Edward's hair. His fingers dug deep into the depths, the strands thick and coarse and yet as silk on Cillian's skin.

"Edward, my dear one," he whispered. "Don't."

"I plead your mercy," Edward said without raising his head. "Cillian, by the Arrow, I beg you for it."

How many times had he imagined a moment like this? Some nights, with the rats nibbling at the edges of his blanket and the darkness pressing into his eyes it was all he'd been able to think of. Edward, his dear one, his friend. Sometimes he'd thought of him with somewhat shameful desire mingled with thoughts of revenge, especially in the long, long days when Cillian had died a little every hour under the care of men whose cure was worse than the disease and Edward did not come.

He'd never imagined that Edward on his knees would make him feel nothing but softness and clear-sighted love unblemished by anything else. He wanted to weep with it, but tears had stayed behind in the darkness with the rats and he could only manage to blink against the sting.

"You have ever had it, Edward. How could you not know it?" Cillian's hand stroked down the dark hair and over the braid at the base of Edward's neck. "Rise you up, my dear one. You don't have to do this."

Edward heaved another sigh and raised his face, and Cillian saw tears had not deserted his friend. He handed Edward a handkerchief from his pocket, but Edward only swiped them from his face without shame. He didn't get off his knees.

"You will be king, Cillian, and I shall bend my knee to you then." Edward said it without any doubt, so firmly Cillian could believe it himself. "And you will be a fine king. Better even than your father. I know this."

The tumblers of a lock deep inside him shifted, like tiny gears moving at last after long being rusted tight. Something moved in his heart and in his head, like a flower unfurling or the glimpse of sunshine through black clouds, or the parting of a curtain on a play long-delayed.

Cillian opened.

"Rise you up, my dear one," he murmured with a smile, "else I think you'd like to spend an hour on your knees in a different sort of service."

Edward grinned. "If I were to serve you in that way, my prince, I guarantee it would not take me an hour."

Cillian's hand found Edward's neck and pulled him close. He kissed Edward's mouth with his lips closed and his eyes open, and only for a moment. Then he did it again softer. And then, he let Edward go.

"You have ever been my dear friend," Cillian said. "And I am fair grateful you will always be."

"Then let me help you," Edward said, still on his knees.

"Have you signed Devain's petition to bring me to trial?"

That sent Edward to his feet. "No! Of course not! By the Void, Cillian, how can you ask that of me?"

"Sign it," Cillian said calmly. "Have Alaric sign it. Have Persis, though he might be more hindrance than help, I'm uncertain. Have all the lords who would serve me sign it."

"Are you mad?" Edward cried, aghast.

Cillian stood, his laugh genuine. "Well, yes, I've heard it said so."

"If we sign Devain's petition, you will come to trial for your seat."

"And all those who sign it will be made to sit upon the voting committee, Edward. I need a majority to rule in my favor. Now, what do you think I'd rather have? A small list of men convinced I need a trial to determine my worth? Or a long list of those who know I'm worthy of the crown?"

Edward stopped, shook his head in wonder and then again. "So simple."

"Not all intrigue needs be complicated," Cillian said.

Edward looked impressed. "I daresay Devain wouldn't have thought of it."

"Even if he has, he can't stop you from signing."

"You, my prince, are a marvel."

"More than merely handsome, yes?" Cillian shrugged. "I lived more of my life than not being groomed to rule, Edward. Devain forgot that."

"I forgot it, too."

Cillian gave another shrug. "Well, it's a good thing I never did, yes?"

Edward came close and clapped his hand on Cillian's shoulder. "I'll go now and make it so. We'll shake him up, Cillian. We'll put that rat back in his hole."

"And bring me word of my father, will you?" Cillian asked quietly, pleased with Edward's reaction but unable to forget the only way any of this would matter was if his father died.

"Yes. Of course."

They embraced again, without lingering, and Edward made to go.

"My regards to your wife," Cillian said with a smirk, if only because some things would never change.

Edward didn't rise to the bait. He made a rude hand gesture, instead. "I may have to remind her who you are, first. She does tend to forget every other man's name."

Cillian laughed so loud and long the guard opened the door. Edward grinned and left. Cillian ordered a fresh plate and a jug of wine, and the guard looked surprised but nodded and closed the door.

Cillian smiled to himself, well pleased for the first time since Devain had shown up at Edward's door. The guard brought more food and more visitors. Alaric had come, and Edward, and a few of the fabric merchants still seeking boons though imprisoned Cillian was unable to do much for them. Friends and enemies had all been to visit, but Honesty had not. And in the end, he mused, had it mattered? For he'd found his solace in forgiveness, the giving and the getting, both.

Nothing so bold as a signpost marked her leaving one province and entering another, but nevertheless Honesty drew in a deep, slow breath of the sea-scented air and slowed her horse. Ahead of her she could see the mountains overlooking the Belloran Sea. Her father's house was a hard two hours' ride in that direction, and though they'd been riding for the past two weeks, Honesty didn't at once set her heels to the horse's side. She reined it short and stared down the road, neatly lined though unpaved this far out into the country. At this time of year her parents would be in their country manor, not in the seat of state, in the city. She was glad of that, at least. The chance to meet them once more amongst the orchards rather than buildings and noise. She'd been glad for the excuse to ride instead of taking the train so she might return the way she'd left, bearing nothing but herself and a desire for change.

"My lady?"

The Order had given her Gilbert to attend her, for she no longer wore the gown of a Handmaiden and couldn't expect its protection. He'd been the perfect traveling companion, saying little but making the way as easy for her as possible. She might have made her own arrangements, bartered at inns and found her own supplies, but she would be infinitely grateful she'd had Gilbert to do it for her.

"In a moment or two, Gilbert, please. We're almost there."

Gilbert looked past her to the mountains beyond. "The sea is past them, isn't it? I've never seen the sea."

"Perhaps you should go the long way home," she offered. "It would be a shame to miss it, since you're so close."

He laughed, the corners of his eyes crinkling. "I might, at that."

They rode in silence after that, keeping the horses to a steady pace that wouldn't wear them out, and though she'd estimated the journey's final length as two hours, it took them four. They rode into the courtyard in the purple hues of twilight. Gilbert took the horses to the stables.

Honesty went toward the manor.

Her hair was longer than it had been when she left, her waist narrower. Her eyes, like Gilbert's, bore the lines of her experience. She was no longer a fresh-faced girl. She wasn't a child.

Yet her knees quaked like a child's when she pushed at the front door, unguarded though her father's men would be close by him

and her mother at all times. The great open entryway was un-
changed. She hadn't thought beyond this point, where she'd go and
what she'd say. With nobody to greet her, Honesty wasn't sure what
to do. So she did what she'd have done in any patron's house had
she arrived with no one to welcome—she went to the kitchen.

"Dina."

The older woman looked up from the pan of rolls she was buttering for baking. Her brow furrowed. She stepped back, a white-
floured hand over her heart, leaving the imprint on her black dress.

"Holy Mother. Erista?"

"It's me."

"Erista . . ." Dina's head went side to side in her amazement.
"By the Quiver, child, what are you doing here?"

Erista. The name felt strange in her mind, the same number of
syllables, even sounding somewhat like the name she'd worn for the
past many years but strange all the same. She wasn't sure she felt
like an *Erista* any longer, even as she was certain she no longer
could answer to the name *Honesty.*

"I came home." She gave a simple answer to what had been a
simple question, but Dina again shook her head and proved there
could be no such thing.

"Ah, lass." Dina wiped her hands on her apron and came forward to clutch at Erista's shoulders and pull her close. "Ah, lass,
you've grown so. And so much has changed since you've been
gone."

A small thread of alarm wove its way through her innards and
tangled up into a knot greater than the one that had been there
already. "What do you mean? Are my parents well?"

Surely she'd have heard if they'd taken ill or died. Dina sighed,
her shoulders lifting, and went back to the pan of rolls as though
Erista had only been there yesterday, despite what the older woman
had said. But then conversation could wait, and the rolls could not.

Erista wouldn't have known that before leaving, but her time in the Order had taught her how to discover that which needed the most attention at the moment.

"They're as well as they've been, lass, at least in the times I see them. They don't oft come here any longer. Your lady mother prefers the entertainments in Bellora City and your lord father wishes to please her. This place is more oft used for guests who've come to view the seaside than anything else any longer." Dina looked up, her mouth working on words that wanted to come but would insist on being bitten back.

"And the boy?"

"And . . . the boy," Dina said. "He comes here with his father."

Erista's heart failed in its rhythm for a moment before starting violently in her chest. "Yes. I imagine he does."

"You'll not know him," Dina said. "He's near a man, now."

He would be ten and four, near a man as Dina had said, but Erista wouldn't have known him had he still been an infant. She'd left him while he was still at suck. "And the Lady Bevins?"

Dina looked confused. "Oh, Caspar Bevins never married."

Erista's heart skipped another beat. "He's never had a mother? But . . . they told me . . . they assured me . . ."

They'd told her if she left, gave up her place, Bevins would raise the boy as his own son and as her father's heir after her two older brothers. Bevins would marry some hand-picked noblewoman somewhere in the line of succession, so Erista's son would have two parents and be raised a nobleman, regardless of his bastard's birth. They'd told her to leave him if she wanted him to have the best life he could have, and she'd done what they told her to do.

"They did raise him a nobleman, did they not? They did that, at least?"

"Oh, aye. Gave him your father's name and everything a boy could wish for."

"Wait . . . my father's name?"

Dina looked sad, though with a grief long put aside. "He's been made your father's heir, lass."

"What of Eynan and Egart?" Her brothers, both so much older they'd been more like uncles. Erista's heart pounded. "Both . . . gone?"

"A fever took Eynan. Egart fell in a hunting accident. Your father had nobody, lass. He gave the boy his name, as I said. And everything a lad could ever need."

"Except a mother. By the Void." Erista knotted her fingers into the length of her gown, the one Cillian had given her. The finest she'd owned since leaving this place.

Dina again looked confused. "He has a mother, of course he does."

"But you said Bevins never wed . . ." Her mind reeled, focusing more on her brothers' deaths than anything else. "Nobody told me. I didn't know."

Of course they hadn't. She'd been sent away, dead to her parents, who'd had two sons more important than a daughter they were unable to wed to their advantage. They'd told her she was doing the best thing, and she'd believed them.

"And here you came back. I can't say as I'm sad to see you, lass, but I'll admit I'm surprised. I thought for sure you'd never come back. I don't know many who would."

Erista looked around the kitchen, smaller than she remembered it but as impressive as any she'd seen in her travels. She looked at Dina. "The worst they can do is put me in gaol, yes? They've not named me a traitor while I was gone? I've not been tried in my absence for treason?"

"No, I don't think so!" Dina looked shocked and then busied herself with the pan of rolls, putting them into the oven. "By the Arrow, I should think not."

"I think I'll see my father and mother now. Do you know where they might be?"

"They might be in the gardens," Dina said reluctantly. "You're just going to jump in on them without warning, the way you did me?"

"I came home," Erista repeated. "There's no sense in skulking in corners or waiting to be called to an audience. So far as I recall I'm no longer their daughter, so I suppose I'll be considered a guest. It would be rude not to introduce myself to my hosts."

Dina had no reply for that, not that Erista thought she would. Dina was a talented cook and ran the manor as strictly as any general, but she was a simple woman for all that. Erista left her there and went to the garden to find her parents.

They were old.

They'd been old for a number of years, she realized, noting the gray in her father's beard and the silver glinting against the gold of her mother's hair. They sat, clothed in garments playing at being peasant garb though sewn of the finest fabrics. It had ever pleased her mother to play the part of country housewife when they came to stay in the manor. Time hadn't changed that.

"Mother," Erista said and surprised herself when the word broke on her tongue.

Her mother turned, the smile slipping from her lips. She was on her feet at once, lifting her skirts and running toward Erista, who froze, uncertain of her mother's intent. When her mother embraced her, tears flowing, Erista wept, too.

Her father was more reserved. He walked with a cane now, and slowly, but he nodded at her as though days and not years had passed. "Daughter."

"You've come back, oh, you've come back. They told us there was no way to get in touch with you, that you'd entered the Order and only you could decide to contact us should you desire it . . . We had no recourse!" her mother babbled, hugging Erista and holding her at arm's length to look her over at intermittent moments. "We had no way of knowing where you were, if you were well or ill . . . or if we'd ever see you again!"

Erista hugged her mother hard, but looked her father in the eye. "I was not aware I'd be so welcomed."

"Would you have returned sooner, had you known?" Her father had always known her better than her mother had.

"No, Father. I don't think so." She watched him carefully, this man who had taught her how to rule a country though he never intended she should need to do so.

"Why come back now?"

"Eslan, hush. She's back now. She's back and we have so much to say and do, it's been too long. Don't start up with all that . . . nonsense. Yes, nonsense," her mother said and linked her arm through Erista's. "She's home now. That's all that matters."

"I'm sorry, Wife, but it's not, and she knows it. Don't you, girl?" Her father jerked his chin at her.

"I'm not a girl any longer," Erista said, glad for the years of training the Order had provided in temper-keeping.

"No. I don't suppose you are." Her father opened his arms and she went into them. Once she'd fit just right beneath his chin and his embrace had meant safety. It was different now.

He looked down at her when she stepped back. "Welcome home, Erista."

"That's all? Nothing more?" She smiled at them both, though warily. "You'll welcome me back with open arms and hearts, nothing to be spoken of again?"

Her mother frowned and looked at her father. "We've longed for you to come back."

"You sent me away in anger. I wasn't to assume you'd wish me to return. And . . . there was the matter of the boy." Erista forced her voice to calmness.

Again her father and mother shared a look.

"He is well," her father said. "You would be proud of him."

"I have no right to pride," she said quietly. "I didn't raise him."

Her mother blinked. "You might pretend, Erista."

Erista—the name still felt strange, like clothes a size too small—shrugged. "I've borne the name Honesty since joining the Order. They chose it for me. I've learned to live up to it, I suppose, Mother. I mean no offense, but I can't take credit for anything my son has become."

It hurt her to say it, for she remembered the softness of his skin and the baby-sweet scent of him. His tiny hands and feet. The feel of him at suck.

"I didn't come back to take him," she said. "I know I have no right. I just . . ."

All at once it was too much. The travel. Cillian. Leaving the Order. Erista crumpled, the grass soft under her. She Waited, finding peace in the position which had been the staple of her existence for so many years. She pressed her face into the grass in Waiting, Remorse.

"I just wanted to come home," she whispered into the grass. "I needed someplace to come to."

"Get her up," she heard her father say. "Before someone sees."

She hadn't noticed any servants but had forgotten her parents would never have been far from those who waited on them. Hands lifted her gently to her feet and Erista shook her head. "I'm all right."

"You should go inside and have a warm bath. New clothes. Some sleep," her mother said.

Erista didn't argue with any of that. "You told me I had to go. That it was the best choice for him. And for me. You gave me no other choices."

"Erista," her father said, "we were wrong."

Chapter 16

Though the room rustled, anything but silent, Cillian heard nothing. Saw nothing. Felt nothing.

He made certain of it.

Chin up, eyes straight ahead, face a blank, bare mask. He wore his finest clothes and carried in one hand a copy of the Sacred Book, leather-bound and tied closed with a ribbon. The other held a single coin, printed with the face of his father. The Book was for show. The coin was for comfort.

Three Temple priests, heads shaved and skin oiled, their red tunics bright against the room's white walls, sat impassively in one corner. Across the back of the room stretched a single long table, behind which sat the lords who'd signed the petition to see him here. Devain crouched in the center seat, a spider in the center of his web and Cillian the juicy fly he intended for his supper.

Edward was there, too, along with Persis and several others who would support him. Alaric, unless he'd hidden himself behind the gross-bottomed Lord Beals Defentaine, was missing. As for the others, Cillian could name them all as his father's men, now Devain's. One to one, if put to a vote, they might come out evenly matched. Or he might find himself deposed before he'd even made it to the chair sitting now empty across from him.

He lifted his chin. "Devain. The proceedings should start. I've long been kept from my lord father and would see him for myself."

He refused to allow any one of them, friend or enemy, to see how he knew he'd been prevented from sitting at his father's side not because of his arrest but because his father hadn't seen fit to send for him. Edward, who'd also been kept from the king's side, said the word from the medicus attending him was that Cillian's father couldn't speak, though he was awake and could write simple instructions. They'd bled and steamed him, and forced him full of potions and powders, but nothing seemed to help. The word was he was fading fast, and Cillian meant to see him before the old man passed, if it meant breaking down the door to do it.

The Temple priests muttered and shifted, but Devain didn't spare them a glance. Whatever he'd paid them or whatever he anticipated, it was nothing compared to his apparent glee at being able to lead this trial. Cillian kept his gaze steady, fixed on Devain and not daring even to flicker toward Edward. He wouldn't give Devain the satisfaction.

Fear had sat in his gut like a stone for the entire imprisonment, but had gone the moment he entered this room. There was nothing Devain could do to him that could be worse than what had already been done. Cillian could survive losing his place. His wealth. He could even survive the death of his father, when it came, so long as he had his freedom.

If Devain managed in some twist of circumstance to wrest that away from him, Cillian would take his own life before he ever went back to the asylum or any place like it.

Devain stood and read the list of charges, one after another, the list so long it took him more than a full breath to finish. There was no point in Cillian pleading his innocence though Devain paused to give him time. With every eye on him and every tongue held in anticipation of how he'd respond, Cillian clutched the coin in his palm until the metal was as warm as his own skin.

"I have done all these things, yes. But I deny that any one of them makes me incapable of becoming King of Firth."

Thus it began.

The commentary was exhaustive. Every lord who'd signed the petition had the right to speak against Cillian or in his defense, and each had the right to call up to three witnesses to prove his stance. Devain watched every one of them with avid, greedy eyes, even while the rest of the room drooped as hour after interminable hour passed and the stories unspooled and unraveled.

Cillian could not speak for himself but had to listen to men who'd nearly crawled up his ass to eat his breakfast for him a few weeks ago now denounce him as a lecher, a cretin. A madman. He wanted to be insulted but found he could only be amused. The more he smiled, the harder Devain frowned.

The charges of debauchery and lechery soon held no weight. Too many men had themselves found pleasure in wielding or submitting to a flogger to comfortably chastise Cillian, especially when none of the girls they brought forth from his hareem said anything but that they'd had only pleasure from his touch.

One of them, a petite brunette with tawny skin who'd come to Firth from far away and had never spoken more than a few words to him threw herself at Cillian's feet and begged him to allow her to return to his service.

"No, beauty," he told her, lifting her to her feet with a tug on her hand. "I'm sorry, my pretty one. But I can't."

And no matter how Devain would seek to twist Cillian's reasons for it, he was unable. Fists flexing, he addressed the room. "A man doesn't give up his penchant for cruelty as though it were a hobby he tired of."

"No," Cillian replied, thinking of Honesty. "But sometimes he might no longer find it necessary."

The vote came as night fell. They did it the modern way, pulling the lever of a counting box that kept track of each vote, one side apiece for *yea* and *nay*. Cillian watched them, one by one, and at last let his head drop and his eyes close. In the end, he didn't want to see who stood against him.

"My lord prince." Devain's voice, strangled with fury, raised Cillian's head. "It would seem you have managed to garner the support of enough men to keep you in your place a while longer."

Cillian had no room for relief; to give in to that or joy would open the way to every other emotion he'd stamped so deep down. He was bone-weary from sitting so stiffly and now he stood, his jaw unlocking after being clenched for so long. At first he had no voice and had to clear it, but when he spoke it rang throughout the room. More than one man flinched.

"I will see my father now."

Devain's lip curled and he took his hand from the counting box. "Let us not forget what is perhaps the most important accusation. You have no wife and no prospect for one."

"I have a year to take one. If at the end of it I'm still unwed, you can try to wrestle my crown from my head again, Devain. But until then, I would see my lord father." Cillian stepped off the dais, his every joint aching but irrepressible lightness trying to bubble up from inside.

"Wait." The tallest priest spoke, rising. "There is yet the matter of your faith."

Cillian had been weary before, but the brief respite had lifted him. "What of it?"

It wasn't the response the priests had been looking for. The tallest spoke again, calmly. "Do you have any?"

Devain shot them a glowering, thin-lipped stare, and Cillian thought perhaps the man had overstepped himself with the priests. "It's been documented the prince doesn't attend Temple services aside from holiday gatherings."

"This is ludicrous!" Edward spoke up from amongst the milling lords eager for their suppers. "The king himself never set foot in Temple, as it's well-known, and he's been on the throne for years! You have your results, Devain, accept your loss and let the man go see his father before it's too late!"

Cillian met Edward's eyes at last. Edward didn't return his smile at first, all thorns and bristles on Cillian's behalf. Cillian teased him into one, finally, tiny but real. Just like across the schoolroom when both were meant to be paying attention to the teacher but instead were plotting how they'd spend the cash in their pockets.

The priest moved between Cillian and Devain. "A man can have faith without ever attending a formal service, and he can worship every day without having any faith at all. But a king without faith cannot sit upon the throne of Firth. We've not yet been so hobbled we can't prevent that. The Temple has final say in any appointment. Simply because my brothers haven't found it necessary to deny any doesn't mean we can't do it. You can read the Law of the Book and see what I say is true."

Devain's grin split his lips back and turned his face into something monstrous. He made a small, reaching gesture with his hands as though grabbing the imaginary crown off Cillian's head. The priest didn't pay any attention to him, his focus on the prince.

"So I ask you again, my lord prince. Do you have faith?"

It was no simple question to answer, and Cillian didn't try.

"You were sent a Handmaiden. The Order doesn't send Handmaidens to those they don't deem worthy." The priest ticked off a list on his fingertips while his brothers watched, quiet. "But what sort of man is unable to find solace even when assisted by one of the Order?"

"A man unfit to rule," Devain began, but the priest's upheld hand silenced him.

Cillian faced the priest, sewing together his reply from words he plucked one by one from his mind. He knew many reasons why Honesty had been unable to complete her task. Why he'd sent her away from him before she could. And why he didn't deserve for her to try. He had many answers for the priest, who now waited with his head tilted, listening for Cillian to speak.

Even so, Cillian didn't know what he meant to say when his mouth opened. But then Bertram appeared in the doorway.

"My lord. Your father. He's gone."

And Cillian found he need say nothing at all.

Y ou don't have to go." Erista's father leaned heavily on his cane, breathing hard.

He was too proud to ask her to slow the pace or even take a break, but Erista did it anyway. "Sit with me, Papa."

She arranged her skirts around her ankles and made room on the stone bench for him. Their seat at the top of the garden path gave her a clear view to the ungroomed meadow below, where young Eslan practiced some sort of swordplay with his mentor. Taller than she by half a head, he had her eyes set in the features of his father's face. It had startled her upon seeing it, for she'd forgotten how he'd looked, her first love. Eslan mingled the best of them both, though he didn't know it.

"You don't have to," her father repeated.

"Of course I have to." Erista's voice stayed steady. She watched her son learning to be a man. "How can you look down there and see what I see and not understand that?"

"We could tell him the truth."

She turned on the bench to look at him. "Now? After all this time? You've raised him as your own son, not as grandson. You told him his siblings all died. He thinks I'm a distant cousin come to stay, not your daughter returned from the grave. The boy has lived his entire life being fed a lie. What purpose could it serve to tell him the truth, now?"

Her father sighed heavily and slouched. "I'm growing older. Your mother, too. What will happen if I die before he's ready?"

She found more pity in her heart for him. The man had lost two sons, after all, to accident and illness. Yet she couldn't forget he'd lost his daughter, too, and by choice. "The fact I'm all you have left is no good reason for me to do what you wish."

"How about for mercy's sake?" Her father gave her a solemn, piercing look.

Erista didn't answer. Time had passed and she'd found a large measure of forgiveness for her parents, but there would always be a space between them.

"But to a madman, Erista?"

Her father's anguished tone turned her head.

"Cillian's not a madman."

Her father shook his head. "Only a madman would advertise the position of bride as he would for a new chatelaine."

He would have to, Erista thought. He only had a year to find a wife or be deposed without any effort from Devain at all. "There are women aplenty who will overlook his past for the position he offers."

"But to send a mailing to every noble house in the closest hundred miles! It smacks of desperation at the very least. Low breeding. What sort of woman is he seeking, that would answer a call such as this?"

One like her, or so Erista hoped. She'd never told Cillian where she'd lived. Who she was. It might be foolish of her to think he was trying to find her, but she'd been foolish before.

Eslan, smile wide, raised his sword and turned to them. Sunlight slanted across his face. There was no way Erista would ever do anything to take the smile from it. Honesty had ever served her well, but not this time.

"You could have a kingdom as fine as any right here," her father said.

She leaned to pat his hand, then turned back to the sight of Eslan now back to battle with his teacher. She looked around the garden and to the fields where the orchards had once stood. She'd never regret returning, but this was no longer her home.

"It's not his kingdom I desire," she said, and for that her father had no answer.

The Princess Erista Bellor," announced the footman, stumbling over the pronouncement of her name. "Formerly of Bellora."

That drew the attention of every eye in the room. Erista straightened. She'd faced scrutiny often enough, but it had always been easier to withstand when wearing a Handmaiden's gown. Looking at her in uniform, most people saw her function. In more fashionable clothes, they saw her as a woman.

Woman I began, and woman I shall end.

She lifted her chin to face them all.

Cillian's court was different than his father's. Women had been allowed to join, and Erista straightened further. How many of them had come for her same reason? How many vied for the seat beside him?

"Approach the king and present yourself," said the footman, as though every day trembling, anxious women arrived and had to be reminded of protocol.

Perhaps they did.

Erista moved forward on silent slippers, gliding carefully toward the dais at the end of the room. Cillian hadn't even turned his head at the sound of her name. He spoke idly to the man next to him. Edward Delaw, she saw, and was glad to witness the easy way the men smiled and laughed.

Cillian didn't look up until she'd dropped to a low curtsy in front of him, her head bowed. When she looked up, she watched his expression slide from boredom to surprise to wariness. It stopped short of the joy she'd hoped to see.

The room had been abuzz with talk but slowly fell quiet as Cillian stared. Erista held the curtsy for longer than necessary, her eyes locked with his. Her head swam at the sight of him, his red-gold hair shorter and worn loose around his shoulders. He was still so lovely.

"You're here," he said finally, and all the tension she'd been holding whooshed out of her in a sigh.

"I am."

Cillian got to his feet and took her hand. "Walk with me."

Ignoring the buzz of whispers following them, she followed him out the pair of glass doors to the gardens beyond. A glance over her shoulder showed the press of many faces to the glass. They had an audience.

"Don't mind them," Cillian said. "It pleases them to watch me as though I were an exhibit in a menagerie."

He took her along the crushed stone path to a more private place sheltered by flowering shrubs. He turned, stepped back. Gave her space.

"You came," Cillian said. "I didn't know if you would. I didn't . . . think you would."

"Did you hope?" She let her gaze drink in every inch of him, not bothering to hide her appraisal.

Cillian nodded, solemn. "I did."

"Have many others come, too?"

"Oh, more than I could have imagined," he said with a familiar smirk that faded quickly into seriousness. "I find it most merry how many who'd have been hard-pressed to dance with me at a ball now offer themselves to dance between my sheets."

Thin-edged jealousy sliced at her. "I believe you."

"And yet none of them were you," he said as though the very idea were unbelievable. "Lovely story makers all of them, well versed in telling tales designed to make them seem to be everything I could ever want, and all of them naught but stories, in the end."

"Surely not all of them are dishonest."

"And none of them are you," he said again and took a step closer. "Honesty."

She laughed, heat rising in her at the look on his face and the memory of his taste on her tongue. "I don't use that name any longer."

"You've left the Order."

"I have." She looked down and gestured at her gown. "I find myself in civilian garb once more."

"It suits you." He took another step.

She took one, too. "So you've not yet filled the position?"

"My dear one, it has been so long since I've filled any position I'm fair to bursting."

Erista's laugh became half a sob. She drew him closer that last step and tipped her face to his. "I plead your mercy. I meant to fail you and I did."

Cillian shook his head. "No, sweetness, you didn't. You went away and left me alone."

"So I failed in more ways than one." Her voice cracked as months of grief flooded it. "I shouldn't—"

He stopped her with a soft brush of a kiss. "I made my peace with Edward. I had no one, and he was there. If I'd had you to lean on, I'd never have done that, and he and I would still be estranged. I found my solace, Honesty, and it's lasted longer than a single moment."

Again, the cut of envy sliced her, but only a little and of a different sort. "I'm glad for you. For both of you."

"And you are here, now." His green eyes flashed. "That says something, does it not?"

She smiled, though her throat had gone tight with emotion. "Cillian, I cannot promise you I will be any better a wife than I was a Handmaiden."

He smiled. "I'm fair certain I shall be as equally unreliable a husband as I was a patron. We are well matched, then."

A shiver ran through her. "Do you think so?"

"I think we can learn to be, if nothing else." He kissed her hand.

She thought of the playroom and the sting of leather on her skin. She shivered again but looked steadily into his eyes. "As a Handmaiden I would have bent my back for your pleasure. As wife . . . I'm not sure I'd be able."

Arousal flared in his eyes, but deep within and not frighteningly. "As you once said, there are more pleasures to be had than at the end of a whip."

She studied him, looking for any sign of insincerity, no matter how well meant. She found none. There was more to him than there'd been before, she thought as she reached to stroke his hair from his face. The Cillian she'd known had worn himself like a costume. The man before her stood easily in his skin.

"Shall we marry, then?" she asked him. "Men and women have wed with less acquaintance and for worse reasons."

"Indeed they have, though I should hope ours will be better than that." Cillian's mouth quirked. "And as for acquaintance, I have the better part of a year left before I'm required to marry."

Erista raised a brow. "Oh?"

Cillian reached into his pocket and drew forth a length of silken white ribbon that tangled, then dangled tantalizingly from his fingers. He looked down the path to the glimpse of the entrance to the hedge maze and the bower decorated with braggart's laces. Anticipation crawled along her spine, tightening her nipples and sending heat between her thighs. Wielded by any other man the ribbon would have meant nothing, but in Cillian's hand it reminded her all too well of how it felt to be bound with his desire.

"I had hoped to have time to woo you," Cillian said.

She took the ribbon and wound it around her wrists, watching how his eyes lit and his tongue wet the center of his bottom lip.

"Then I say we find the center of the maze," she told him, already backing in that direction and watching him follow. "And perhaps we might have reason to hang this ribbon on the bower when we come out."

She'd begun to love him when he needed her, but standing before him now, Erista discovered how much better it was for him to want her instead.

Determinata

Chapter 17

I t's highly irregular." The Mother-in-Service, Compassiona, peered over the rims of her spectacles at Mina, then tapped the thick sheaf of papers on the desk in front of her. Her pen, as ever, left not so much as a dot of unwanted ink.

"I don't suppose it's for me to judge such a thing. If the Mothers say I am to go, I go." Mina shrugged.

Compassiona sighed and steepled her fingers beneath her chin. "Determinata, my dear, I know you've no qualms about the assignment. But I do. It's highly irregular, and it chafes me to know that simple rules are broken for the promise of a coin. It's not the way the Order should be run."

Mina reached to snag the top paper and ran down the list upon it with her finger. "He looks a worthy patron, Mother. And the application is thorough."

Compassiona shook her head. "But he's not the one who filled it out, Determinata. No matter his need, he wasn't the one to request it. I don't like it at all, but who am I to go above my fellow Mothers-in-Service who've decided to allow an exception to this case? They say it's because he is worthy, as indeed you've said, but in the end I fear their reasons are baser than that. And I hate to see . . ." She stopped herself and shook her head again. "But never mind. It's not your worry."

Mina smiled at the older woman, whom she'd known since she'd been a Sister-in-Service along with Mina. "I told you. I don't mind."

She more than didn't mind. The man's case had intrigued her enough that no matter how unorthodox the procedure had been to approve him as a patron of the Order of Solace, she was willing to take him. It had been too long since she'd been assigned anyone at all.

Mina looked at the other woman carefully. Compassiona had ever been one to fret but something on her face prompted Mina to ask, "Has there been a question of my ability to serve?"

She had wondered as the months passed and she'd remained behind while others came and went, if there'd been a reason beyond that which she could know. The Mothers-in-Service didn't often choose to explain themselves. Most of the Sisters didn't care—but most of them had little enough rest between their patrons. A few weeks, a month. There were not so many of them in service that the demand could be outstripped by the supply. If anything, more of her Sisters craved a break from their work. For Mina it had been longer than a full twelvemonth since she'd returned from her last assignment.

Compassiona looked surprised. "No, of course not. The other Mothers agreed unanimously you were the best suited for this patron."

Mina, as was her constant habit, kept her back straight and didn't give away her emotions in her expression. She and Compassiona had known each other for many years. If anyone at the Order knew how to understand Mina, it was the woman in front of her now.

Yet Mina often got the impression her longtime Sister-in-Service didn't understand her at all. That few of them did. She was different than the others. No less qualified, no less committed. No less, as her given name proved, determined.

"The other Mothers? Not you?"

Compassiona hadn't become a Mother without effort and experience, and now she leaned her chin in her hand to stare across the desk. "Oh, I'm sure you'll suit him just fine. I've no doubts about that at all. But will he suit you?"

"Is that ever a question of import? Do you doubt me?" Her voice didn't shake, but Compassiona had been well named, as they all had, and she didn't need to hear anxiety to sense it.

"I've never doubted you. Worried for you, yes. Many times."

Mina got up from her chair and went to the window to stare down at the lawns below. In the distance she could see the bare, stripped fields. "You needn't. But if my vocation is in question . . ."

She let her voice trail off, not making her statement a challenge. Compassiona sighed. Neither spoke for a few moments, long enough for Mina to draw herself inward. *A flower is made more beautiful by its thorns*, she thought. *But what of the thorns? Did not the flower's beauty make their sting all the easier to bear?* She had ever thought herself the thorn and not the bloom.

"I daresay nothing you do could be questioned, Sister."

Mina turned to meet her friend's gaze. "Do you suggest I believe myself better able to decide my actions than the Mothers?"

"No. I know you understand your place here. I just want you to be certain you wish to take this patron. You can refuse. You always can refuse."

"But I've been deemed the best for him, yes?"

Compassiona sighed. "Yes."

"Then I shall go."

"If you're sure," Compassiona said doubtfully before laughing. "What am I saying? Of course you're certain, Mina. I've never known you to be anything else. And it's not often we are petitioned for a patron with his . . . needs. He does seem to require your special touch."

Mina's fingers twitched at the thought. "I hope so."

Compassiona cleared her throat and shuffled the papers. "All is in readiness, then. I suppose you'll be off in the morning?"

She wouldn't wait so long as that. "I plan to leave this afternoon, actually."

This surprised the other woman for only a moment. "Ah."

Mina shrugged again. "It's been a long time since I've been able to practice my vocation, Mother. I don't like feeling useless."

Compassiona frowned. "No Sister is useless, no matter if she's serving patrons or assisting here in the Motherhouse."

"Dull, then. Weary. Unused. Is that a better description?" Mina gave a smile the other woman returned. "I don't like feeling unused."

"That I cannot argue against. Go. And may the Invisible Mother herself attend you," Compassiona said.

"And you." Mina gathered the papers and tucked them all together, then put them under her arm.

Already smiling, she headed to her room to finish her preparations. Her journey would be long, but she had little enough to pack. The afternoon carriage couldn't come fast enough.

But of course there would be no hurrying it, especially not when she could think of little else but heading away from this place. During her years in service she'd lived in several of the sisterhouses scattered throughout the Seven Provinces, and once for a few delightful months at a seaside house as well appointed as a resort. Technically, they were all her home and had been since the moment she walked through the front gates of the Motherhouse, but she'd stayed the longest here.

Long enough to hang a portrait on the wall of her cell and fill the drawers with clothes she'd bought for herself rather than relied on a patron to provide. Long enough to have worn a spot in the carpet where she paced before the window as she read from the book of poetry she now packed in her bag. Long enough that it was time to be out of this room, this house, this province, in fact, and away from the mountains and familiar smells of the flowers. She might return to this house, this room, but while she was gone they'd clean and paint it, scrub it down, so even if she did come back to it, she'd no longer feel like it had ever been hers.

Many of her Sisters-in-Service couldn't abide this sort of change, but so few of them remained long enough in any one place they could never begin to feel like they owned any of the rooms, anyway. Sisters like Mina, those with not-oft-requested specialties, had more chance to stay longer and leave their marks on the rooms they left behind. She'd leave no marks on purpose and be glad to know they swept away any remainder of her.

She slipped a gown identical to the one she wore into her hand-trunk along with a pair of sturdy leather slippers. She wore her good traveling boots and her traveling gown, and simply slipping into both had filled her with warmth. She also packed the carved ironwood box, polished to a high sheen, in which she kept her collection of teas. Some for pleasure, some for health. The mix all Handmaidens drank daily to prevent not only pregnancy but also the monthly flow could be brewed from ingredients likely to be found in any household, but she'd included an ample supply anyway. Mina added another small box filled with salves and lotions she'd mixed herself, scented with gillyflower oil from her own garden bed.

Compassiona had said no Sister was useless, but Mina wasn't convinced. She'd been much neglected since leaving her last patron. She'd spent too much time with such activities, the growing of flowers and grinding of herbs. Not that it wasn't necessary to know how, and not even that she hadn't enjoyed keeping herself busy with such matters, but they weren't what she'd joined the Order to do. There was ever much to learn and Mina was no different, no matter how long it had been since she'd been in service or how accomplished she knew herself to be. She'd worked at training new Sisters-in-Service. She'd begun studying the hand-harp, simply because it was one skill that took a long time at which to become proficient and she could spend many hours a day on it.

She had been useless and unused, and tired of it. She'd been ready to go the moment Compassiona'd sent for her, and now, completely packed, she still had to wait. Mina paced the familiar route in front of her window, taking comfort in the swish of her hem and thud of her boot heels on the wooden floor.

The carriage did not come.

When at last she could no longer stand waiting, Mina took herself through the halls and down the stairs to the house's large, open entryway. The massive double front doors, closed now as evening fell, resisted her hand but she forced them open anyway. The slate rang beneath her heels as she went onto the front porch and looked out over the yard and driveway, and to the road beyond.

"Mistress?"

She turned at the low male voice. The man in the doorway stood a full head taller but kept his gaze down and away from her. "Yes, Stephan?"

"You're leaving us?"

"If the carriage ever arrives, I suppose I am." Mina looked again toward the road.

Stephan took a step closer. "Can I bring you something? Food or drink? You might be waiting a long time. You've missed the dinner chime . . . and it's getting dark."

Though the trees crowded close against the lawns of trimmed grass, Mina didn't fear the forest or the encroaching night. There might be beasts in the woods but they rarely ventured this far. Still, she favored him with a smile.

"I'm fine." He didn't expect more, which was why she gave it to him. "Thank you."

He looked at her, then, a large man with a plain face and big, work-worn hands. He'd come from the fields to serve in the house and had never quite grown used to it. He smiled, and it was not difficult for her to remember the taste of his mouth. "You're welcome.

"I'll wait with you," Stephan said. "Until you leave."

He didn't have to, of course, and she wasn't even certain she required company. But she didn't deny him this small thing, more for his benefit than hers. They waited together in silence as dusk turned to darkness and there seemed little hope of the carriage ever arriving.

She'd thrown her cloak on top of her hand-trunk and now shivered as the night breeze soughed out of the trees. Stephan covered her shoulders with the cloak at once and stepped back again. She gathered the soft material around her throat and looked at him.

"You're not needed inside?"

"I'd rather be out here." He roughed his hair with one of those big hands.

Mina understood that. Inside, the Order ran with swift efficiency. The halls overran with women going about their business, and the young, giggling girls unlike she herself had ever been were enough to try the patience of anyone, much less a man like Stephan who'd never quite accustomed himself to the bustle of it all. Out here was only the darkness and the wind, and the scent of the earth in the fields stripped of their harvests.

She had nothing to say to him, but Stephan didn't require speech. She appreciated that about him. Mina looked again to the road where the far-off clip-clop of hooves alerted her to the carriage's arrival. "Finally."

When the carriage at last arrived, he helped her into it and loaded her single, small trunk.

He kissed her hand.

Mina waited for more, but Stephan stepped back from the carriage and gave the driver the signal to go. She looked out the window at him as they drove away. He lifted a hand in a wave she didn't return.

L ight cut through the darkness and Alaric put up a hand to cover his eyes. From far away, farther than the light had come, a groan rumbled in his ears. His own, he guessed, tasting it on his tongue before it faded. He thought he might be muttering, but if words formed on his tongue and not mere nonsense syllables, he couldn't tell.

"By the Void, he stinks."

"This entire room stinks."

Something nudged him and the light shone bright again. Alaric burrowed deeper into softness, seeking his self-made cave. At the next nudge he cried out and swatted at the unseen tormenter. His hand connected with nothing and he fell silent.

Listening.

He recognized the voices. Edward and Cillian. Conspiring against him? What did they mean by "get him up, dump him in it?" Some small, clear part of his mind insisted he try to figure it out, but the rest of it, most of it, remained fuzzed with the delightful numbness brought on by herb and wine and some other small potions he'd picked up from he could no longer remember where.

And with oblivion, the source of which he knew all too well. He tasted it with every breath and heard it whisper in his ears. How long had it been since the last dose? Too long . . .

The frigid water closed over his head and he knew he should come up sputtering, but though it set his teeth to chattering at once, all he did was let his body weigh down deeper into it. Cold and darkness, unbroken by any light. That was what he wanted. That's what he wished for.

Cold, unbroken darkness.

Two pairs of hands grabbed him beneath his arms and hauled him upright. Someone pounded his back. Someone else held his head over a bucket while his guts surged up and out, emptying him. Except he was already empty, he thought, his mind clearing too much. His body heaved again.

His mind went black.

Mina looked good in black. It was not her favorite color—she preferred red. But black suited her just as nicely and was better, for many reasons, at portraying the image she wished to uphold. A Handmaiden in red might as well be a whore, as far as she was concerned, though it wouldn't do for her to say so out loud. Someday she might wear red again, but not now.

Now she had a purpose, and black suited it. She smoothed her hands down the fine cloth of her traveling gown, admiring the severe cut. The high neck. The long sleeves. She'd had it made with buttons of black ironwood, faintly shining, and she admired them too as they ran from her throat to her hem. Not a thread out of place, not a line hanging uneven. Not even a hair dared uncurl from the braid into which she'd pulled it. It hung now over her shoulder and across her breast, and Mina flipped it back to hang straight and sure the way she stood.

A chair, its cushions looking soft, had been waiting when they showed her into this room, but she didn't take it. Her trip had been long, the ride rough enough that standing felt good for a while. She smoothed her gown again and adjusted the sleeves.

Where were they, by the Void? To have sent for her and be told she'd arrived, yet do nothing to greet her? Intolerably rude. Mina sighed and but didn't shift from foot to foot in her impatience. She kept herself still and stern though she wanted to pace. It had been long enough, waiting to be sent to a patron. The hours of the journey had been long enough, too. Why was she being kept waiting?

When at last the door opened, she'd already made several circuits of the room. She'd looked out the window. Perused the rather shabby and unimpressive collection of books on the shelves. This office was for show, not function, and it told her much about its owner, King Cillian. He didn't spend much time in here, which led to an interesting string of thought about where he did his business, if not in an office.

"Your Majesty." Mina greeted him with her stiffest curtsy, as was appropriate for a man of his stature. To the unknown man coming into the room on the king's heels she made a slightly less formal gesture.

"Oh. They said you were in here, but I wasn't expecting . . ." The king's gaze swept her up and down, and he grinned slowly. He elbowed the man with him. "Edward. What say you?"

His companion gave her the same sweeping gaze. "Perfection."

"No," she said. "Determinata. Perfection was not assigned to this house."

Neither man laughed and she sighed inwardly at the confused looks they gave one another. "Gentlemen. I am Determinata, most often called Mina. Or *my lady*. Sometimes, should I decide it appropriate, *mistress*."

The materials she'd read had provided great detail about the man to whom she'd been assigned, but next to nothing about the men who'd done the acquiring. One a king, she knew that much. His friend a nobleman of some sort, clearly a long-time companion, and with something there beyond mere friendship. She watched them closely. The King of Firth was new to the throne and not much about him had come as gossip to the Motherhouse.

The one called Edward rallied first, making a half bow and inclining his head. "My lady, I am Edward Delaw."

"Cillian Derouth," said the king without using his title. His gaze turned admiring. "By the Arrow, you will whip him into shape, won't you?"

"By *him* I assume you mean my new patron? Alaric Dewan, yes? Your friend. I wonder, sirs," she said casually to them both, "what sort of friends you are to send away for a Handmaiden when he is either incapable or uninterested in procuring one for himself."

"Incapable," said Edward.

"Uninterested," Cillian added. "But that doesn't mean he doesn't need one. He does. Desperately."

The men shared another look she couldn't interpret. Mina plucked a barely visible speck of dust from her skirts. "The Order must have agreed, else I wouldn't be here. But I think I shall be the one to decide, ultimately, if he deserves one."

Both of them stared at her with frank appreciation, but it was Cillian who spoke. "Of course."

They took her to a set of rooms that would have been impressive if they didn't reek of sour breath, darkness, and intoxicants. Mina looked around the outer room, small but furnished with exquisite and expensive taste. She ran a finger over the fireplace mantel and brought it away coated with dust. Alaric Dewan, the son of a merchant farmer, had risen to favor as one of Cillian's consorts before he became king. Yet the papers the Order had given her said her patron hadn't held a position of any worth within the court.

"Who pays for this?" She gestured at the furnishings, the books, the accoutrements of a gentlemen's life.

Edward and Cillian shared another look, but Edward spoke. "Alaric doesn't pay rent to live in the palace. He's ever been Cillian's friend."

"Since school. I know. But who pays for the rest of it?" She lifted a pile of what might have been rags, though made of velvet and sateen. "These clothes are fine, as is the whiskey in that decanter over there on the window, if it indeed came from the bottle I spy beneath the chair there. These books are all fine-bound and read, real books, not for show. The furniture is well crafted."

"Alaric has an income from his father's estate. I think much of the rest of this came from . . . gifts," Cillian said.

"Love gifts." That made sense. The room did have a definite, feminine touch to it. "A woman with exquisite taste, yes?"

Edward's lip curled. "A woman, yes. Her taste is a matter of opinion."

From the adjoining room came a rustle of fabric and a snorting groan. Edward and Cillian turned, but Mina moved between them and the door. "You can go."

"We should introduce you," Cillian said.

"I don't think so." Mina smiled at him to take the edge off her response. The man was a monarch, after all, and it didn't do to be rude.

"But he's not been himself," protested Edward.

"I imagine he is more himself now than ever he has been, else you'd have no need of me." She looked toward the half-open door but made no further move toward it.

Cillian also looked toward the door. "He's not been well, is what my friend meant. But you will help him, won't you? He's sore in need of solace."

"He wouldn't be the first. I know what I'm doing. You can go."

Again from within the other chamber came a groan. Mina wrinkled her nose. Whatever aid her patron's friends had provided, it hadn't been the sort she intended to give.

"Edward," said Cillian after a bare half moment. "She's right. Let's go."

Edward didn't protest again. He shot a glance through the door but nodded and sketched another bow in her direction. "We shouldn't doubt you, my lady. Your mercy."

Mina regarded them both calmly, her mind already working on the puzzle of her as yet unseen patron. Much to learn and more to do. She smiled at them both.

"Sometimes," she said, "they call me that, too."

When they'd gone, Mina looked once more around the room. It would have been easy even for an untrained eye to see that despite the luxury, there could be no solace found here. Once it might have been a room of relaxation and peace, but someone—her patron, no doubt—had done his level best to turn on its head anything that might remotely provide comfort.

She knew how that felt.

However, his past was her problem only in how it related to his present; his future was her concern. Her duty was to give this man solace, whether for but a moment or something rather more, something upon which he could build a lifetime. She never knew in advance which she could provide, but there was no doubt in her mind she would satisfy them both during her stay here.

Rummaging in the desk pushed haphazardly kitty-corner by the window, she found a box of fine writing paper. Another search of the drawers turned up an inkwell and pen of carved wood, the nib showing no signs of even normal wear. Not a writer, then. Well, she didn't require poems or love letters, and she would be the one making the lists, not him.

Mina straightened the desk until it sat squarely in front of the window, then pulled the high-backed chair from in front of the fireplace and set it behind the desk. There wasn't much else to tidy there. Alaric Dewan had been a man of much leisure from what his papers told her. A few receipts, a bundle of letters in a masculine hand and tied with a piece of twine. No accounting books or ledgers, nothing to indicate he'd done much work. At least not the sort most fancy gentlemen of her acquaintance had ever done, the sort that required much conversation and very little physical effort.

Mina believed strongly in the benefits of physical effort.

When the desk had been sufficiently tidied enough to suit her, and her lists had been written, she stood and brushed off her hands. She tugged the bellpull and waited an entirely inappropriate length of time for the plump-cheeked maid to knock on the door. The girl looked around the room with wide eyes and didn't bother with even a curtsy.

Mina didn't waste her time or breath correcting the chit. It wasn't her job to train other peoples' staff. Instead, she spoke slowly and clearly so as not to be misunderstood. "I need a pot of cocao along with a basket of yesterday's bread. If you haven't any from yesterday, fresh will do but make sure it's crusty. I need a pitcher of milk, as well, and the things on this list."

The girl took it and made to read it, but then shook her head. "I don't know what this says, miss."

Oh, by the Arrow, what sort of place was this? "Take it to your chatelaine, girl. Bring me what I asked for before the five chime."

The girl goggled, eyeing Mina's long, dark gown. If she had any idea at all about Mina's function here, it didn't show. "Yes . . . yes'm. Will you be needing anything else? Lord Dewan hasn't had anyone into his rooms in a right long time. They could use a good cleaning."

"They could, indeed, but we won't need anyone for it. Thank you."

The girl looked around the room again and opened her mouth as though she meant to speak, but a look from Mina stopped her. "All right, then, miss."

When the girl had gone, Mina took one last look around the room before slipping through the doorway into the bedchamber. Dark curtains blocked the light. A lump huddled in the center of the bed, not even covered by the blankets that had been tossed into a heap on the floor. The room stank, not the worst reek she'd ever encountered, but one strong enough to assault not only her nose but her sense of propriety.

The first thing she did was go to the window and let in the light. It showed the disorder in greater detail as well as illuminating the lumpy figure on the bed, and Mina's lip curled. Disgusting, that a man should allow himself to sink so low, and because of what? Love?

He didn't move. She hadn't expected him to. The low, irregular in-out of his breath told her he wasn't even conscious. It would take more than light to rouse him.

She went back through the study and to the attached bathing chamber where she filled a pitcher with water. She studied him for a moment or so with it in her hands. Would he scream? Thrash about? Or would she have to rouse him more thoroughly?

A small smile stole across her lips at the thought.

"Wake up," Mina said, and tossed the contents of the pitcher on Alaric's head.

He muttered, arms and legs swimming against the bed's dirty bottom sheet, but he didn't get up. His eyes fluttered and closed again, his mouth lax. The water spread in a darkening stain on the sheet.

Mina put the pitcher carefully on a side table. She walked just as carefully to the side of the bed, leaned over, and studied him. Alaric Dewan, beneath the dirt and despair, was a handsome man, but if he'd had a troll's features it wouldn't have mattered. What caught her breath would not be the shape of his mouth or breadth of his shoulders but something rather less tangible. Something . . . subtle. And as always the first time she met a patron, Mina wondered if he would have that silent, subtle something she craved.

Obedience.

She took his earlobe between her thumb and finger, the nails pressing into the tender flesh, and squeezed. Hard. Alaric squirmed under the sudden pain. His eyes opened wide. They were blue, she noted without releasing his ear. A lovely, pale blue. He struggled, but was no more able to get away from her grasp than if she'd had him bound with ropes.

She pulled.

He moved.

"Wake up," she repeated calmly.

"By the Void!" he cursed in a thick voice and swung his arms as though he hoped to push her away.

Mina stepped to the side, releasing him at the same time so he tumbled from the bed onto the floor. He found it first with his face and not even the thick rug could mask the sound of his nose crunching. He let out a stream of mumbled curses that made no sense and cradled his head in his hands, legs askew. Mina watched him calmly for but a moment, just long enough for him to take a few deep breaths.

"Get up."

He looked up at her, blood leaking from his nose, and spat to the side. "By the Mother's invisible tits, who are you?"

"I am your comfort and your grace," she said without a hint of irony. "Now. Get. Up."

When she'd drawn three breaths and he'd made no move to obey, Mina reached and grabbed his earlobe again. She pulled. He got up, not easily and not without stumbling and cursing and flailing, but she got him on his feet.

Standing, he was taller than she, but that didn't matter. She had a tender part of him in a painful grip, and he was still too groggy headed to get away. Mina marched him one stumbling step at a time into the bath chamber, where she let him go and he fell to the damp floor over the drain with a strangled cry.

"You vile bitch," he managed to sneer through the runner of blood still dripping from his nose.

"Bold words from a man on his hands and knees," Mina replied, unmoved. She nudged him with the toe of her leather boot, and Alaric cringed back. "Your body is as filthy as your mouth. You will be cleaned immediately."

He gaped at the tub but didn't move until she reached again for his ear. Then he scrambled back faster than she thought he'd have been able to just a few moments ago. Mina kept her smile locked tight. Alaric put up a hand against her, and she drew back.

She turned to the spigot with the bucket beneath and twisted the handle to let the water pour forth. She didn't bother waiting for it to warm. She opened the small cabinet to find soap, a brush or cloth, bath oils. She found scant supplies of everything, though all were of high quality and must have been costly. When she turned again to face him with a stoppered bottle in one hand and a cloth in the other, Alaric became gape-mouthed again.

"Who, by the Void, are you?"

"I told you. I'm your comfort and your grace. Take off your clothes."

He shook his head, fist clutching the front of his shirt. "I will not—"

She tossed the overbrimming bucket over him. Spluttering, Alaric made as though to grab away the bucket, but Mina was faster.

He fell short, his palms hitting the wet floor with a smack that sounded as though it must sting. He let out a low groan.

"Why can't you leave me alone?"

"You've been left alone. It hasn't served you very well, has it?" She put the bucket beneath the tap again to fill once more with cold water. "Take off your clothes or I'll do it for you."

The dual dousings had revived him, or perhaps whatever he'd dosed himself with had begun to wear away, for now Alaric stared up at her with a clearing gaze that swept her up and down. Recognition dawned in him. "I didn't send for one."

Mina allowed herself to smile, just a little. "I am not a one."

"I didn't send for you!"

"No. And yet here I am. Now, will you get undressed, Alaric Dewan, or shall I be forced to strip you like a schoolboy and put you over my knee to get you to comply?"

He had to know there was no way she could do it, really. Not by sheer force. He was bigger; she was not small but she was still smaller than him. A look crept across his face and anchored at the corners of his mouth, turning down. In his eyes, too, a half-sullen glare that sparkled nonetheless with a vigor missing moments before.

Mina lifted the bucket.

Alaric, with trembling fingers, undid the buttons on his white shirt. Soaked, the material clung to his skin and made it more difficult for him to remove it, but he managed. His trousers next, the sodden fabric squelching as he tossed it. He wore nothing beneath, not even hose, and since he'd had to get to his feet to remove the trousers, Mina had a full-length view of his body.

A fine, broad chest and shoulders, slim hips, flat belly. Muscled thighs. He'd once been a gentlemen's gentleman with a body honed from horses and hunts and leisure. It didn't look as though he'd sat a horse for some time.

His cock, surrounded by a thatch of thick golden hair, stirred under her perusal. At least it still worked. A man might be led by many things, but a cock could always serve as the finest of leashes. Mina admired it openly and then lifted her gaze to his. Alaric had clenched his fists and his jaw, but he was looking at her, too.

"Sit." She indicated the small, three-legged stool with a jerk of her chin.

He sat.

Mina, mindful of his eyes upon her, unbuttoned her gown and hung it carefully out of the way. She pulled her shift to her thighs and buttoned it into place at her hips. She didn't want to get her clothes wet.

She filled the bucket again and dipped the cloth in it before rubbing it briskly with the bar of soap she'd also found in the cabinet. When it had risen to a rich, creamy lather, she faced him.

And then she began to wash him.

His skin hunched at once into dead man's pimples at her first touch. By the time she ran the cloth over his chest and belly, Alaric's shudders were clacking his teeth together. But he said nothing, just allowed her to rub him with the soapy cloth. Even when she reached his thighs and the rising head of his cock, he said nothing.

Mina murmured instruction to him, to raise an arm, shift to the left, open his thighs wider that she might find the places on the backs of his legs. He was no longer combative. In fact, she couldn't recall ever having so pliable a patron, for he did whatever she wished with no more than a shudder or shiver to mark his reaction.

She rinsed, then soaped him again. She washed his hair thoroughly, taking the time to comb out the tangles carefully, without pulling. He moaned when her fingers dug into his scalp, and again when they found the knotted tension of muscles in his shoulders and back. He'd been abusing himself for some time, and his body was paying the toll.

When her soap-slick fingers found the root of his prick, now fully erect, Alaric groaned aloud. His hands bore down on the stool as his hips pushed his cock into her fist, but Mina's hand on his shoulder kept him still. His eyes flew open and met hers, only a few inches away.

Without looking away from him, she stroked downward. She felt the beat of blood in his erection against her palm, but she didn't look down to see it, not even when she twisted her grip around the head and down again, all the way to his balls. She locked her gaze with his. When his lips parted, she allowed the tiniest furrow to appear between her eyes, a crease she felt and knew he saw.

Alaric, if he'd been about to say anything, fell silent. Mina stroked him again. The stool shook as his body did. She let go of his shaft to move a soapy hand down to his sac, which she weighed in her palm. His eyes fluttered closed. His thighs trembled as his feet pushed on the floor and every muscle tightened.

Her body responded to the sight of his arousal. She was unable to control that reaction—the sight of a man responding to her touch was sweeter to her than any lover's caress. Having a man respond to her command was sweeter still.

She let go of his cock and stepped back to dunk her hands in the pail of clean water. Her voice dropped to husky purr. "Rinse yourself. I'll be waiting in the other room."

And then, with his mouth still agape and his cock still erect, she left him.

Chapter 18

The near-frigid water did little to tame his erection, shameful as it was. Alaric doused himself thoroughly with a couple buckets of water. His head had cleared, though most every part of him ached and his mouth tasted disgusting. He swiped wet hair back from his face and took a few extra minutes to rinse his mouth with flavored tooth polish.

He wrapped a towel around himself and went to the bedchamber where she said she'd be waiting. That woman. That . . . *Handmaiden*, he thought with a shiver. She was a Handmaiden, but like none he'd ever heard of. What was she doing here? Had he, in the midst of his darkness, sent for one without knowing? How could he?

And he didn't want one, he reminded himself as he kept a firm hand on the towel at his waist. Even when she turned from whatever she'd been doing at his wardrobe and looked him up and down, and even when that look sent a shock of sensation straight through him, Alaric reminded himself he did not want her.

He wanted no woman, ever again. If he couldn't have his lady, he would die alone. The sooner the better.

"Get dressed." The woman indicated something laid out on the chair by the window.

Alaric looked at the pile of cloth, then at her. "These aren't mine."

"They are now."

He reached to finger the rough, poorly cut trousers. No shirt. He held them up, but while the fit seemed right, they were the trousers of a servant. Not a gentleman and a lord in the prince's service. He tossed them down. "Those aren't fit for me."

Mina looked at the trousers but didn't bend to get them. She moved a step closer to him, and Alaric, though he'd faced greater dangers than the slim, stern woman before him, stepped back. "They are fit for a man who doesn't know how to appreciate what he has. And they'll better suit the work you'll be doing, which is likely to ruin your fine gentleman's clothes."

Her lip curled on the word *gentleman,* and Alaric's back stiffened. He let the towel fall and stood, his heart beating fast, naked. Her gaze flicked over him without lingering, and she showed no signs of arousal or intimidation.

Alaric held the trousers to his skin, which crawled at the roughness. He'd stopped counting the years that had passed since he'd worn anything as low quality as this, if ever. Yet his fingers twitched the cloth, and his skin crawled in expectation of how it would feel.

The woman surveyed him with calm eyes and when she spoke her voice was firm but not unkind. "You would rather have them than go about naked, and you would rather not ruin your fine, expensive clothes. Whether you believe it or not, this is done for your benefit."

He hated himself for thrilling to the simple words, the tone. He held up the trousers. "Just these? No shirt? Is that for my benefit as well, to be half dressed in peasant's garb?"

"Oh no," she said with a hint of a wicked smile. "That is for *my* benefit."

She reached to flick his nipple, which defied him by standing upright at once. Alaric bit back the sound that tried to lurch from his throat and only half succeeded. She heard him, and her smile tipped her mouth, that lush mouth, he was helpless not to notice, higher at the corners.

She noted his shiver. "Don't fear me."

"I'm not afraid."

She smiled. "Good. Now. I've laid out a tray in the other room. You'll eat and feel better with something more solid in your gut than what you've been giving it. And drink. You need to nourish yourself."

Of course he did, if he wanted to live.

"And then," she said with a sudden gleam in her gaze, "you'll get to work."

"Work? What . . ." Alaric shook his head, mind still fuzzy enough to confuse him.

"You've sent away all your maids, and at any rate, I hardly think a maid could make much of an impact upon the mess you've made. Your rooms are in an atrocious state, Alaric. You balk at wearing a peasant's clothes yet you have no complaints about living in rooms you've made into a hovel."

"Surely you don't expect me to . . . clean."

She studied him. "Your arms and legs are not broken, nor your back so far as I can see. You're capable of the work, and as you made it, I see no reason why you ought not be responsible for taking care of it. At any rate, *I* refuse to share quarters in this state, and as I'm to be provided with appropriate clothes, food, *and* living space, I'd suggest you get started."

"Who are you?" he whispered.

"I told you. I'm your comfort and your grace. I'm your Handmaiden, Alaric. Sent for by your friends Edward and Cillian, which I should tell you is not at all the usual manner of things. They must have pleaded quite a case for you, or else spent quite a bit of coin. I daresay I can't imagine how much it must have cost them to get the Order to agree to send me at their request and not yours."

Edward and Cillian, of course. Alaric's mouth thinned and he stepped into the trousers not so much because he believed what she'd said but because he no longer wished to stand before her without even the barrier of this cheap cloth. "They shouldn't have."

"Ah, but they did. And here I am. They must love you very much to make such an effort on your behalf."

His fingers fisted. "And you?"

The Handmaiden raised a shapely brow. "What of me?"

Alaric's firsthand experience with the Sisters of Solace was limited to two, exactly. Stillness and Honesty were both sent to soothe his friends and both had stayed. If that was what his friends had in mind for him, he wanted no part of it.

"Love." He sneered the word and stood at his full height so she'd have to tip her head back to look at him. So she could not possibly look down on him. "Is that your intent? To make me love you so I find peace and help you fill your bedamned Holy Quiver? You wish to use me to help you fulfill some stupid prophecy? And you'll do what it takes, won't you," he added without giving her a chance to answer. "I know how you work."

Alaric staggered at the force of his words, still unsteady on his feet despite the cold bath. His gut churned and his head pounded in sick-making counterpoint to his heartbeat. He could taste herb on the back of his tongue and below it the flavor of worm, but below that, even more terrible and lovely, the scent and taste of oblivion clung to his senses as though his blood had been turned to it. His fingers curled again to scratch at his belly, where the sleeping dragon was waking. He needed more. It would soothe the itch and the ache and take him away into darkness better than any woman ever could.

"I will never love you," he spat out. "No matter what you do."

All traces of amusement slid from her expression and all warmth left her tone. "I do none of this for love, Alaric. I do this as my duty and my purpose and on occasion my pleasure as well, but I do none of this for love."

"You should go," he muttered with a rub of his eyes.

"Alas for the both of us, I'm bound to stay until I fulfill my duty or I'm dismissed."

"Then I dismiss you," he said.

She shook her head. "You didn't hire me."

They faced off, and though she did, indeed, have to tilt her head back to look at his face, Alaric couldn't shake the feeling that her look had put him at her feet. "You will never be a comfort to me, nor my grace."

He wouldn't allow it.

Her lip curled. "By the Arrow, you are a stubborn fool. I offer you a chance at something few men ever hope to reach, and you don't even need to know how to take it, for I'll give it right to you."

Desire and hunger flared inside him, and Alaric swallowed a burst of bitterness. "Go away. I need—"

"It's gone."

"What?" He could manage no response wiser than that.

"Your supplies of that drug are gone." She gestured at the wardrobe. "You'll get no more. I imagine the sickness has begun, but it will pass soon enough. You'll have to suffer the pain for longer, and I've heard it can be immense, but I'll be here to help you through it."

He had never raised a hand to a woman in his life, but now Alaric pushed her aside with such force that she cried out and stumbled. He barely heard her, so caught with discovering if what she said were true. He flung open the wardrobe doors, dug through the scattered piles of his clothing, and came up with nothing. No small porcelain box, no stoppered bottle, no jeweled spoon or needle.

Vomit burned in his throat, but he barely felt it. He turned and grabbed her by the front of the dress, but his fingers slipped on the smooth material and the buttons cut at his palms. With a cry he grabbed her upper arms and shook her so hard her teeth rattled.

"Damn you to the Void!" he shouted into her face, spittle dotting her cheeks. Her arms were taut with muscle for all they were so slim, but he could wrap his fingers all the way around them, and he squeezed tighter. Tighter still when she made no reply. "Damn you to the Void, you stupid, ugly whore! How dare you?"

The sickness rushed through him, setting him on fire, making him shake. He bared his teeth to make her flinch.

She made no move to get away from him, not when he shook her again. Nor when he shouted, and nor when he snapped his teeth so close to the flesh of her throat he swore he could taste the flavor of her soap. She made him a dog with her gaze, and that was what he became. What he'd been.

"You live in filth!" she shouted into his face, her voice dipping low when he let her go. "Everything you have of beauty has been broken or dirtied, and you live within the trash like an animal that knows no better, but you *do* know better, Alaric. You squeak about love but what I see here tells me you know nothing of it. You know only selfishness and spite. I know naught of the man you were, but of the one I see before I wish to know little more."

He let her go. He stepped back. She looked him up and down and sneered.

"No wonder she left you."

The words shot him surely as an arrow and he went to his knees. His forehead found the floor. Alaric was aware of pain but it couldn't compare to the agony ripping through the rest of him.

When he looked up, she was gone and he was unable to tell if an hour had passed, or a day. Sunlight shafted through the window and hit the same place on the rug it had always done, but that told him nothing. He cradled his head and his palm came away spotted with dried blood. The sickness had passed, at least for the moment, though pain deep within his muscles still locked them tight. His stomach clenched on emptiness.

No wonder she left you.

But she hadn't left him. If she'd left him, she would be gone. He would not have to see her, or listen to her laughter from across the room, or hear her name on someone else's lips. He wouldn't have to suffer knowing she'd sent him away.

He got to his feet, every muscle screaming, but bit back the moan. His joints creaked as though age had settled onto him all at once instead over the passage of years. His stomach no longer leaped up to burn his throat, but the nausea had been little worse than this constant, nagging pain that flared into agony with every step.

He went to the door to the hall but the knob wouldn't turn. Locked in? As though he were a common prisoner? Alaric kicked the door, heedless until the pain that ripped through him indicated that he wore no boots. He fell to the carpet and pounded it until his fists bruised, but that didn't open the lock.

Nor did it bring back the Handmaiden.

He curled into a ball on the floor for a long while, but then got to his feet. He looked around the room, and it tilted every which way as his head swam. He blinked away the red haze and drew in breath after breath until he no longer felt he might fall.

Alaric paused when his bare foot crunched against the remains of a puzzle box of shaved and polished wood. Once the pieces had fit together so smoothly they appeared as one solid block, but at some time over the past few weeks he'd torn it apart and ruined the tiny, coiled springs inside that held it together. What had looked solid and unyielding had proven to be fragile and all too easy to destroy.

He drew back his foot to kick it aside but stopped himself. Instead, he bent to lift the shattered frame with its dangling shreds of wood. He cradled it for a minute in his two palms. Larissa had given him the box. The center, seen only by someone clever enough to undo the puzzle, had held a miniature portrait of her. He looked for it now, knowing the sight of her face would hurt, but looking anyway. It wasn't there, but he didn't throw down the box. He took it to the woodbasket next to the fireplace. It would burn as well as any log.

Alaric turned, his sore foot one more complaint to add to the list, and looked 'round his room. He'd never cared overmuch for the sorts of expensive furnishings Cillian craved. It had never mattered to him what hung on his walls or the name of the maker who built his chair. But it had mattered to his lady, who'd been the one to pick out almost every item in these rooms. It had given her pleasure to use both her coin and his for such a project, and Alaric had never minded, no matter the cost or how he might have to put himself into debt for it. She'd made these rooms more than a simple apartment in a king's castle. She'd made them a luxury.

Broken now, a paradise no longer. Alaric toed aside a stack of papers he couldn't recall throwing to the floor. Beneath rested an inkpot, its contents spread across the carpet upon which he'd once made love to Larissa for an entire afternoon. He could still taste her, and his fingers came to his mouth unbidden at the memory.

Alaric stood, eyes closed, in the center of the room as he fought for one breath. Then another. And the next, each as sharp and hot in his lungs as breathing fire.

When he opened them, nothing had changed. No lady stood waiting, beckoning. No room full of sunshine and laughter, no table laid with food for them to share. She had sent him from her, the laughter that once had suffused him with joy turned horrible in its mocking.

He looked around the room again and breathed deep but found no trace even of her perfume. The stink of spoiled food reached him, and the subtle odor of dirt. He'd have stunk of it himself, had that . . . woman . . . not cleaned him.

Even now his cock twitched at the memory, and he cursed his body for a fool. A disloyal fool at that. She had a soft touch, yet there was no forgetting she could be harsh, too.

He hadn't even asked her name.

Had it mattered? He hadn't sent for her and didn't want her, no matter how his traitorous prick tried to prove otherwise. Now he reached past the drawstring of the trousers she'd forced upon him and pinched his inner thigh hard enough to bring tears to his eyes and a grunt from his lips. Then harder, fiercely enough to bruise.

The desk had already been tidied. She must have done it. Dull anger knocked his innards as he moved toward it, intent on scattering the neat piles of papers she'd made, but his hand stayed at the last moment, and at the sight of the tray of bread and milk she'd told him about. His stomach rumbled and he put a hand on it. Stale bread and milk would have made him retch not so long before but now it looked as good to him as any meal he'd ever eaten.

He fell to without manners, wiping his mouth with the back of his hand. He could eat only a little before his stomach protested and he stifled a belch. He paused, waiting to see if his makeshift supper would exit the way it had arrived, but nothing came up but a sour taste.

He still wanted oblivion. His hands, in fact, shook with the wanting of it. In a few more hours the craving would be very bad, he thought. But not the worst he'd ever undergone.

He might even be able to get through it, if he had to. If he wanted to. As Alaric looked around the room again, he thought of the Handmaiden's smooth touch and her cool gaze. She didn't know him at all, and never would, if he had his way. But he wouldn't give her the pleasure of being right about him.

He was no beast, bound to live in squalor. His lady had not left him, and though she'd turned him away, it was not because of how he lived or dressed or kept his chambers. That Handmaiden was wrong. It was naught he'd done that had ruined his lady's favor . . . Alaric stopped, aware he'd been stooping to lift a pile of books to put them back in their places on the shelves.

Back aching, he held on to the bookshelf with one slim volume in his hand. He stared at it for some long time before sliding it into place, aligned with the others. Then the next.

He'd done nothing to make his lady abandon him. He had, in fact, done everything she wanted, no matter how she pushed. No matter what she asked. Any humiliation had been hers for the taking, any punishment she granted, he'd borne. She had a heavy hand and a sharp tongue, and her sadism was finely honed. She'd always known just where to prick him to force the blood, and which places to pinch to leave a bruise. And he'd given it all to her, whatever she'd asked.

In the end, she'd laughed, her arm looped through another's. A man Alaric didn't even know, some minor lord from an outlying province, come to town in his out-of-fashion boots and his hair too short. He'd looked at her with adoration, though, the same as Alaric always had, and she'd looked back.

He should never have been surprised. He knew her, after all. Lady Larissa was not a woman without reputation. Alas, just as he'd never dreamed she'd give him her favor, once she had he'd never dreamed she would take it away. He'd fallen into the crevasse of her affections and hadn't cared how deep. She became his light, his dark, his everything. He'd given up everything he had to her command and been glad to do it.

He'd left lovers aplenty, some of them brokenhearted though he'd ever been truthful about his whims. If the warnings he provided hadn't sufficed, he'd always supposed it to be their own fault if they lost themselves in him. How different it was with the ribbon on the other wrist.

He loved her, and she no longer loved him, if she ever had. And thinking back, Alaric believed it quite possible she had not, no matter what she'd told him. He ran a fingertip over the leather volumes, put back in their places, and thought how easy it had been to set them right, after all.

The rest of the room took him little longer, for the ruin he'd caused left him little to save. Anything torn or too harshly abused he set aside in a pile to be given out to the pauper's hostel. Anything still in good condition he returned to its place, but even though he had to pause often to catch his breath or ease the ache in his muscles, by the time night fell he'd finished.

He was just ringing for a maid when the door opened. The Handmaiden came in, her arms full of sheets and towels and followed by a maid bearing a tray of food. His stomach rumbled and he stepped forward at once, but a look from the Handmaiden silenced him.

The maid, also silent, set down the tray and retreated at once. The Handmaiden disappeared into the bedchamber, where he'd not yet gone. She came out a moment later, dusting her hands. She looked around the room.

"You did a fine job, Alaric."

He straightened at the familiar way she, a stranger, addressed him. "I thought for sure you'd gone for good."

She looked at him solemnly, her eyes narrowed, before she shook her head. "No. I haven't gone."

Unexpected relief rushed through him, and he cursed it as much as he'd cursed his prick's interest before. He didn't want to wish to impress her, no matter how nice it had been to hear her praise the job he'd done. His gaze fell upon a few of the items he'd yet to tidy—one of them a small portrait of Larissa he hadn't been able to figure out where to put.

Larissa had ever wanted what she didn't have; she thought nothing of stealing a lover or wheedling someone out of a bauble if she thought it would suit her better than it would a companion. She'd kept Alaric longer than many of her suitors and accepted his proposal, but she hadn't become his wife.

Yet how would she feel should she see him on bended knee to another? She could scarcely bear to watch her favorite horse being ridden by a groom or her cast-off gowns on the backs of her servants. How would she feel to see Alaric bent to another woman, even one hired for the purpose?

Perhaps especially one such as that?

Alaric looked the Handmaiden in the eyes. "I plead your mercy for my behavior earlier. It was inexcusable."

"It was excusable," she said quietly. "Perhaps not pleasant, but you had your reasons. However, I expect we shall not need to ever have such a discussion ever again."

By the Void, he'd struck her, hadn't he? If not struck, shaken. A flash of the memory came to him and the heat of shame sent him to his knees without a second thought. "I plead your mercy," he muttered. "I should never have taken a hand to you in that manner."

After what felt like a lifetime, he felt the soft touch of her hand on top of his head. He lifted it to look at her. The Handmaiden, whose name he still didn't know, gave him such a look of sweet compassion he wanted to weep.

"I forgive you. Make no more of it, Alaric. What matters is not what you did but what you shall do."

"And . . . what shall I do?" he asked.

She smiled. "Why, whatever I tell you to, of course."

*L*ove. Alaric had claimed he would refuse her even the hope of it from him, and his words had sliced open a wound in her Mina didn't wish to notice. Not because she longed for such a thing from him, by the Holy Family, no. Mina was a woman of faith; she believed in much she couldn't see or hear or touch . . . but she did not believe in love.

She knew the power of it, certainly, for more than one man had declared it from his knees in front of her. She'd taken it as her due, or as something necessary to lead them to the solace for which they'd depended on her. She'd even believed they meant it. She simply didn't believe it was real. Men had begged her to stay, and she had always gone. She would always go.

But still it was more pleasant to be craved than despised.

More proof she'd been too long without a patron if she was allowing her emotions to get in the way of what she knew must be done. *Selfish is the heart that thinks first of itself,* Mina reminded herself firmly and turned her attention back to Alaric.

He'd not been trained to act the part of serving maid, ladies' maid, or any other type of maid, and it didn't particularly please Mina to have him act as such. It wasn't the act of cleaning she required from him. It was obedience.

If his mind were occupied with organizing books and sweeping the floor, he'd be less apt to worry about the pain in his guts from the lack of the drug. It was gnawing, she knew that, and the pain would be just beginning. She'd had little enough experience with addicts, though she'd brought her entire collection of medicinal teas. Some would help. Some wouldn't.

But for now his belligerence, some part of it from the drugs, the rest from his other pain, had faded. She'd seen a glimmer in his gaze when she returned and knew what it meant. She'd have been more surprised had he greeted her on his knees and with a bent head. If he'd been in that sort of place, he'd scarcely have needed her at all. No, wherever his former lady had taken him, it was not a place Mina wished to go.

She would take him to her own places, in due time.

"Alaric." She said it quietly from her place in the chair by the fire where she'd been watching him go about the tasks she'd set.

He turned, the peasant trousers riding low on his hips. They'd lit no lamps and the fire's red-gold glow reflected off the sheen of sweat covering his chest. He'd become almost frantic in his efforts as the sun dipped lower outside the window and finally disappeared. She didn't think either of them believed it was from his desire to please her.

He blinked and swallowed hard, then wiped the back of his hand across his lips. His chest heaved with a breath. His nipples tightened, though it was hard for her to tell if it were from arousal or the chill of fever.

"Rest, now."

He shook his head. "No. I . . . you were right. I've made a mess and I need to clean it up. This is an intolerable mess. It's not fit for you . . . not fit for me . . ."

His voice scratched and rasped. Alaric waved a hand when his voice failed him. He closed his eyes, bit his lower lip. He cried out and went to one knee, a hand clutching at and toppling the nearest chair. It landed with a crash.

She was on her feet at once. "Alaric, you must rest now."

He shook his head, the blond locks lank with sweat. He bent his head, so she couldn't see his face. Mina went to him. "Come."

She took the hand still holding the chair and helped him to his feet. Took him to his bed, which she had fitted with fresh sheets while he'd been cleaning. She laid him down and he went without protest, his body already twitching. She took his trousers down over his hips and off, then undressed quickly and slipped in next to him with nothing but skin between them.

His prick rose, though she doubted he meant to make any sort of love. She curled herself against his back and stroked his shoulders when the muscles spasmed. She crooned to him in wordless songs when he muttered and cried out. When he sweated through the top sheet, she got up and replaced it with a clean one.

All through the night she eased him as best she could with everything she could do. None of it was enough, but it was all she had. When morning broke, so did the fever, and so did he.

She followed him to the bath chamber while he was sick. She cleaned him up without a moment's hesitation. When he begged her for the oblivion, she gave him tea mixed with herbs, instead. When he made to leave and found the door still locked, he raged at her for the key.

He called her the worst names and made the most evil threats, none of which moved her. When at last he collapsed on the wet, cold floor of the bath chamber, she covered him with a cloth and rang for breakfast. She took it from the maid when she arrived and sent her off with a note for Cillian and Edward. Then she bathed herself quickly and dressed in a fresh gown identical to the one she'd worn the day before. She smoothed the fabric on her arms and bodice, and over her belly. She combed her hair and brushed her teeth, all while Alaric moaned and jerked on the floor in a fitful sleep.

And when he woke, she brought him a bowl of hot broth and spooned it into his mouth. She bathed his brow with cool cloths and got him back into bed, again with fresh sheets she'd put there. She sat with him until he slept again, this time without twitches and jerks and maybe, without dreams.

She slept herself and woke to find him sitting, staring at her. Shadows circled his eyes, but his gaze was clear. He'd dressed in a pair of loose-fitting linen trousers of the same cut as the peasant garb she'd given him, but clean. He'd brushed his hair, too, and bound it at the nape of his neck with a length of cord.

Mina sat. "You've been up and about."

Alaric nodded. "I . . . yes."

"How do you feel?"

"As though I'd been trod on by wild boars."

She sat up and stretched, aware she'd slept in her clothes. "That well?"

Alaric ducked his head. His laughter pleased her, weak as it was. "It was a long night."

"Yes. Have you eaten?" She watched him carefully. He looked tired, but not ill, his muscles without the twitching that indicated craving.

"Yes. Thank you."

"And did you try the door?" She smiled at the way his gaze shuttered just before he ducked his head again and grinned. He had a charming manner that seemed mostly unfeigned. She could work with that.

"If I say no, will you know that I'm lying?"

"I will, indeed."

"And what would you do?" He tilted his head to slant her a look.

Mina moved to the edge of the bed to put her feet on the floor. She looked over her shoulder at him as she got up. "Do you want me to say I'll punish you?"

"Would you?"

She stood. "What do you know about Handmaidens, Alaric?"

"I know you believe that for each person you bring to absolute solace, another Arrow will go into Sinder's Holy Quiver. And that when the Quiver's filled, the Holy Family will return. I know you're trained in providing solace to your patrons. But I'll confess, I've met only two of your Sisters and . . . neither was as . . . bold as you."

She raised a brow. "Perhaps their patrons didn't require them to be."

"No," he said after a bare pause. "I don't expect any Handmaiden given to Edward or Cillian would be."

Mina smoothed her gown. "You might not know much about me or my Sisters, Alaric, but you are far from my first patron. And you are not the first to ask me such a question. So I shall tell you what I tell them all. If I felt it would bring you solace to punish you, I would do it. But I don't wish to be your mother or your nursemaid, so I hope there shall be no punishment for naughtiness needed."

Alaric nodded. "But you . . . you know me. They told you about me, else you'd not have been so . . ."

"Bold?" She laughed. "My sweet one, I know no other way to be. Think you this is all for your benefit?"

"Isn't it?"

Sinder bless him, the confusion was both adorable and expected. "We were matched, this is true, and it's true as well I am able to bend myself to fit a patron if necessary. Such is my purpose. But the Order doesn't send me to patrons who don't need what I can best provide. I am who I am at all times, not merely because it's what you need."

He blinked, understanding swimming up into his gaze from someplace deep inside. "But you are what I need?"

"I hope to be."

"For at least one small moment, yes?" He stood, also.

She hadn't forgotten the words he'd shouted the day before, or the way he'd put his hands on her in anger. It was reason enough for her to leave, even if the drug had forced the actions, but he'd apologized. She believed he meant it. There was hope here, even if it was not for love. "That is the goal, yes."

He moved within an arm's length, but didn't touch her. "You took care of me, all through the night."

"Of course I did. I am your comfort and your grace," Mina said quietly. "I told you that. I'm your Handmaiden."

"My . . . lady . . . My lady Larissa would never have done such a thing."

Mina brushed a tendril of golden hair off his face and let her hand linger on his cheek. "Then she was no true mistress."

He moved from her touch, and though it wasn't unexpected, it did sting her pride just a touch. They stared at each other for the space of a few breaths. He looked away first.

"If you clean yourself up appropriately," she said finally, "I think you might escort me around the gardens. I've heard they're lovely."

Chapter 19

She'd taken his arm as though it were the most natural event in the world. They fell into step beside each other even more naturally, his gait shortening to make sure he didn't walk too fast. Her head came only to his shoulder, and he was shamed to recall how fragile she felt in his grip. He could have broken her, but she walked now beside him as easily as if they'd known each other for years.

"I don't even know your name," he said suddenly, surprised he hadn't even thought of it before now."

"My name is Determinata."

He stopped so short his boots left a mark in the grass. "Truly?"

"I don't lie."

Alaric pondered this. "It suits you, I'll say that."

"It's meant to. The Order doesn't give out names lightly. But you needn't address me by that name," she said with a smile.

"What should I call you?" A small burst of unease twisted in his stomach. Now she would command him to call her *mistress*, or *lady*. He couldn't do it. Not in the way she would have it.

She looked up at him and let go of his arm. The breeze tugged the fringes of her hair. Sunshine, just a hint too bright, slanted down across her face. In his chambers he'd thought her eyes dark, but here in the light he could see they were mostly green. And frank, he thought as they studied each other. It was easy to believe she didn't lie.

"You may call me Mina."

Alaric watched as a cloud passing overhead cast her face into shadow. "Mina?"

"It's also my name." She took his arm again and started walking, the hem of her gown sweeping across the short-clipped grass.

"But you don't wish me to call you something more formal?"

She stopped again to face him. "Such as my lady?"

Alaric shuddered. "No. Not that."

It was what he'd called Larissa, his one true lady. Mina—and it would take some effort for him to think of her that way for Determinata suited her so well—narrowed her eyes to watch him, as though she understood. He thought perhaps she did, better than anyone.

"I don't hold the use of my name as a privilege. Anyone can call me by it, and many do. It's not what you name me but how you behave for me that matters."

She wasn't like the other women of his acquaintance, most who simpered and flirted behind their fans. She wasn't like Larissa, who'd met his gaze as boldly but had held her favor above his head the same as she'd lift a treat to make a dog leap. Alaric's guts tensed at the memory, then again with a sudden flare of craving.

She noticed. "Walk with me."

He forced himself to the steady pace she set, though the sunshine had become far too bright and the wind too chill. It had been how long since his last needle-full of oblivion? Too long. The crunch of stone beneath his boots raked at his ears, but Alaric kept his head high.

Mina's grip tightened on his arm. "Tell me the names of those flowers, there."

He looked to where she pointed as they drew closer. Red-petaled heads danced on the breeze and sent even chillier fingers down his spine. Next to them a bush of spiked green leaves bloomed with yellow flowers. "Mother's slippers."

"And the yellow?"

"Something buttons. Captain's buttons, I think."

"You know your flowers. Very nice." Her touch should have been too light for him to feel, yet each caress of her fingertips pressed him through his coat and shirt. "And the blue ones, farther down the path?"

They walked. In the distance he saw the flowers she mentioned. His mouth opened to answer but a voice from behind them called his name. Alaric turned.

"Cillian."

Dressed as always in the height of fashion, Cillian sauntered down the path toward them. "Alaric! And . . . my lady Determinata."

Alaric had never seen Cillian at a loss for words. Now his friend looked back and forth from Alaric to Mina and spread his hands, silent. Alaric's guts took another slow tumble, thinking of how low he'd fallen, that his friends should have taken it upon themselves to fit him with a Handmaiden. He swallowed a surge of emotion and blessed the Quiver Edward wasn't there to see him. He didn't think he could face him. Not yet.

"I've just had the most delightful letter," Cillian said. "From Edward. His lady wife has had their child, Alaric. Our dear one is a papa."

The earth slid a bit beneath Alaric's feet, though why the news of Edward's fatherhood should so rock him, he didn't know. He'd seen the man with Stillness. He knew how much Edward loved her. But somehow, knowing it before when he'd had his lady to hold him up had made all the difference.

"Please send him my congratulations." The words slipped out from numb lips.

Cillian looked at him askance. "You might present them yourself. They're not opening the house to guests just yet, but I'm to go there in a few days. You'll come along."

Alaric said nothing and Cillian only stared. Mina's fingers tightened again on his arm.

"Alaric," she said. "I would know the name of those blue flowers. Go and wait for me by them."

He thought of balking, for who was she, after all, to order him? But he wasn't so far gone he couldn't see what she meant to do. Give him the space he sorely needed. Some time. He nodded and gave Cillian a half bow that set the other man back a step, a startled look upon his face.

He looked back over his shoulder to see Cillian and Mina locked in serious conversation. Cillian was frowning, his arms crossed, the familiar "I want" look on his face. Mina didn't look as though she meant to bend to whatever Cillian was proposing, and a smile flitted across Alaric's mouth. He'd known her just a day, but she would be a formidable opponent even to the King of Firth.

At the end of the path he stopped to stare at the blue flowers. He didn't know the name of them. He'd never cared. He didn't care now, but for the fact she'd asked it of him and it was more natural for him to answer than to refuse.

"M'lord." A bramble-rough voice edged out from behind the bush, and Alaric startled.

He'd never learned the man's name, though once it had been

Larissa's pleasure to have the stranger suck Alaric's cock while she watched. Alaric shuddered at the memory, and then again at the smile on the other man's face. He had dark, lazy eyes and a grin that left them cold.

He'd been the one to give Alaric his first taste of oblivion.

"M'lord," the man repeated. "I've not seen you about lately. You've been absent even from court. And from our lady's chamber. Ah, your mercy. I misspoke. She is no longer—"

"Choke on it," Alaric gritted out.

The stranger lifted a brow and pursed his lips and cocked a hip, though he seemed not as casual as he wanted Alaric to believe. His gaze flicked over Alaric's shoulder. "Your master is going to work himself into apoplexy by something that chit is saying."

Alaric didn't turn. "You speak of the king with so little respect? You should mind your tongue."

"You can mind my tongue any time you like." The stranger swiped the tongue in question across his teeth.

Alaric had no intentions of doing any such thing, but as much as it disgusted himself, he leaned toward the man. "You still serve her?"

The man raised a brow. "As I ever have. Of course. As I always will."

She'd put Alaric from her, but not this man. Knowing it only knotted his guts further. Alaric spat to the side. The man smiled again with another lick of his teeth.

"You shouldn't let it wound you so. I have no fear in telling you she keeps me around because I cost her nothing and bring her much. It's not your fault she let you draw too close."

Alaric didn't answer, just turned to focus his attention on the blue flowers.

"It's eating at you, though, innit?" The stranger's hot breath blew on the back of Alaric's neck. "Not just her. But the other, yes?

I know. I know how it feels, brother. But why make it so? Why not just let me help you with that?"

Alaric looked down to the box in the man's hand. It might have been costly, but now the white porcelain was grimed, some of the jewels missing from the design. The gold hasp was broken. The box fell open in the man's palm to reveal a faded inner lining and a clear glass bottle in which the yellow liquid shimmered.

He was already reaching for it when he heard the crunch of footsteps on the path behind him. The man turned, his smile a lie on his lips. Alaric's fingers twitched, but he withdrew without taking the box.

"The flowers, Alaric," Mina said as her gaze moved smoothly back and forth between the two men. "I asked you the name."

"I bid you good day," the stranger said and fled.

Alaric watched him go and even took a step toward him, but stopped himself. He knew enough to recognize his need was artificial, that it could be ignored. Oblivion tempted him but if that man knew so plainly of Alaric's need for the drug, that meant Larissa must, as well. And though he didn't care if Cillian or Edward or even Mina knew he'd given in to its dark embrace, suddenly it very much mattered if his former lady knew it.

She'd laugh behind her fan at the news. Mocking. He'd seen her do it before, about lovers she'd spurned. One had thought to end his life from leaping off a bridge. He hadn't died, but Alaric thought he must have wished he did. Larissa had gone to visit the poor wretch and come home beaming, cheeks flushed and eyes sparkling, to regale her inner circle with the story of how he'd clung to her hand even though his fingers had all been broken.

"The flowers, Alaric."

"Blue . . . blue . . ." He stumbled on the name, tongue searching for what his mind refused to give. His fists clenched. He looked at her.

"Take a breath and think," Mina said.

"I don't know it! I don't know the name of your bedamned flowers!" He tore one from the bush and ripped the petals from it.

Mina's cool gaze served to make him feel even more ridiculous. "I would have the name, sirrah, and no further discussion."

"And what will you do if I cannot give it to you?"

She stared in silence.

Alaric spat again to clear the taste of oblivion rising on his tongue. If his action offended her, she showed no sign. She kept her gaze upon his face.

Had she demanded his obedience with threats, or sneered, or given him any indication she thought ill of him for not performing, Alaric thought he would simply turn on his heel and walk away from her. But Mina kept up her steady gaze. She didn't point out to him how she'd nursed him through the night, nor offer to remind him of her purpose. She waited.

"Blue . . . bonnets," he said at last. "No. Blue slippers. No. No. Blue coats! They're called blue coats."

Relief sighed through him. The taste of oblivion didn't dissipate, but his stomach settled. He moved to the next bush in the row.

"Roses. Named for the king's mother, Ingrid. These are also roses. I don't know what breed, but they come in white and pink as well."

He turned to her, triumphant. Mina smiled and held out her hand. He took it.

She was lovely, but her smile made her the more so. And she was, whether he wished it or no, his. And he hers, he supposed, for the time. Alaric brought her knuckles to his lips and kissed them, helpless all at once against the impulse to bring another smile to her face.

It worked, and he let out a sigh. "Thank you."

"You're welcome," she said.

Chapter 20

Three days had passed since her first arrival, and so had the worst of Alaric's illness. He'd suffered the shakes, the nausea, the mood swings, but ultimately, Mina thought, it was not the drug that had turned him so desolate. He was heartsick, not drug-sick. Oblivion had been a means of easing his pain and later an easy excuse for further downward spiraling. She'd eased him through the initial drug craving. Now she needed to get him past his heart's wound.

He'd taken to her simple commands more easily than any patron she'd ever had. More than any man, she had to admit, watching as Alaric paused to check the level of her glass with his gaze before turning his attention back to the papers on his desk. She had set him to the task of organizing his accounts and settling his debts, for just as no soul could find solace amongst a mess, neither could anyone find peace with creditors banging on the door.

If indeed they should, she thought and turned the page of the novel she only feigned reading. If Alaric's friends had thought it no financial burden to acquire her services, they would surely keep the debt collectors at bay. Someone was keeping everyone away, she knew that, for aside from the maids who brought and took away their meals, nobody else came knocking.

If he felt abandoned by this, Alaric didn't say. He seemed glad enough to stay sequestered with her in his chambers, aside from their daily stroll in the gardens. Though Edward had sent an invitation to his home and Cillian had left a note encouraging Alaric to join him and some other young lords for evening entertainments, he'd refused. As for attending court, he'd made no mention, though she knew he'd gone often in the past.

She finished her glass of cool honeyed tea deliberately and turned her gaze to the words on the page. In a moment, Alaric was there with the pitcher, though he didn't pour until she looked up and nodded. He had a natural inclination toward service, tempered with a lack of assumption that he could know exactly what she wanted. He was there to fill her cup or pull out her chair, to offer her the best cuts of meat, but he didn't overstep.

She watched him pour the glass full and set the pitcher aside, and her pulse throbbed with sudden fierceness in her temples and the base of her throat. Between her thighs. They'd shared a bed every night, skin to skin, and not once had he laid a hand upon her.

"Alaric."

He paused at the low, throaty sound of his name. His eyes widened, just barely. When they left the room, he dressed as a gentleman, for it didn't suit her and wouldn't help him to be displayed as anything else. Here in private, however, he wore no shirt, his drawstring trousers dipping low, the way she'd told him pleased her. Mina saw the vein in his throat throb, the same as hers just had.

She set aside her book. Alaric's gaze followed it, then moved back to hers. When his tongue crept between his lips, her breath caught.

"You have well pleased me these past few days."

He bent his head. "Thank you."

"I thought you might fight me more," she said.

He smiled. "I thought I would, too."

"But you haven't." She didn't mention that first day, though they both knew of it. "You have done just as I told you, to the best of your abilities."

"Because you seem to know what is best for me," he said somewhat gruffly. "I don't have to be a scholar to know it."

"Knowing something doesn't necessarily mean you might accept it, and so readily."

"Have you had other patrons who didn't?" He seemed curious rather than jealous.

She thought of past patrons who'd been less able to bend to her whim or to accept the need to do so. There had been few who did not eventually accept her as mistress, but Mina considered it their loss. As she'd told Alaric, she might take a strap to a man's back if she believed it brought him the peace it was her purpose to provide, but it was not her pleasure to do it for any other reason.

So far, Alaric had done what she told him to do because, as he'd said, he could see she had his best interests at heart. It meant he was smart, a trait she admired in anyone but appreciated even more so in a patron. In a lover.

"Tell me I've not been your most difficult patron." His voice held a hint of teasing.

Mina appreciated that, too. A man on his knees was particularly arousing to her, but not if it meant he never knew how to rise to his feet. "You haven't been. I assure you."

"Nor your best, I'd wager." She heard a hint of something in his tone and knew it well. For an instant sorrow gripped her at how like other men he was. She shouldn't expect him to be different— she must needs remember that though there might be many patrons in her life, she was his only Handmaiden.

"Never mind," Alaric said. "I know you said you wouldn't lie to me. I shouldn't have asked such a question simply to feed my own vanity."

"All my patrons are different and unique to me," Mina said.

Alaric took in a slow breath, and she watched the play of muscles in his shoulders and chest with heat filling her.

She pushed him to the ground in front of her with her gaze. "I would have you please me further."

A slow ripple, a current of tension, passed over him. "I would like to."

"How would you please me?" She breathed.

Alaric sank to his knees in front of her and didn't touch her. She watched him, her breath coming faster. Her nipples tightened. She'd grasped his cock and stroked him, that first day, but had never touched him with passion.

"I would like to taste you," he murmured, gaze moving down over her body to center for a moment on her lap, that she might have no doubts as to his meaning. His eyes caught hers again. "If I may."

In reply she inched up the hem of her gown to her ankles. Alaric went onto his heels to watch her. He put his hands on her ankles and followed the path of her skirt as she lifted it. By the time he reached her thighs, his fingers trembled and his every breath caught.

Hers, too. It had been overlong since she'd had a patron she'd allowed to touch her. Most, though they believed otherwise, didn't require sexual congress with her and no few number of them would have been set back by it. It had been a long time, too, since she'd taken a lover, and his was a lover's touch when he pressed his mouth to her inner thigh. Mina's mind knew the difference, but her body, traitorous though it might be, didn't seem to.

"Ah," she breathed when his lips caressed the smooth skin. And again, "ah," when his tongue crept out to swipe along it.

Her fingers clutched at her gown, bunching it so she had something to grab. Alaric shifted closer. His hot breath found her flesh, and then the heat of his tongue. He tasted her, oh yes, with lips and tongue and tender kisses the likes of which had her hips rocking upward within moments.

Her hand slipped from its nest in her gown and found his hair. Her fingers twined, pulling. Alaric groaned, and Mina's body leaped at the noise.

His lips fastened on her clitoris and gently suckled. His fingers found their way inside her to probe and stroke, lifting her higher. Pleasure built and spread within her, filling all the spaces that often felt so empty. She rocked herself against his mouth.

Mina looked down at him, that man on his knees. She watched the muscles of his shoulders shift and bunch as he worked his tongue against her. She watched the pleasure on his face as he made love to her with his mouth. Many men would've had their hands on their pricks when they did this, but Alaric had focused all his attentions on her. That was what tipped her over the edge more than the skill of his mouth and hands; his unwavering devotion to her pleasure, with no hint of a reward for himself.

She climaxed with an unstifled shout. He cried out, too, maybe because of the fierce tug she gave his hair. Alaric spent another few moments with his mouth between her legs before he looked up, smile glistening.

Mina drew in a slow, long breath before she pulled him upward with a hand on his shoulder. He came willingly enough, looking a bit confused. She kissed his mouth and he pulled back, gaze wary. He didn't protest, but it was clear he'd not been expecting the embrace.

She let her hand linger on his cheek before she drew him closer to kiss him again. His mouth softened against hers this time, his lips parting when she urged them to. His hands slipped to her waist, holding gently.

He broke the kiss and ducked his head against her shoulder, pulling her closer. Mina held him with her legs tucked tight to his sides. The chair wasn't the best suited for such a position, and she knew his knees had to be fair aching at this point, but she didn't push him away. She stroked a hand down his bare skin, feeling the bumps of his spine. His mouth worked against her throat but he didn't speak.

She Waited.

Most often Handmaidens Waited in a variety of kneeling positions, but Mina had never been the sort to kneel for any reason other than her own comfort. She drew in a breath and let one out and counted the stars of infinity in her mind. She opened her mind to emptiness and floated on it. Her body had been sated, which helped. She gave him the comfort of her silence and embrace.

"I know it's wrong to be so grateful for you," he whispered at last. "I know a man must needs stand on his feet and determine what path is best for him to take. I know this. And I have ever done so. But . . ."

Mina turned her face to press her lips to his shoulder. He tasted of sweat and the faintest residual tang of oblivion still rising from his pores. She gave a low, wordless hum. He buried his face deeper against her.

"Sometimes, it is of great relief to need not guess what is required of you. Yes?"

He nodded then, and got to his feet to pace in front of her. Mina pushed her gown down to her ankles and watched him. The front of his trousers still bulged, but she didn't think he was thinking of his prick. Alaric ran a hand over his hair and his fingers caught, tangling.

"Yes. Yes, it is a relief. There is much expected of a man. Learn in school, gain a position. Take a wife." He laughed, bitterly, and didn't look at her. "Yet I've never had a head for schooling and my position in this court is because of the benevolence of my friend, not any skills I've ever had. And I can accept that, for it makes my parents happy to know their son has risen beyond what they could provide. What they still provide, as a matter of fact, with my yearly income."

He went to the window and looked out, one long arm stretched out above his head. "And I don't care, as others might, that I'm not smart or skilled or that I'll never gain great wealth from either."

She would've refuted his lack of intelligence or skill, but Mina only listened.

Alaric turned, one hand splayed on his belly. "I will only ever be what I am."

"As will any of us," Mina told him.

"I have been so very, very stupid," Alaric said.

Mina got to her feet and offered her hand for his kiss. "Shhh. There are few mistakes that cannot be repaired."

He needn't, if he's not able." Cillian shook his head with a frown. "If he's not well."

"Alaric isn't ill," Mina said.

Edward shifted in his chair, one long leg crossing over the other. Shadows dusked his eyes and he hid more than one yawn behind his hand, the consequences, perhaps, of the child his wife had so recently borne. "Perhaps he's not suited for it, then."

Mina lifted a brow to show him what she thought of that, and Edward shrugged. Cillian tapped the table with his pen, spattering ink over his clothes, his hands, the paper. Mina sighed and got up to hand him a blotting cloth, which he took with a startled glance.

"He's not ill, and he's suited to any task you should provide him, I think. He's certainly capable of it, at any rate. You did it, after all." Mina let her judgment rest on Cillian's shoulders.

The king, who had the far-reaching reputation of temper, didn't rise to her bait. His brow furrowed and he chewed at his lower lip. "I hated being the Minister of Fashion. I thought it a position my father fobbed off on me to keep me out of the way."

"Is that why you granted it to Alaric?"

Cillian and Edward exchanged looks, and Cillian nodded. "He wasn't . . . well. But I wanted him in my cabinet. You understand."

She didn't, not beyond the most limited knowledge of how such matters worked. Mina shrugged and fixed him with a steady gaze she wasn't surprised to note he ducked. "You gave him the position but allowed him to lie fallow in it. He's not done a lick of work on it, based on the papers I saw on his desk. He's done naught but wallow in his grief and self-indulgence. How could you, his friends, allow him to sink so low?"

They shared another glance, those two men who fancied themselves lords but who were acting like lads. Mina bit back a smile at their shamed faces. These were men who ruled their households—one of them ruled a country, for Sinder's sake! And yet neither could look her in the eye.

"You must have thought it would be so simple," she mused aloud. "Having me come to clean him up, yes? It would be so much easier, and would set your minds at ease, to know you'd done whatever you could for him."

Edward, no longer yawning, frowned. "You should watch your tone."

"Should I?" Mina stood taller, lifted her chin, let her hands hang open at her sides. She didn't miss the way they both looked her over from neck to hem, how the severe lines of her costume impressed them no matter how they tried to hide it. She was far from their ideal woman, she had no trouble seeing that, but they respected her.

"You should, for no other reason than mercy." Cillian's quiet tone turned her toward him.

"I should grant you mercy from what? The knowledge you behaved badly, or that you were so caught up in your own lives you neglected a friend?" Mina's lip curled, just enough.

"We didn't mean for it to be that way. Have you never focused on yourself to the exclusion of others?" Edward leaned forward in his chair.

"I'm a Handmaiden. I do not exclude others in favor of myself."

Cillian nodded. "And you're here to help him, yes? So help him. We want our friend back, that's all. The way he was."

"Not the way he was," Edward contradicted quietly. "None of us are the way we were. But yes, we'd like him back. He's been too long lost. And before you judge us again, I can tell you I do take responsibility for it. I know the part I played. But I feel helpless to do more than I've done."

Mina believed him. Both of them, actually, for both were sincere in their expressions of love for their friend. "If you love him, as you say, then you must insist he again take up his work. Give him an assignment as simple as balancing the accounts if you don't feel he's ready to leap into responsibility for writing new taxes. There are others in the Ministry of Fashion, yes? Working while he doesn't?"

"Alaric is my minister and as such has the right to appoint others to serve under him in the council, but he hasn't. All those who served me continue their work," Cillian said.

"Without the minister at work, how much has been accomplished?"

Cillian gave her a rueful grin. "Not as much as needs finishing. I thought of the job as near to useless, but now I know better."

"So you do need him at work, then. It's not simply a throwaway job you granted him as your friend."

"Some would say so," Edward muttered, and Cillian shot him a look.

Mina didn't know Edward's position in Cillian's cabinet, or if he had one beyond councilor and friend. Whatever he'd been assigned, however, it seemed assured he was competent enough at it. As Alaric would be, she knew, if only he found it necessary to be.

"I can do much with him, my lords, but I can't force him to attend to his duties to you."

"No?" Cillian arched a brow. "I would think you could force him to attend to anything you wished."

She smiled. "You know that's not true."

Edward smiled, too. "Perhaps Cillian only wishes to imagine it for his own pleasure."

Cillian made a rude gesture, but Edward only smiled fondly. Watching them, Mina was struck by their closeness. Edward had a wife and Cillian was in the midst of the drawn-out dance surrounding a political engagement, but to look at them one might never know they were married. Not that she believed either to be unfaithful, merely that together, the pair had a closeness not all men shared.

"You three," she said, watching yet more closely. "You were close friends, yes?"

"The best," Cillian said stoutly, and at once.

"Not were. Are," Edward replied as firmly.

"But something happened. You're not as close as once you were." She pressed an unseen wound, and both men stole their glances from hers. "Think you Alaric's problems are not only because his mistress put him so cruelly from her?"

"Perhaps it could be said Alaric did ever wish for something . . . more," Edward allowed, grudgingly and without looking at her.

From Edward, then. Not from Cillian, who scowled and tapped his foot in its pretty shoe. Mina studied the dark-haired man thoroughly, not seeing what was so splendid it could command such love and loyalty from not just one man, but two . . . and from a former Sister, besides! He was handsome enough, and perhaps could be cordial, but so far as she was concerned his value had been vastly inflated.

"And did you tell him it couldn't be?"

Edward shook his head slowly and met her gaze. "I thought he understood."

"I'm sure he did. But that doesn't mean it felt any better to him. And then to give himself wholeheartedly to that woman, as you say he did. No wonder he despaired." Mina didn't quite shake her finger at the two of them, knowing they were men and only so much could be expected of them. "This is not solely for me to repair. I will do my best, but . . . woman I begin and woman I shall end. I'm not a magicreator."

"Nobody expects you to be!" Cillian cried, affronted.

Mina stared at him long and hard until high color crept into his cheeks. "You'd be surprised at how many people do."

Alaric looked up when Edward entered the room and his hand arrested itself at once in its journey across the top of the desk. His fingers clenched hard on the cleaning rag. He wanted to toss it aside but kept it clutched tight. His chin lifted, waiting for Edward to take note.

Edward looked tired . . . and mussed. "Alaric."

Alaric put down the cleaning cloth and dusted his hands. "Where's Mina?"

Edward had lied too few times to him for Alaric to be certain he was doing it now, but he thought his friend might be. "I don't know. I thought she'd be here with you?"

"No, she . . . left me here." She'd left him with strict instructions about what he must do while she was gone, but no mention of where she was going or when she'd return. He knew that game for what it was, and it had still lifted his cock with every passing minute, wondering if she'd be pleased when she came back.

Edward looked uncomfortable, as though he'd come upon Alaric in some sort of compromising position instead of polishing the wood of a desk. He shifted from foot to foot and looked every place but at his friend until finally, Alaric moved round the edge of the desk to stand directly in front of him.

"What fly's gotten into your guts?"

Edward still looked everywhere but at him. "I came to see how you were feeling."

Alaric looked around the room, tidied and organized by his own hands to Mina's exacting specifications. He'd lived in these rooms long enough for them to become familiar, but he'd never quite come to feel they were his alone. Larissa had chosen them and encouraged him to petition the king for them, and she'd been the one to furnish them to her taste. Edward had rarely visited Alaric there, and seeing him now only accentuated Alaric's lack of attachment to them.

"Better. Thank you." He knew Edward couldn't ignore his friend's loose trousers or the lack of shirt.

Was that the reason for Edward's hot cheeks? His shifty gaze and shiftier stance? Alaric shifted his own gaze to try and catch Edward's but it eluded him.

"Good. That's good. Cillian sends his regards."

Alaric waited for more, but Edward went to the window and looked out, seemingly satisfied with silence. "You look tired. I'd think your lady wife would take better care of you than that. At least, she used to."

Edward's laugh was muffled. "She's been rather more busy taking care of our son, a more demanding man than I dare to be right now."

Alaric hadn't forgotten about Edward's son, but it had slipped his mind. "Your mercy, Edward. I should've sent my regards. I should've come to see you. Cillian said you'd had an open house to welcome the babe."

Edward turned, frowning. "You weren't well. I hold no grudge on it. You'll come see him as soon as you're . . . able."

Edward's hesitation and the dance of his words hurt worse than the craving for oblivion. Once, and not so long ago, he and Edward had been able to share anything and everything, had even been able to share thoughts without the need for words. By Sinder's Blue Balls, they'd even shared more than one woman, the last being the one now become Edward's wife.

Was that Edward's concern? That Alaric should visit them to pay his respects to Edward's wife and child but overstep his welcome with improper advances? That Edward might think such a thing churned Alaric's guts and angered him, as well.

He joined Edward at the windowsill, leaning with one arm up to stare through the glass at the night falling beyond. Edward didn't inch away from him, but his body tensed. He kept his gaze on the scene outside, even when Alaric leaned closer.

"Edward, what by the Void is wrong with you?"

Edward kissed him.

Hard, and long, and unexpected, the kiss stole Alaric's breath and threatened to strangle him. In all the years he'd dreamed of such a thing, it had never felt like this. He must have gasped in shock, because in the next moment he tasted Edward's tongue, felt Edward's hand on the back of his neck as his friend pulled him closer. Stunned, Alaric couldn't even protest. His eyes fluttered closed and his hand came up to press on Edward's chest.

Sanity returned with his next breath, and he pushed Edward away. "What the . . . why . . . what are you doing?"

Alaric touched his mouth, which felt bruised. Edward, breathing hard, tried to kiss him again. Alaric shoved him back and looked automatically toward the door, hoping he wouldn't see Mina watching.

Edward let out a slow, strangled sigh. "Alaric. I have ever been . . . we have ever . . . I am . . ."

It was so rare a thing to see Edward struggle so for words, Alaric could only watch for too long before he took pity on his friend. He put a hand over Edward's mouth, hushing him. Edward quieted, then put his hand over Alaric's and took it away but didn't let go.

"I plead your mercy, Alaric."

"For what?" His heart had beat in a thunder a few breaths before but now settled like stone inside his chest.

Edward blew out a ragged breath. "For never admitting I knew how you felt about me."

A sudden, horrendous memory of school ripped through Alaric's mind, and he took a half-staggering step back. He'd been hiding beneath his covers, prick in his fist and breath coming fast, eyes closed, imagination filled with thoughts of Edward as he'd seen him only moments before, bare-chested and wet from the baths. Laughing. Hair falling too long over his eyes and being flung back with one hand while Cillian slapped at his arse with the edge of a towel. In his mind Edward had reached a hand to pull him close.

In his mind, Edward's kiss had never made Alaric feel like this.

They stared at one another until Edward once again looked away. Though the room was warm from the fire, a chill rippled over Alaric's bare skin. He'd been bare dozens of times in front of Edward, barer than this, but he suddenly felt more naked than he ever had. He grabbed up his shirt from the chair and slipped it over his arms, buttoning it with stiff fingers.

"You're my friend," Alaric said when it seemed silence would strangle them both. "I've never doubted you knew it."

Edward cupped Alaric's cheek before letting his hand slide down to rest on Alaric's shoulder. The weight of it shouldn't have been as heavy as it was. Alaric couldn't bring himself to pull away.

Edward had ever been an ideal. Taller. Stronger. Smarter, handsomer, richer. Better loved. There'd been times with the two of them, Cillian and Edward, Alaric had felt as though he were running along three steps behind. But that had been in school, when they were boys and young men. Though they were scarcely older now, things had changed.

Alaric took a step back at the thought of it. Things had changed. Between them and within himself. Edward, seeing the step, perhaps mistook it for retreat and moved forward to snag Alaric's wrist.

"I have been unfair to you, Alaric."

Alaric had never thought to be here, this way, with Edward staring from misty eyes at him. He'd never thought he might not wish to have his friend's hand in his own, or that Edward's ever-present face might have been replaced in his mind with that of someone else. Even on the floor at Larissa's boots, performing like a lapdog for her every whim, Edward's face had sometimes swum up from the darkness to remind Alaric there was more.

Things had changed, indeed.

"You haven't," Alaric said. "Truly, Edward, you haven't."

In Edward's dark eyes Alaric caught a flash of a bed, entangled limbs. A woman's blonde unbound hair. And the sight of his own face, twisted in passion. It was all in his head, of course, his imagination as vivid as it had ever been, but somehow, he thought Edward might be thinking of the same moment.

"I don't know why it's been me. You and Cillian both . . . you both have ever been my dear friends."

Even now Alaric expected the flash of envy that always came when Edward spoke of Cillian. "As you've both been to me."

Edward let go of Alaric's wrist. "Did we leave you behind?"

Hearing it put out that way, Alaric could only swallow the rush of emotions. Mostly anger and envy. No small part grief.

"Yes. You did."

Edward sagged and turned again to lean against the window frame. One hand came up to cover his eyes. Alaric watched him for a moment as the world spun beneath them, but unlike it had done in the past when he spun with it, now he stood still.

"But should you have waited for me? Instead of moving on to find your solace with your lady wife, should you have stayed behind to wait until I caught up?" Alaric shook his head. "Should Cillian?"

Alaric laughed. "Could he have? I've seen you both with those women, and I don't believe you could. No, Edward."

"But all of this—"

Alaric's voice grew stony. "All of this was my own doing. And I have nobody to blame but myself."

Edward stared until a small smile crept over his mouth. "She's done it, has she not? Done this to you."

At first Alaric thought Edward meant Larissa, that she'd sent him spiraling down into a mess of drugs and despair, and that was no small part true. But the rest of it had been him, and would have been him, no matter what. Because he'd chosen to embrace pain instead of fighting it.

He looked round the room again, the floor swept and books tidied, the fire stoked and lit, and he realized who Edward meant. "Mina? Yes. I suppose she has."

Edward laughed and rubbed at his eyes again, looking wearier than ever. "By the Arrow, they do work magic."

Alaric wouldn't have called it that. He believed not in such a thing. "Go home to your bed before you fall over."

Edward yawned so broadly his jaw cracked and scrubbed again at his face. "I should. My lady wife is patient, but not so patient she doesn't miss me."

From far off, Alaric heard the faint sound of the hourly chime. Several had sounded since Mina had left him, and though she hadn't promised any sort of punishment should he not have finished all the items on the list she'd left, he couldn't help the itch of restlessness when he realized how many tasks remained. Well aware this came from within himself and not from anything she'd said, nevertheless he looked toward the door and no longer at his friend.

"Are you happy?"

Edward's question, such a strange thing for another man to ask, stopped Alaric stone solid. He turned, thinking of how to answer. He knew how happy felt, or thought he had. Mina had given him focus, which wasn't the same.

"I might be," he told Edward cautiously.

"She's meant to bring you solace," Edward said in a low voice. "They do that."

"That's not the same as happy, Edward."

"I know it." Edward laughed.

Alaric laughed too, after a moment. "You and Cillian found yours. The Order does know its work. I'm sure Mina will do just what she's meant to. But I don't expect to gain what you and Cillian have."

"No. I suppose you shouldn't expect such a thing." Edward yawned again. "Your mercy. I should go. But one more thing, Alaric, before I do. Cillian would have me give this to you."

The envelope, sealed with red wax and Cillian's stamp, was too heavy to be an invitation, and knowing his friend as he did, Alaric rather doubted it was personal correspondence. "What is it?"

"Think you I know the king's business?"

Alaric smiled. "I think you know it better than he does, some-times."

"He wants you to return to take up your duties as his minister."

Alaric blinked and tapped the letter before setting it on the table. "Does he? This is an official summons, then?"

"The seal would make it so, yes. He's asking you not only as your king but as your friend."

"He could have come to me and asked in person." Alaric knew this was splitting hairs and beside the point, but the thought of going back to court, to facing them all, to actually doing something undictated. On his own.

Edward frowned. "Alaric—"

"Never mind." Alaric waved a hand. "I'll read it. Thank you for delivering it."

Edward nodded and looked as though he meant to say more, but whatever words rose to his tongue were shoved aside by another yawn. Pushing for an argument had never been Alaric's way. In the time it took for Edward to yawn again, for Alaric to breathe in and out, he thought of pricking at Edward to give himself reason for anger.

"Go home," he said in the end, with a gentle push of his friend toward the door. "Go."

The door opened just before they reached it. Mina stood no higher than Alaric's chin yet she filled the doorway top to bottom, side to side. Or so it seemed to him. Edward perhaps had a differ-ent view, though he gave her a half bow and a murmured greeting.

Mina nodded at him with a smile, but didn't offer her hand. She stood aside as he left and only when the door had closed be-hind her did she turn to Alaric. She said nothing.

She didn't have to.

It was not the way it had been with Larissa. Larissa had ever done what she could to make him yearn for her, and he had, willingly enough. She'd taunted and teased him into a fever for the pleasure of pulling his strings, and he'd allowed that, too, because Alaric couldn't recall a time when he'd not been overcome with one or the other.

Only the subject of it had changed. He'd traded his longing for Edward and to a lesser extent, Cillian, or at least his closeness with Edward, and replaced it with Larissa. What now had replaced her?

"Tell me, sweetheart, what has you looking so pensive?" Mina drew him to her with a glance, not a pompous jerk of her finger. She sat, her head tilted, watching him.

If he didn't go to his knees for her, she wouldn't mock him. It made him want to be in that place all the more, but Alaric kept to his feet. "I'm almost finished with your list."

Firelight glittered in her dark eyes. "Almost?"

He nodded.

Mina looked around the room and back at him, no trace of a mockery in her expression. Nor anger. "Have you done your best?"

He didn't need to be untruthful when he replied. "Yes."

"That's all I could ask."

For the first time in as long as he could remember, doing his best was good enough, even for him.

Chapter 21

Mina was not in the habit of making mistakes. Not that she believed herself incapable, for such a thought would be a mistake in and of itself. But she wasn't in the habit of mistakes, so when they occurred she was not often prepared to deal with the aftermath.

Watching Alaric sleep beside her, Mina wondered if she'd misstepped. She'd taken him firmly in hand, and he'd responded, but that wasn't the error. It was in enjoying this so much.

There is no greater pleasure than providing absolute solace.

Mina knew the principles of her faith more than simply by heart—they had become so much a part of her every thought they were as much a part of her as the color of her eyes. She rarely had to think on them, or what they meant, or how she made every choice based upon them. She was a Handmaiden in every part of herself.

But one of the five principles stood out for her now, resounding in her head so loudly she had to get out of bed. In the moonlight she went naked to the window seat, covered now in soft, clean fabric. Alaric had turned the cushions to hide the stain and tears and she had no fear of her bare flesh on it. She looked through the glass.

Alaric's rooms overlooked a small stone-laid courtyard and the lawns beyond. Not the gardens where she'd allowed him to take her walking, though she knew where they were. Vast, rolling slopes that would be green in the sunshine, in the summer, but now shone silver in the autumn moonglow.

Selfish is the heart that thinks first of itself.

Mina had long known what that meant but believed herself above such a statement. Prideful, perhaps, but also true. Until she came here, anyway.

From the bedroom she heard Alaric's soft, in-out breath. He slept without tossing or turning, and if he dreamed he did it in silence. She'd given him that much, at least, and if it were prideful to believe so that, at least, she knew was no mistake.

But there was no denying her selfishness, as well. She'd been thinking first of herself ever since Alaric had gone to his knees and made love to her with his mouth. Thinking of ways to reward him for his obedience by allowing him to get on his knees again. Knowing from deep within her soul that he gained even more from so pleasing her didn't change the fact that she was not acting solely with his solace in mind.

Even now, thinking of his mouth on her flesh, Mina shifted on the seat. Her skin heated, her nipples peaked. His lovemaking had been exquisite and perfect, as though he'd been trained to know just where and how to touch her. Tipping back her head and closing her eyes, she cupped her breasts and then ran her hands over her belly. Her thighs. Over the soft curls between her legs, her clit and cunt.

"Mina?"

Without opening her eyes, Mina smiled. "Alaric. Sweetheart. You should be sleeping."

"So should you."

She heard the pad of soft, bare feet on the carpet and felt the swirl of air heated by his warmth as it caressed her skin. She opened her eyes. Moonlight painted him in silver gilt the way it had done everything else in the room, but on Alaric the soft streams of light seemed to add an extra glow. Even his hair had turned silver instead of golden.

"I woke up and you were gone. I thought maybe . . ."

"I would never leave you without telling you first," Mina said. She held out her hand and he came forward to take it. The soft brush of his lips across her knuckles sent a shiver through her.

"Because it's against your Order's rules?"

"Because it would cause you unnecessary pain," Mina told him quietly. Sincerely.

His eyes flashed. "Will you come back to bed?"

"In a while. I want to sit here." Sleep would still elude her, no matter how soft the pillows or warm the blankets. She smiled. "The window seat is big enough for two."

Alaric kissed her hand again and went to the bed, tugged off the top blanket, and brought it with him. He settled onto the cushion with his back against the wall and covered them both with the blanket against the chill. She wasn't sure how he did it, but Alaric maneuvered her between his thighs, her back against his chest and his hands on her hips. So settled, Mina couldn't help the sigh of contentment.

Most of the men of her acquaintance hadn't been much for talk, but with Alaric the silence wasn't the same. She didn't believe he stayed quiet because he had nothing to say, or because his thoughts were rambling off into his own head, trying to figure a way to get what he wanted from her. Alaric was quiet because she was. Because the night called for it. Because . . . he understood.

"I've been summoned by the king."

She knew this, of course. She put her hands over his and drew them up to cover her breasts. Against her back, the pole of his erection thickened, and Mina smiled. "I would be surprised if he hadn't called for you. He is your dear friend, after all."

Alaric snorted lightly and rubbed his chin against her temple. "It's less than a social call he requests. He wants me to work for him."

"You don't wish to work?"

He gave a low murmur against her hair. "I've not been idle these past few days."

She laughed. "Sweetheart, this is not the sort of work that will keep you in silk and velvet, and you well know it."

"And if I don't care about being kept in silk and velvet?"

She moved his hands over her breasts and her belly. Along her thighs. His cock got harder. Sweat slipped between them. She moved his hand between her legs.

"You should care about something beyond this room, Alaric. Beyond the gardens. This is not your life."

He didn't answer, and she didn't push. His fingers found her curls and parted them to stroke her clitoris. Mina shifted her knees, tenting the blanket. She arched a little to tip her head back and offer her mouth for his kiss.

His tongue slipped just right between her lips. She sucked on it, and he moaned, his fingers moving faster. They dipped into her well and slid, slick with her juices, over and over her clit.

"I like this room. When you're in it."

She allowed a small groan from her lips to urge him on. "I would be remiss in my duties to you if I allowed you to remain a recluse."

He kissed her again, then murmured into her ear, "So I should not balk you in your wishes?"

"You should not."

Mina rocked her hips against his hand and pressed the other one to her breast. She closed his thumb and finger over her nipple, urging him to pull it tight and taut. He'd learned her body so well she really didn't need to tutor him, but it added to her desire to do so . . . and to his, she could tell.

Alaric's breath came faster, harsher in her ear. She rocked against him, the sweat between them lubricating his cock in the groove of her spine. The fingers on her clit mimicked the pinch she was making him give her nipples. The sudden, unexpected burst of sensation forced a cry from her, and the sound of that loss of control was as erotically charged as his touch. His kiss.

He'd surprised her, taken what she taught him and used it to expand her desire, and he hadn't needed a command to do it. Coherent thought had left her but even if it hadn't, Mina would have been hard-pressed to recall the last time any patron had learned her as well as she'd learned him. Or any man.

He pinched her nipple again and fucked his fingers deep inside her. Then out to slide over her clitoris and tweak it, too, until Mina gasped aloud and cried his name. He moaned but his pace didn't stutter.

His cock jerked against her. They moved together. Her climax swept over her and she lost herself in it.

When her breathing slowed, Mina licked the salt from her lips and shifted to kiss Alaric's mouth again. Between them his prick rose, proud and stiff, but she didn't touch it. His eyes gleamed again in the moonlight, which had begun to soften and fade toward full darkness.

He leaned toward her for another kiss. Mina pulled away. He smiled. She smiled, too.

She got off the window seat and pulled the blanket with her, leaving him to shiver in the sudden chill. "Come to bed, now. It will be morning soon, and you have work to do."

Alaric let his head fall back against the wood of the window frame and groaned. His erection stood out in silhouette. Mina bit back a grin and fell onto the bed to crawl toward the pillows. In the next moment, the bed dipped and Alaric got in beside her.

He lay on his back, not touching her. Mina covered her smile with her hand, though he couldn't see it. "You might move a little closer, sweetheart."

"If you wish me to sleep, I think it would be better if I stayed over here."

"Indeed," Mina said from around the yawn taking control. "I did suggest you needed your sleep. You have work to do in the morning."

"Not the work I've done for you," he said, grudgingly, but in the next moment she heard a small, low and reluctant chuckle.

Mina turned to drape herself across him, her arm over his chest and a leg across his thighs. She kissed his shoulder. "I think you shall find, sweetheart, that the work for your king will bring you rewards you don't expect."

And then with a long, deep yawn, Mina settled into sleep.

Alaric had spoken true about not being a scholar. His position in King Allwyn's court had been done as a favor to his father for the service the man had provided and because of Alaric's relationship with Cillian. When Cillian took the throne, Alaric had been granted a minister's title but had done naught with it.

Now he raked a hand through his hair and studied the sheaf of documents scattered across his desk. He tallied the numbers, and they all made sense. He worked them again, a list of shipments of fabrics and laces, and again the amounts matched in both columns.

"By the Arrow," he said. "I've done it."

"Of course you've done it." Mina looked up from the small square of her embroidery. It was a lady's task, and her delicate fingers had created a pretty picture of threaded flowers on the background of white linen. She'd been at it for hours, he realized, noting how close she seemed to finishing.

Which meant he'd been working for hours, as well.

"It's no great task. Minister of Fashion." Alaric looked again at the papers, expecting the figures to swim and blur as they so often had when he'd been in school. They stayed firm. The subjects even made sense, a peck of this, a barrel of that.

"The king held the title before his father died, did he not?"

"How did you know?" He put down his quill to smile at her.

Mina gave him a small, secretive smile and a shrug. "My goodness, Alaric, you'd think I knew nothing of this place before I came here."

"Did you?" He tidied the stack and stretched, noting the ink stains on his fingers, and reached in the drawer for a box of sand to scrub them clean.

"It's my task to make myself aware of anything I might need to know before I attend a patron. Aside from the information provided to the Order, I have my own resources."

He found it difficult to believe he'd known her but a week, so familiar had the curves of her face and sound of her voice become. She bent back to her embroidery, and he watched the steady, sure in-out thrust of her needle into the fabric. He looked to his work again. She'd done naught but encourage him gently in a tone that brooked no arguments to take up the task, but he had no doubt that somehow Mina was the reason he'd been able to get through it.

Alaric's mother had raised him to serve the lady in the room before himself, and it had ever been his nature to do so. If asked to list what Mina had required of him this past sevenday, he'd have been unable to put it into a format the way he'd added and subtracted the columns of goods and services his position required him to track. Every day she eased his service from him.

"Thank you," he said aloud.

She looked up, her needle clutched in slim fingers. "You're welcome."

He liked that she didn't play coy with him. She knew her place and made it easy for him to know his. As he watched, she pricked her finger on the needle and let out a small gasp.

He was on his feet before she even had time to tuck the finger into her mouth to suck away the crimson drop welling on the end. He took her hand and drew the wound to his own lips to kiss away the copper-tang taste of it. He'd moved without thinking beyond the moment, but as always when on his knees in front of her, his cock began to fill.

He'd not forgotten her touch and how she'd stroked him that first night. He'd dreamed of it, in fact, waking with his cock rigid and aching for release. But Mina had not offered it, and Alaric hadn't asked permission for it. He'd contented himself with pleasuring her, spending hours licking her to climax, making love to her with every part of him but his cock. He'd never thought he'd rise to another woman's touch again, but all she had to do was look at him and he got hard.

Now he sucked gently on her fingertip and withdrew it. Mina's eyes gleamed. Her breath quickened. She murmured his name.

"Have you finished your work?" she asked next when he didn't release her hand.

"Yes."

She made a show of looking round the room. "And look how nice and tidy this room has become."

He laughed. "For my lady's pleasure."

Her gaze flared brighter at the words he spoke, and Alaric let go of her hand. He'd called her by the title he'd used for Larissa; it had slipped out before he could think. Had he overstepped?

"Go into the bedchamber," Mina said.

A cold fist clutched his throat for a moment. "I plead your mercy."

"Alaric. I said for you to go into the bedchamber. Take off your clothes, and wait for me. Now."

He might well have refused. She couldn't make him. But he got to his feet at once and nodded, his prick thickening in his trousers despite the flush of guilt heating its way up his throat to his cheeks. He didn't want to disobey her, even if she meant to punish him. In the bedchamber he stripped out of his trousers and hung them carefully, mindful of Mina's insistence on neatness.

Alaric had long known he was different than his friends. When his friends cringed at the stern demeanor of their teachers, he'd squirmed in his seat and fantasized about being naughty solely to risk punishment. It was not the pain that twitched his prick, but the idea of pleasing someone and being held accountable for providing that pleasure.

Later, when the three of them had taken to the sorts of escapades only young men with privilege and money can afford, they'd gone to the whore. With coin in hand and unused to anything but being given what they wanted, they must have amused her, but she took them anyway.

She'd ordered them to strip and when they stood in front of her, pricks at attention, she'd spanked them all until their buttocks turned red. Cillian and Edward had suffered beneath her touch . . . but for Alaric it had been as though the heavens had sent a bolt of lightning just for him. Even when his friends had moved on to other whores, other pursuits, he'd spent many joyous hours under the tutelage of that first mistress.

It had gone bad for his friends, one who'd forgone that which aroused him and the other fanning his desires to flames high enough to consume him. Only Alaric had walked the same path, never regretting or trying too hard to lose himself in it.

Until Larissa, he thought now. From outside the door he heard Mina's soft tread and he tensed, waiting for her to come in. She didn't. He heard her tug the bell cord. He heard the door open and a maid's voice, but not what was being said.

Alaric had long loved Edward, even though Cillian had always outranked him in Edward's affections. When they'd fallen out, with Cillian gone mad and Edward locked deep within the self-made prison of his guilt, it had been Alaric to whom he'd turned. And Alaric, fool he was, had allowed himself to imagine . . . well, it hardly mattered now. There had been Larissa to ease the sting. And later, there had been oblivion.

And now, Mina.

He heard again the sound of the maid and Mina's low murmur. The sound of the outer door closing. And at last, the swish of her gown in the doorway.

"Get on the bed. On your hands and knees, facing the wall."

He dared not look at her, for fear his cock might spill from the vast and overwhelming surge of excitement flooding him. It had been days, nay, weeks since he'd had release, so long he couldn't recall the last time. He did as she said, aware as always when he submitted of how ridiculous he might look in his submission. Aware as well any who might think so didn't matter.

The rustle of cloth alerted him that she might be undressing, but even so when her bare belly pressed to his buttocks, Alaric couldn't hold back a moan. When Mina tugged free the ribbon holding his hair and it fell around his face, another low sound slipped from his lips. His cock could have drilled through brick.

"I adore the sounds you make," Mina murmured, getting into

place behind him on her knees. Her belly pressed his ass again. Her hands settled onto his hips. "Tell me, sweet, are you afraid?"

"I'm afraid of many things," he admitted, holding himself still even when he longed to thrust his cock into even the bare relief the air would bring.

Her low, slow chuckle trickled over his skin and sent another surge of arousal through him. "I do adore your honesty."

"I'm afraid you won't be able to . . . do . . . for me. What you're meant to do." The words scratched at his throat but came out anyway.

"Hush," she said, not a mother chastising a wayward child, but a lover easing an inconsequential fear.

"It's been a week."

Her hands clutched his hips harder, and her belly pressed harder, and his cock got harder. He let his forehead press into the bedclothes, his elbows bent. Again, he thought of how ridiculous he must appear, ass in the air and a woman standing over him. But he didn't care. All that mattered was the feeling of her body against his and the sound of her voice.

"I appreciate your trust in me, but I assure you, Alaric, sometimes it does take longer. We're talking about reaching absolute solace, sweet, not a few minutes of ecstasy. It doesn't matter if you think you don't deserve it, or if you believe anything you've said or done could make me not try my best to serve you."

A small, strangled gasp escaped him. "You're not the one who serves."

"If you think," she said as she grasped his cock, "that the only way to serve is on one's knees, you know nothing about service."

He cried out as she stroked a dry hand along his erection. She hushed him again and palmed the head of his cock until his hips bucked. She stroked him again and withdrew, and he looked over his shoulder.

Mina held up a small bottle, which she uncorked and tipped over her palm. Thick, fragrant oil oozed out. She painted her nipples with it while he watched, then slipped a finger through the curls between her legs. Her eyes became sleepy lidded.

He had grown as familiar with her body as her face and voice. Her high breasts, the size to fit into his hands. Her pink nipples. The slope of her belly and thatch of dark pubic curls. She displayed herself more proudly for him now than she had ever before, but when he made to get off his hands and knees, she shook her head.

"No."

Alaric put his forehead into the cradle of his palms and closed his eyes. Mina's hand, coated now with oil, slid 'round to stroke him. Mindful of her professed adoration for his noises, he moaned without holding back.

"Lovely," she breathed. "Beautiful."

He was a man, and though he knew of many who'd found his countenance pleasing, he'd never have said he was beautiful. Yet Mina speaking it made it so, without anything ridiculous about it. He breathed and caught her scent. The scent of the oil on her hands.

Her hand moved up and down his shaft. Her other caressed his buttocks. One slim finger ran down the seam there and he tensed at the delicate probe of her fingertip against his anus. His breath gusted out of him on a sigh.

Mina's fingertip pressed against him in counterpoint to every stroke. No woman had ever touched him there. Even Larissa, with all her fondness for watching her playmates suck and fuck each other, had never herself explored his body in this manner. Mina's touch wasn't timid, not rough, and the sweet pressure in time with every stroke had him on fire in moments.

She paused and withdrew, and Alaric shuddered with wanting. She murmured an endearment. He heard the dull sound of the bottle uncorking, smelled a fresh burst of the oil's distinctive odor, and he tensed in anticipation.

Mina drew it out, that sweet, slow twist of time before she touched him again. This time, she grasped him harder, and instead of applying only pressure to the tight ring of muscles, she entered him. He thought for sure he'd cry out, there seemed no other way for the force of his reaction to be expressed, but all that slipped from his lips was a sigh.

"I will never do anything to cause you harm, Alaric. You must tell me if there is anything I do you cannot stand. I am not much interested in pain for its own sake, but there is much some call pleasure and others cannot abide." Her finger slid deeper inside him to stroke a hidden place that sent lightning shocks of desire exploding inside him. "You must tell me if anything I require is too much."

He'd never been fucked this way; never fucked another that way either though amongst the group of young lords Cillian had ever kept 'round him this sort of play was common enough. He'd taken his pleasure with men more than once, but this . . . this was something so different and unexpected he could only bite the sheet beneath him and thrust forward into her hand.

Alaric closed his eyes and gave up to her touch. Mina used both her hands in tandem, and the bed dipped as she moved behind him. With every thrust, he felt the press of her belly against his buttocks as she moved inside and around him. She'd taken the man's place in the bed, but nothing she did made him feel less masculine. He'd never felt more a man than at this moment, giving up everything because she asked it of him.

Alaric was fair certain he'd spill into her grip as quickly as a boy with his first woman, but Mina knew how to stretch out his pleasure, to keep him on the edge of desire for so long he lost track of all time. The world narrowed to her murmuring voice and her touch.

His body became her instrument and she played him with infinite skill.

She made him senseless with desire. Words fell from his mouth, one not matching the next. Compliments, then curses, and finally, pleas for release. Each time he felt he could hold back no longer, she changed her stroke to keep him from it.

"Please," he panted, finally, hoarsely, gasping in a breath.

It took only two strokes after that for her to finish him. He spurted violently into her hand as his body convulsed. Behind his closed eyes bright sparks flashed and universes were created. He lost his breath and found it. He collapsed onto his belly on the bed, spent.

Some moments later her touch on his shoulder turned him onto his back. Mina, smiling, had brought a cloth and basin of warm water. She cleaned him thoroughly and set the cloth and basin aside, then stretched out beside him, naked.

He thought he should speak but had used his words too freely before. Now only silence left his lips. Mina hushed him once more as though she knew he meant to speak, and Alaric stopped trying for a while.

"Is this absolute solace?" he asked at last when sense returned.

Mina laughed into his ear. "If sexual release was all it took to provide it, do you not think I'd have provided it and been gone already?"

He tried to rouse himself to sit but, boneless and sated, could only pull her closer to press a kiss to her temple. "How can you be so certain? Maybe I'm such a simpleton that's all it takes."

"The next time you refer to yourself as a simpleton, Alaric, I will punish you, and I assure you it will not be in a manner you'll enjoy."

He had no doubts she would. "But . . . how do you know, really? When it happens?"

"Absolute solace is not some magical, mystical event," Mina told him. "There's no sudden spark or divination that determines it. The fact you're asking me if you've achieved it means you haven't, that's all. When it happens, you'll know. And I'll know."

"Have you ever been wrong?"

"No."

"Not once?"

He wouldn't have blamed her had his questions put a frown on her lips, but Mina only stroked his hair back from his face. "No, Alaric."

"Have you ever . . . failed?" He'd failed at much in life and wouldn't judge her for it.

"Not often. But yes. Of course. There are some who sought my services for the wrong reasons. They'd lied to themselves, so it was impossible for them not to lie to me. And I'm neither mystical nor magical myself. Nor perfect."

"You are as close to perfection as any lady I've ever met," he said sincerely, and she touched his face again.

"Since I find false modesty offensive, I will not disagree except to say I will accept being practically perfect, if not ultimately."

His cock lay soft on his thigh and he touched it briefly. "Still, it had to be a start."

"Mmmm," Mina said, which he couldn't tell was concurrence or dissent.

"Thank you for it, at any rate."

She laughed again and kissed his shoulder. "Did you think I would keep on allowing you to bring me such pleasure without ever returning the favor?"

"You could have," he said, thinking of Larissa.

Mina's laugh became a sigh. "It was time."

Sleep tempted him but didn't overtake him at once. He managed to pull a blanket over them both to ward off the chill. With

Mina in his arms he thought he might sleep well for the first time in months.

"Tomorrow, you shall go to court and attend your king so that you might present him with the results of your efforts."

He sat, refusal on his tongue. At the sight of her expression, he stilled it. It had been overlong since he'd gone to court, since he'd performed the duties of his position, few as they might be.

"If for no other reason than to prove the king's enemies wrong about his choices," she continued.

"Who speaks out against Cillian?" Alaric thought he must know already. Devain had ever been against the prince before he took his father's place, and though the man had been tossed into prison for his attempts to overthrow the succession, he'd had many support-ers. "And how do you . . . never mind."

He should know better than to ask how Mina knew anything.

"He shouldn't have given me the position of minister."

"Since there have been kings there have been men put into posi-tions because of friendship and not value, Alaric."

A flash of irritation bent his mouth. "You agree? And yet you tell me not to call myself simpleton."

"Because you're not," Mina said. "And I didn't say I agreed with you. I'm saying you must attend court so that you might prove wrong those who speak against your friend. After what he's done for you, it's the least you can do."

Nothing she'd done so far had shamed him, but these words did. "Has he suffered because of me?"

"Suffered? Your friend seems fair immune to suffering such mi-nor stings as snide remarks, but I daresay your persistent absence has hurt him. He's worried about you, as is Edward, whom you've also been ignoring. And him with a new son to coo over."

She'd given him no new truths, but having her say them meant he couldn't easily continue to ignore them. "You're right."

"Of course I am."

He lay down again and she tucked herself up close beside him. The slowing pattern of his breath soon matched hers. Sleep was not so tempting this time.

He thought of the man with the jeweled case and for the first time in days the craving woke inside him. "If I attend court, I'll be expected to appear at evening entertainments, as well."

"And what a merry time we shall have," she murmured sleepily.

"There will be people there I don't wish to see."

Mina slung a leg over his and kissed his shoulder. "I'll be with you."

Knowing it did ease some of his worry. What she said next took away the rest.

"It pleased me to have you call me your lady," Mina said.

And then at last, Alaric was able to find sleep.

Chapter 22

There would always be those who stared, Mina thought without a blink to betray she was even paying attention to the way heads turned as she passed. Her high-necked, long-sleeved gown, with its buttons from throat to floor, stood out amongst the dresses of sateen and frothing lace. Add to it the fact that her attire was more than merely out of fashion but marked her profession, and she couldn't be surprised at the attention being paid to her.

There would also, she mused, ever be those who chose to be unkind rather than silent. For them, however, she had even less interest in response. She didn't need a title or a family line to outrank all of them. She was a Handmaiden and above their petty comments.

Alaric had called her bolder than the Sisters he'd previously met, but Mina wasn't particularly bold in public. She drew enough attention simply walking into a room; she'd gain nothing by behaving in any manner designed to create more. And it wouldn't serve her patron to cause a scene, no matter how many insults came to her ears in voices making mockery of whispers.

Alaric had performed superbly earlier at court. Any who found fault with his discussions on the current import and export laws being written would have done so only from spite, for his every suggestion had made sense and been backed by scads of documentation. Even Cillian had been fair impressed, clapping Alaric's shoulder and grinning with bared teeth at the lords who made to oppose them.

Mina hadn't, of course, taken part in any of the work, but had been there for every glance Alaric gave her. There'd been fewer as the hours wore on. He'd needed her less.

And such was how it was meant to go, she thought now as court dispersed and the lords and ladies who'd lingered with nothing to do but gossip made to leave. She was meant to bolster him so he could stand on his own. No matter how much they both enjoyed each other's company, it wasn't meant to be forever.

Alaric, flushed and laughing, was bent in conversation with Cillian. The men drew envious glances and she heard mutters of favoritism from a few, but there were many who'd left the room praising the work done that day.

There'd be more to do, of course, more than Mina cared to think on, for politics and the working of government held little appeal for her. She learned what was necessary, and that was all. Still, it satisfied her to watch the pair of them, golden head and amber, talking with such affection. It would do Alaric more good than anything to be back in the bosom of his friends again. Better even than the release of climax, she thought with a small smile.

"Look at him prattle on as though anyone but his school chum could bear to pay attention."

Mina didn't turn her head at the snide, feminine tone. She didn't have to see the speaker's face to guess the look of it. A pinch-mouthed, narrow-eyed huss, no doubt. Too bitter and too convinced of her own worth to keep her meanness to herself.

"One might become convinced he's actually managed to teach himself somewhat of business," continued the voice.

Mina turned. She knew the Lady Larissa not from her portrait, which in truth had been painted with a more favorable hand than she deserved. In reality the cut of the lady's lips and ridge of her nose created a much sharper-edged beauty. Her hairstyle belonged on a much younger woman and her clothes, though costly and well-tailored, also hinted at pretentiousness.

Or else, Mina admitted to herself, she could simply not form a decent opinion of the lady, knowing what she knew.

"I don't believe we've met." Women didn't shake hands as men did, so Larissa flicked her fan in Mina's direction. "You're the Handmaiden."

Woman I begin and woman I shall end, Mina thought. It was never truer when facing another woman over a man. "I am. And you are?"

There must have been too few who dared put Larissa in her place, for that lady blinked rapidly as color stole into her fashionably powdered cheeks. She flicked her fan again. Ridiculous, Mina thought. Fans are meant for heat and evenings, and we are having neither.

"I am Larissa Darshan."

Mina said nothing.

Over Larissa's shoulder she saw Alaric, stopped by the same weasel-faced man who'd accosted him in the gardens a fortnight before. They'd bent their heads together over something Mina couldn't see. Larissa shifted to block Mina's view of anything but herself.

"You think you have him," Larissa sniffed, "but you don't. Not if I want him back."

Mina had ever faced jealous lovers with compassion, for it couldn't be easy knowing they'd failed the person they claimed to love. For Larissa she had only contempt and didn't bother to hide it. Apparently the woman was unused to seeing it, for she actually took a step back and closed her fan with a snap.

"I am a Handmaiden," Mina said. "I need not squabble over the favors of my patron with the likes of you."

Larissa staggered as though she'd been struck. She put a hand to her heart, and her cheeks flamed like fire. Mina took a dangerous amount of enjoyment from the sight.

"And even if you want him back," Mina said, "you can't have him."

The metal box rested against the skin of Alaric's belly. It scratched with every movement. He couldn't stop thinking about it.

He'd not been sick in days, too busy with the tasks set him first by Mina and then by Cillian. He'd discovered much about himself, as well: for example, that he wasn't as dense with numbers as he'd always imagined. He'd taken to his work as Minister of Fashion and he'd taken to his private life as Mina's patron, which was far different from being anything he'd ever been to anyone.

"Just a hit," the stranger had said and offered the box. "You needn't overindulge. You can hold back. Can't you?"

And he could, indeed. Herb, worm, wine . . . these were the indulgences of gentlemen and not considered vices. He'd spent hours in the pleasant haze of intoxication.

He could handle one, small dose of oblivion.

It would be sweet, he knew that. First the taste would flood his tongue, then heat would flood his veins. In another heartbeat, no more than two, he'd stand taller, walk a straighter line, pontificate with a brilliance that failed his normal mind.

With just one hit.

And then, after, when he came down, the sickness would come back twice as fiercely as it had before. The only way to stop *that* from happening would be to take another dose. And another.

For now, he satisfied himself with a glass of Cillian's fine wine. He took another to Mina, who'd declared she didn't dance, at least not in public and not unless it was necessary for her patron. He'd been unable to convince her a turn in the reel would benefit him, and she'd sent him to fetch her a full glass, instead.

He didn't mind, though he enjoyed dancing. King Allwyn's court had been a bit duller than Cillian's, for the new king sponsored entertainments every night. Since his appearance in court, Alaric and Mina had attended the entertainments every night for close to a full sevenday.

"Your wine, my lady."

"Thank you." She took the glass and sipped. She might not dance, but her toes tapped in merry time to the music and her cheeks had flushed rosy to go along with her gleaming eyes.

She was the most beautiful woman in a room full of fine-featured ladies, and he could only stare like a sudden, gape-mouthed fool when she smiled.

"Alaric?"

He'd worried her. Knowing it warmed him more than her smile. He took the chair next to hers. "You are like no other woman in this room."

She laughed. "I stand out amongst all the others?"

"To me."

She cupped his cheek. "You're very sweet."

The music changed from a simple country tune to one of the newer, more fashionable dances Cillian had commissioned. Alaric hadn't yet learned it, but he looked to the dance floor anyway.

"Are you certain I can't convince you to allow me to escort you for a dance?"

Mina patted him. "I'm sure. But you go. There are a number of unaccompanied ladies who look to be fair itching for a partner."

This suggestion puzzled him. "You'd not . . . mind?"

"Why should I mind, sweetheart?" Mina lifted a brow. "It's custom in Firth as in other places, is it not, for men and women to dance together even if they're not wed or betrothed?"

Neither of which they were, he was reminded. "Yes, but—"

"Then go enjoy yourself," she said.

She wouldn't be jealous, was what he thought she meant to say, but knowing that was true didn't sit well with him. Reminded she was with him for a purpose and not from pure desire, Alaric frowned.

"Oh, don't put the pout on," Mina teased. "Go. Dance."

"Do you order it of me?"

Her smile faded and something dark crossed her gaze. "Do you push me to do such a thing, here, in front of your peers?"

"And if I do?"

"Then there are many other demands I could make of you that would better suit me than to have you dance with other women."

The thought of it, of being so attuned to her command he would follow even in public, aroused him. She saw it, he knew she did, and it echoed in the rise and fall of her breath and the slide of her tongue across her lips.

"But I shall make them later," Mina breathed. "Now. Go."

So he went, if only to prove to them both how obedient he could be.

Alaric joined the dancers as they lined up across from one another and found himself partnered with a sweet-faced girl he thought he might have known, if only she'd have kept her eyes on his face and not at the floor. She had a familiar giggle, but perhaps he only thought so because she sounded so much like so many of the women there.

Had he made love to her? The touch of her gloved hand told him nothing, nor the sly smile she gave him as they turned and went down the row to the end of the line in time to the music. She fluttered her eyelashes at him but made no move to speak, though a good part of the dancing was usually spent conversing with one's partner.

This dance, though, switched off partners readily, and in the next round he stood across from another woman entirely. This one he had no doubts he knew. This one didn't waste her time with a simper. She gave him her hand, though.

"Puppy," Larissa purred as they moved close and then apart. "What a pleasure."

Even a week before he knew he'd have reacted, maybe even making a spectacle of himself right there on the dance floor. And she'd have eaten it up, he saw by the gleam in her eyes. She'd have reveled in watching him perform for her. Of watching him make a fool of himself in front of his peers.

Not like Mina, who might have asked him anything with the assurance he'd do his best to comply, but who'd required nothing that might make him look the fool.

Larissa loved having reason to condescend and even better, reason for anger. She must have been expecting a different reaction from him. In the past she'd have left him no room to wonder about her feelings but now she only stared.

They bowed and circled one another. Larissa eyed him. "You look . . . different."

"And yet you look exactly the same," he murmured as he took her hand to move down the row.

It wasn't time to change partners just yet, though he might wish to escape her. Larissa squeezed his fingers and pulled him closer than the dance required. Alaric allowed it but only because he could see Mina from across the room.

He might have made a scene, before, but now there was no need. Nothing Larissa could do or say could prompt him to it. Not even when she pulled him closer and the metal box pressed again at his belly.

"Your lady keeps you on a rather long leash."

"Perhaps she knows I'll come back to her without being short-tethered."

The music ended just then, and before they could begin to call the next, the crowd parted and closed around them. Larissa made him move to the side of the room. Against his belly, the metal box scratched.

Larissa leaned close and put her hand on his waist. The metal pressed him. She had to feel it. Larissa smirked.

"My, my. Has my boy been visiting you? I didn't think you still . . . indulged. I heard you'd gone off all that."

Alaric swallowed his retort. Larissa studied him. Really studied, not just swept him up and down with her gaze to make him feel as though his appearance was lacking.

"You never used that garbage when you were with me."

Alaric slid a hand into his shirt and pulled out the box. It fit just right into his palm. Inside, the contents rattled. "No, Larissa. I never used it when I was with you, no matter how hard your 'boy' pushed it."

She ran her tongue over her lips in a gesture that had fascinated him in the past but now left him cold. "I heard you went deep, Puppy. What a shame."

"I wish you wouldn't call me that."

"If wishes wore saddles, I'd have no need of a pony." She laughed, a bright and tinkling sound like chimes of glass. Larissa lifted a brow and looked purposefully at Mina. "You might have done more for her, Puppy. You might have at least dressed her properly. It is your place, you know, to provide for her."

The crowd dispersed around them, another dance starting. Alaric didn't join it, and neither did Larissa. She ran a finger across the lace at his cuffs.

"She's kept you tidy, I see. But then you always did clean up rather well. It's a pity you haven't seen fit to do the same for her."

Before he could reply, she laughed in his face. "You've no idea what I mean, do you? Oh, by the Arrow, you do so amuse me more when I need not tolerate your simple head every day."

The words stung but he only smiled.

Larissa's laugh died in her throat. "She's a Handmaiden. Yours. You're bound to provide for her. Clothes appropriate for the season and activities. Food. Shelter. Whatever she requires, it's yours to provide. And yet you parade her about in the same shabby gown she's worn most every day since her arrival. What, she has but the two, yes?"

Alaric's eyes went to Mina, now chatting with Cillian's betrothed. It was true, she wore the same gown, but he'd become so accustomed to the sight of it he hadn't noticed it was the same one. Larissa laughed again.

"You serve her quite poorly. More poorly even than you served me."

"I served you with everything I had!" he cried, pricked at last into anger.

Larissa blinked, then reached a hand to flick the lace at his throat. "Ah. The puppy bares his teeth."

"You chose to end our relationship after accepting my ring. You chose it, Larissa, not I. You agreed to become my wife and you . . ." He couldn't continue, not without raising his voice and drawing attention to them both.

"You've not learned a thing," she told him. "Don't you know there's no joy in requiring submission from a man who never, ever, bites back?"

"I never wanted to bite you," Alaric said. "I loved you."

Larissa could be cold, and she could be cruel, but now she looked at him with a fondness he'd never thought to see again. "If you'd loved me less, I would have loved you more."

Thoughts swirled, but no words came out. Alaric felt the touch of her hand on his cheek but it was gone before he could react. She sighed and shook her head.

"Take care of her better," she advised. "Responsibility goes both ways, Alaric. Spend all the time on your knees before her that you desire, but don't forget to take care of all she might need, as well."

The music swelled and Larissa left him, only unlike before, this time, Alaric was still standing when she went.

Chapter 23

"Tell me about yourself."

Mina looked into Alaric's grinning face and leaned back on the pillows. They'd spent a leisurely hour in the bath, after which he'd rubbed her skin with fragrant oils and carried her to the bed. Now he was feeding her grapes. It was a bit of silliness, a role-play with him the part of the hareem boy, but it pleased them both and did no harm.

"Hmmm," she mused. "What would you like to know?"

She had no quarrel with talking about her past. Unlike many of her Sisters who chose to come to their patrons as unmarked parchment, Mina had ever believed her duty required her to give her patrons of herself, a task made too difficult if she kept herself locked away.

"Anything. Everything." Eagerly, he knelt in front of her on the bed.

"What's gotten into you? Invisible Mother, if you don't stop wiggling the bed, I swear we'll both fall off." She studied him, looking for signs of the drug in his eyes and skin, but saw none.

He leaned in to stroke a hand down her side to rest on her hip, and when she tilted her face up, he kissed her mouth. "I just want to know you, Mina."

She laughed against his lips. "Oh, Alaric. What do you think you might need to know?"

His mouth moved across hers and over her cheek, down her throat, across the tops of her breasts. He kissed a path down to her belly and rested his head there. "Something you've never told any-one else."

This gave her pause. She touched the softness of his hair but didn't stroke. "If I've never told anyone else, what makes you think I'd tell you?"

"Because soon you'll go away. And I'm safe."

His breath slipped across her skin and warmed her. So did his touch. She couldn't deny what he said was true, though how he'd guessed it, she didn't know. "I would imagine I'm less interesting than you believe, but very well. Something I've never told anyone else. Let me think a bit."

He kissed her belly and slipped his arms around her. He hummed with his lips on her skin. Tickled, she laughed and tugged at his hair until he left off to look at her with that same mischie-vous grin.

"I lied about my age when I joined the Order."

This was clearly not anything like what he'd thought to hear. Alaric sat upright, eyes wide. "Did they ever find out?"

"If they had, sweetheart, do you think that would qualify as something I never told anyone?" She did, in fact, believe at least a few of the Mothers-in-Service suspected she wasn't as old as she'd claimed, but none had questioned her.

He laughed, chagrined. "No. I suppose not."

Alaric settled back against her and Mina contented herself with running her fingers through his hair. So soft, the color of good, rich butter . . . no, sunshine, she decided. Summer sunshine. And, amused at herself, she sighed into laughter.

He looked up at her again. "Why did you lie?"

"Because I wanted desperately to become a Handmaiden. It takes a long time to train for the position, but unlike many other vocations, the Order won't take a girl under the age of ten-and-six into apprenticeship."

He hummed again on her belly and slid a hand up her leg. Alaric nuzzled into her as though he couldn't bear to have one measure of his skin not pressed to hers. She liked it, Mina thought as her fingers stroke-stroked along his scalp. This closeness.

"Why did you want it so desperately?"

"Because nobody believed a girl of ten-and-three could possibly know her own mind. I could be betrothed, even wed should my parents will it. I could bear a child. But command myself? Never." Mina shifted and her voice lowered as her fingers twisted. "And command another? Unthinkable."

He stretched against her, not pulling from the tug on his hair but leaning into the embrace. "You knew, so young?"

"Oh, my sweetheart, I have ever known I was meant to control, not be controlled. I knew it from behind my mother's skirts, I knew it when my body changed and first drew the hungry glances of my father's friends. I knew it before the first time I had a man on his knees before me."

She didn't miss Alaric's small groan. She smiled and pushed his head lower. He obliged at once, sliding on the sheets to move between her legs. She parted her thighs for him, already arching her back to press herself into his hot, wet mouth.

"But at ten-and-three, nobody would believe I could know this. So, I left my house and went to the Order, and I . . ." She sighed as his tongue found her clitoris. Her words expanded, melted, dripped from her lips without making sense.

With Alaric's mouth on her, working her flesh to ecstasy, Mina's mind opened to the first time she'd been so pleasured. The Mothers-in-Service who'd accepted her into the Order hadn't pressed her for her age, but they'd kept her in training long enough it didn't matter if she wasn't of consent when she joined. Years had passed while she studied. More years than most of her Sisters had to face, but then her natural inclinations had led her down some more . . . strenuous . . . paths.

Stephan, the man brought from the fields to the house, had been the one they chose for her, the first man to act the part of patron. Mina had never asked him how many young women he helped to initiate into the role of Handmaiden, but she knew without question she'd been the first to take him instead of the other way 'round.

Alaric shifted and added the stroke of his fingers inside her. Mina moaned his name, urging him on. His mouth worked in time with his hand, bringing her fast to the edge but holding off at the last moment, keeping her burning.

"I learned how to make people give me what I wanted in a way that satisfied us both." She drew in a breath and ran her tongue over her lips, tasting salt.

They rocked together. She let him take her away with his touch. She let him bring her back with it as well. She cried his name when climax shook her, and it tasted right as though she couldn't have said anything else.

When he moved up her body to slide inside her, his kisses tasted of her desire. It sent another surge through her. Her hands found the hard muscles of his back and buttocks, urging him deeper. Harder.

Alaric gave her what she wanted. He pushed up on his arms, angling so deep inside her sweet pain mingled with the pleasure. She cried out again as her body clenched in the onset of another climax. It rippled through her. Mina wrapped her legs around Alaric's waist, holding him to her until he lowered himself to hold her just as tight.

They kissed. They breathed. He shuddered and bent his face against her throat, and she felt the pulse of him inside her.

They lay, quiet, for some moments until he moved off her to rest by her side. "I always knew, too."

Mina, drowsy and sated, turned to press her lips to his temple. "Did you?"

"Yes."

"Then we were well matched, yes?"

He tilted his head to look up at her, his hair stuck to his forehead with the sweat of his efforts. "I think so."

Mina thought so, too.

"You know, what I said before," Alaric said after a few more quiet moments. "That first day . . ."

"Yes?" Mina, drowsing, didn't care to think too much upon it.

"I didn't mean it."

"Oh, sweetheart, if I believed you meant it, I'd have walked out that day. There are words men say when they are sore in need of solace, or deep in their grief. You didn't even know me, then. And many men think Handmaidens are equivalent to whores."

He shifted and got upon his elbow to look into her eyes. "I shouldn't have said that, either, but that's not what I meant, now."

Ice bloomed in her belly, and Mina sat, too. She drew away from him, just barely, aware more than ever of how selfish her heart was being. "Hush, Alaric."

"When I said I would never—"

"I said hush!" She shook her head, and he obeyed.

She settled down into the pillows again and he followed after a few minutes. The rise and fall of his breath told her he slept, and once again Mina crept from the bed. This time not to sit at the window but to creep to the bath chamber where she ran the water as hot as she could stand and scrubbed herself clean of anything to remind her of his touch. His taste.

She got into the tub, overbrimming, and sank down until the water covered everything but her mouth and tip of her nose. She could hear her heart beat, slow and steady in her ears. She could hear each breath as it sighed through her nose, down her throat, and into her lungs. She closed her eyes and floated.

Not dreaming.

Before creating the world, Sinder had walked the Void alone. The texts didn't say for how long, and priests and scholars had argued over the number of years for as long as the texts had been a matter of study and not pure belief. He walked the Void, created the world and came across Kedalya in the forest—nobody had ever explained to Mina's satisfaction how she came to be there, if Sinder was the Allcreator, but that's what the Book said happened, so she believed it was true. Sinder saw Kedalya and fell in love with her, and they bore a son together. The Holy Family.

And then the versions of the story diverged, some claiming Kedalya sinned with their child, others blaming Sinder for abandoning his wife and son. No matter what the reason, the Holy Family had been broken, on that they all agreed. They'd gone away and wouldn't return until Sinder's Quiver contained enough arrows to fill it.

Mina's entire faith was based on love and the loss of it.

She ducked entirely beneath the water, holding her breath, and wondered how long she could stay there before she had to come up for air. Heat soothed her, as did the water's cradling embrace. She wasn't afraid of drowning. She'd never been afraid of anything in her whole life, but she was afraid now, her heart squeezing in her chest, her fingertips and toes numb despite the water's heat.

Mina fully believed in the principles of the Order. She understood them so deeply she needn't think on the meaning; she simply lived them. She knew how to find beauty in imperfection and how to think first of what another needed to bring the best pleasure to them both. She believed without question she'd begun and would end as a woman, and that utter solace was not only attainable but should be the goal of every person in the Land Below. She had spent her entire adult life doing her best to provide it, and now, here, for the first time she feared she would be unable to finish her task. Her failures had been few before, and not of her making, but Alaric was different than any patron or man she'd ever known. If Mina couldn't bring him to solace it wouldn't be his fault, but hers.

Love had ever seemed weak to her. So many had claimed it, held it out like a prize in which she had no interest. That she was worthy of love she had no doubts, for Mina had ever lived above reproach. She was fair of face and form. All that men claimed to love about her, she couldn't disagree with. But to love another based on his features had seemed ridiculous. To love him for his bended knee equally as silly, for of all the men of her acquaintance, even those who claimed to serve her had done so out of hope she would serve them, in the end.

How could she be expected to love anyone when even the All-creator and the Invisible Mother couldn't manage to maintain the emotion?

It had been easier when he'd claimed he would never love her. When she'd believed he meant it. Now something stretched between them, unseen and unheard, untasted, or unsmelled.

But not unfelt.

"And you must make sure to use your best stitching. Nothing sloppy." Alaric gave the seamstress the list of measurements and instructions and watched her look them over.

There were benefits to his position as Minister of Fashion he'd never considered, he thought with a grin as he left the woman's shop and headed out to the street to next find the sweet shop. Mina had mentioned desiring a certain kind of toffee not commonly found in Firth, but he knew where he might find some. It had been some time since he'd been inside, but once through the doorway Alaric paused to breathe in deep the scents of candies and pastries. He ordered a pound of the toffees, imported and expensive though they were, added a few other sweets to the bill, and arranged for delivery.

Then back out to the street again, where he lifted his head to the scent of snow in the air and thought about how many minutes it would take his carriage to get him back to the palace. He wasn't watching where he was going, and there was no excuse for the way he trod upon the lady's gown as she came out from the milliner's. He grabbed at her arm to stop from jostling her further, but let go at once when he saw who she was.

"Your mercy," he said.

Larissa's broad-brimmed hat was not in the latest fashion, but she made it seem so. It shaded her eyes. Were they more shadowed than they'd been the last time he'd seen her?

"You're alone," she replied. "She lets you out alone."

"She doesn't own me, Larissa."

"Yet you'd be owned, if she wanted it." Larissa glanced down the street. "You've been to the seamstress?"

"Yes." He gave a glance down the street, too, then moved away from her. "Good day."

"Alaric, wait."

He paused but didn't turn at first. When she didn't command him again, Alaric softened. Turned. Larissa gestured and he moved closer.

"You look well," she said.

"I am well. Thank you."

He could remember he'd once wanted this woman, but he could no longer remember how it felt, that desire. Now he stared at her pretty face, the fine clothes, and felt nothing. She might have been an acquaintance from long ago, so unmoved did she leave him.

Larissa wasn't stupid. He knew she saw his lack of emotion in his face, where he wore it the way he'd always worn every feeling. She blinked rapidly, and Alaric caught the sheen of tears.

"She'll leave you soon. She'll have to. I can tell how much better you are, already."

He swallowed against the words rising like bile in his throat. He wouldn't give her the satisfaction of getting such a reaction. Yet when he looked at Larissa longer, Alaric wondered what reaction she'd been hoping for.

"When she does . . ." Larissa didn't move toward him. No longer even looked at him. He recognized that habit, of staring at something else to draw attention away from what she wanted.

"Good day, Larissa."

She looked at him then, the bright blaze of her eyes familiar even if she no longer seemed so. "She *will* leave you, Alaric. It's what she's meant to do. And when she does, what will you do, then? Go back to oblivion? I'm telling you that you needn't do it. You can come back to me."

A pony, a gown, a book. A set of rooms. A servant. What Larissa could not have, she wanted, and for the first time, instead of anger or grief, Alaric was moved to pity for her. She had wealth and beauty and the love of many, and none of it was enough. It would never be enough for her.

"I don't want to come back to you," he said, but gently.

She blinked again and he thought this time the glitter of tears might be real. "You do. Of course you do."

"No. I really don't. But . . . thank you, Larissa."

She took a step back, a hand going to her throat as though he'd made a grab for it. "For what?"

"For not loving me."

Her lips moved in silence. Alaric made a leg. He'd have kissed her hand this one last time, had she not snatched it close to her body and taken another step back. Her shoes gritted on the gravel as her voice ground out her words.

"You are not supposed to thank me for that!"

"But I do," Alaric said. "For if you had, we would ever be gnawing at the ties binding us to each other and would never be happy."

She drew in a breath and curled her lip, but said nothing. Perhaps she had nothing to say. Alaric put his fingertips to his heart, and then to his forehead, and at last his lips in the traditional, triple gesture of farewell.

"Now if you'll excuse me," he said, "I must return to my lady."

He didn't bother to wait for Larissa's reply.

When the knock sounded at the outer door to the chamber, Mina didn't move. Alaric did, hopping out of bed as though shot from a cannon. He wrapped a spidersilk robe around his waist but left his chest bare. The look he gave her over his shoulder as he went out of the bedchamber had her pushing up on one elbow, brow furrowed.

What on earth was he about?

At this time of afternoon, it was the height of laziness to be abed, but Mina doubted they were the first couple to ever pass the hours making love. Not even the first to spend a week in such leisure, as they'd done, she was sure. She settled back onto the pillows, still listening for sounds of who might have come visiting and hoping with a yawn covered by the back of her hand she would not have to leave the comfort of Alaric's bed.

The murmur of voices reached, but didn't rouse her. She snuggled, tucking herself against the pillow that smelled of him. She breathed in, her eyes closed, thinking of how little time it had taken for her to recognize it.

The murmuring grew louder and softer as she dozed. The thud of the door closing woke her but not enough to force her from the blankets. She waited for Alaric to come back, and when he didn't, Mina again sat up to call his name.

He appeared in the doorway. "Mina."

"Mmmm?"

"Come see this."

She yawned and blinked, then fixed him with a look meant to intimidate him back to her side at once . . . though gently. He didn't waver. He grinned, gesturing, but the look in his eyes was what swung her feet over the side.

"What is it?"

"Come," he said. "Please."

She was not above granting requests, particularly when made so nicely, so even though the soft bed was more appealing than anything else at the moment, she got out of it. "Do you have a surprise for me?"

He said nothing, just took her hand as she came through the door. Mina stopped on the other side of it, made suddenly breathless by what she saw. She turned to him, questions trying to tumble from her tongue but tangling it, instead.

He'd brought in a hanging rack a dangle with gowns in every color. Below it, a rack of slippers, shoes, and boots to match. A jewel case on a stand stood next to it. Boxes brimming with hats, gloves . . . a cloak caught her eye and she went to it at once to press the luxurious fall of soft velvet against her bare skin.

"What . . . what is all this?" She turned to meet his gaze and found herself unable to keep her vision clear.

Alaric came forward, expression concerned. "Don't cry."

Was she weeping? Mina swept at her cheeks and blinked away the blur. "What have you done?"

"What I should have done at once, if I hadn't been in such a state. I'm providing for you. Clothing appropriate for the season and activities." He drew her by the hand to the rack. "It should have been done immediately, and I plead your mercy for failing you."

"You didn't. I have ever preferred my own gowns to those my patrons chose . . . oh!" She stopped herself at the sight of a blue dress, hem hung with spangled gold beads. Matching beads decorated the short, puffed sleeves and the wide band of ribbon that would cross just beneath her breasts. This gown was of the highest fashion, the loveliest fabrics. She touched it, her heart thudding faster with longing to put it on.

"You would be beautiful in that. You're beautiful in anything," Alaric said from behind her.

"There are so many!"

He chuckled. "I do have some small influence in the realm of fashion."

She faced him. "You've done too much."

"I haven't. It's my responsibility to provide for you." He looked over the clothes, then back to her. "And my pleasure, Mina."

"Purpose and pleasure," she said, her throat thick with emotion. How often had she heard that said? How often had she been required to believe it of herself?

"Yes. Purpose and pleasure, both." Alaric moved closer to take her hand and bring it to his lips. "Are you displeased?"

"No." Mina leaned against him, her cheek to his chest, before pulling away to look again at the treasures before her. Simply because she chose her garments to create a specific appearance didn't mean she never longed for beauty for beauty's sake. "I'm far from displeased."

"Try them on."

He looked so eager she couldn't refuse, though she insisted upon bathing quickly, first. She had no lady's maid to help her as she would have had she been as grand a lady as the gowns would insist, but Alaric was as swift tying laces as he was untying them.

"Practice provides perfection," he told her with an unashamed grin.

There were many choices but only one she could imagine making at that moment. With its simple cut, the lack of lace and frills, the gown would have been plain but for the color. Crimson silk, hemmed in gold. It was not the gown for a Handmaiden.

It was the gown, however, for a woman.

When she stood before him in the dress, her high-heeled shoes a perfect match, the soft gloves rising to just above her elbow, Mina thought no mirror could better reflect her than Alaric's eyes. Men had gazed at her with wonder before this, and with adoration, but none had ever looked upon her with such utter satisfaction.

She was brand-new before him.

"This gown . . . it fits me. Perfectly." None of the others she'd ever been granted had done so. All had sagged or pinched, needing tailoring. Many had been the wrong color, what her patron preferred and not what would suit her. But this dress hung on her as though it had grown from her own skin. The shoes fit so well she scarcely noticed them. Mina twirled, slowly, to bell the skirt. "How did you do it?"

Alaric looked confused. "Do what?"

"How did you know exactly what I would like best? How did you make sure it would fit me just so?"

"I gave the seamstress measurements." His brow furrowed, as though her question made no sort of sense. "And as for choosing what you'd like the best, I simply . . . well, I simply thought about it."

She smoothed the fabric with her fingers and looked down at it. So simple a thing and yet so full of meaning. "But how did you know the measurements?"

He shrugged and held up his hands slightly apart. "I showed them. I said, 'This is the span of her hips, this the shape of her breasts.' They fit them from that. And I told them to use their finest stitches, as my lady deserves nothing but the best."

This might have been his duty, part of the requirement of having her, but he'd done so much more. Mina blinked again to clear her eyes and swallowed hard. Alaric stood, clad now in the peasant trousers in which she so enjoyed him.

"It was no great effort," he said. "Because I know you."

She'd had patrons who'd bent themselves to her, the bending giving them what they required to find peace. Patrons who'd obeyed her and followed her lists. She'd never had a patron who so simply became everything she required without her having to ask it of him.

"You do know me," she whispered. "Oh, yes. You do."

It happened. Mina had said it was no mystical, magical thing, the finding of solace. And she no mystical, magical person. Yet when it fell between them, sudden as a cloud passing across the sun or a wave licking at the shore and retreating, she felt it. They both did. But it was not Alaric's solace they'd found.

It was hers.

Mina didn't know the moment he went to his knees before her, only that he was there. Alaric bent his head over her hands. When he looked up at her, his eyes gleamed, his mouth wet.

"How could I have spent so many years believing I had everything I needed?" Mina asked him. "When I was only waiting to find it?"

Alaric smiled and stood. "Let me give it to you."

"Sweetheart," Mina said, "You already have."

Purpose and pleasure. It had brought solace to them both. Neither of them needed to ask if it had arrived.

They both already knew.

Don't miss the next Order of Solace novel
by Megan Hart . . .

No Greater Pleasure

Coming October 2009 from Berkley Sensation!